Praise for *No Salvation*

"Truth, as they say, may be stranger than fiction, but novelist and award-winning editor Jeffery Hess manages to masterfully blend both in *No Salvation*. Based on actual events from another era, Hess's novel with page-turning cinematic appeal sizzles with gritty realism and uncomfortable truths regarding racial tensions aboard a U.S. Navy carrier. I dare readers to walk away unchanged"
—Tracy Crow, author of
Eyes Right: Confessions of a Woman Marine

"In a skillful fictionalization of the racial discord aboard the USS Kitty Hawk in 1972, Mr. Hess has created an unflinching picture of life aboard a Navy carrier forty-seven years ago, in a work that builds in tension with each chapter to a decisive climax, bloody, but prescient with hope."
—Raymond Hutson, author of *Finding Sgt. Kent*

"From the opening chapter Hess plunges you deep within a Navy aircraft carrier with characters rich enough to have stand-alone stories of their own. Powerful is not only the first word that comes to mind when describing *No Salvation*, it's the *best* word."
—Jonathan Brown, author of the Lou Crasher series

"Hess, himself a Navy veteran, knows exactly what he's doing, and ⸻⸻⸻ a riveting ⸻d compelling story firmly base⸻ ⸻⸻⸻ ⸻⸻ closing days of the Vietnam wa⸻ ⸻⸻⸻⸻ ⸻⸻ ⸻⸻⸻⸻ e Cold War memoir ⸻: *At Play in the ASA*

NO SALVATION

ALSO BY JEFFERY HESS

The Scotland Ross Novels
Beachhead
Tushhog

Cold War Canoe Club

As Editor
Home of the Brave: Stories in Uniform
Home of the Brave: Somewhere in the Sand

JEFFERY HESS

NO SALVATION

Down & Out Books
3959 Van Dyke Road, Suite 265
Lutz, FL 33558
DownAndOutBooks.com

Cover design by Zach McCain

ISBN: 1-948235-86-2
ISBN-13: 978-1-948235-86-0

*For all who have been haze-gray
and underway (in good times and bad)*

CHAPTER 1

USS Salvation (CV-44)—Yankee Station—Tonkin Gulf
October 31, 1972

Of all the ways Commander Robert Porter had witnessed death, he never expected this. It was 0200. All lights aboard ship had been switched to red following taps four hours earlier. Porter double-timed it along passageways and down ladders and sprinted aft, all through the dim red glow that radiated off every pipe and cable run. Breath came easy and deep despite his heightened alertness. With each urgent step the odors of wet iron and jet fuel made his mouth hot with the taste of rust. He slowed along the starboard passageway on the second deck, where broken glass crunched beneath his boots. Shadows in the red light played tricks. He stopped and leaned forward. Lengths of inch-and-a-half fire hose lay unspooled, their nozzles missing, as were various dogging wrenches—except for one sticking out of a fuel transfer gauge attached to the portside bulkhead. He cleared his throat of the rising heat.

This main thoroughfare should've been wide open with less than a third of the ship's crew awake to get in his way.

"Make a hole," he called out, intent on resuming his pace.

No one moved.

Farther down the passageway, through the red glow, those

1

crewmen were not milling about, but rather slumped along the deck, many motionless with open wounds leaking blood. Porter's stomach felt like it had been kicked and his nervous eye twitched.

There had been no alarm or missile impact, not even heavy seas, yet dozens of casualties surrounded him. Those who were able applied direct pressure or tourniquets.

As he stepped over Seaman Runyan, a young striker from postal, his boot slipped in a puddle of blood. Gravity almost dragged Porter to the deck with his wounded crewmen. The kid looked nearly unconscious sprawled on the deck.

"Someone apply direct pressure to the postal clerk's head," Porter called out. "Now!"

Despite blood pouring like hydraulic fluid from his scalp, Runyan's eyes opened in time to focus on Porter. The blood covering the kid's pale face made his skin look as dark as Porter's. Runyan waved an arm, as if weakly mocking semaphore performed topside—on the flight deck and signal bridge. Blood and confusion filled his face.

"Mr. Porter, please," he called out. His head wound percolated into his mouth. "*They* ran aft."

The way he said the word "they" made Porter's windpipe grow tight. He looked past the multitude of injuries, contusions, and smeared blood and wished it wasn't true. The red light obscured colors, but the contrast was plain enough.

All the casualties were white.

"Mr. Porter," Runyan called out in a voice that might not live through the night. "Please, sir. Make the other blacks stop."

Porter's neck shivered beneath the weight of the kid's words. To keep himself upright, he reached out a hand to the yellow casing of an emergency light fixture.

As an airdale with a broken arm pulled his T-shirt over his head and used his good hand to staunch the blood flowing from his buddy's face, synapses in Porter's brain fired with the message to keep moving. First aid and mass casualties had procedures, but there was no script for being attacked from within.

Nothing of the kind had been part of Porter's crises-at-sea training. He had to keep going, despite the wet puzzlement on that postal clerk's face.

Nervous energy propelled Porter faster despite the heaviness threatening to drag him to his knees. With each step, his stomach churned more. He wondered if the color of his own skin would help or hurt his efforts to restore calm aboard the ship. A dozen frames down the passageway, red lights made a tunnel leading to white lights.

His eyes adjusted to the brightness the closer he got to the mess deck. The smell of blood mixed in the air with fumes of jet fuel, old coffee, BO, pot smoke, and bad breath. Instead of the empty tables and chairs where twelve thousand meals were eaten daily, Porter arrived in time to see a firefighting nozzle swung as a weapon from its brass handle. It shined in the light of fluorescent bulbs overhead as it spun midair toward a blond kid's head.

"No!" Porter called out.

The crowd buzzed with cheers and rage. Bulkheads vibrated with animosity.

The kid had kneeled on the deck beside an ammo elevator, surrounded not by missiles or bombs but by a hundred fifty black men—one hundred fifty-one counting Porter. They were in various degrees of uniform, some bare chested with blood smeared on their faces; some with dilated pupils from smoking, snorting, or shooting smack; many others high from the fog of marijuana in the air. Their fists were still clenched. The blond kid's face bore wounds pounded and kicked into it earlier. As Porter noticed the hula girl tattoo on the kid's forearm and the anguish in his young eyes, that ten-pound nozzle struck the side of his blond head—ruptured skin, shattered bone across the eyes and the bridge of his nose—opened up his skull like a can of dog food.

Porter gagged low in his gut and covered his mouth with his fist.

The kid's body slumped and his shoulder hit the deck without sound. His opened head thudded wet upon impact. Porter's first instinct was to call for a corpsman, but it was already too late.

3

During his career Porter had dropped ordnance on villages, so death was nothing new to him. He'd made his peace with it so he could have a chance of sleeping at night. But seeing something so senseless, so violent, up close and personal made him want to vomit.

No one spoke. The only sound was heavy breathing and an icemaker along the far bulkhead as it pulled water and coughed a handful of cubes into its gray storage bin. Halfway between that icemaker and Porter stood Rufus Applewhite, a pissed-off brother all of twenty years old, in a blood-stained T-shirt and faded dungarees with a monkey fist key chain hanging out of his pocket. He dropped the nozzle. The brass thunked hard onto the deck. He walked toward Porter, his stare full of defiance.

The black sailors shifted side to side, opened and closed their fists like athletes preparing to compete. They stood in random packs like wolves among the tables and chairs where they'd eaten every meal for the past two hundred seventy-four days. Only a couple of them tried to conceal weapons improvised from firefighting equipment, dogging wrenches, and aircraft tie-down chains. Porter recognized a few faces, but every one of them knew who he was and what he might be worth to their cause. He watched the dead kid's blood puddle widen beneath his head. The men stared at Porter as Applewhite ambled up slow and cocky.

Pressure built in Porter's chest where wise words should have been.

Applewhite walked the long way, going around the group instead of cutting through it. The ball of the monkey fist bounced with each step.

Applewhite stepped up, toe-to-toe—so close Porter smelled pot on his breath and felt the rage radiating from the angry crowd and into the deck plates and up the bulkheads. It made Porter feel like he was plummeting through the air. He spread his feet to give himself a stronger base, digging in, intent on manufacturing the power to calm his black crew.

* * *

Ten weeks earlier, a CH-46 Sea Knight helicopter flew a dozen miles off the Vietnam coast. It was near noontime. The sun radiated across the cool blue water of the South China Sea and bounced off the haze-gray paint of two US ships. At that distance, the helo's only passenger, Commander Robert Porter, guessed the ships out there were a carrier and maybe an oiler from the battle group. Without binoculars he couldn't be sure. At distances like that, he'd always had a hard time distinguishing between smaller and farther away. That had gotten worse over the years the less he flew. Blame might rest on the aging process, but he was only forty-one and not ready to admit that to himself. It seemed like only a couple of years ago he had flown across the same water in an F-8 as one of the Navy's only black pilots. Now he was being chauffeured.

"Are you comfortable back there, Commander?" the lieutenant flying the helo asked over the headset built into Porter's helmet.

"It's not a limousine, if that's what you mean," Porter said, "but it's a hell of a lot more comfortable than the jump seat of the AC-47 I rode all the way to Singapore one time."

Laughter filled his headphones. "That's a good one, sir," one of them said.

During his nineteen-year career he'd been on the receiving end of a lot of admiring and flattering attention—more than he would guess white men of the same rank might get. Before his commission, most white people treated him like everybody else. That's how he grew up. That's what he was used to. Some kids in class had called him names, but by the third grade there were a hundred black kids in his school.

This new assignment, this role of executive officer, carried the weight of four thousand men and officers who would demand his full attention. It didn't worry him though. His confidence was rooted in rising to the occasion every time. He never understood where that trait came from. He damn sure didn't have an example of that growing up.

As they got closer to the ships, the carrier's superstructure, what they called the "island" and civilians called the "tower," came into focus, but the array of RADAR antennas and glass around both bridges and the flight control tower remained too far to see clearly.

The Sea Knight passed over a supply ship sailing away from the carrier and within seconds the carrier went from looking as small as a shoebox to being the real deal. A dozen F-8s lined the port side of the flight deck, with a squad of F-4s grouped in pairs along the starboard side, aft of the island. The center of the flight deck stood crowded with pallets of food, ammunition, replacement parts, and sundry supplies following replenishment at sea.

The Navy had been good to Porter, the progeny of a janitor and a librarian's assistant, who'd given him the gift of reading, which led to his interest in college and traveling the globe. Because his father worked at Sacramento Municipal Airport, where young Porter had spent every summer between the third grade and being commissioned as an ensign in the Navy, he'd begun flying planes at fourteen years old.

Catching sight of the familiar hull number painted on the flight deck transported his mind to the last time he'd landed on the *Salvation*—wing a little shot up—back in sixty-eight. This was a different kind of happiness now, but no less powerful. This was also the first time he'd flown onto a carrier without his hands on the controls. He felt everything in him clench. He trusted this lieutenant because he trusted all Navy pilots. And he was excited to get back aboard that ship.

And that ship was a workhorse—from all the reports he'd read, she was consistent and expert, exceeding goals every day during this deployment. The thought of being in charge of a crew with high morale made him anxious to get aboard. He leaned forward, tried to hide any display of unease. If anybody accused him of being nervous, he'd deny feeling anything but honored to assume his position as second in command of that beautiful ship. This was an opportunity of a lifetime, and just one step away from being captain of such a ship himself someday.

The Sea Knight carried a crew of three highly trained Marines and came equipped with machine guns mounted on each side for self-defense. They were loaded, but unmanned. The cargo bay was empty and the internal winch in the forward cabin had nothing attached. The helo's sole mission on this day was delivering the *Salvation*'s new executive officer—the first black man to attain this position on an aircraft carrier. They circled in anticipation of clearance to land.

Porter twisted in his seat, strained against the harness tethering him in place, trying to catch a clear view of the ship. She steamed below him churning a foamy wake in the same patch of cool blue water as she'd been every day since leaving San Diego seven months prior. Porter adjusted his sunglasses to see out the window. Each glimpse made his heart rate accelerate to match the rhythmic thwacking of tandem rotors as they fanned the air overhead. The *Salvation* was as long as four football fields put end-to-end, and it towered more than fifteen stories from the waterline. This aircraft carrier displaced 85,000 tons fully loaded as she was with eighty planes, six helicopters, and four thousand men and officers, whose mission was launching and recovering aircraft to support our troops in the jungle.

Porter remembered the first time he landed on that flight deck. It seemed a lifetime ago when he missed all three wires and had to double back. He'd never been that nervous again in his life, until now.

"I hope this works, Commander," the pilot said.

"Yeah," his copilot added. "Those dumb shits need all the help they can get."

"Don't say that," the pilot said.

"What? I'm not saying just the blacks. I mean all of them, Commander. Both. You know? It's a powder keg lately. Worse than usual, is all I'm saying."

Porter's stomach dropped though their altitude hadn't changed. He'd heard of tensions amongst the crew second hand. Tensions were to be expected on a long deployment.

In the helo, Porter adjusted his microphone. "You're talking about racial tension," he said, playing along.

"Can you imagine, sir?" the pilot asked.

"It's not that big a problem, gentleman," Porter said. "All our bones are the same color. There's nothing more to it than that. We'll all be one big, happy family before Old Sal sails back to San Diego."

"Sounds like you got it all figured out," the pilot said.

Porter cleared his throat to buy some time. He needed to come across as confident and in control. "I usually do, boys," he said with a laugh into his helmet-mounted microphone. "I usually do." He cupped his hand over the microphone, so his touch could convey the sincerity missing from his statement.

"They'll need that," the copilot said, "especially since the captain has been bearing down on them."

"Yeah," the pilot said. "The last time the *Salvation* got liberty there was a big dustup at one of the nightclubs. Nasty fight." The pilot's helmet reflected the sun as he spoke.

The copilot pivoted partially to face Porter. "A couple crewmen stayed behind 'cause of it."

Porter's research had mentioned a couple hard landings and widespread crew testiness, but he had no idea what the pilot meant about "bearing down" or how severe it might be.

"No better man for your new job. You gotta admit, Commander. Right?"

Porter didn't know which one said that. A wave rolled inside his ribs and he had a fleeting sensation that he might vomit. He kept it together by thinking this was his lucky ship. She'd always brought him success, and he'd be successful now as well. He always was.

"Isn't that right, Commander?" one of the voices asked again.

Porter's right eye twitched and he was glad they couldn't see him. The weight of it all seemed to press down on his shoulders in that moment. Surely, he was there based solely upon merit. His father had always called guys like this "jive turkeys," but that didn't change the question.

"You bet your ass," he said. As soon as the words left his mouth, he couldn't be sure if he'd conveyed confidence in his leadership or his race.

The helo hovered twenty feet above the deck. Blades thwacked, and Porter's heart raced even faster. They lowered to ten feet, then five, and hung there for what seemed like an hour. Porter's throat ran dry. He exhaled so that his next breath would be the mixture of jet fuel, scorched rubber tires, and sweat that comprised that *Salvation* air.

When they did touch down, it was more gently than he'd ever managed in his old Crusader. Porter removed his helmet and set it on the seat beside him.

The crew chief opened the clamshell door with the roar of rollers in tracks. "Sir," he yelled through the noise of the blades chopping the air above their heads and the wind washing across the deck. He gestured the "all-clear" for Porter to exit the aircraft.

Porter stepped onto the deck in khakis instead of a flight suit, then signaled a thumbs-up as he crouched and looked back at the helo. A strong crosswind flapped the slack in his khaki sleeves and pant legs. He adjusted his sunglasses and leaned his weight into the wind to move forward.

Awaiting him just outside the down draft were the chief engineer—a skinny man with a big, genuine Midwest smile; the chaplain—a young lieutenant who had a baby face and cynicism in his eyes; and the command master chief—a salty senior chief who must have been around since World War II. He had hands like baseball mitts and squeezed Porter's hand the hardest by far but avoided making eye contact.

Porter stood tall and proud on the flight deck of that ship— felt the surge of strength he'd previously known as a pilot taking off and landing on that very deck.

The chaplain and the chief engineer said, "Welcome aboard, Commander Porter," in unison, while the senior chief said, "You got big shoes to fill here, sir."

Porter thought he misread the tone of the man's voice. He looked over the top of his sunglasses at him. Dismissed the notion. Assumed his words had gotten caught in the wind blowing past their faces.

On the flight deck, a dozen airmen in color-coded shirts hustled around the helicopter, refueling the helo and assisting the flight crew with any additional items or services they needed prior to their return flight to the airfield outside Da Nang.

Porter did his best to keep up with the questions from the chaplain and chief engineer. "Yes," he said, "it was a good series of flights to get here. Yes, I am excited to be back aboard the *Salvation*. No, I didn't mind being called away from my cushy gig in Newport, because this is where I truly want to be."

All the while, the grizzled old master chief looked off toward the horizon and muttered under the weight of the wind.

CHAPTER 2

Elliot Brackert had seen the helo circling. He was a defrocked petty officer with a Fu Manchu mustache, hair longer than regulation, a wrinkled uniform, size-twelve boondockers, and a mission of his own. He slipped down to the hangar deck and stood in the shadows.

The hangar deck was the largest covered space Brackert had ever seen, at sea or on land. It was the space below the flight deck where all the planes were stored, maintained, and repaired. This was the place where the crew assembled for special events. As an aviation electrician, Brackert had spent most of his days in there. Knew his way around the hangar bays as well as he knew the woods back home in Knoxville. His access had been revoked two months ago, after his crow had been taken away when he'd officially declared himself a conscientious objector.

While the helo circled and the mechanics and ordnance men rode up the elevator platform to get a closer look at the new XO, Brackert took advantage of the diversion to get up close to an F-8 Crusader. As he approached one of the planes, a stocky, redheaded guy everyone called Hydrant walked by.

"Hey, Elliot. My son took his first steps the other day. He's walking, man. Can you believe it?" Hydrant was the only one aboard the ship to call Brackert by his first name.

Brackert shook his head. "Seems like only yesterday that

giant tapeworm was slithering out of your wife's hairy snatch."

Hydrant laughed. "Tell me about it."

Up close the red hair was kind of orange, and Brackert wondered if the guy's wife was redheaded, too. As good buddies as they were, Hydrant had never shown Brackert a picture of the woman.

"That kid is going to be a handful. The night we made him, I fucked my wife so hard my hipbones were bleeding and her whole undercarriage was black and blue."

"Jesus, Hydrant." Brackert rarely flinched in these kinds of exaggerated conversations, but the image of bleeding and bruises surprised him and formed too clear a picture.

Hydrant ignored Brackert's shock and punched him lightly in the arm. He had the smug crease across his face that guys get when they'd one-upped you. Instead of giving Brackert the opportunity to turn the tables, Hydrant changed the subject. "How's things in the chaplain's office?"

Brackert slapped his hands together. "It's skate duty, let me tell you. And that old boy only quotes the Bible in Sunday services and at Bible study in the evenings but, I swear, if I have to hear one more hokey story about how to be a well-behaved and patriotic young man, I'll yank the Bible out of his hands and beat myself to death with the damn thing."

Hydrant shook his head. "Easy, tough guy." He pointed a grease-stained finger. "That kind of talk will land you in hell."

Brackert shrugged. "Too late for that."

Hydrant pulled a screwdriver from his back pocket and dug grease out from under his thumbnail. "So, what are you doing up here now, anyway?"

Brackert nodded his chin toward the flight deck. "Why aren't you up on deck watching the new XO arrive?"

Hydrant leaned to see up and over the open hangar bay. "He's here?"

"I reckon if you hurry you can see him standing up on deck."

Hydrant waddled the fifty yards toward the ladder leading to the flight deck, leaving Brackert alone to hurry and do what he came to do.

August 3, 1972

Seaman Elliot Brackert
USS Salvation (CV-44)
FPO San Francisco, CA 95660

Dear Elliot,

I got so excited reading your last letter. I love your plan to stop fighting and declare yourself an objector. This is the best news ever. I wish Nixon was as bright as you and would come to realize the same thing instead of sending you boys over there to kill those poor babies. I'm going to reward you like you've never been rewarded before!

How long until you get out and come back? Mission Beach isn't the same without you. Professor Williams asked me to go to the homecoming formal at his school. We'd just be going as friends, but I told him I'd have to ask you first. Since I didn't go to my high school prom I thought it might be fun to be Cinderella one time. I don't know. You can say no if you want. It doesn't matter to me. As long as you're safe and you come back soon.

Ok. Got to go. You-know-who just got back with groceries and if I'm not there to help her put everything away and listen to her complain about the "Damn prices, man!" I'll never hear the end of it.

Stay well and peace baby,

Chrissy

* * *

After a fifteen-hour day of flight ops and underway replenishment, the air crew went below deck to grab chow before showering and sleeping, just so they could wake up and do it all again.

In the chow line, Rufus Applewhite found himself separated from his buddies farther down the line by white boys from the flight deck. He ran a finger around the monkey fist dangling out of his pocket. The edges had gone dark from wear and tear. It was connected to a key ring that held just two keys—one to his locker and the other to the main door of the forward laundry, from where he was happy to be getting a break now.

Applewhite hated lines as much as he hated the smell of stroganoff, which failed to cover the fumes of jet fuel stuck to the crew's color-coded shirts as they filled the passageway that formed the chow line. Each color represented their job on the flight deck. Guys in purple shirts, the grapes, refueled the planes and always reeked head-to-toe of JP-5. Blue shirts handled the planes above and below decks with elevators and tractors. Anyone in green was responsible for the steam-driven catapults that launched the planes like a slingshot, as well as for the arresting gear that stopped the planes on a dime as soon as the tail hook caught the wire. The guys in red were the ones everybody wanted around when takeoffs and landings didn't go according to plan. They were the crash and salvage teams. In-between emergencies they also served as ordnancemen who loaded and reloaded all the aircraft firepower. The brown shirts were the air wing petty officers. White shirts were safety and medical personnel.

Applewhite didn't have a colored shirt. Unless you counted his white T-shirt, which time and too much bleach had turned the same yellow shade as his teeth. The funny thing about that was he worked in the ship's laundry, where he'd loaded and unloaded more of those damn colored shirts than he could count. Too much of his day was limited to washing skid marks out of underwear and snail trails from sheets—ten hours a day for the past ten months. Dissatisfaction combined with a closed-in feeling from the cramped living spaces and the Navy's shower policy—water on, water off, soap up, water on, rinse, done, all in two minutes, maximum—had him on edge. The lack of female companionship and being cooped up with all these white motherfuckers had him feeling like his head would explode. And today he was fucking hungry. Three square meals per day were the only thing that made shipboard life bearable.

He followed behind one of the grapes and tapped his empty tray on the rail, partially so his boys could see him keeping it real up there, but also daring the cracker-ass grape to say something about the noise or the vibration in his tray as he slid it along.

As the line moved, Applewhite passed on rice and runny stroganoff that looked redder than it should. He looked farther down the line and noticed a tray of sandwiches. He was hungry. Hungrier than he'd been in his entire life. He'd been forced to miss noon chow because one of the machines in the ship's laundry was down and it took A-gang a day and a half to fix it. Applewhite had worked straight through to get the forward goat locker's sheets done so he could stay on schedule and not have to hear the chief's mess bitch about getting their racks made up before taps.

Applewhite slid down the line, closer to the sandwiches. He lifted his tray. "Hold me two of those."

The mess crank behind the line was a husky, blond-headed striker with the remnants of acne on his cheeks and forehead and a hula girl tattoo on his left forearm. "Only one each," he said, plopping one on Applewhite's tray. He clapped together the wire tongs twice like a puppet's mouth as he said, "Bye bye." Each clap made the hula girls hips sway.

"Another cracker on a power trip," Applewhite said.

"Just doing my job." The kid clapped the tongs five times.

Applewhite didn't even know what kind of sandwich it was, but he wanted another one. He pointed over the guy's shoulder.

"That cook is calling you." When the guy turned around, Applewhite grabbed another sandwich.

The guy turned back. "Who?"

Applewhite shrugged. "He gone now, man."

The mess cook didn't suspect a thing, but the line hadn't moved, and Applewhite hadn't bothered to conceal the extra sandwich.

"You thieving coon!" the guy hollered. "I said only one."

Heat shot up Applewhite's neck and into his ears. He'd been called that a few times growing up in Lawrence, Kansas, but he never could accept the hate white folks put behind the word. He leaned into the tray rail, his chin hovering over the sneeze guard. "How about you just let the fucking sandwich go." Applewhite wasn't the biggest guy on the ship, but his voice filled the passageway.

The blond kid shook his head. "Can't."

Applewhite looked down the line to his buddies. All eyes were on him. His boys, a group of unlikely sailors from Watts, the south side of Chicago, and Birmingham, Alabama, always looked to him to set things right. He didn't have any rank to speak of and he didn't make a lot of money but having the respect of a group of brothers made every breath he took aboard that ship smell cleaner. It made him feel bigger. Stronger.

Getting called "coon" and not getting the sandwich would cut the legs right out from beneath him. Without that credibility, he'd be left in the stink of bleach and jet fuel with every inhale.

Everyone in line had spread out to watch what would happen next.

Applewhite dropped his tray and lunged for the kid—reached through the food service opening and grabbed the guy by the front of his T-shirt with one hand and yanked him so fast his head smacked on stainless steel. Applewhite flexed the same muscles he used to heft laundry bags stuffed taller than him from the deck up to one of the machines he ran every day. The same burst of energy pulled the kid all the way over the serving line. Applewhite had him on his back on the chow line deck. The kid's arms flailed and smacked at the stainless steel as he tried to break free. The crowd backed up to give them more room to do whatever they were going to do.

"Let go, man," the guy shouted.

Maybe it was anger, maybe it was the expectation in the air, but Applewhite's heart raced like an Eldorado's V-8. He reared back his fist, cocked it for maximum velocity until one of his buddies shouted, "Heat!"

Every man in the crowd exhaled audibly in relief or disappointment.

Applewhite lowered his arm, lugged the kid up to his feet and smoothed the front of the kid's T-shirt. Nothing could be done to hide the welt swelling on the kid's forehead. Applewhite's jaw clenched as he ground his teeth. He'd made his point with this zit-faced kid but mixing it up in front of a master-at-arms would get him locked in the brig and taken to Captain's Mast, where the old man would bust him down a pay grade, again. His stomach knotted up even tighter. This was no longer about a damn sandwich.

A squared-away master-at-arms with forearms as thick as mooring lines walked toward the aft mess deck, anxious to get a quick bite and then hit the rack for at least five hours. The badge affixed to his left shirt pocket slapped against his chest as he stepped over every knee knocker. *Byrd* was stenciled in perfect black letters over his other pocket. As he approached the food service area, he heard commotion from the chow line.

He closed his eyes, hoping he misheard some other noise, but there was no mistaking the hoots and hollers of a crowd just before a fight. He fast-walked along the passageway into what looked like a standoff between a mess cook and a black sailor.

"All right, everybody shape up!" Byrd said, putting himself between the black guy and the white mess cook. Byrd had never seen the blond kid before, but he knew Applewhite from their first night at sea when a game of craps in the corner of the mess deck got out of hand.

"What's going on here?"

"This boy here," the blond kid said, "stole a sandwich."

"I didn't steal shit," Applewhite said. "I don't want none of that other slop. I should get two sandwiches."

"The Navy doesn't give you what you want, Seaman Applewhite. Only what you need." The blond mess cook's voice came out low and he stared Applewhite in the eye.

Applewhite lunged for the mess cook again and got him in a headlock.

Byrd shoved Applewhite twice by the shoulders and hollered, "Knock that shit off this fucking minute." But Applewhite didn't let go.

The crowd chanted, "Let them fight!"

Without backup Byrd was outnumbered. He couldn't count on white guys helping him, because after eight months at sea, many in the crew wanted any kind of entertainment they could get. Their appetite and expectation bounced off the bulkheads.

In the old days, a fight between two sailors would be allowed to continue for a minute or two before being broken up. Back before that, the crew would hold smokers in makeshift rings and let guys battle it out in a clean fight. But in the past few months the chain of command had zero tolerance for altercations, especially between black and white sailors. And by this point in his career Byrd had disappointed his share of bloodthirsty sailors by keeping the peace. He hooked Applewhite's left arm and twisted counterclockwise. This tactic might not make him release his grip on the mess cook's head, but it was just a matter of time until he wouldn't be able to withstand the tension on his shoulder and fear meat would tear from bone.

Byrd had to hand it to the guy for hanging in there so long before releasing the mess cook and raising his other hand in surrender. Byrd didn't let up. "Show's over. You fellas enjoy your meals."

He kept the pressure on the shoulder and used it to propel Applewhite off the mess deck and down the starboard passageway toward repair locker three.

Applewhite struggled less and less the farther down the passageway they walked. Once out of site of the chow line Applewhite went slack as he unclenched his fighting muscles. As tired as Byrd was, he wanted to just let the guy go, but he deserved to spend the night in the brig and let the command master chief decide what to do with him.

As they walked down the passageway toward the brig, Byrd began thinking about the incident report, the intake forms, and the forms the Marines made them sign before taking custody of a sailor. It would make for another night of only a couple hours' sleep. He'd lived on that little sleep, but was really looking forward to an extra hour or two.

He looked at Applewhite. A young, strong kid. Had seen him around the ship hundreds of times. Poor bastard had spent some time in the brig already this deployment. Byrd rationalized that he'd witnessed no punches thrown. No bones were broken. There wasn't any blood. He recalculated the extra sleep time.

"Why you gotta be like that, Rufus?"

"Man." Applewhite shifted his weight. "Honky boots always stepping on nigger necks. Even you got to admit that. This bird farm ain't nothing but the USS *Plantation*. I ain't picking cotton, but all the let me do is wash, dry, and fold that shit for the white man."

"On a purely color level, I'll remind you the new XO of this ship is the epitome of that and there's only one job higher on this whole fucking ship that you fuckers call the Plantation."

Applewhite looked surprised, but also indifferent. "You taking me to the brig or what?"

"You know what?" Byrd said, and let Applewhite loose. "I should take you to the brig, Applewhite. You're in violation of articles one-twenty-two and one-twenty-nine of the Uniform

Code of Military Justice. That's enough to get you lonely and hungry again. But we don't want that, do we?"

Applewhite looked away and shook his head.

"I'm doing you a favor," Byrd said. "Least you could do is pretend to be thankful."

"That's because I ain't done nothing wrong."

"Are you shitting me? I saw you. You were a cunt hair away from pounding that mess crank's face in. I fucking saw you. Jesus fucking Christ, man."

Applewhite crossed his arms and looked down the passageway.

"Save that attitude shit, Applewhite, and listen to me. If you want to go around representing your people like that all you'll do is convince every white man aboard this ship that's all you are. Half of them are already sure of it. Keep on giving the other half reasons to take their side instead of yours. Go ahead. Just don't act surprised when shit turns from bad to worse."

"Come on now, Byrd, man. It ain't like that. You doing me a solid. No brother gonna forget that, but don't be preaching at me, man. It ain't cool. You don't know how shit is."

Byrd felt amusement rise into his lungs, which forced a smile. He shook his head and crossed his arms over his chest. "I know way more than you think, Rufus." Byrd used the guy's first name as a way to make the conversation more personal. "Now make yourself scarce. Don't let me catch you near the mess deck anymore this evening. You got it?"

"Appreciate the solid, man," Applewhite said, making only brief eye contact. "And tell your buddies they don't have to be such assholes all the time. They should be cool like you."

Byrd appreciated the compliment. He nodded. "You can say the same exact thing to your men." Byrd laughed as he rested a hand on Applewhite's shoulder. "Go on. Get where you need to be without causing any more trouble."

"Fuck that. I'm a go eat."

Byrd grabbed Applewhite's upper arm and was surprised how

dense it was with muscle. "Seriously! Stay away from the mess deck. You hear?"

Applewhite shook his head. "Shit. I'm just playing. You being cool. I be cool."

Byrd let go. "If we don't take care of each other out here, who will?"

May May
Barrio Barretto
Olongapo City 2200
Baloy
Olongapo City, Philippines

July 22, 1972

PO Harry Byrd
USS Salvation (CV-44)
FPO San Francisco, CA 95660

Long time you no here. Gone to long. I no like you way. Come here soon.

Until, look my picture. Come for me.

Mahal kita,

May May

CHAPTER 3

After evening chow, Porter stood on the bridge wing, nearly a hundred feet above the water, but still close enough to smell the fumes of jet fuel and hydraulic grease that filled the air topside and below decks.

He slouched a little from years of bending to better hear shorter men. He corrected his posture whenever he caught himself relaxing into it.

Even up there, the vibration of the ship's kinetic energy worked into the rubber soles of his steel-toed boots and into his hips and on up to his eye sockets. There'd always been comfort in that. Now, having a far greater responsibility, that sensation excited him as well.

Extreme pride to Porter was something to be felt, not displayed. That was the one positive lesson his father had taught him. "If you got something good, don't show it to nobody because they'll try and take it." Even as a kid, Porter saw the value in the words, but as he got older, he pointed it inward to make sure he never got cocky. Even the best pilot in the world could be taken out by one well-placed round or surface-to-air missile. That way of thinking guided him now. It wasn't just about having the job, but about doing it well and getting man and machinery home safely.

Darkness had settled, and the *Salvation*'s flight deck was

quiet as the planes sat in position in the hangar deck for the next day's work. Porter rested his elbows on the railing and stared at the horizon, which was as faint as a crease in a blue-black sheet. The ship had been sailing the waters of Yankee Station in the Gulf of Tonkin for the better part of a calendar year. A surge of worry shot through him, making him question if he was as qualified as he needed to be to deal with the problems he'd encounter among the officers and crew. He'd never been responsible for the sheer numbers he was now. But he never lacked confidence, especially when he flew. He stifled the worry, stowed it until another day.

His bags had been delivered to his stateroom, but they remained zipped. This was the first opportunity he'd had that day to exhale. It felt good. He felt good. Tired, but powerful. He didn't recall what he'd eaten for dinner, but it filled him now as fully as the pride for being where he was. This ship. This job. One step away from commanding his own ship.

On the bridge, a lieutenant that Porter hadn't met had the CON, but instead of introducing himself Porter stood outside on the bridge wing. There was something about the sound of wind and water brushing past gray steel that spoke to him. This was the first chance he'd gotten to be outside since he'd helo'd in from Da Nang that morning. It seemed like days ago already. And he hadn't even met the captain yet. He looked out over the flight deck. A sight he'd seen from all the good angles, but in that moment he simultaneously feared he wasn't prepared for such a giant step, while he also dreamed of the day he was captain of his own carrier. The dichotomy was nothing new to him. He'd felt the same mixture of emotions when he entered college, then again at Navy flight school, and on every sortie and mission he flew.

The metal-on-metal sound of a hatch opening broke him from his thoughts. He turned, expecting to see the lieutenant from the bridge. Instead, he saw thick gray hair as the captain stepped through the hatch onto the bridge wing. The top of his head barely reached Porter's nose. His torso formed a rectangle bisected by a khaki web belt.

The captain held out his hand for Porter to shake. "Robert Porter, I presume," he said with a Southern accent that surprised Porter. It shouldn't have, since he'd read the captain was from Mississippi.

"It's a pleasure to meet you, Captain Holt."

A moment later, a third-class boatswain's mate stepped out with a silver tray carrying two crystal highball glasses and a bottle of Jim Beam, which he placed atop the gyrocompass repeater. He had a neatly trimmed mustache and never made eye contact with either officer. Without being told, he poured two fingers worth into each glass and then ducked through the hatch, pulling the watertight door closed behind him.

"My apologies for being unable to welcome you on the flight deck personally." The captain's accent seemed less pronounced as his voice floated on the wind in Porter's face along with the aroma of bourbon.

"Your plate being full isn't exactly a secret," Porter said. They'd never met and Porter didn't fully know why the man had selected him to be his second in command, but he didn't want to believe the helo pilots either.

"I trust the greeting you received on my behalf made you feel most welcomed."

It didn't strike Porter as a question, but he lied anyway. "Absolutely, sir."

The captain picked up one of the glasses. "Join me in a drink," he said, and then climbed into his conning chair on the forward end of the bridge wing, where he crossed a heel over the opposite knee.

Porter felt the wind gust again and tasted jet fuel, though it could easily have been the booze.

Porter wasn't much of a drinker. He wasn't a stick in the mud at parties, but none of his problems had ever driven him to the bottle. This wasn't any gift of restraint, but quite the opposite. He'd learned to stay away from the sauce by watching his father down twelve cans of Brown Derby Pilsner every night between getting home at six and passing out by ten, usually with a cigarette dangling from his lips.

Despite the awkwardness of silence with the captain, Porter remained still. He'd had a drink or two aboard ship before, but never with the captain, and never so openly. He didn't know if this was a bonding moment or a test. If he drank, he could be judged as unreliable. If he didn't, he could be dismissed as a tight-ass. Standing there any longer would make him look like a pussy.

The captain removed a toothpick from his breast pocket and worked it into a molar. He stopped, pulled out the toothpick, looked at the end, and flicked whatever he'd extracted into the wind. "How's your first day, so far?"

Porter fought a sudden desire to yawn as the lack of sleep caught up with him. Before the helo ride that had delivered him aboard, he'd spent two days in cargo plane jump seats, trying to doze in spurts between air pockets.

"Easier than the last time I was out this way," he said.

The captain breathed with a laugh, tucked the toothpick back into his pocket, and reached for the other glass of bourbon. He held it up to Porter. "To easier days."

Porter took the glass and echoed the captain's toast.

After a hearty swallow, the captain said, "You went to USC, yes?"

Porter lowered his glass from his lips. "UCLA. Mechanical engineering."

The captain nodded. "That's what I studied, too. Five years before you, if I recall."

"I read that," Porter said. "Brown is impressive."

"That was graduate school. My heart will always be with Ole Miss."

Porter tried to swallow his embarrassment. The lack of sleep made that detail slip from his mind. "But you've got to admit, Providence is a fun town," he said in an effort to change the subject.

"That's right." The captain nodded, as much to his bourbon as to Porter. "You spent time at the War College."

"Newport is scenic, but..."

"But when the sun goes down..."

They both laughed.

The captain uncrossed his legs and leaned forward. "I'm mighty glad to have you here."

A swell of pride washed around Porter's ribcage and he was convinced the helo pilots were full of shit. Porter nodded. "Thank you, sir."

The captain settled back and looked out over the water. "Do you know why I selected you for this job?"

Porter let the alcohol ease down his throat. He wasn't the type to mince words, but he couldn't allow himself to blurt out the rumor he'd heard on the helo.

Before Porter could answer, the captain looked over to him. The wrinkles around his eyes deepened as he expressed enthusiasm. "We surpass every goal CINCPAC lays out for us. And I intend to keep it that way."

"Why mess with perfection?" Porter asked.

"You flew planes off this very flight deck."

Porter nodded and took another pull of bourbon. He didn't want to think about the past. Everything going forward mattered more than what he'd accomplished up to now. Most of it was exemplary. As recently as ten days ago, it was the best it had been since his divorce. He recalled the severity of the moment-within-the-moment he'd been in bed with a dishwater blonde he'd met at a convenience store. Porter always dated white girls. His father called him out on that every chance he got. On his son's wedding day the old man had said, "Black women need strong men in their lives. White girls done got enough in this lifetime. It ain't right for them to snag all the smooth brothers, too."

Trails of bourbon clung to the sides of Porter's glass.

The captain looked out toward the horizon as he spoke. "You're a shit-hot pilot."

Porter appreciated the present tense.

"Squeaky clean."

Porter looked down at his glass. It was the same kind of rhetoric he'd heard at every turn of his career. "Lots of commanders have the same track record," he said.

"Well, none that I can think of who wants the best for this ship almost as much as I do."

"It's no secret this ship holds a ton of memories for me," Porter said. "But make no mistake, Captain, I wouldn't have accepted this billet if I didn't think I could learn a lot from you."

The captain nodded and pulled his glass away from his mouth. "I'm flattered you took the time to do homework on me."

"I couldn't help noticing you have an amazing way of staying on mission despite some hefty obstacles." Porter took a bigger swig than he'd meant and coughed once in response.

"Well, there's no need getting emotional about it," the captain said. "I just live by two simple rules. One, do your job. Two, don't let anyone get in your way of doing your job. If everybody does the same, why there's nothing we can't do."

Porter felt himself smiling even before he registered the goose flesh traveling up his forearms. "This is going to be an exciting deployment."

"It already has. And that's another thing, you're joining us late into this deployment. Some may resent you being new. Others will hate you simply because you're not Jimbo Lamply. Don't let them get you down."

Porter's stomach soured at that. He tugged on the collar of his shirt; it was hard to get a good fit over his shoulders. He never viewed it as a nervous tick, just something the tailors were limited in resolving. It would eat at him later, wondering if the captain was being delicate in implying a racial bias of the crew.

The captain crossed his legs again. "You heard about the altercation on the mess deck earlier tonight?"

"The command master chief briefed me. And I have to ask, why is he only a senior chief?"

"That's a story for another day. The real story we need to discuss is the substantial tension among the black crew."

Porter squeezed his glass. There it was, out in the open. The helo pilot was right and Porter was a fool for thinking he'd received the position solely on merit. This too, he had to hide from the captain despite boiling inside. "Totaling three hundred men?" he asked.

"Give or take. And I'm not going to lie to you. There've been a few incidents, mostly on the beach when booze was involved. I don't know what their problem is."

Porter felt the sting of the word "their." He wondered if the captain would break out more colorful terms or mind his manners. "But you're hoping I'll keep *them* calm," he said.

The captain removed the toothpick from his shirt pocket again and worked it between his upper molars. "If you think about it," the captain said, "I effectually bet both our careers on it. But it's not a reckless wager. We're both bright, capable Naval officers. I'm sure your presence will remind them that good things happen to good sailors no matter their skin color."

Porter didn't like the insult or the cadence in which it was spoken.

"Let's make no mistake, Mr. Porter. Your ethnicity factored into my decision. But trust me, you're a rising star. Destined to achieve great heights in the Navy."

The praise surprised Porter. He rested a hand on the life rail. "My career ambition is no secret. And as long as we're speaking frankly, sir, I don't give one shit about anything preceded by the words 'first' and 'black.'"

"Take it easy, Smokey. I'm on your side. Remember?"

Porter winced with a contraction of neck muscles. He resented the captain's use of his old call sign. That name was given to him without choice back in flight school. As a naïve young pilot, Porter had protested the name by declaring, "I've never touched a cigarette in my life." The squadron commander had laughed. They all laughed. It took two weeks for Porter to catch on to the brown bear reference.

The captain raised his glass and Porter raised his and they sipped at the same time.

"Are you familiar with Jesse Brown?" Porter asked as the burn eased down his gullet.

"Did he play for the Cincinnati Reds?"

"No, but since you mention baseball, I'll say he was like Jackie Robinson to me when I was a kid. I read an article about him in *Life* magazine shortly after he became the first black man to earn his golden wings. I thought about him every time I lowered into a cockpit."

"So, you're talking about the Navy's first black pilot?"

"I am."

"Didn't he crash in Korea shortly after?"

"The point is that he was the first. I'm just another guy doing my job."

"But you're on pace to be the first black man to get command of his own ship. Maybe this ship, someday."

Porter couldn't help smiling at the thought. "Well, that would be a dream come true, but I have no control over that."

The captain laughed and inhaled the liquid in his glass. "I suppose a good word from me, when the time comes, will go a long way in making that happen."

"That goes without saying, Captain."

"Well then, all you have to do is exceed my expectations and you can consider that signed, sealed, and delivered."

Such a phrase would normally excite Porter, but the way the captain said it made the bourbon taste like JP-5.

"It's not about what color you are or where you're from as far as I'm concerned. I mean to say, to my knowledge there are no two red-blooded gentlemen who agree on absolutely everything, outside of the merits of booze, money, and pussy, yet they always remain gentlemen."

Porter had never heard the speech delivered quite that way. "If you're implying disagreements between us be discussed privately,

I'm in complete agreement."

"Well," the captain slapped his knee, "that was awfully easy, then, wasn't it?"

The smile on the captain's face made Porter feel like he'd just lost a negotiation. He wondered if the captain had sat in the same seat and had the same conversation with his last XO.

A moment later, the rush of an inbound plane's thrusters caught Porter's attention.

"You've got a bird coming back?" Porter asked. "Sounds like an F-8."

The ship turned into the wind and increased speed.

Porter didn't know what kind of intel the plane might've gathered, if any. That wasn't his concern as the ship's XO. The ship's true task was carried out in daylight when visibility was better to lay down cover fire for ground forces. He looked at the sky, moon and stars mostly hidden. Night landings were hard for most pilots. Setting down a bird at night on a surface that never stayed still required timing, precision, and balls the size of boulders. Porter had flown hundreds of sorties himself in that same model plane back in sixty-five as a thirty-four-year-old lieutenant, proud to be the only black pilot in his squadron—one of only a handful of black pilots in the Navy.

The captain looked at his watch. "It's early." He picked up the handset beside his chair. "What's going on, Johnson?" The captain nodded and grunted, "Uh huh," and then, "Very well," as he hung up.

"Everything okay?" Porter asked.

"Inbound bird took an arrow or two over the coast."

Porter looked at the *Salvation*'s flight deck lights from the vantage of the bridge wing. Lights delineated the four and a half acres of darkened flight deck. Without those, the entire ship would be invisible to a pilot on a night with no visible moon.

He watched the F-8 Crusader wobble on approach. Even at

that distance, the wings' downward slope revealed either fear or overconfidence. The pilot had dropped to ten thousand feet and zeroed in. His angle of approach was off and his attitude wasn't correct. Porter had always relied on the optical landing apparatus affixed to the port side of the landing area—what everyone called the meatball. The color-coded datum lights in relation to his plane's flight path were indispensable. They never misled him, and without the depth perception that darkness steals, his best odds required utilizing the tools at his disposal.

The pilot in this damaged inbound plane likely used TACAN radio navigation to find the carrier's beacon and headed for it. He had his IFF code and the approach controller in his ear issuing instructions. He held the abeam position but not the optimal glide slope. The pilot would have to call the ball and ignore his urges to look at the deck. His eyes would tell him he's too high. As the pilot made his final approach, he'd have to trust the meatball to reveal his true approach. The follicles on Porter's skin dilated, ready to sweat. He felt his pulse throb. Surely the pilot would utilize the meatball. Wouldn't he?

As a precaution, a search-and-rescue helicopter, generally referred to as the "angel," hovered three hundred feet off the starboard side.

The sound of the F-8 engine was familiar, comforting, distant at first, but rapidly increasing to full power in case he had to bolter. The pilot needed to ignore the red glow of his altimeters. He was high and crooked. Porter angled his hips and held out his hands, as if body English could overcome the yaw instability and correct the plane's attitude. The pilot reduced power to control his rate of decent and landed hard, just past the first wire, where a rear tire blew like a shotgun blast. The plane listed and skidded.

The tail hook missed second wire because of the angle at which the plane listed. If it missed again, the pilot would normally raise his flaps and take off, but with this plane's tire situation that wasn't an option.

The plane continued sideways across the deck to the port side in a metal-on-metal symphony. As it skidded across the flight deck, the downed titanium wing snagged an ordnanceman, pinned him down and dragged him the length of the tarmac. The deck was like a cheese grater on human flesh. Friction cooled by the blood and bone of the guy's pelvis.

Porter resisted the urge to look away.

As the wing dug harder, a leg broke loose at the top of the femur. The severed limb spiraled for a moment before it lost momentum and came to rest on the deck. The tail hook skipped along and caught the severed leg just below the knee. Momentum carried the skid along, lubricating the deck now with the kid's torso and the back of his head.

When he was younger, Porter had understood guys around him were going to die. It came with the territory. Porter wasn't brave about that, but rather hopeful that it didn't happen to him. His selective reasoning allowed him to believe that the more pilots who did, the better were his odds. As he got older and took on the responsibility of a squadron and hundreds of men's lives, he grew to realize that even in wartime, when men were killed every day, that the news of each shortened life would break somebody's heart.

He exhaled when the plane came to a halt. The distance was too great to see the particulars, so Porter used binoculars. Before he could inhale again, a spark ignited the fuel leaking from the plane's damaged tank. A magnified flash seemed to melt his eyes. He couldn't see clearly, but flames roared high enough and hot enough that he felt the heat from his position on the bridge wing.

As his eyesight returned, black smoke filled the flight deck and the air all around them.

In its immediate horror, even from that height and through eyes throbbing from the flash, Porter saw the burning plane not as it was, but rather as the plane his buddy, Sully, crash-landed back in sixty-six. He'd died on impact. There was no way Porter could forget the night he'd lost his friend. Every subsequent landing event served as a reminder of that loss.

The captain sprang from his chair and set down his glass on the gyrocompass repeater. He bolted through the hatch to take his place on the bridge.

On the flight deck, the damage control team sprinted into action with their fire nozzles and hoses applying foam from one side, while a team washed it away with high-pressure water from the other side. The pilot was still in the plane.

Porter knew what the captain had to do. Porter knew what was required of the air wing commander. But he had no idea what his role might be in that moment.

He looked down onto the flight deck. The damage control team had the flames extinguished and the canopy open. The pilot climbed out and down to the wet deck. Apparently shaken, but unharmed.

Porter walked onto the bridge, where the captain had a sound-powered phone handset pressed to his ear.

When the captain saw Porter on the bridge, he lowered the phone, looked at Porter.

"I don't have my bearings, sir," Porter said. "How can I help?"

The captain laughed. "No need to worry, Smokey. You've had a long day. Get some shut-eye. This is all under control."

For the first time in Porter's sea-going life, he wanted to vomit. It wasn't the severed leg that got to him, but rather a pressure in his throat that built until he panted through a sensation of falling overboard, choking on the chopping waves. A kid just died a horrible death. A death that would devastate his mother, or girlfriend, or wife, or some other family member or friend. It was never easy for people to let go. He couldn't blame them. His instinct was guilt. While the plane that killed that boy had flown closer, Porter had been drinking whiskey. It felt like a knife in Porter's side. And that knife twisted upon the realization the captain wasn't equally disturbed by the tragedy.

He didn't care if the captain was heartless and using him. Porter would make the most of this opportunity.

CHAPTER 4

The night of the F-8 crash, Brackert sat on his bottom rack in the berthing compartment. Uneasiness rampaged inside his ribcage. Not just tears, but moisture from his liver and spleen leaked over his lower eyelids. In quick succession, Brackert raised his hands above his head and swiped the water away with each shoulder. The only thing that traveled around the ship faster than scuttlebutt was the truth. Brackert had learned that his redheaded buddy, Hydrant, was the one killed in the crash landing.

They'd shared stories about their women. Played cards and drank together when they were in port. Brackert didn't want a drink now, or feel the need to vomit, but just wanted to lie down and be left alone with the steady hum vibrating through every piece of metal aboard the ship.

Hydrant had been the last friend he had left since declaring as a conscientious objector. He'd been yanked from his circle of friends to finish out the cruise on his own. That's when he'd been turned over to the chaplain. Brackert hadn't been on liberty since, but Hydrant never let it bother him. The guy remained friendly. Now he was gone.

Dead because of what Brackert had done.

His aisle faced forward and aft and was tucked out of the foot traffic of the main aisle in a maze of racks stacked three-high. Despite the close proximity of the other ninety-eight guys, he almost felt like he was alone. The smell of jet fuel filled his nose. It was in the passageways, even down there. Twenty-four hours a day. That smell was the one thing he'd miss the least when he received his discharge. Everything was covered in a pond scum mixture of fuel and grit. At first, it drove him crazy to have that oily dust on his clothes, in his nostrils, covering his teeth. After a few days, he found himself washing his hands less frequently. Within a couple weeks, he didn't even notice it. Fortunately, Chrissy's letters still smelled like her perfume.

His legs extended into the aisle, his size-twelve boots crossed. He held one of her letters to his nose as he put pen to paper. He had to swipe his eyes with his shoulders again. He wondered if now was the best time to write a letter to his girl back in San Diego.

Maybe it was a naïve perception of time that made him think the letter had to be written that day. Perhaps it was a desire for a sense of connection to something that made him feel good. Maybe a combination. But he wrote, *I miss you*. He really wanted to brag about how he'd wedged the thin steel of his P-38 can opener between the bead of wheel rim and the tire of a Crusader so as not to impede the plane's takeoff, but would cause the blowout upon impact of touching down and essentially crash the plane. Wanted to write in all capital letters: I SINGLE-HANDEDLY TOOK A PLANE OUT OF COMMISSION. But his head was a blender. She'd be disappointed the plane had been able to complete its mission, but he'd locked on to the angle that bothered him. A man died because of him and this made his eyes well up again. He swiped at the water and reminded himself of the pride of plotting it successfully. He never meant to get somebody killed. He never thought for a minute that even the pilot could be hurt.

Guilt hit him with heat inside his ribs—it steamed his intestines, burned his throat. He cupped a palm over his mouth in case he dry heaved. He'd miss his friend, but Hydrant's son was too young to understand what had happened to his father. All he'd know is that his daddy ain't coming home. Brackert experienced that himself in 1961 after his father quit coming home. His mother and the other adults tried explaining it to the scared little boy in his little league uniform, but Brackert couldn't help blaming himself until he was in high school and his composition teacher, Miss Engle, explained how she'd known his father and how he always bragged on his son. The car crash that took him, she said, wasn't anybody's fault. It was an accident. Brackert found out later that year how much the old man had been drinking the night he crashed. That was the old man's fault. Brackert learned to live with that.

Hydrant's son wouldn't have the benefit of wrongdoing on his father's part. He'd have only the randomness of the universe. When Brackert got home, he'd contact the kid. Explain how it went down. Why it went down. He'd bring Chrissy with him and the kid would understand. Chrissy would show him pictures of burned and scarred Vietnamese children and he'd never question it again.

Even if that ever happened, the kid would still miss his father being there to see him graduate high school, get married, have kids. Hydrant wouldn't be able to wow grandkids with fart noises he could make with his hand in his armpit. He would've been the type to always have candy or quarters in his pocket. Hydrant was like a big, wide kid.

Brackert put that out of his mind as he wrote: *Dearest Chrissy, There was an accident with a plane today. It'll be out of commission for at least a week. One guy died, unfortunately.* Brackert needed her to know the seriousness of this thing she had him do for her. Not that they were friends. He didn't trust the system enough to write anything more about it. He was pretty sure the Navy brass had random letters and packages pulled for inspection somewhere along the way, maybe every step of the way. His status as a conscientious objector likely made him more of a target. Everything he did was in an effort to impress Chrissy. But he couldn't risk telling her outright. And he was in no mood to brag. She should get the message. He hoped so.

Chrissy was the first woman to make him feel like a man—not just a testosterone-driven animal, but like he *was* something. Not just a product of what he did for a living, but what he had to contribute to the world. Like all he'd done in his life amounted to something. Like she believed in what he had accomplished to that point and in what he could become. No one else on the planet had made feelings of pride rise up in him that way. He'd do anything to prolong that feeling.

He signed off the letter with *I love you*, even though she never said those words to him. Brackert knew she meant it. She signed her letters with a heart and that had to count almost as much as saying it. His mission in life was to do something that would make it impossible for her to keep the words hidden in her mouth.

Right then and there, he resolved to tuck away his friend's death. He couldn't let himself get weak with guilt over that dumb bastard who got caught in the crossfire.

Brackert folded his letter and reached into a shoebox where he kept stationery and stamps and her letters. He stuffed and stamped one of the envelopes he'd addressed twenty at a time for later use. He picked up her most recent letter and held it to his nose. The paper felt slick from wear and the perfume smelled faint, but familiar. He didn't know the name of it or how much it cost, but the musk reminded him of sitting close on a blanket in the sand on Mission Beach.

The smell and the memory calmed his nerves. Mission Beach was where they'd met one night at a bonfire near the roller coaster. Brackert had walked right up to her and introduced himself and teased her about being drunk even though it was obvious she wasn't. She protested as playfully as he'd accused. They shared a joint, held hands, walked with their feet in the cold surf, and had been a couple ever since.

He often thought of her near the water. Her hair half-wet

from the ocean. Her skin tan, tight, and salty. He grew rigid just thinking about her. In that moment, he was no longer sitting on his rack, but rather reclined on her bed in the house in Lemon Grove she shared with a fifty-year-old yoga instructor and a cellist from Austria. He loved that bed, saw it now, covered with a green and yellow afghan knitted by her grandmother, positioned beneath a window he liked to leave open at night. Cool So Cal air drifted in and he curled beneath the comforting weight of the afghan. It was the exact opposite of his rack aboard ship, and not just because of all the love they made there, but rather because he slept better in that bed than anywhere he'd ever been.

He clicked off his rack light and covered himself with his Navy-issue wool blanket. Held the letter to his nose with one hand, while pleasuring himself with the other. It was the closest way to be with her. Until he saw the image of Hydrant's leg getting gigged by the tail hook and dragged into an unrecognizable cut of beef that landed ten feet from the lumpy puddle that used to be his torso.

The more he sniffed her scent, the easier it was to convince himself that he didn't kill his friend, but rather got himself a notch closer to Chrissy. Any life was worth that. That thought made it worthwhile. This sudden comfort allowed his eyes to close and his mouth to smile.

Sharon Wickes
462 ½ Hope Street
Bristol, RI 02804

August 28, 1972

Commander Robert Porter
USS Salvation (CV-44)
FPO San Francisco, CA 95660

Robert, Robert, Robert.

Why did you have to ship out so soon after we met? I wasn't nearly done with you yet. Eddie didn't have any right to say those things to you. He isn't like that. He was just mad. He was dealing with it okay with his hang-ups about you until he caught me singing "That Old Black Magic." I wasn't even aware I was doing it. I just can't get you out of my ever-loving mind. There's never been anything particularly romantic about our open marriage until you. Maybe it's the color thing. Maybe it's your life-risking position in the military, I don't know. I can't believe I never even saw you in uniform. Can you send a picture or something? Having one tacked to my vanity mirror would make Eddie's head explode, I suppose. So never mind. I'll just have to keep my memories of you where they're safest and most vivid and most accessible when I want you. It's not the same, of course, as having you here, but it's better than nothing. I hope I get to see you again sometime soon. And I really, really, really hope the world hasn't changed us too much by then. I better get going. I want to get this into the mail before too much more time passes and you forget about me. You stay safe over there, Robert. And don't pick up any women at convenience stores. Haha.

XOXOXO

Sharon

Early in his second week aboard the *Salvation*, Porter took a shortcut through the officers' lounge. He moved fast so he could get back to his stateroom to use the head before the galley inspection he had scheduled for 1500. This was the downtime between meals and he'd planned the occasion to be a morale-boosting, goodwill event for the men who fixed most of the ship's meals. His purpose there would be to tell them they made the Navy proud, as a way to motivate them to hang in there and do their best for a while longer.

His goal accompanied his need for positive PR. To this point, Porter felt everyone was keeping him at arm's length. Made him feel like a salesman in someone else's territory. He didn't know if it was loyalty to the former XO or if it was his race, but he acted like everything was okay all the time, like he always did.

With ten minutes before the galley dog and pony show, his shortcut stopped him in his tracks. This wasn't because of the off-duty ship's officer in a bathrobe leaned over a crossword puzzle from the pages of the *New York Times* someone must have sent from back home. Rather, it was a scene unfolding through the glare of the nineteen-inch television mounted on a steel bracket in the corner of the room. The camera angle was over the captain's shoulder, tight enough to catch his profile in the foreground and wide enough to show the black sailor standing before him.

"What the hell?" Porter couldn't imagine why the captain had chosen to allow cameras inside his Captain's Masts.

As executive officer, it would be Porter's job to determine which sailors brought up on charges would be worthy of the captain's time, but this case must've been held over from the previous XO's tenure.

Someone should have told him there was a Captain's Mast that day, and he should have been informed it was being broadcast over the ship's closed-circuit television station. It was a fluke of timing that he'd seen it at all.

The Navy's rich history of punishing men at sea was no secret. Captain's Masts dated back to the wooden-hulled, triple-masted vessels at the dawn of America. Captain's Mast proceedings regularly resulted in demotions, pay cuts, and time served in the brig.

Porter looked around the officers' lounge. The officer with

the puzzle looked up and nodded at him but went back to filling in the blocks. Such a puzzle would be a welcome distraction on the toilet if Porter could only tear himself away from the television. He held it in and watched the pleading of a black man whose name was too faded to read on his chambray shirt.

"It was self-defense," the man said in response to the captain's question of why he'd hit a petty officer with a chair.

Porter stood there rubbing his dry fingers over the part of his arm exposed beneath his short khaki sleeves. The smell of coffee filled the space strongly enough that he tasted it.

After some back and forth about the events leading up to the altercation, it was clear the young man on television had meant to say he'd been provoked. "That cracker can't go 'round talking about a man's mama like that, Captain Holt. It just ain't right."

The captain didn't seem impressed with the defense.

Porter watched the captain sentence the black man to three days in the brig.

The brig was a series of cells four-feet by seven-feet with nothing but steel in each. At night the Marine Corps guards issued foam mattresses for the prisoner to put between them and the steel deck as they tried to sleep. In the morning, the mattresses were ripped out of the cells and the prisoners began cleaning their cells, the head, decks, and bulkheads. After lunch, they cleaned the whole brig again. On hands and knees, with toothbrushes.

Most of the traffic down there was younger guys, young enough to be Porter's sons. They were the impetuous crowd with no grip on their tempers. There were some older guys, occasionally, being punished for dereliction of duty and the like.

The captain didn't stop there.

Porter stared at the television and witnessed the man being sentenced to the fullest extent allowed by the Uniform Code of Military Justice.

The captain added, "Three days on bread and water."

"Bread and water?" Porter asked aloud.

The off-duty officer in the robe nodded again but didn't seem surprised or even impressed. He continued with the crossword puzzle.

Porter pulled a green notepad from his shirt pocket, clicked a pen, and jotted a note reminding him to find out the frequency with which the old man gave out such severe punishments. He returned the pad and pen to his pocket and watched the television with his arms crossed. There was no way to know if the captain had the temerity to continue with another case after that, but the next minute, a white sailor—a skinny airman with red hair—stood before the captain. He'd been caught throwing a mallet and a crescent wrench, both hitting a helicopter mechanic.

Every muscle in Porter's body clenched in anticipation of another bread and water sentence. Instead, the white guy got off with a stern talking to about respecting the chevrons and exhibiting self-control. "Don't let me see you here again," the captain said. "Dismissed."

Tension shifted from Porter's shoulders and shot into his forearms as he squeezed his fists. He'd made himself twenty minutes late for the galley inspection, not by enjoying the lengthy bowel movement he'd planned—that mood had passed—but by standing in front of the television hanging his head at the captain's injustice.

Brackert checked his watch. He was five minutes late already. He tucked Chrissy's dog-eared letters into his locker and ran out of the berthing compartment. The passageway stood empty as he sprinted toward the aft mess deck. The escalator there was meant for such occasions, but it was a nonstop shot to the arresting gear machinery room just below the flight deck, and he only needed to go as high as the hangar deck.

He ran up ladders with chain rails that rattled as he took them two steps at a time. His boots slapped the vinyl tile through passageways all the way to the hangar deck, which was filled with the metal-on-metal sounds of maintenance and preparation, voices shouting and whistling. Jet fuel fumes hung heavy in the air along with the exhaust of forklifts and plane movers. The space was lit daylight-bright by the yellow glow of a thousand fluorescent tubes overhead so that work could be done around the clock.

Most of the guys would go up there any chance they got. Brackert was no different. Since the flight deck was off-limits to nonessential personnel almost all of the time, the hangar deck—almost three football fields long under a roof thirty feet high—was as close to being outside as they could get.

As he made his way through the hangar deck, he heard the slaps of a ball bouncing, the raised voices of the group playing four-on-four.

The chaplain arranged the weekly game for the group of ne'er-do-wells he'd been tasked with rehabilitating. Brackert knew the guys from the Bible study he'd been obliged to attend since declaring himself a conscientious objector, and he was familiar with most of them and the infractions that got them included in this group of troubled or at-risk sailors with histories of bad decisions, but nothing purely criminal. All minor offenses—fighting, booze-related issues on leave, threats of suicide, that sort of thing. He didn't judge them for any of it. And if they judged him, they didn't let on. There were plenty of other guys for that on the ship. Brackert was assigned to the group while he waited to process out of the Navy. This, of course, was taking longer than he'd anticipated and he needed the chaplain on his side to help with the paperwork and all the official stuff.

The basketball noises blended with the engine rumbles of forklifts driving various loads. And despite being opened up, the hangar deck smelled of jet fuel, gunpowder, sweat, and burnt metal from the charred remains of the F-8's twisted carcass—the one whose crash landing he'd caused. His stomach twisted as he looked at it in the far corner of the hangar deck; it reminded him of the dead shipmate zipped in a bag stuffed in one of the walk-in freezers below decks.

The ball players hollered various calls for Brackert to hurry and get in the game.

Flight ops were done for the day, but pallets of ordnance took up the second half of the basketball court. Brackert knew little about the munitions—didn't know what caliber went with what plane—but Chrissy was convinced each round would kill a Vietnamese child.

Brackert unbuttoned his dungaree shirt and tossed it toward the pile of others draped across a stack of empty pallets by a water fountain. He untucked his T-shirt and rolled his shoulders forward and back a couple times. Leaned his head side-to-side to stretch his neck.

The chaplain had been sitting out, leaning on a pallet of bombs. "It's about time, Brackert," he said.

When Brackert nodded, the chaplain pushed himself away from the pallet of ordnance and hopped onto the court of play. He crouched, hands out wide, guarding Brackert. He stepped on Brackert's size-twelve boondockers a number of times. Sometimes hard enough Brackert fell to the deck. The chaplain did it on purpose every time but calling foul would look weak. And it wasn't like Brackert had the liberty to stick an elbow in his ribs or get a hand in his face to send a message.

He worried that the chaplain was on to him about his involvement with the plane, Hydrant's death.

The edges of the deck were gray painted steel, while the rest of the surface was covered with a thick, black, nonskid coating the texture of ten-grit sandpaper. The ball didn't bounce true and once in a while it would hit a smooth patch and carom in an unexpected direction. Brackert lost two possessions because of that.

With quick glances toward the damaged plane and away from the game, Brackert saw a black guy hauling ammo on his shoulder. The guy was likely a basketball player himself. Most of the black crew liked the game and were better at it than these talentless misfits. Brackert had watched groups of blacks play a number of times. Those guys dunked and sank twenty-foot hook shots like the pros. There was no chance of that kind of play with these two teams. They all played in dungarees and boots and were clumsy from lack of practice. The best guy on Brackert's side had played JV ball ten years earlier.

The chaplain brushed past Brackert and scored an easy layup. As the opposing team hooted and high-fived in celebration, Brackert's teammates remained quiet and passed the ball inbounds.

The chaplain elbowed him in the ribs. "What's wrong with you, Elliot?"

Brackert couldn't stop thinking of the letters delivered in the underway replenishment that had brought all these bombs and bullets. Chrissy almost always wrote about wanting him to stop killing babies, but her most recent letter urged him to make others stop as well. She threatened to end things with him if he didn't do something right away to save as many lives as he could. He was willing to do everything she said because he was that into her.

The chaplain was Brackert's height, but he was slower to change direction. Usually, Brackert had a great free throw and passed the ball better than anyone else. Today, he snuck glances at the planes parked on the far end of the hangar as he took more shots, missed more baskets than ever before.

"Where's your head at, man?"

The question surprised Brackert. "Give me a break, sir. I'm making you look good, ain't I?"

The chaplain laughed but didn't allow his expression to change. It was a look Brackert had never seen before. Did he know or not?

They played for the better part of an hour, until a pot-bellied chief waddled over and whistled them to clear the area. "Sorry, Chaplain. Time's up. Got to stage the next load."

"Okay, Chief," the chaplain said. "Guys," he called out,

"that's it for today. Good game. See you tomorrow in the forward conference room for Bible study. Read Leviticus and be prepared to discuss."

The group of troubled sailors shook or slapped hands and went their separate ways down different passageways and different ladders to their corners of the ship.

The chaplain stopped at the water fountain on the starboard side and drank.

Off to the left, firefighting equipment lined the bulkhead near the ladder well. Brackert admired stations such as that around the ship as art installations. Twenty-five-foot lengths of hoses stood rolled and ready for action. Above them was an array of nozzles—brass, lever-action nozzles, as well as four-foot-long bent pieces of pipe, which would apply a wide shower of water instead of a straight stream in order to cool down a wide area quickly.

The chaplain wiped his mouth with the back of his hand and nodded at Brackert. "Walk and talk," he said.

Brackert wasn't surprised by the invitation. Could this be the signal that that other shoe was going to drop? He followed the chaplain as he stepped through a watertight door and down a passageway not wide enough to walk two abreast.

"Did something from mail call bother you today?" the chaplain asked.

Brackert froze for a moment, mentally and physically. It was a long enough pause for the chaplain to take a few more steps down the passageway but not long enough to make Brackert gasp once he realized he'd been holding his breath. He shifted his focus to a cable run lining the bulkhead and thought about reaching out to hold on. "What makes you think I got something at mail call? You ever suppose maybe I'm just sick to death of still being out here? I was supposed be to stateside weeks ago." He didn't want to talk about the letters but receiving something from Chrissy every mail call was a point of pride for him and that was the one thing he wasn't shy about having people know.

The chaplain stopped and walked the steps back to Brackert. "You know you can't lie to me. I see right through it."

"Two letters from my girl."

"Is everything okay?"

Brackert leaned his hand on an I-beam running fore and aft. "In the first one it was."

"I see where this is going."

Brackert leaned his head back and exhaled at the overhead. "You say that, it's not true. You don't know. You have no damn clue."

The chaplain crossed his arms. "Brackert?"

Brackert didn't know if he should run or play dumb. The tilt of the chaplain's head indicated he wasn't shocked or insulted, merely interested in the letter that had him upset. He didn't know about Hydrant's blood on his hands. That freed Brackert somehow. And for some reason Brackert never consciously knew, he told the truth. Told about Chrissy, the letters, Hydrant. All of it. "She's got me damaging planes and shit. But that's not enough for her. She wants me to be more in the moment."

"I beg your pardon," the chaplain said.

"Living in the moment."

"What is that?"

"I think they call it philosophy." Brackert made it sound like he wasn't sure because something in the back of his mind told him that as a fancy college boy, the chaplain knew that's what it was.

"Where did it come from?" the chaplain asked.

"I believe it's Eastern philosophy."

"You mean like New England, New York, Maryland, maybe?"

That tickled Brackert enough to make him snort. "No," he said. "Far East, not East Coast."

The chaplain's nod involved cords of muscles and veins bending and straightening, as they pumped even more blood up to his head. He looked Brackert in the eye, his face red, his eyes laser focused. "If so, just remember where everyone in the orient stacks up on the food chain before you go misinterpreting them."

Brackert didn't care for the way the chaplain's facial features got stormy all of a sudden. He'd been lucky to get through high school on time, but he wasn't going to let anyone insinuate he was stupid. "I'm not misinterpreting anything."

The chaplain raised one hand to halt Brackert's protest. "The most important thing you need to leave this room knowing is that living in the moment means you're supposed to be present, to feel everything there is to feel and register everything without ignoring or blocking out anything or escaping it through drugs or alcohol. So, if that appeals to you, more power to you. But if you use it as an excuse to do bad things, you're only deluding yourself. And nothing is more pathetic than that."

"But..." Brackert said.

"Trust me, Elliot. I wouldn't lie to you."

Brackert felt vibration in the deck from a fan motor kicking on somewhere in that passageway. He covered his chin like he was thinking on it, but Brackert was mostly confused because the chaplain had never called Brackert by his first name before.

The chaplain took it all in without moving a facial muscle. He had listened without judgment as Brackert told his side of things, then nodded for them to get moving again.

Brackert didn't know if he'd be escorted down to the MAA shack or taken directly to the captain for admitting such things. He didn't care anymore. His chest felt lighter and he'd said everything with eyes completely dry. Still, being locked up would be better than killing another innocent man.

As the passageway tile turned from green to blue, the chaplain came to a stop, signaling Brackert that he wasn't welcome in officers' country. Brackert braced himself for yelling or orders to turn himself in.

"Are you okay with people getting hurt?" the chaplain asked.

Brackert's first thought, back in the beginning, was that he could make himself okay with people getting hurt. It was wartime. Casualties occurred all the time. The synapses of his brain fired in a way that told him he didn't know those soldiers and Marines fighting in the jungles. That distance made it easy to think of them as nothing but numbers in newspaper articles and on newsreels. He didn't live with those guys around the clock, every day. He never had to attend their memorials on the flight deck of the ship they once shared.

Brackert's mind focused on Hydrant, as it often did now. Sometimes in his rack, Brackert felt tears sliding down the sides of his face and into his ears. Killing his friend was the one thing Brackert regretted more than anything else in his entire life. But he couldn't let that emotion show now, and he couldn't risk hurting other shipmates.

"Ain't never been my intention to hurt no one. Just the opposite."

In as even a voice as Brackert had ever heard, the chaplain said, "A single plane only does so much damage." He looked over his shoulder into the passageway of officers' country, then turned back to face Brackert. "But if you take out a catapult you can reduce our capabilities by twenty-five percent."

Brackert's mind didn't readily believe what he'd heard.

The chaplain stared into Brackert's eyes. The intensity almost backed him up a step until the man looked down and then up before he walked away.

Brackert was left standing across the threshold of blue and green title, stricken with the paralysis of surprise.

Eugenia Phillips
4462 Peck Drive
Providence, RI 02905

August 1, 1972

Chaplain Kenneth Phillips
USS Salvation (CV-44)
FPO San Francisco, CA 95660

Heavyhearted greetings Kenneth,

You know how I loathe being the bearer of bad news, but I must tell you that Patches joined the glory of the Lord peacefully two nights ago. He crawled under the house and didn't wake your father or me. He was always a considerate canine companion and he'll be missed. Your father buried him beneath the sugar maple in the back-yard and will mark the site with that square rock he found at Yellowstone.

I'm sorry to burden you with this sadness. I toyed with the notion of not telling you until your return, but I didn't want to keep this news from you. I also assumed that it would be better for you to get through your grief now, while you're at sea, instead of wasting time with sadness upon your most triumphant return. So my advice to you is the same with any bad news. Simply acknowledge it, accept it, and move on. You'll do that for me, won't you?

Until then, stay safe and keep the faith. Your father and I miss you terribly and pray for you daily.

Love,

Mother

CHAPTER 5

In the moment Harold Byrd's eyes began to close, a ruckus took place on the deck above him. Instinctively, he leaned his head through his rack curtains and looked at the overhead lined with cables and pipes. After a silent moment, he leaned back into his rack. He was tired and wanted to get at least four hours sleep.

Byrd worked the longest hours of anyone on the MAA staff. Whether he had duty or not, he'd break for chow, but get right back to patrolling or filing paperwork or just hanging out in the MAA shack. He never understood why other guys bitched and moaned about working long hours at sea. As far as Byrd was concerned, he wanted to bank all the bonus points he could get while at sea. Why wouldn't he? He wasn't going anywhere. The ship had him. No matter if he was in his rack or watching a movie or whatever, he was still stuck within the confines of that ship. It was in port, however, where he was able to put off time to good use. And the harder he worked at sea, the more easily his liberty requests were approved, the more slack he got when returning late or drunk, or both. He'd even gotten slack once after being so hammered that he pissed on Colman's bottom bunk thinking he was at a urinal in the head and then climbing into his rack and barfing into the aisle. That only happened once, and he wasn't proud of it, because of his stellar work ethic no one would've covered for him and kept the information from his division officer and the XO. That was the day he vowed never to drink anything stronger than beer. He'd stuck to it, two years to that point. But he was likely to hop a slow jitney from the barrio and get back late to the ship. He knew he should leave earlier, but he got so little time with May that he wanted to spend every minute he could with her.

Before his eyes closed for the second time, he heard the noise again.

A moment later someone stormed into his berthing area asking for MAA help.

Byrd leaned out of his rack. "Wilson is the MAA on duty," he said into the aisle. "Go get him."

"You're closer. And it's black on white."

Byrd closed his eyes to get one more glimpse of his girl, May, bare-chested with the rum and coconut milk among the palm fronds. The image wasn't there so he swung his legs over the side of his rack and slid down in one fluid motion until his feet hit the deck. He stepped into his boots and ran up the ladder in his underwear.

Inside the berthing compartment, two guys in the TV area pushed and shoved each other and knocked chairs around. A couple dozen guys, also in their underwear, stood around the perimeter to watch the fight. It looked like a fair matchup though no punches apparently had been thrown.

"All you fuckers better shape up!" Byrd hollered as he inserted himself between the two fighters. "What the fuck's going on here?"

The white kid said, "I had the April issue under my pillow and now it's gone. On my way back from the head, I look over and this spear-chucker just so happens to have the same issue."

"It's a coincidence," the black kid said.

Byrd felt cool air through the gap in his underwear fly. If he were in uniform, he'd have had dungarees to cover the slack and a shirt with his badge. He'd be official.

"What are you going to do about this tar baby coming into

our house and taking what ain't his?" one of the bystanders hollered.

Byrd wasn't on duty. This wasn't supposed to be his problem tonight.

"Gentlemen," Byrd said, "why don't we all just calm the hell down for a minute." He rested his hands on his hips, because he didn't have pockets. "You fellas been going at it pretty good up here when we should all be asleep, so why don't y'all just cut your losses and say good night."

"Why you talking up for this lawn jockey?" one of the guys shouted.

As Byrd had gotten older, he'd learned diplomacy. "Give it a rest. I don't have an opinion about race for the same reason I don't have a wife—the Navy ain't issued me one yet. Okay?" Truth was, his own opinion was heavily influenced by stories of how his paternal grandfather treated his Italian mother. "The only black and white I care about is the ink filling the pages of the UCMJ."

He walked over and picked up a magazine from the deck near the water fountain. It was a *Playboy* open to page one-fifty-eight with three photos of a pair of breasts paler than but the same size and shape as May's. He closed the magazine and held it up. "Is this the magazine in question?"

"It damn sure is," the white guy said.

Byrd tossed it to him underhand.

The guy caught it and smoothed the cover.

"Looks like there's no crime then. Now let's clear the aisles. It's past lights out."

"This is bullshit."

"That's the way it's going to be," Byrd said.

He guided the black kid toward the ladder and walked behind him. Once they were up and out of earshot, Byrd said, "I don't know what happened down there, but you might want to avoid getting yourself into those situations."

The black kid couldn't have been more than eighteen. "I

wasn't looking for no trouble. I was just on fire watch and got bored."

"Then I recommend you watch for fires more intently."

In the black berthing compartment near the forecastle, Applewhite shifted the ball of his monkey fist as he crouched at the end of an aisle. He wasn't wearing his chambray shirt. He almost never did anymore. A couple of buddies from engineering leaned over him as he pitched a penny off the standup locker dead-ending the aisle. They passed a joint around and Applewhite took as deep a hit as his lungs had room for.

This was a low-stakes game he wouldn't normally bother with, but he'd taken a pay cut when he got busted to E-2 back in June and he needed an inexpensive way to kill a couple of hours until his buddy, Wooly, got released from the brig.

Applewhite wouldn't say it to anybody, but he missed the man. They had slept across the aisle from each other this entire deployment, except those nights they had spent in the brig. Applewhite heard him snore so much he could barely sleep without the noise. Knew that Wooly's stank-ass farts meant he'd had double dessert at chow because he always drank extra milk when he had extra desserts and cow juice didn't agree with him.

Neither of them would forget their time being locked up already on this cruise. He'd stayed angry the whole time, no breaks. Not even while sleeping on nothing more than a piece of pipe-lagging foam to cushion his shoulders and hips. The worst part for him wasn't the bread or the water, it was the isolation. Aside from the counseling he received, he had no interaction with anyone but the brig officer and supervisors, who spoke only to issue commands. Visitors were prohibited.

They'd been allowed to write and receive letters, though the brig staff would open and read anything coming or going, inspect it for the faintest whiff of impropriety. Applewhite didn't get a lot of mail. Didn't have many people back home in Lawrence.

Didn't even have a home. He'd been raised by his grandparents. Never met his mother or father. His grandparents had been gone for a few years each. But there was one person he could count on come mail call.

Applewhite looked around the berthing compartment—glad to be there instead of locked up. He pulled a roach clip from his pocket and clipped it on a pinch of the rolled paper. Simpson and Washington each took their turns pitching pennies while Applewhite leaned on a middle rack with its blanket folded almost the regulation way, lit his roach, and exhaled. He wasn't sure if this was Slide's rack or if it was where that fat brother, Willie, parked his big ass to sleep. Neither man seemed the type to waste his time on regulation rack making. Not many of the racks were made up to regulation. Some had sheets. Many had nothing but their striped mattress covers showing. This was where Applewhite and a hundred of his brothers slept, gambled, jerked off, farted, and talked shit. The black berthing compartments were off-limits to white crewmen, unofficially, and none of the zeros bothered to exercise their authority and inspect the place, least of all that Uncle Tom XO. The smallest of the four berthings was kept relatively clean, but no one inspected that either. The brothers there keep it nice because they're a bunch of fussy fuckers.

Applewhite wasn't fussy. Knew little of hostility and rebellion. Upon arrival, he'd punched lockers and threatened to storm the captain's cabin and tell him this segregation was bullshit. He was all of a hundred and twenty pounds, barely needed to shave, and right out of Lawrence, Kansas, where he'd seen his high school buddies gunned down by racist cops during a riot. He and all his friends had taken it personally. Some were scared, but Applewhite had courage enough for all of them. His public defender and his grandparents had recommended he take the military deal the judge offered.

Applewhite rubbed the charred remnant of the joint between his forefinger and thumb and pocketed the roach clip. Washington bounced the copper too hard off the painted steel.

Just then, footfalls rang off the ladder outside the berthing compartment and Wooly entered with his head hanging and gave an exhausted wave. Applewhite reached out his hand to dap Wooly, but there was no strength in his friend's hand.

They'd been on the ship together for almost two years, met at the official indoctrination on the pier in San Diego before even walking the brow to the main deck. Wooly came to the Navy from St. Louis, for the same reasons as Applewhite.

"Three days of that shit," Wooly said. "Bread. Water. It's torture, man."

"I know, brother-man. I know." The first thing Applewhite did the day he got out of the brig was go to the galley and have a couple of brothers hook him up with some cold chicken, French fries with gravy, and coleslaw. He wanted to give his buddy the same treatment.

"Come on," he said.

"What?" Wooly said. "I'm going to hit my rack."

"You can sleep after."

"After what?"

"Let's go, man." Applewhite pushed Wooly's shoulder to get him moving. It felt like nothing but bone.

Applewhite guided Wooly, who struggled with his confidence going up and down ladders, from deck to deck.

"My legs are a little rubbery," Wooly said, and stopped in the middle of the passageway.

"No, Wool. Nah, man. We cool." It was wrong. Wooly's discomfort was Applewhite's discomfort, and this pissed him off.

To change the subject, Applewhite asked, "You hear about the crash-landing that snuffed out a redshirt like a cigarette?"

"I'm glad he dead," Wooly said. "That's one less honky punk-ass we have to deal with. I wish more of them roof rats got killed. Be less motherfuckers clogging the chow line."

Applewhite laughed as they continued up another ladder and down a long passageway to the aft mess deck, where they saw

Grimes swabbing the deck just outside the bakery.

"Hey man, you missed a spot."

Grimes dropped the swab handle to *clack* on the deck and gave Applewhite an abbreviated dap. He pointed to their mutual friend. "He looks like shit."

Applewhite held his arm around Wooly. "Nothing some meat and gravy can't fix."

"I don't know," Grimes said.

Applewhite looked over his shoulder. "We need to get him fixed up." In Applewhite's mind there was no reason to make Wooly wait until midrats to get some solid food.

They walked through the main galley, a long and wide kitchen with low overhead clearance and filled with stainless-steel workbenches, shelving, and appliances. Even the exterior of the walk-in refers were silver. Half a dozen mess cranks cleaned their various stations with white rags dipped in buckets of bleach water. They all had attitudes. While the cooks chose that line of work, the cranks were victims of ship policy to have the lowest ranking new arrivals serve three to six months in the galley and on the mess deck regardless of aptitude or choice.

Grimes didn't speak as he guided Applewhite and Wooly to one of the refers and pulled open the door and emerged with a tray of cooked chickens.

"Get him started on this," Grimes said, setting the tray on one of the stainless-steel tables near the row of ovens.

While Grimes walked back into the refer, a white mess specialist walked over pointing to the tray of chickens. "What the hell is this?"

Applewhite whispered to Wooly, "Get you some big-ass bites, man."

"No!" the mess specialist hollered. "No, no, no." He walked closer as Grimes emerged from the refer holding a tub of coleslaw. He got in Grimes's face. "This is absolutely unauthorized. Put that back."

Applewhite signaled for Grimes to remain quiet and let him

handle it. He was pretty sure something like this would happen, but he hoped Wooly could get his fill before they got kicked out of the galley.

"I understand this is unauthorized," Applewhite said, "but my partner here just got out of the brig a few minutes ago. He ain't had shit to eat but bread. We weren't going to feed him much, just enough to hold him till midrats."

The mess specialist had a second-class crow on his arm and a face that looked like he fell asleep in an ant pile. He shook his head. "There're plenty of people who get to tell me what to do, but you sure as hell ain't one of them."

Applewhite flashed a smile, hoping to convey some goodwill. "I was asking, man. Come on. Be cool for a few more minutes. Let him eat."

"No, goddamn it."

"Maybe you just pretend you didn't see us." Applewhite looked over his shoulder and then back. "We'll be out of here in two minutes."

The mess specialist slapped a hand on the table, rattling the tray of chickens. "Are your ears full of shit, boy?"

Applewhite ignored the snarl of the fucker's lip and checked on Wooly. He was sucking the meat off a chicken leg, his lips and cheeks smeared in grease. It smelled like baked chicken does. Must have been warm still from evening chow.

Grimes looked scared.

Applewhite said, "Hold up. If my man here was white, I bet that would make a difference."

"If he was white he wouldn't be coming out of the brig half-starved."

Wooly had devoured a whole chicken by this point and Applewhite was sure that would hold him, but still.

"What are your names?" the mess specialist asked, pointing from Applewhite to Wooly. He looked at Grimes standing in the refer doorway. Didn't seem to recognize him. "Tell me your names," he said.

Applewhite held his hands out to his sides. "We don't need to make nothing personal."

The mess specialist leaned in. "Thieving niggers."

Before Applewhite could react, Wooly lunged across the table and grabbed the mess specialist by the belt buckle and punched him in the balls. The guy went down hard. His head thudded on the deck and he groaned, hands over his genitals. The guy rolled, facedown. Wooly dropped a knee into the guy's lower back and whaled hard rights into the side of his head with fast and sharp punches that made Applewhite wonder what was in that chicken. But it wasn't the bird. It was the word. And Wooly continued punching the guy until one of the other white mess cooks rushed in.

Applewhite could fight the guy and go back to the brig with his buddy, or he could try to save them both from having to go at all. He grabbed Wooly by hooking his elbow, struggling to pull him away. Wooly switched to throwing lefts and wouldn't stop.

Grimes left the refer and looked down the passageway. He turned back and hollered, "I ain't going down for this."

Applewhite released his grip on Wooly and nodded at Grimes. They left Wooly to throw his punches and ran down opposite ends of the same passageway.

Tonya Washington
5521 Old Plain Pass—Apt 3C
Lawrence, KS

August 19, 1972

SN Rufus Applewhite
USS Salvation (CV-44)
FPO San Francisco, CA 95660

Thank you Rufus for sending money. Willie is going through diapers faster than I can keep up and the money you sent will go long ways to helping. He's good. A good boy. Like he remembers you telling him before you left. I show him your picture and he says Dada. It makes me cry every time cause so many boys don't come back from over there and I worry about you. We all proud of you. I hope you no that. You best come back too. Soon. We don't got to get married or nothing if you don't want to, but Willie needs his dada. I need you too baby. So stay safe and call us when you can. I no they ain't got no phones on your boat but if you get to land I hope you find a payphone so you can call.

Derk and LaFonda look in on us all the time. They's good to us. You might could send them a post card or sumthing to say thanks. They's good people to have in the building.

You still haven't told me what it's like out there for you. You never give me much information or nothing. Tell me more about it than everything is fine and work is going good. I don't even know what you do. Tell me!

I write again soon. You stay safe baby.

We love you,

Tonya and Willie

CHAPTER 6

The ship coasted through the sea quietly before the crew was fully awake and filling the air with sounds of jet engines, chipping hammers, and voices of praise, instruction, and hate.

With the benefit of a few days to have calmed down, Porter knocked on the captain's sea cabin door.

"Enter," the captain's voice called out.

The captain's sea cabin was a windowless room in the center of the ship's island. It was convenient to both the bridge and flight command should the need arise in the middle of the night. And while not as spacious as the captain's in-port cabin, he had a sitting area with light-blue couches and pale-yellow carpet. Gold, the Navy called it. The space included a vestibule that housed a mahogany desk, and a separate bedroom space with built-in nightstands and a private head. Porter found the captain standing beside his desk wearing khaki uniform pants and a new white T-shirt perfectly tucked in. He had a rectangular shape, but his body was lean. He was only ten years older than Porter, but from the neck up, he looked like a man well into his sixties—gray and with deep wrinkles around his temples and on his forehead. His eyes were farther apart than anyone Porter had seen, and he imagined the man had excellent peripheral vision. The captain's ears seemed large, with fleshy lobes that shook when he moved his head. Despite, or perhaps because of these characteristics, he commanded attention as he spoke.

There was only one thing on Porter's mind, but he couldn't come into the captain's cabin frothing at the mouth and tell his boss what to do. On the other hand, Porter assumed that if he told the captain he was upset he hadn't been invited to observe the mast and that no one told him it was scheduled, then the captain would apologize and enact a plan to prevent that from happening again. There was no guarantee.

The position was foreign to him. He wanted to feel connected to the Navy, to the captain, as much as he felt to the ship he sailed aboard. He needed that to further his career. In the back of his mind, he'd always had the fear that he was being rushed up the ranks because of his skin color. He was along for the ride. He absolutely wanted to achieve as much as he could, but it would only mean something if he earned it. That had been easy as a pilot. Not so much now.

The captain cleared his throat. "What can I do for you, Robert?" Without waiting for an answer, the captain bent at the waist, placed his hands on the deck and, one at a time, raised his legs to rest his bare toes on the edge of his desktop, forming a decline push-up position.

Porter was surprised to see the captain's bare feet. He didn't know if he should answer the question or wait for the man to stand.

In that silence, the captain banged out twenty decline push-ups, then stood and grabbed hold of an I-beam in the overhead. His grip was wide and he pulled himself up ten times before dangling there, coping a stretch. The captain then dropped and assumed the push-up position again, but this time his feet remained on the deck. Instead of regular push-ups, he pressed himself hard, propelling his hands, arms, and torso off the deck high enough to clap his hands before landing with his elbows coiled to push himself up again—he repeated this twenty times. Following that, he hopped up to bang out ten more chin-ups, then grabbed a white towel from the top of his television. He wiped sweat from his face and drank from a yellow coffee mug from the mess deck.

"I'm impressed, sir."

The captain waved it off. "You've got to take your exercise when you can get it."

Porter noted the old-fashioned expression for physical training but didn't comment.

"You look like you exercise regularly, Robert."

"I play squash when I'm home. And some golf," he said. "At sea, I run around the flight deck when I can. Sprints, not jogging."

"Good. That's good. No basketball?"

Porter shook his head.

"Well, you should join me for some push-ups."

Porter didn't feel like he had the captain's attention. Took exception to that. Felt disrespected and even more paranoid than before. "Maybe one day we can workout together."

The captain lowered his towel from his face. "No time like the present, Smokey. Why should new recruits have all the fun?"

A short laugh escaped Porter. He never saw exercise as fun. It was just an essential part of life, like eating, sleeping, breathing, and brushing his teeth. He coughed as a way to buy himself time. His choice to accept this bizarre invitation or risk alienating himself further reminded him of the booze on the bridge wing. He wondered if he'd remember this for the rest of his life. If he'd pull this kind of shit someday after he became captain of his own ship.

"Straight-up push-ups," the captain said. "Let's see how many we can do."

Porter pointed to the captain's torso. "But you're already warmed up."

The captain pulled his T-shirt over his head and tossed it toward his desk. On his chest, over his heart, was a Confederate flag tattoo in bright red and blue. The stars were finely outlined skin breaks.

"You're young enough." The captain hit the deck in position.

Breath caught in Porter's throat. The captain's allegiance was no real surprise, but the tattoo was. Porter tried to brush it aside as he removed his khaki shirt, tossed it toward one of the sofas, and assumed the position. He had no way of knowing if the captain was of the hood-wearing, torch-bearing variety, but angry as Porter was, he wasn't about to assume anything in judgment. Yet.

The first push-up felt awkward. The second one pinched his neck a little. The third through tenth reminded him of his football days.

The captain barked out each repetition, "One-two-three-four…"

After thirty-some push-ups, the captain slowed. Porter's chest and triceps were engorged with the rush of blood to them, but he slowed to match the captain's cadence. Halfway into the forty-first push-up, the captain was petering out. Porter was younger, stronger, and had adrenaline flowing now. He felt indefatigable. This, combined with his rage over the televised masts, made him feel like some sort of hero out of a Saturday matinee.

The captain stopped at fifty.

Porter was pissed and into it, but he wondered if he should stop and give the captain the victory. Beating him could only piss him off—no man liked to lose. But beating him might make him respect Porter's physical abilities, at least. He didn't know which held the better odds.

Porter stopped too.

"That's pretty good, there, Smokey."

"It felt good."

The captain looked up, grabbed the I-beam, and performed ten solid chin-ups. With his feet back on the deck, he said, "Your turn," and stepped out of the way.

Porter hadn't done a chin-up since graduating OCS, but he wasn't about to confess that. He reached up. The spots where the captain's hands had been were still warm and slick with his sweat. Porter widened his grip to find cold steel, squeezed tight, and pulled himself up. It was difficult at first. His fingers were uncomfortable on the painted steel and the muscles in his back seemed to protest the activity.

It reminded him of his freshman year at UCLA, when he'd made the team as a receiver and kickoff returner. A shoulder injury sidelined him for more than a year. It was in that time away from football that he fully developed his passion for flying.

He clenched his shoulder blades together and yanked nine and a half pull-ups before his grip wore out.

"I'm impressed again," the captain said.

Porter picked up not surprise or anger in the captain's voice, but something else—competitiveness.

"Okay," the captain said, "let's see how you handle the equalizer."

"The equalizer, sir?"

"Hit the deck," the captain said, once again getting into push-up position.

"More push-ups?"

"No. Get on your elbows."

"My elbows?"

"Like this." The captain demonstrated. "Make one straight line with your body. Keep your ass level—don't let it dip, but don't raise it either."

Porter did so, which required the muscles in his lower back and his entire abdominal wall to contract. Sweat that had formed on his brow now dripped rapidly onto the carpeted deck between his clenched fists.

"Right about now," the captain said, "you should be pressing your heels back to keep the weight distributed properly." He demonstrated. "Your back is starting to sag. Your abdominals are fatiguing." He spoke these words while maintaining the perfect form of a straight line.

Porter's shoulders began to shake. His hamstrings quivered. Sweat absorbed into the carpet beneath his face and neck. After what seemed like eternity, Porter collapsed into that puddle and exhaled.

The captain maintained his position and laughed. "You're very athletic people. You've got brute strength, but you're not fit enough to last one full minute here, Smokey."

Porter was too strained to control himself. He rolled over and called back, "At least I'm not dumb enough to tele..." He bit into his tongue hard enough to draw blood. The taste calmed him. It was a fair trade for not going too far.

The captain lowered his knees to the deck and then rose. He whisked away sweat from his eyebrows with his index fingers.

Porter watched water droplets arc through the air and land on the carpet. For a minute, he thought the captain might ignore that last sentence.

The captain looked down at him. "You were saying?"

Porter's breathing still hadn't returned to normal. He regretted opening his mouth. That wasn't how he planned to broach the topic, but it was out there now. "Pardon the tone," he said. "I'm heated by the spirit of competition and my words may have come out incorrectly."

"You have something to say, so say it."

Porter feared it might be too late to salvage this. "With all due respect, captain, the only guys televised masts will scare are the guys who would never do anything wrong to begin with. The others? Well, you're just stoking their fires."

The captain never said it, but Porter always felt that the message was, "I'm not asking for your input on running my ship. I just want you to convince the problematic black crew that everything is how they say, 'cool.'"

Porter ignored the attempt and continued his pitch. "James Wooly was released from the brig today."

"Ah, yes." The captain draped his towel over his shoulder. "So?"

Porter made his way to his feet, trying to hide his surprise that the captain wasn't aware of what had followed Wooly's release.

He walked to the sofa, pulled on his khaki shirt. As he buttoned it, he said, "Wooly and two of his compatriots raided the galley. It appears Wooly was so hungry he ate from a tray of chickens and assaulted the mess cook who tried to stop him."

The captain was judge and jury in a town of four thousand residents and a shitload of rules. He spread his feet shoulder-width apart and began a new exercise of squatting and standing in a cadence similar to the push-ups earlier. "Did the Marines catch them?"

Porter tucked in his shirt. "One of the master at arms caught Wooly red-handed beating the hell out of a newly frocked E-5."

"What about the others?"

"Still at large."

"And you think this has something to do with my sentencing the man to three days in the brig?"

"It was the very same man, sir, and a couple others."

The captain continued his squatting and standing. "Sounds like that lunkhead didn't learn anything in the brig."

"He maintains that he was just hungry and trying to get some food to hold him over until midrats."

"That's bad enough. And the fighting?" The captain started to sound a little winded.

"It appears one of the mess cooks took exception. The situation escalated."

The captain stopped. "We serve four meals per day. Virtually around the clock. This sailor couldn't wait? That's his problem. He'll come before me again and will be met with much harsher penalties."

"But sir," Porter said, not knowing if this new mast would come as swiftly as the next day or as delayed as weeks.

The captain flicked sweat off his eyebrows again and placed his hands on his sides. "See here, Mister Porter. We're not out here to coddle a bunch of disgruntled mess cooks or boiler techs or even the pampered radiomen. We're out here for one reason, and one reason only—sustained air operations against the North

Vietnamese. This crew and this ship and these planes are here to help win this goddamn war once and for all, and by God I will use my last breath in service of that mission as long as I'm in charge here."

Porter stood tall. "We've all dedicated our time and risked our lives in support of that mission, sir." He thought about all the sorties he'd flown off that same deck, all the action he'd seen in the same airspace. That was his true connection. "I'm with you one hundred percent."

"Then what's your goddamn beef?"

"The crew," Porter said, pointing to the door as it represented all four thousand of them. "They, like the steam turbines and the catapults, are made up of various parts. If parts of any system are broken, the performance and reliability are going to suffer. That's all I'm saying. The reason you brought me here."

The captain dabbed his towel at the creases beside his mouth. "Discipline is for the good of the crew."

A trail of sweat rolled down Porter's back. He rotated his shoulders hoping his shirt would absorb it; he didn't need the distraction now. He swallowed, cleared his throat. "The black crew doesn't understand the process. They don't know you factor in each man's civilian records in your sentencing for current infractions. They don't realize I wasn't here for Wooly's investigation or preliminary hearing or his case review."

"And why is that our problem?"

"I'm prepared to serve as the shit-shield between you and the crew. But that shield has two sides. How many more masts are scheduled that I'm not aware of?"

"You want to be briefed on all pending cases you weren't here to investigate?"

"I think an extra pair of eyes can be helpful, yes, sir."

The captain rolled the towel and placed it around his neck. "And what is it you'd have me do, Mr. Porter?"

"With all due respect, sir, I just worry this kid's anger will fan the flames, so to speak."

"What is it that you're not saying? Out with it."

"Can I speak frankly, Captain?"

"Of course."

"The black sailors are already enraged about the differences between the punishments you distribute."

"It's my duty, Mr. Porter, to maintain order and the highest possible situational readiness that CINCPAC expects from this vessel. I will not allow an immature sailor with no control of his temper to go unpunished. I don't care what color he may be."

Porter tried to believe him.

"You've seen the records on some of these boys. Some of them have been brought up on charges in the civilian world a dozen times or more. Hell, some of them were offered a choice of our Navy or jail. I have to take all that into consideration."

"I understand," Porter said. He didn't want to go through all that again. "But that notwithstanding, sir, I fail to see the benefit of having the proceedings televised."

The captain sat on the edge of his desk, where his toes had rested earlier for his decline push-ups. "My predecessor began that business. I'm continuing what he started to show the crew that there's nothing to hide. Plus it's a hell of a deterrent, regardless of what you say. Few men are as foolish as Airmen Wooly."

Porter adjusted his gold wings on his khaki shirt. "There's no way to have you reconsider this?"

The captain drank from his coffee mug. Lowered it. Raised it and sipped again.

Porter wanted to smack the mug out of his hand and demand an answer.

As the captain lowered the mug, he licked his lips, exhaled, cleared his throat. "Perhaps you've gotten wind of a drug problem aboard my ship."

"I've heard numerous reports," Porter said, grateful for the return to conversation. "I plan to make it one of my top priorities."

The captain sat in his desk chair and laid his hands flat on his desk. "I'll make a deal with you," he said.

"A deal?" Porter asked.

The captain picked up his coffee mug again. "You get the main guy behind the drug problem, I'll turn the cameras off."

Porter felt as if the deck had given way beneath him. His hands dropped to his sides as he stared at the captain. He couldn't stop himself from staring. "Is this—"

"Blackmail? Extortion? Politics? Incentive? Extra motivation? A friendly wager between admittedly competitive men?" The captain said as he matched the stare, without resisting the smirk spreading across his face. The captain gripped his mug in one hand and rubbed his other palm on the desk as he spoke. "We're simply asking for your cooperation."

The implication made Porter's throat run dry.

"We don't need to put labels on anything, Smokey." The captain leaned back. "We're just CO and XO—two guys with the same goal of bringing this ship and all her crew home safely. How we achieve that is strictly up to us." He looked at Porter. "And by us, I mean me. Do you follow?"

Porter's pulse sped faster than it had during the workout. Sweat rolled down his back in a stronger current too. His jaw ached from grinding his teeth. He tried to relax and draw a full breath. "Aye, sir," he said.

He turned, walked to the door, where he paused before exiting, and closed the door behind him.

Gina Holt
1155 Star Park Circle, 2A
Coronado, CA 92118

August 20, 1972

Capt. Davis P. Holt
USS Salvation (CV-44)
FPO San Francisco, CA 95660

OK Dave. This is way beyond ridiculous. I knew you'd have to go from time to time, but not this long. I'm done. I can't do this. Being all alone. I visit my family again they will make me move back. They are none too happy either. This is not a life. I am at my ropes end. Now I know why your first wife left you. I just wonder how she put up with it for so long. And the other wives are embarrassingly phony.

I know you have important things to worry about, but I am important too. Think about that for me and come home soon or the condo will be empty when you get there.

I love you, but this is too hard.

G.

CHAPTER 7

Reveille hadn't been called yet. Byrd had gotten up early and had coffee and a fresh, hot roll with the guys in the bakery. He licked the taste of yeast from his lips as he walked up and aft, headed toward the master at arms shack for the morning muster they called Quarters.

The MAA shack occupied a space near the fantail, but Byrd took a detour and pushed open a watertight hatch and stepped onto the open-air landing looking out from the back of the ship. The crew generally referred to the fantail as the patio—an outdoor space about sixteen feet above the water and covered by the flight deck.

The open area often turned into a workspace, with airplane engines on stands and crewmen with tools in their hands, but today all that stuff remained inside allowing Byrd to stand alone at the life rail. Salt air mixed with the yeast on his lips and he washed it down with a mouthful of fresh air. He welcomed the rising sunlight into his eyes. Humid air coated him with moisture. He watched blue water churn into white. These moments were sanity breaks. He needed this once in a while. It made him remember the whole wide world existed out there and wasn't limited to what happened in the confines of that ship. He loved being at sea. Craved the horizon in his future.

As he listened to the sound of waves and the calls of distant birds, he heard footsteps. He turned to see his boss walking toward him. Senior Chief Rawlings served as the chief master at arms and also as Command Master Chief—the highest-ranking enlisted man on the ship. He'd been in twenty-five years, so if he joined at seventeen or eighteen that put him in his early forties. His face was a melon, with a hack for a mouth that always seemed to have a fuck-you slant. Word around the ship had him advancing to master chief before they returned to San Diego.

The senior chief raked his oversized fingers through the pomade holding his black hair in place. He stood and walked like he enjoyed being the sheriff in a town of four thousand men.

His presence put Byrd on edge enough that his fingers drummed on the life rail. He'd never been one-on-one with the man before. The guy stood only five-ten or so, but he seemed movie-screen big. Byrd liked it better when there were at least a couple other guys around to deflect the attention.

Senior, as everyone called him, said, "Well, good morning, Byrd. I see you came for some fresh air, too." In one hand Senior held a coffee mug with the number 5 bold and black on it. In the other he held a pouch of Beech-Nut chewing tobacco.

Byrd took a gust of wind up the back of his neck. It made him shudder like a piss-shiver. His fingers stopped drumming the life rail. He always felt like Senior saw right through him. Like he knew every questionable thing Byrd had ever done and sat in judgment. "Nothing beats the oxygen of open spaces, Senior."

Senior nodded while looking around. "Listen," he said. His face had a way of flattening out when he was being earnest or otherwise saying something he wanted people to remember. With his face flat, his eyes made contact. His mouth moved fast. "I planned to tell you this in front of everyone at Quarters," he said, "but I guess I can tell you now." He drained the remaining coffee from his mug and wiped his mouth with the back of the paw he used to hold his bag of chaw. "You heard about the fracas in the galley."

"I sure did," Byrd said. Thinking about it made his back

hurt. "They're saying fifteen kicks to that poor bastard's back and sides. Damn shame that mess cook was attacked like that."

"We got the main nigger," Senior said, stuffing his cheek with a handful of brown tobacco leaves from the open pouch in his hand. "Swanson caught him red-handed—eating chicken after beating that poor dumb mess cook. But here's the thing, Byrd." He paused and looked toward the open hatch before continuing. "There were two others that got away. We need to catch them. That shit-for-brains mess cook didn't get the names of the other two, but expects he'd recognize the porch monkeys if he saw them again."

Byrd didn't appreciate the name-calling, but it wasn't foreign to him. A lot of the crew talked like that. "You know, Senior," he said, "an investigation will rub some people the wrong way."

Senior stared out at the water and sort of nodded. "I don't give a shit."

"You still want to do it?"

"I want *you* to take the lead on this." He spit a dark stream into his coffee mug and wiped his lip with the rim. "Penalties must be paid. I need you to get to the bottom of it."

Byrd felt his adrenal glands flood his system with energy. The recognition that accompanied such assignments always sped him up. If circumstances were different, being handpicked by his boss would mean the man had faith in him, recognized the potential. Instead, Byrd couldn't shake the look of revenge on Senior's face.

Instinctively, Byrd suspected Applewhite. After a moment, he said, "I'll damn sure try."

"Try?" Senior spit again. "It's your sole responsibility for the next two days. Forget everything else. You've got the best investigative skills out of every swinging dick with a badge on this ship."

Byrd felt his face flush. He couldn't help liking the way Senior pep talked.

"I mean it. You're a damn fine investigator. You've got a

level head. You'll make a fine chief in the not-too-distant future."

Byrd shaped up, might've flushed a little more. Praise did that to him. "That's good of you to say, Senior."

Senior pointed at Byrd. "Nothing but the truth, Petty Officer Byrd." He lowered his finger, spit into his mug. "And you're good with the crew. Wish I had ten more like you."

The praise seemed heavy to Byrd. It made him wonder why he was getting it now, but he couldn't help being flattered by it.

"That means a lot to me," Byrd said through a smile.

"Now, look here. You can be as overt or covert as you please with this investigation. Keep in mind an overt approach could get messy, you sure are right about that. But..." He stopped talking and nodded his head in Byrd's direction for emphasis. "I know you've built relationships across the color line. That might be one of your strengths in getting this done with minimal fuss. You follow me, son?"

Byrd got it, but he didn't like the way the chief knew the score. Knew that Byrd applied a great deal of discretion throughout a day. This meant he'd have to go at this and take down the two accomplices. Each of the sailors would lose a stripe, each would take a pay cut to match their lower rank, and depending how many strikes they had against them, maybe get kicked out of the Navy with a dishonorable discharge—the whole nasty horseshit pie. But without order, there's anarchy. With a soon-to-be-master chief on his side, Byrd had a leg up on advancing to his next pay grade and becoming a chief himself.

"Fucking-A, Senior," Byrd said. "I'm on it."

"That-a-boy!" Senior poked him in the sternum. "Make me proud and bring me some nigger heads on sticks."

Byrd smiled big to convey a sense of happiness about the assignment. "Leave it to me, Senior." Byrd looked down. Saying what he was about to say made his stomach feel as frothy as that whitewater churning in the ship's wake. He braced himself. Cleared his throat. "I'll have a pair of coons confessing in your office within the next forty-eight hours."

Doris Rawlings
1934 Frost Line Rd.
Atlanta, GA 30304

August 24, 1972

Senior Chief Richard Rawlings
USS Salvation (CV-44)
FPO San Francisco, CA 95660

Dear Dick,

You need to get to a phone and call this god damn house. Your the god damn chief of the boat and you aught to be able to tell the captain that your crew needs a god damn break. You don't have to tell him its so you can call your god damn wife once in awhile just as long as you do. And pronto. The dentist is saying that Betty Ann needs braces and it is so god damn expensive I'm not willing to put all that money in her teeth just so some guy can rake his dick across them someday. I'm going to leave it up to you though since she's your favorite and all. The longer we wait the more time and money it'll take. Let me know as soon as you can.

And by the way the water heater gave us some problems last week but I changed the rods in it. Your son was no help by the way. Just stood there banging the monkey wrench on the washing machine. Little bastard dented the god damn lid for no reason. Anyway we should be fixed for hot water for awhile. But we'll need to replace the whole god damn thing before too long. Just so you know.

So your doing good? Has the Chaplain kid been staying out of your way? Or have you had to set him straight yet? You're probably tired of the god damn water by now. I know I am. When are you coming home? Soon? It better be. In the meantime get that captain to make a port visit so you can get to a phone and call me about Betty Ann. I miss you. We all do.

Kick some ass and get yourself back home.

All my love,

D—

September 17, 1972

In honor of Constitution Day, Chaplain Phillips delivered a special pre-meal grace in the Chiefs' Mess. At the end of the grace, seventy-five chiefs stood around their tables and applauded. The sound and energy in the room surprised him. It wasn't often he'd gotten applause, and it left him with a sense of floating as he waved on his way out. It was the first lighthearted mood he'd felt in recent memory. If he didn't know better, he'd suspect that a smile had creased his mouth. Regardless, he was excited to have something positive to write in letters home to Mary Alice and Mother.

As he walked down the passageway, his moment of elation was interrupted as his ear passed directly beneath a loudspeaker the precise moment the boatswains mate on the bridge blew his bosun's pipe to signal mess call over the shipboard announcing system. The whistle cycled through a high pitch, low pitch, warbling, and an insufferable trilling for less than a full minute, but it felt like being stabbed with icepicks in his ear holes.

Most of the crew loved the lunch whistle that announced the noon meal from every loudspeaker throughout the ship. To most, it meant nourishment and a brief distraction from steaming in circles, arming and launching planes around the clock. To others, it meant another hour until knocking off because the crew was so large it had to eat in shifts. To others still, lunch was dinner before hitting the rack for a few hours' sleep. To others, it was breakfast.

As he leaned away from the loudspeaker, the chaplain heard a grunt and a thud from somewhere in the passageway. He followed the direction of the noise to a ladder well leading down to a vestibule, where he saw bare feet below. He leaned over the chain and saw a sailor in dungarees sprawled at the bottom of the ladder, legs opposing one another, a boot in each hand. The chaplain hurtled down the ladder, his hands sliding along the chain.

"Oh, God, don't be dead," the chaplain said.

He sank to his knees and put his ear to the man's chest. He didn't readily hear a heartbeat, but after a moment of nausea, he saw the rise and fall of a full breath in the guy's ribcage. The chaplain remained on his knees and sighed. "Thank God."

The downed sailor coughed drily and licked his lips, as if they were coated in caramel. He wore his boots over his hands and began laughing.

The chaplain didn't know what he should do, and indecision wasn't like him. His left knee rested on a bolt fastening the ladder to the deck. He didn't feel it digging into his skin until he stood and looked at the hexagon shape etched into his khaki pant leg.

"Are you okay?" He read the name stenciled above the guy's shirt pocket. "Martindale?"

Martindale groaned. The sleeves of his uniform shirt were rolled but sweat dripped off his head and face. He clutched his boots to his chest but didn't speak.

"Did you fall down the ladder?"

Martindale laughed again, though he didn't seem fully awake. Laughed hard enough that his thick black hair shook over his forehead and into his face. The laugh was a high-pitched kind of giggle that didn't reach a second note. Aside from that outburst of noise, Martindale didn't speak. He was only a few years younger than the chaplain, but he'd probably sailed on a couple deployments already.

"Hey." The chaplain tapped the backs of his fingers against Martindale's face. "Hey," he said. "What are you doing down here?"

Martindale didn't answer.

Chaplain Phillips leaned forward. Got a closer look. The guy didn't smell of black-market booze, but his pupils dominated his eyeballs. The chaplain grabbed the guy by the bare ankles. "Where are your socks?"

Before the guy responded, the chaplain dragged him toward the bulkhead so he'd be less conspicuous if someone looked down from the deck above.

Martindale, with his boots still over his hands, rolled his head side to side in the rhythm of unheard music.

The chaplain didn't know if coffee could help his condition. Didn't know if the guy needed to vomit to save him or if he just had to ride out the narcotic. He could fireman carry Martindale up the ladder, but then what? There was no way he could lug dead weight without being seen, and even if he could, he wouldn't know where to go.

Martindale lifted his head, looked at the chaplain with a dull, glazed stare.

The chaplain stood and slapped an open palm on the front of the watertight door immediately to his left. He grunted. "I've been holding hands with weak-willed people like you this entire damn cruise and I'm sick of it." The chaplain looked up the ladder. "I earned a master's degree from Vanderbilt University. In theology. Specializing in ecumenical ecclesiology. I shouldn't be in a position to find a junkie with no self-control. I shouldn't even have to talk to somebody like you."

Martindale laughed again and continued waving his boots, which were shined, except for where he'd drooled on one of them. His hair shook over his forehead. He looked like he might have been a good sailor before this deployment, maybe even up until recently.

"Are you out of your mind?" the chaplain yelled through

clenched teeth. "The XO is gunning for guys like you. Is that what you want?"

There were no tinks, thunks, or pings of chipping hammers, as the boatswain's mates had forks and spoons in their hands at the moment. The air smelled of lubricating oil and bearing grease. There were three watertight doors on the different sides of the vestibule. Each room sounded like a tractor engine idled inside. That hum might or might not have been the source of the type of vibration all over the ship that made the chaplain's cheeks shake.

He didn't know exactly what those compartments down here were for, but he felt positive someone would happen by sooner or later. He wished he could turn back time and take a left turn as he left the Chiefs' Mess.

Martindale laughed again. This time it was louder and hearty enough to make him drop one of his boots. He didn't seem to notice. He waved his hands like a conductor.

"What are you on, Martindale? What did you take?" The chaplain grabbed him by the collar. "What did you take?"

By this point, the chaplain had begun to sweat too.

Martindale's eyes opened and stayed open. Saw Phillips for the first time. "You look like the chaplain," he said.

"I am the chaplain," Phillips said.

"Oh shit."

"Oh shit, is right. Do you realize you could get busted and kicked out for this?"

"Nooooo," Martindale bellowed. "No, no." His eyes were half open and he breathed through his mouth.

"You would've been smarter pretending to be unconscious from the fall," the chaplain said, checking again up the ladder.

SOP dictated the chaplain call sick bay and get a corpsman down there ASAP. He'd already been down there long enough. He couldn't risk someone seeing him there with a man high on drugs. He should run back up the ladder, grab the nearest phone and call the corpsmen to the scene. "I'm going to call sick bay and get a doc down here. You might want to practice acting like you're unconscious."

"No!" Martindale bellowed again. "Please," he called out, though he made no visible effort to raise his head.

"Save it!"

"Sir. Please," Martindale said in a tone the chaplain recognized as sincere—not sober, but sincere. "I joined the Navy to make a better life. Doesn't look like it now, but that's what I want." He pulled a tinfoil packet the shape and size of a deck of cards from the boot in his right hand. Without looking at the chaplain, he said, "Just take it. I quit now. Don't turn me in."

The chaplain peeled back a flap of the foil. Inside, white dust collected in the creases—spilled from the cellophane from a cigarette pack filled with white powder. There were also four hand-rolled cigarettes he assumed were marijuana, six white pills, three red pills, and a pack of matches. He sat on the bottom step of the ladder.

Martindale sprawled on the deck with his hands in the air, a boot beside his head.

The chaplain leaned to look up the ladder again. "You're in luck," he said. "I know exactly where to dispose of this." He turned his back to Martindale, folded up the package, and slid it in the front pocket of his khaki pants. His pocket had enough room, but the fit was neither comfortable nor inconspicuous.

"You help me?" Martindale asked.

"I'll do what I can on the condition that you get cleaned up. This garbage will ruin your life. Now, if you go back and use again, well then, you deserve to get caught and kicked out on your ass. A dishonorable discharge following you everywhere you go. You don't want that."

"Fuck no...sir."

"Okay," the chaplain said. "Are you with it enough to remember this?"

Martindale nodded.

"You fell down this ladder, plain and simple. You'll take

some ribbing, I'm sure, but it's better than Captain's Mast and getting thrown out. Stay here until you sober up. Then swing by sick bay and have a corpsman document the lump on your head. Tell them you must've knocked yourself unconscious in the fall. Don't mention the drugs. No one needs to know anything about that. If you stay clean and sober from now on, you'll be all right."

Martindale lifted his head. Raked a shaky hand through his hair to pile it up, like Elvis Presley. "Can I have booze on liberty?" he asked.

"Within reason. While on liberty. Never aboard ship. And no more drugs. Ever."

"Deal," he said as his head leaned back to the deck. "Won't let you down."

"Stay here until you're at least fifty percent." Chaplain Phillips squeezed the package of confiscated drugs. "I was never here. You understand? And if anyone asks me, I've never even heard of you."

CHAPTER 8

Byrd stepped into the goat locker to find Senior. The chiefs sat around tables of four, and a couple from each table turned to look at the blue jacket entering their domain. Just as quickly they turned back to their meals. They ate from real dishes instead of the yellow compartmentalized trays used on the mess deck. Byrd was still one promotion away from attaining their status, but he'd been in there frequently over the past year, bringing business for Senior to sign off on.

In a room full of khaki and gray hair, Byrd didn't have to look hard to find Senior. He was mid-sentence, holding court at a table in the corner. His voice was deep and carried enough to fill the room even when he wasn't addressing everyone. The chiefs around him laughed in response to something Byrd caught only the last couple words of. Senior continued speaking while he waved Byrd in.

"You missed Padre Phillips," Senior said. "That old boy laid us all out. I wish somebody would've thought to record that."

A number of the chiefs in earshot nodded agreement.

"It's extra special, being a Sunday and all. Who else feels like they went to church services without having to have gone?"

The chiefs at his table concurred.

"Sorry to interrupt, Senior," Byrd said as he squatted to ear level. He resented this game, but it was his job and he would do it out of a sense of paying his dues. "The XO called and I wanted you to know as soon as possible."

The others in the room continued to talk amongst themselves, but he had Senior's attention.

"He didn't call me here. What the hell does he want? Why didn't he call me here?"

"He wants you to go with him to remove the contents of the most recent fatality's locker."

"Who? The airdale that got crushed in the crash-landing?"

"That was a month ago, Senior."

"Has it been that long? I heard about that. Awful."

Byrd nodded his "no-shit" nod to hurry it along. "The new XO thinks it'll be a good idea if you're both present at the pack-out for Petty Officer Pruitt. Ceremonial, and shit like that."

Senior tilted his head toward his shoulder deep enough for his neck to pop like an oversized knuckle. "When?"

Byrd's knees felt like they were going to fail. The right one quivered. Byrd stood and tried to shake out his legs without being obvious. "Sixteen-hundred, tomorrow."

"Why so late in the day?"

"That wasn't discussed, Senior."

Perhaps it was the chaplain's sermon, or whatever it had been, but Senior actually smiled. Being in a good mood was the only time he treated anyone adequately. Byrd never trusted it, because he could go back to being a hard-ass at the drop of a ball cap.

"I'm not crazy about the situation, but this is this XO's first onboard fatality. I hope he doesn't plan to make this a regular thing." Senior slapped Byrd's shoulder as he laughed.

Byrd laughed in the lowest register of genuineness.

Senior wiped his mouth on a crumpled paper napkin. "You know something? I appreciate you coming down here to give me the news as quickly as you did. That's a sign of respect. You're very respectful, Byrd. Have I ever told you that?"

"Not in this lifetime." The flood of energy through his limbs might have come from Senior's words, but were likely the result of his own. He'd never displayed such frankness with his boss.

Instead of calling Byrd out on it, Senior said, "Well I'm telling you now. In fact, I'll tell all my brethren. Gentleman." He raised his voice as he stood. "Pipe down a minute. I want to tell you all to keep an eye on this bright bastard because he's going to be in here with us very soon." Senior clamped his massive hand on Byrd's shoulder and shook him a little. "He's a hell of a sailor and the best deputy a sheriff could have."

Byrd felt heat climb his neck and flood his head. The sentiment was even more surprising than the public announcement of it.

The chiefs all slapped their tables a number of times in some sort of applause, firmly enough to rattle the utensils and the dishes.

Byrd felt air on his teeth and gums before fatigue set into his smile. "I don't know what to say to that, Senior."

"Say goodbye so I can get back to my goddamn lunch."

All the chiefs within earshot laughed.

Byrd's smile returned as Senior punched him in the arm.

"And go get some food yourself," Senior said. "I hear they're serving ice cream on the mess deck."

Byrd left the goat locker feeling good. He whistled a tune of his own composition as he walked down the passageway. He had forty minutes left on the noon break and he could've gone to the mess deck to eat. Instead, Byrd headed to the brig, where he planned to check arrest records down in the brig office. He had the information of who was arrested, but he needed the brig's logbook to see how each of them served their time. Before he got very far, he ran into Chaplain Phillips.

The chaplain's chin went tight. He stood straighter, like he had something to hide. "Hello," he said. "How are you, Petty Officer Byrd?"

Byrd nodded and smiled as placating a smile as he could. Normally, religious people made him uncomfortable, but the chaplain was younger than him. Byrd remembered the baby-faced guy walking up the brow with wonderment in his bright blue eyes. Over the course of the deployment, the chaplain had changed. That wonderment had faded into his cheekbones, graying out the glow he'd had there. Even his eyes were gray now.

"I was down here delivering grace in the Chiefs' Mess," the chaplain said.

"Senior said it was an amazing grace. No pun intended."

If the chaplain got the joke, it didn't register. "I just went down a deck to look around and then I run into you. Funny. How have you been?"

He seemed to compulsively check something in his pocket. If this had been an enlisted man, Byrd would've been suspicious. As it was, Byrd thought the chaplain was playing pocket pool. That or maybe the guy had crabs. Either option was awkward to think of the ship's chaplain.

Byrd crossed his arms and looked at the silver bars on the chaplain's collar—a lieutenant. He wasn't playing with himself and he wasn't scratching either, but he was definitely messing with something in his pocket. Whatever he had in there was about the size of a deck of cards, but not a consistent thickness. Byrd's respect for officers made him dismiss any notion of impropriety, but he couldn't help wonder what the man was so fidgety about.

"Hey, Padre," Byrd said to break the awkwardness. "I been meaning to thank you for welcoming those kids from A-gang into your Bible study group. They've really shaped up. They haven't had a lick of trouble since."

The chaplain stared off down the passageway a second or two before answering. "We have a good group of young men who know what they've done is wrong." Sweat rolled down his temple and Byrd couldn't imagine why the chaplain might be so hot in an area so close to a forced-air vent.

"Well," Byrd said, "I hate to cut this short, Padre, but I've got a short time to get something done."

* * *

The next day, Porter had to deal with the most recent casualty aboard the ship—a black sailor who'd overdosed on heroin. It had been only twenty-eight days since the last crewman died, the one on the flight deck. Porter would never forget having witnessed that one on his first day aboard.

He hadn't thought of it all those days ago, but beginning with this most recent death, Porter instituted a policy that he and the command master chief would be present during all deceased crewmen's locker pack-outs. This pack-out took place in one of the berthing spaces where a couple of black sailors had permission to be in their racks at that time of day.

"This is one space I haven't made it to this entire cruise," Senior said, raising his coffee mug to spit.

From what Porter had been told about Senior's coffee mug, at half full, Senior went to the head, dumped the spit cup and rinsed it out with tap water, but no soap, and dried it with a paper towel. He'd throw that and his wad of chew into a trash can and walk into the goat locker—or the mess deck or any workspace big enough to have their own coffee mess—and pour overcooked, black-as-tar coffee into the same mug. If he wasn't spitting, he was sipping. Porter couldn't help worrying that spit would spill.

As they descended the ladder and entered the berthing compartment, Porter wrinkled his nose. "This is appalling."

Senior spit into his cup. "The captain relaxed the standards hoping everyone would have more energy to do their jobs."

Porter paused, looked over at Senior. "Who's been doing the routine inspections of all berthing spaces?"

Senior led them through the maze of racks. "That's one thing you're going to have to learn. Some places aboard this ship don't get inspected."

"What kind of spaces are those?"

"Well, black berthing spaces, obviously."

Commander Porter felt his teeth grinding. To hide his tensing facial muscles, he nodded without speaking for a few seconds. "Um hm," he finally said. "I see." As his head stilled, he leaned toward Senior. "Can I speak to you privately for a moment?"

Before Senior answered, Porter was on his way to the ladder well on the other side of a watertight door. He left it open. As Senior walked through, Porter indicated for him to close it behind him.

"What's this about, Commander?"

Porter pointed at Senior. "Oh, so you do remember my pay grade."

"Of course, I do. What's going on, here?"

"I will not tolerate any of your insolent bullshit, and I damn sure am not about to let my command master chief buy into some racist policy of ignoring the needs of the black crew."

"Racist policy?" Senior held up his hands before resting a palm on the door's dogging handle. "You might want to get all the facts before you go accusing people of shit like that."

"Is that right?"

"They've got their own berthing spaces and they're very protective of them."

"Segregation is an outrage!"

Senior spit into his mug. "Clam down, sir. The coloreds did that themselves." Senior looked at Porter. "The blacks. They want to be together. And they don't like whitey coming down here at all."

The XO stepped into Senior's face. "And you're in the habit of allowing crewmen do what they want, is that what you're telling me, Senior Chief Rawlings?"

"Ah, no, sir. I'm not."

"Not stopping a known problem is the definition of allowing it."

"Well, sir, I guess it depends on your definition of the word problem."

"What the fuck does that mean?"

Senior held up his hands. "We had full integration when we

got underway, but it didn't last long. They want it this way. And the old man doesn't want to upset the apple cart."

"Then you're both guilty in this kid's death."

"Get real, Commander. We abide as a way to give them one thing less to bellyache about."

"Bellyache?" Porter couldn't believe what he was hearing. "You're placating these men by ignoring Navy standards in their living conditions? Is that what you think?"

Senior nodded his chin at Porter. "That was the last XO's policy. Take it up with him."

Porter ignored the derision implied and tried to keep his voice calm. There were junior enlisted men within earshot, some watching them in the throes of this confrontation. "Look," he said, "any group of men left to their own devises will have pockets of illegal activity."

Senior's head cocked sideways, and an eyebrow went up opposite of his cheek with the wad of chewing tobacco. "So, you're saying the coloreds are to blame for the drug problem?"

Porter nodded. "They very well could be."

Senior's expression leveled off and he stood straight. He held his spit cup at his side, his jaw gone slack, which made it obvious he never expected to hear such words from a black man.

Porter felt this was a good opportunity to continue the barrage on the salty bastard's defensive reflexes. "I don't care what color the criminals are, Senior Chief. I'm going to clean up this goddamn ship."

Senior didn't move.

Porter was tempted to share the deal he made with the captain. Wanted to confess the urgency had two purposes, but he didn't trust the man any farther than he could heave him. Instead, Porter took a step. "Now let's go honor our fallen shipmate."

"Even though he don't deserve no honors."

Porter stopped. "That's a horrible thing to say."

Senior spit into his coffee mug. "It's a drug thing, not a black thing."

Porter turned to face him.

"What?" Senior asked. "If that feller bought the farm on the flight deck like that kid last month, well then, that would be something to honor and remember. But drugs? This goddamn guy was either weak-willed or stupid or both. I'm not interested in memorializing that."

"See here, Senior Chief. That was our shipmate who lost his life in a time of war. Period. That is very worthy of memorializing. Some of these boys, black and white, weren't blessed with the same fortitude and ingenuity you and I share. They didn't leave home with the plan of getting hooked on drugs and taking too many. None of them did. Do I make myself clear?"

"Yes...sir. But he didn't die for his country like a hero. He took his own life by shooting that devil powder."

Porter looked at Senior. They were both stone-faced for a moment until the corner of Porter's mouth twitched into a grin. "I'm glad you agree," he said. "We need to redouble our efforts of stamping out the drug trade aboard this ship."

Senior held up a hand. "That too is a case of not rocking the boat, XO."

"But it's a problem for our crew."

"For a small portion of our crew."

"You mean the black men of our crew."

"Your words, XO, not mine."

Porter slammed the dogging lever open and slung the door wide. Inside the berthing space, he flipped on all the overhead lights and ripped open the curtains on a rack immediately to his left. The rack wasn't occupied, but the mattress was covered only in its striped mattress cover. No sheets meant it should've been rolled to one end, but there was a blanket and a pillow clearly left in place after a restless night's sleep. Porter yanked out the blanket—which released a few wads of crumpled tissues to fall to the deck. Porter dropped the blanket and turned to the next rack. This one had sheets, but it was unmade and the blanket was similarly curled to the far side instead of folded at the foot of the rack as per regulations.

Porter yanked everything out, leaving the little yellow curtain to flap back and forth. He reached up on tiptoes and found the top rack in the same state. He threw that to the deck as well. He squatted and shoved everything off the bottom rack. As he sprang up, he announced, "Unacceptable, Senior Chief Rawlings. This is patently unacceptable, and it will change as of today."

"Hold on there, XO."

Porter didn't give him time to gain any traction. "See here. I want you to get word to every petty officer on this ship that you and I will be conducting health and comfort inspections in every berthing space at least once per month, with surprise inspections peppered in. Any space that fails isn't just the fault of the offender, but the ten most senior enlisted men living in that space will also be charged with dereliction of duty and will find themselves in front of the old man at mast."

"Hey now, sir. How about we all just take ourselves a good deep breath?"

"Save it, Senior Chief. My mind's made up. Can you remember everything I said or do you need someone to write it down for you?"

Senior stared at Porter for a moment looking like he might take a swing. Instead, he grunted through clenched teeth, "I've got it."

Porter ignored the contempt. "Reinspection here will be one week from today."

"Aye, sir," Senior said.

"I'm glad that's settled. Now let's go pack-out this locker so we can send our shipmate's belongings to his loving family."

Back at the fallen sailor's rack, the junior MAA and both guys with permission to be sleeping were huddled there, clearly eavesdropping.

"Okay," Porter said. "We're going to open Petty Officer Pruitt's rack locker and box up the contents. This is a difficult time for all of us as we have lost a shipmate, a sailor, an American. He gave his life for the protection of his country and that's as high an honor as anyone can have."

Senior Chief coughed, but Porter was convinced it was a laugh covered up.

Evans, the young master-at-arms, cut the lock with a pair of bolt cutters as long as his arms. Inside, cracker crumbs, two used hypodermic needles, and civilian clothes mixed in with working dungarees lay scattered about. There were a couple of letters, a small Bible that looked like it had never been opened, a shower kit with a green and white canister of shaving powder, and a folded picture of Angie Dickenson ripped from a magazine. Underneath it all was his dress blue uniform—folded perfectly, inside out, ready to flip and wear.

Senior said, "This one makes number three, if I remember correctly."

The junior MAA counted off on his thin fingers. "Besides that poor bastard on the flight deck last month," he bowed his head and added, "and that Howdy Doody kid from Albuquerque that got blown overboard by the blast of an F-4. Oh, and four if you count the old XO had a heart attack that same night and had to be airlifted to Da Nang. I heard they recovered the Howdy Doody kid's body and they made the same helicopter flight."

No one said anything for a moment.

Senior broke the brief silence. "They really start to pile up on you when you're not looking."

Porter didn't have anything to say about this callous way of looking at the world. It was immoral, but it wasn't against Navy regulations, so Porter said nothing. Instead, he shook his head while watching the young MAA roll up the dead man's mattress, leaving it at the foot of the rack. This poor kid was zipped in a bag in one of the walk-in freezers below the mess deck.

While Evans boxed it up, Porter pulled Senior to the end of the aisle by his upper arm. "Let's get one thing clear. Your world will be a happier place if the two of us are friends. You want a happy world don't you, Senior Chief?"

Senior was clearly caught off guard. But he didn't hesitate to say, "Let's get something straight, sir. I respect your position, your rank, your achievements as a pilot and an officer—regardless of your skin color. The only people I have a hard time with are those who aren't trying hard enough. And where I come from, it don't matter who or what you are as long as you're trying to better yourself and everything around you. That's the standard I live by, Commander Porter. That's the standard I hold this ship to. Ninety-five percent of the crew meets or exceeds those standards." He stopped talking and shook his head. "What are we even talking about this for? The answer to your original question, that you never bothered to ask, is my problem with you is that you're coming in here on the tail end of all the work we've all done for so damn long and will serve as second in command for a couple line periods, three months tops, and then you'll end up taking some kind of credit for our success."

Porter was taken by surprise, but his split-second reaction time allowed him to mask his initial feelings. He nodded. "You feel your old XO should be here."

"You got that right." Senior stared at Porter as he said it.

"You two were close?" Porter lowered his voice to make Senior lean in to hear. Make him closer when he answered. It was a tactic he'd learned for navigating the rigors of cocktail parties, dinners, and other official events.

"I knew Mike when I was an airdale bosun aboard the *Yorktown* working the rigging in the hangar bay. He was a newbie pilot who liked to walk around the other planes. Said he did the same thing at car lots even after he got a car."

"Sounds like a good guy."

"Yeah." Senior spit into his cup. "You write the letter to this kid's family yet?"

Porter shook his head. He wanted to get a sense of the dead guy since he had to write a letter to follow those sent by the Department of the Navy. He would write it and he and the captain would sign it together and it would be shipped in a presentation binder. He imagined some heartbroken mother or aunt somewhere would cry harder when they saw it.

"Well, don't put yourself out," Senior said. "There's nothing you can say to make it easier to take, trust me."

"That's pretty cynical."

"It's a fact."

"You receive training in psychology or are you psychic?"

"The letter I got from the Marine Corps a couple years ago when my oldest son stepped on a landmine and ended up decorating the limbs of a tree didn't help me or his mother one damn bit."

That was the last thing he expected to hear in that moment. Porter's heart felt like it exploded and decorated the inside of his ribcage. He couldn't imagine being in this situation with that kind of pain echoing in his head. It didn't excuse Senior's attitude, but it explained it. Either way, Porter's hope deflated. Senior Chief Rawlings would not be an ally.

CHAPTER 9

Chrissy Lane
426 Carnation Ave.
Lemon Grove, CA 91945

August 23, 1972

Seaman Elliot Brackert
USS Salvation (CV-44)
FPO San Francisco, CA 95660

Dear Elliot,

They had a big protest down in Miami. Tear gas and shots fired into the crowd that was protesting the war and demanding women's liberation. Nixon is there with the Republicans. Such a huge mess. Most of them look like they've been doing it too long and are stuck in their ways. They don't understand that they have to take control with their own hands, like we're doing, right Sweetheart?

Professor Williams is talking about staging a demonstration here. He is a force of nature. I forgot to tell you in my last letter that there's a rumor he's going to ask me to marry him. I'd rather have you, but you're gone and still haven't done anything that really makes a big difference in saving the innocent babies over there. I don't know, Elliot.

I won't make any decisions until I hear from you. Hopefully you'll have some news good enough to keep me waiting for you.

Sorry this is so short, but I got to go now. Make something happen for me. And stay safe.

Chrissy

Brackert walked into the aft section of the hangar bay. He knew two catapults lined the flight deck near the centerline of the back half, while the other two angled off the port side, but he didn't have any idea where the catapult equipment was. Instinct told him to keep moving. He swallowed his frustration as he searched for any indication. The topic had probably been covered during Indoc that first day aboard the ship. He wished he'd paid attention, but his mind had drifted during the lectures and tours. He'd been with Chrissy the night before and there hadn't been much blood flow north of his hips for an entire weekend and he was understandably dehydrated. He wished he could feel that way right now. Instead, he had to do something he never thought he'd do, just so he could have a shot at feeling that way again once he got released and sent home.

With any luck, the equipment room would proclaim itself boldly in yellow reflective paint. In his back pocket he carried a screwdriver large enough to pry off a padlock should the equipment room have one, but he didn't know what other kind of damage he could inflict with the tool. He walked fast as he searched, anxious to get busy and find out. Aside from the difficulty finding the place, he was confident this damage could be caused without harming a single shipmate.

Brackert didn't understand all that peacenik stuff going on in the States. Why would somebody in California or Florida, say, give two shits about people they never met in Vietnam? Some of his buddies believed the whole damn country should be Nagasaki-ed so decent people could start over. A lot of guys Brackert knew hated the Vietcong. Brackert couldn't directly hate anyone, but he wasn't about to lose sleep if they lived or died. Still, it was important to Chrissy, which was important to Brackert. He had to do something that would make a big enough impact that Chrissy would run away with him, and only him. If he got caught he'd hang for murder and treason, but she was worth the risk and the guilt.

But now, he felt stupid for thinking it would be easy to sabotage such equipment. He'd been so insistent on not hurting another shipmate that he'd convinced himself he could disable a catapult by loosening a bolt or jimmying a gear or something. Render the thing inoperable and reduce the ship's air assaults. Thinking about the catapult made him think of the chaplain, which made him feel alone and filled him with an oppressive sense that he'd fail at the one thing he couldn't afford to fail at.

He walked around the hangar deck, assuming he'd find the catapult eventually. In his mind, he'd be able to do any number of damaging things to interrupt flight ops and impress Chrissy. For every plane that he kept from flying, maybe twenty to fifty kids were kept alive. That's what she told him. He never doublechecked her math because it sounded right, especially in those moments when he thought about the magical things she could do with her tongue. But by this stage in the deployment that mental imagery was growing fuzzy, yet also seemed to magnify with anticipation and urgency into a distorted mess that gave him a headache. They'd been gone long enough for many women to have gotten pregnant and delivered babies.

Two fans attached overhead near the elevator deck that ferried planes to and from the flight deck blew steady wind at about eight miles per hour. The fans were big as Buicks and could be angled to blow fresh air in or to vent bad air out. Brackert kept walking. Ducked under the nose of an F-8. It wasn't the same plane that had killed his buddy, Hydrant, but it looked the same. The downward slope of its wings brought to mind the pain the poor bastard must've felt. Brackert would never erase the picture in his mind as long as he lived. Sleeping from that night on had been fitful, at best. He hadn't felt rested since. He kicked the plane's front tire. With everything in him, he wished he'd only wedged the P-38 beneath the front tire so it would pop while taxiing. The whole point had been to prevent it from taking off and delivering its payload.

As he continued his measured steps he looked around, hoping to see a bulkhead stenciled *Catapult Equip. Access* or something to clue him in. Instead, over on the starboard side, he discovered a compartment that served as a locker for Mk-24 flares. The watertight door was wide open. Despite having a hasp, there was no padlock dangling from either end. Inside were hundreds of aluminum tubes, two feet long and packed with gunpowder as a means to spark the magnesium illuminate. These tubes could be attached to fixed-wing planes or launched by hand from helos. Two-million candlepower each. One was bright enough to turn four miles of dark land to daylight. Two firefighting stations were visible from where he stood. He would've felt safer if there were three or, better yet, four.

He stepped past the open hatch and back into the hangar bay, where he came upon two guys working on the tail rotor of a Sea Night helo. He ignored them and kept walking, but quickened his pace to portray a man with someplace to get to and not a wandering vandal.

Over the din of their conversation about the baseball season they were missing, Brackert heard their wrenches clacking on the helo's bolts. "I'm telling you," one of the guys said, "no-body's catching the Reds this year. They're gonna win it all."

Brackert looked over his shoulder at them as he passed. That brief moment of not watching where he went made him run face-first into an aviation machinist mate named Corrigan.

Corrigan was a thick, pasty guy from somewhere in New England. He looked like one of those guys who missed a good night's sleep more than he missed pussy. Brackert knew the type. They were usually married guys, like Corrigan, who weren't into their wives because they got fat, had kids, or both. Brackert imagined Corrigan had at least one or two orange-haired rug rats back home. Probably carried pictures of them in his wallet, but Brackert was not the kind of guy interested in seeing them.

"The fuck you doing up here?" Corrigan asked.

Brackert didn't know what to say. He didn't want any trouble or to draw attention to himself. They were about the same height and about the same age, but this guy was shaped like a capital Y.

"Nothing, man. Just passing through."

Corrigan's face reddened. "You shouldn't be here in the first place."

Brackert tried to pass, but Corrigan sidestepped to block his path. Brackert had seen the scenario played out with the old boys around the bowling alley, the liquor store, even the Laundromat back home in Knoxville. He'd even faced a couple incidents of his own, back in the day. This pale bastard wanted to fight. Brackert felt it in his urine. He tried to wave him off and leave, but Corrigan grabbed his upper arm. The grip was more skin-pinching than bone-crunching. Brackert resisted the urge to turn into the grab and strike fast and often enough to break free. Instead, he asserted just enough force to shrug his arm free. "It's a big ol' ship," Brackert said. "There's room for both of us."

"I know who you are," Corrigan said. "You're that little corncob fucker been hiding behind the chaplain's coattails."

Corrigan was a couple pay grades higher than Brackert, but that wasn't even marginally relevant in this moment.

"Look here," Brackert said. "Every swinging dick on this ship knows my status is complicated."

Corrigan looked in the direction of the overhead fans on the port side of the ship and then at Brackert. "When I heard we had a sissy onboard, I swore to myself I'd throw him over the side if I ever found him."

Brackert choked on half a breath. He'd encountered animosity in his time since declaring his new status, but this was the first overt threat. "Come on now, shipmate," he said, smiling wide enough to make his own eyes squint. "Let's just go about our business. You stay here and I'll head yonder."

Corrigan grabbed a handful of Brackert's collar. There was no leverage to lift Brackert, so the guy pressed his knuckles into Brackert's neck. "I say we settle this now."

Light exploded in Brackert's head like flashbulbs. A surge of adrenaline shot through him. His arms, neck and legs felt swollen with kinetic energy. In the near distance, the maintenance worker's wrenches tapped around the helo. The deck beneath his boots had the constant vibration he'd all but gotten used to. He felt confident he could kick the shit out of Corrigan, but he couldn't allow himself to prove it. Having declared himself a pacifist, throwing fists now would undo everything he'd accomplished to that point and cancel his pending discharge. Neither would please Chrissy. Deep down, he'd rather punch this motherfucker in the neck than be strong-armed by him.

"You best get your hands off me and get the fuck out of my face, man." Brackert's voice floated out in a pitch higher than he'd hoped.

Corrigan puffed up his chest and grabbed Brackert by the neck.

Acid burned in the back of Brackert's throat. He turned his head in time for a burp to escape him, almost silently, like steam venting from lungs. In that instant Brackert swung a punch that connected with the left side of Corrigan's face. Landed a full-fist shot with partial elbow on the follow through. Corrigan landed like a wet swab between pallets of Teletype paper and replacement parts for F-4s.

Corrigan grunted as he pushed himself up. He struggled to his feet and charged Brackert, clamped him in a bear hug. The hold was fortified with iron. Pressure in Brackert's head squeezed his eardrums. He endured the controlled violence, because with his arms in this position, he couldn't possibly get in another punch and his high school wrestling experience was as useless as the letterman's jacket he stored in the locker beside his rack. Corrigan squeezed harder, steaming breath like well water from his nose, and lifted Brackert's feet off the deck and head-butted him. The collision rocked his vision with stars. Brackert struggled but couldn't free himself no matter the exertion.

Even though his arms were pinned to his sides, he could move them at the elbow and reach behind himself. The first try failed to go far enough. Corrigan's grip tightened. Upon the second attempt, Brackert reached his back pocket and felt for the screwdriver. He kept reaching, trying to lengthen his arm at the shoulder joint. He made contact with his fingertips, and then tugged it close enough to pinch the molded plastic handle between his index and middle fingers. Within seconds he had it grasped it in his fist. He didn't know exactly what he'd do with it, but he needed some kind of advantage.

Corrigan shook him as he tightened his grip and pushed backward. Brackert had done the same thing a thousand times on the mat. This was like tying up at the whistle and Corrigan was already pushing back. All he had to do was block a heel and he'd get two points for a takedown. The options for control after that were virtually limitless. Brackert's boot caught on a pallet, or maybe Corrigan's foot, and he lost equilibrium. He tried to move his arms to brace for the fall on his way to the deck, but there was no time to do so. He hung on as they went down. The deck came hard in the crash and his shoulder landed on a protruding corner of a pallet. Corrigan didn't let go.

The world slowed in that moment. The deck burned through the back of his T-shirt, but he didn't know how severely he might've been injured. He did, however, feel a distinct pressure on his wrist and then wetness on his hand.

He relaxed his fists and rolled Corrigan over—saw the maroon puddle spread across his faded dungarees in a widening radius around the screwdriver.

The pair of turbo fans overhead kicked on with blades clanging every third revolution forcing air over them.

"Shit, man. That there's an accident," Brackert said. His heart rate spiked with the memory of Hydrant and the thought of hurting another crewmen made him queasy. "You know that, right?"

Corrigan sat up, coughed twice and tugged on the handle sticking out of his thigh.

"You ought to leave it in, I think," Brackert said.

In one fluid motion Corrigan extracted the screwdriver and raised it in the air. The screwdriver dripped blood and jellied bits of muscle and fat. Corrigan clenched his grip. Spotlights mounted high on the bulkheads shined across the hangar deck while Corrigan lay in shadow. Brackert watched blood and fat droplets puddle on the deck.

The moment became lost in a fog for a minute, like Brackert had been hit in the head. He didn't know what this meant for his future. His focus returned in time to see a young Marine, the corporal of the guard, a kid named Gomez, standing over Corrigan, who still sat on the deck, screwdriver in one hand, while the other applied pressure to his puncture wound.

"What the fuck?" Gomez said, his arms crossed and a .45 holstered on his hip.

Brackert felt the flush of defeat as he was on the verge of getting busted. He took a step back. "I was just minding my own business."

"That's how most stabbings occur, now isn't it?" Corrigan said.

Gomez had his hands on his hips.

"I ain't stabbed nobody," Brackert yelled. "This feller here charged me and landed on a screwdriver."

Gomez looked to Corrigan who said nothing.

"Well," Gomez said, "the way I see it is one guy has a screwdriver in his hand that matches the new fuck hole in his thigh, and the conscientious objector has a really bad fucking poker face."

Brackert felt the weight of a cinder block on his chest.

Gomez stood beside Corrigan. "Give me your belt."

Corrigan asked, "You going to whip him or strangle him with it?"

Gomez held out his hand. "Give me your belt."

Corrigan opened the buckle and pulled the belt from around his waist.

Gomez knelt and looped it around Corrigan's thigh, right above the wound. He cinched it tight to make a tourniquet.

"I'll live, now go bash that fucker's head into the deck a few dozen times."

"Frankly," Gomez said, "I don't give a shit what did or didn't happen here. All I know is that we've got to get that leg looked at."

Brackert looked at Corrigan to see if he was following this.

"So what I'm saying to you two knuckleheads is let's all be fucking men about it and get on with our motherfucking lives. All right?"

"What about him?" Corrigan asked.

Brackert started to defend himself, but before the first word came out, Gomez had Corrigan by the collar.

"If you would've left him alone," he said, "you'd be fine right now instead of having a hole in your fucking leg."

Corrigan fought against Gomez's help as he struggled to his feet. "So? That's it?"

Gomez let go of the collar. "Just be glad it's me and not one of your MAA dicks."

"What about my leg? I bet I have to get a shot because of this."

Gomez scratched an itch on his throat. "You're going to tell the doc you fell down a ladder and poked yourself with that screwdriver. Aren't you?"

Corrigan's face screwed into a knot. His nose wrinkled and his eyebrows touched, more confusion than pain.

Brackert couldn't help thinking this was too good to be true.

"Nobody needs any trouble," Gomez said. "It's not going to make that hole in your leg go away. Besides, no one needs to know you let a pansy like this get the best of you. Got it?"

Brackert said, "I'll agree to that. And I'm sorry, Corrigan. Really."

"Rot in hell, turncoat."

Brackert ignored him, nodded to the Marine. "This is pretty damn neighborly of you, Gomez." He grasped the Marine's shoulder and was surprised to reach bone. He couldn't tell by looking at this spit-polished Marine that he was just a thin kid under his working uniform.

Gomez shrugged him off and came up pointing in Brackert's face. "Go fuck yourself. I know what you're doing is technically legal, but if Major Kelly didn't order us to watch your back, I'd be kicking your ass myself. You turncoat piece of shit."

Brackert backed away with his hands held up by his shoulders. Something else he'd learned outside the bowling alleys and liquor stores back home is never to argue with a man carrying a gun. He walked off, content with the incentive to postpone the catapult mission for another day.

The bosun blew his pipe over the 1MC to signal an announcement to follow. What came next was the last thing Porter expected.

"This is the captain speaking. Listen up. We have a new rule aboard this fine vessel and that rule is the two-man rule for all black crew. Until further notice, no black crewmen are allowed to move about the ship in numbers greater than two at a time. That means no groups off three walking anywhere at any time. Those found in violation will be brought to me for NJP. That is all."

Upon completing his berthing space inspection, Porter went in pursuit of the captain.

He climbed up to the bridge, checked his sea cabin, popped into CIC, and then finally found him in his private galley. There was no mess cook present, just a stool, a sandwich, and the captain.

"Did you make that yourself?" Porter asked.

"Haven't eaten all day. Didn't want to wait anymore. But that's not why you're here." He took a chomp from the sandwich. With his mouth full, he said, "What can I do you for?"

It seemed an absurd environment to have such an important conversation, but Porter had to take advantage of the urgency. "Sir, can I speak frankly?"

"Of course."

"This two-man rule is a horrible policy and I strenuously advise you to reconsider."

"Advise me? As my XO or as a black man?"

"Both, obviously."

"Obviously? The only thing I'd say is obvious is your inability to bring me the head of the drug ring, to say nothing of your effect on black morale thereby making this new rule necessary."

"Frankly sir, I'm shocked you didn't consult me about this ahead of time." Porter was fuming inside. He recognized he was getting off topic and redirected himself. "There's a fire within much of the black crew, that's no secret, but what is the need to throw gas on it, sir?"

"If you're mad I didn't consult you, don't be," the captain said. "There was no way of talking me out of it. And if you're mad I didn't give you the heads up, don't be that either. I'd been contemplating it all about a month now. I spoke to the DCA earlier and he put a bee in my bonnet to pull the trigger."

Porter wasn't a fan of his terminology as it applied to the black crew, but the words were out and the law had been laid. "This is going to enrage every black man on this ship."

"The thoughts and feelings of any swinging dick on this ship means little," the captain said. "They only know objectives and numbers and exceeding expectations."

"None of that is possible," Porter said, "without the crew working together."

"Good," the captain said with smugness spread across his eyes and his slit of a mouth. "I'm glad you understand that fact. I wholly recommend you make that happen. Do I make myself clear?"

"Clear to the point of transparency, Captain."

"Don't get smart, Bob. *Be* smart, but don't *get* smart." He took another bite of sandwich. "No good will come of that."

Porter didn't have an objective way to judge the tone of his own voice and had no way to gauge how forceful he'd been in his opposition. The cold truth of it was the captain was right.

"Aye, Captain. But Senior and the Marines will have to go easy for the first few days as the crew adjusts."

The captain wiped his mouth. "Consider it done, Bob."

Porter nodded as he contemplated the likelihood that would work out favorably.

"More than ninety percent of the men aboard this ship are white, Mr. Porter. Need I remind you?"

"Being black means I never need reminding."

"I'm thinking more about the safety of the black crew." The captain waved his sandwich. "The blacks might have the element of surprise, but they're so outnumbered they wouldn't stand a chance, even without the Marines."

Porter looked away.

"This is a powder keg, Smokey. We've got to keep the flame from the fuse."

Porter shook his head in reflex to hearing something so absurd. "But don't you understand, Captain? This new rule is the fuse and you've just lit it."

The captain took a swig of milk from his cup and then said, "If that's true, it's a good thing this rule is in place. I'd rather have Senior or the Marines throw half of them in the brig than have to bury all of them."

"Them?" Porter crossed his arms.

"That's all the black sailors are to a lot of guys aboard this ship. I grew up with boys like that. There are easily two thousand of them redneck-types aboard. There's another thousand that wouldn't go looking for trouble but would quickly escalate if provoked. That's what we can't have happen."

"Treating a portion of the crew differently, as if they're subhuman, doesn't seem the best move for morale, Captain."

"This has nothing to do with any of that," the captain said. "We're one crew. A big happy family working together to execute our role as flawlessly as humanly possible. Have to maintain that and motivate all hands."

"Personally, insulting crewmen isn't the best way to reach those goals."

"You're not talking about the risk of hurt feelings, are you, Smokey? I don't care about hurt feelings. I'm just interested in operational excellence. Maintaining order is a huge step in that direction. That's all this is. Nothing personal to anyone."

Porter stood there and absorbed it.

"Is there anything else?" the captain asked with another wave of his half-eaten sandwich.

With a head shake and a casual about-face, Porter left. He took with him a taste like ammonia in the back of his throat and a feeling of bricks on his back.

CHAPTER 10

For two days, Applewhite laid low. Laundry, chow, rack. He kept his head down. He didn't want anyone looking at him. He didn't even talk to the fellas in the berthing lounge area, where he usually joined them to play cards and watch closed-circuit television on a fifteen-inch black-and-white set mounted head high in the corner. It had been seven weeks since the ship's crew last got liberty. Seven weeks since they'd touched dry land. An eternity since they'd gotten drunk or laid. Tensions aboard ship ran so high that black crew members weren't allowed to walk in groups of three or more. On most days bullshit like that sparked his fuse. But recently Applewhite had received a couple letters from Tonya that tugged his stomach up over his slow-beating heart.

One night around 2100 he went down to talk to Surico, the ship's cobbler. The late hour didn't matter to Surico, who worked away in his shop. He told anyone who asked how late he was open, "Unless I'm eating, sleeping, or shitting, I am here."

His bushy hair grayed at the sides, as did his mustache. He wore a white cloth apron over a white T-shirt. Both stretched over his rounding stomach and were streaked with boot black. Nobody knew where he was from, but scuttlebutt said his father was a sailor who knocked up an island girl, and after the baby was born, they went to the States and got married. Surico took his mother's maiden name, Hurasa, and never went by any variation of his first name. He said it was a way to stick it to the man without him even noticing.

He met Applewhite at the door with upper and lower halves that could be closed and opened to serve as a counter for incoming repairs or pickups. He gave him a complicated dap that included multiple hand slaps as well as one on top of the head that said, *Come on in, boy, and let me take you to school.*

The cobbler's workshop was a tight room, barely head height, built out of steel beams and sheet metal, just big enough to house a workbench twice as long as he was tall, a muscular sewing machine—for reattaching boot soles—racks for tools and replacement materials for all manner of shoes and boots. Surico kept a reel-to-reel tape player on the shelf above his left shoulder. It played Magic Sam music, the *West Side Soul* album, if Applewhite recalled correctly. Surico played music all day as he stood at his workbench. The place smelled of bacon grease and turpentine from the polishes he used, as well as the smell of new leather and rubber. A gray safe squatted along the bulkhead opposite the door. It was twice as wide as Applewhite and almost as tall. He leaned an elbow on its top and checked out the deep sink wedged into the corner. Its stainless-steel basin held a hot water bottle bloated with fermenting potatoes. This, more than the sparkling conversation, was a side benefit to Applewhite's visit. He didn't love the taste of the crude homemade wine, but Surico always shared enough with Applewhite to have the desired effect.

Instead of cups, Surico poured potato wine from a jar labeled ethyl acetate into two ceramic coffee mugs. He handed one to Applewhite and crossed over to take his stool by his workbench. Applewhite leaned his other elbow on the safe and raised the mug with his free hand. As he drank, he remembered he was the only other man on that ship to know the combination.

They heard footsteps on the ladder as a white seaman apprentice made his way to the half-open door. Applewhite wasn't surprised to see the kid hand over a wad of cash—mostly dollar bills—that spilled onto the deck. The kid held one hand on top of the wad as he squatted to pick up what had fallen. "I'm sorry, Surico," the kid said. But the kid placed the emphasis on the wrong syllable. It came out Suri-co instead of Sir Rico.

Surico banged his open hand on the half-door's sill.

Applewhite hurdled the half-door and grabbed the kid by the collar. "Say his name the right way."

The kid held up the money he'd retrieved from the deck and Surico leaned forward to take it from his hand.

Applewhite bent the kid forward over the ladder until his mouth was biting down on the bottom steel step. The kid shook and moaned incoherently. Applewhite placed his foot on the kid's head. "If I apply a little more pressure, I can knock out your teeth without getting my boot dirty."

The kid smacked repeatedly on the step beside his head and moaned louder.

Applewhite lifted his foot and pulled the kid up by the hair. "Say it right."

"I'm sorry. Sir Rico."

Surico smiled and stuffed the five single dollars into a canvas bag and locked it away in the safe across from the sink. As he rose, he held his hands on his lower back. He took two side steps and reached slowly for a pair of sneakers bleached white as their new shoelaces. "You better get your shit in one sock before you come down here again. You dig?"

The kid nodded as he collected the sneakers, turned, and hightailed it back up the ladder.

The ship's cobbler was never permitted to charge crewmen for his services. Nor was he allowed to sell drugs. That didn't stop him. And it didn't stop guys from paying for the drugs as well as the work done on their shoes. This gave Surico no excuse for having cash on hand, if it ever came up. It never came up. No one wanted to inspect the cobbler's shop. That had been Surico's favorite part of his setup for the past two years.

And everything that changed hands went through Surico. None of the candy men carried cash. None of the cash men carried the candy. All cash men came down and personally delivered his sixty-percent return. Applewhite had been an enforcer for Surico this entire cruise. He'd gotten a twenty-percent cut of what was owed from every collection, whether the money was collected or if payment was made with a couple fingers caught in a watertight door—hard enough to break bone, but not so hard as to remove them.

If somebody got ambitious and tried to go out on their own, someone would take them out or turn them in. Dropping the hammer and the dime with equal pleasure. The first guy who threatened to rat was a third-class wrench turner with a bad fucking attitude. He had himself a nasty fall down the aft escalator. They flew him to a shore-side hospital on a rickety Sea Knight helo. All his ribs broken, a lung punctured, and his spleen had to come out. Everybody knew the score: "Ain't been no talk of nobody giving up secrets ever since."

Applewhite drank from his mug, then said, "Since you ain't brung it up yet, I got to ask. You need any collecting done?"

The question caught Surico mid-sip. As he lowered his mug, he nodded, and swallowed. "Sorry, young blood. All the brothers are up to date."

Surico's orders included strictly obeying the color line. He had his white guys stick with the white guys. Blacks with themselves.

"What about the honkies?" Applewhite asked.

"We been through this."

"Fuck the color line. They owe money."

"Not going to happen."

Applewhite pounded the side of his fist onto the top of the steel safe. "That's bullshit!" With his next breath, he added, "With all due respect."

"All you young bucks know is anger." Surico laughed. "You best learn to calm your ass. I've got white guys handle that. It keeps the heat off all of us that way."

Applewhite didn't know the ins and outs of what Surico said, but he believed him and that was enough to put Applewhite in a calmer state. "Fine," he said. "Then I want to move product for you again. I've got some of my own left. I ration my stash to make it last. I like to have extra before I sell it or finish what I got."

"Planning ahead."

"No good comes from needing some, you know?"

"That's good, but you're an enforcer. I can't have you selling and collecting, and even if I wanted to, the crackdown has a lot of motherfuckers too chickenshit to get caught with anything."

"I figured maybe you were running out of supply."

"I'm still good. Besides, the next shipment is supposed to arrive on one of the upcoming underway replenishments."

Applewhite wasn't sure how, but Surico's group always knew when a shipment was arriving, down to which pallet out of the hundreds that came across from the supply ship. Applewhite wanted to know, not just because of the drugs, but also because he'd grown determined to find out who exactly it was that Surico answered to.

"How old's the baby?" Surico asked.

Applewhite's breath caught high in his throat and he coughed. That stalled moment wasn't enough for him to come up with a solid lie. "I'll lay it out there for you, Surico, man. She's twice as old now as she was when I last saw her."

"She's walking by now."

"Suppose so."

"You providing for her?"

"Baby and mama. They cut my pay when I got thrown in the brig a ways back."

"I know," Surico said.

"I need to make more so I can send more."

"I hear that."

"What about this wine?"

"You're welcome, by the way."

"You know?" Applewhite said. "With the candy being so hard to move these days, we could make a fortune selling this stuff."

"Not interested."

Applewhite's buzz surged through him. He stood fast enough to make his head swim. He straightened as much as he could. "You have any idea how much money I'm talking about?"

"Don't care."

Applewhite slumped his torso back onto the safe. "How can you not care?"

"I only make enough for me and the people I choose to share it with."

"But you're passing up an opportunity."

"You do it, if you're so damn excited about it."

Of all of Surico's enterprises that Applewhite knew, what he didn't know was how to make the wine. He knew it required unpeeled potatoes, yeast, and sugar, but nothing of the intricacies of each. "I don't know how to make this."

"That's your tough shit."

"Fine, damn." Applewhite looked down at the safe. He could easily find out Surico's sleeping patterns and help himself some night. After that brief moment of wonder, he abandoned the notion because stealing from a brother was the opposite of his every belief. There were too many white people fucking with the lives of his people. He couldn't become one of those guys who does harm to a brother, especially one who worked hard to earn his money. He sipped his wine. The burn in his throat made him think of gin, but there was no pepper, no flavor other than the burn.

Surico took a sip and came up nodding.

"If it wasn't for that damn Uncle Tom motherfucker," Applewhite said, "we'd both be sitting pretty right about now."

"Come on, now," Surico said. "You got to cut brotherman some slack. And lower your fucking voice. We don't need nobody picking up an echo on the shit you be saying."

"You're the last person I figured would kiss ass."

"Yes," he nodded. "You bet your ass I am."

Applewhite's spine throbbed from a rush of heat that passed through him. The sensation left him stunned for a second, wondering if it would return.

"The brother just got here. Besides, you can't expect the whole world to completely reverse their policies and plans for us. All that shit is gradual."

"He ain't no real brother."

"You don't know nothing about that man's struggles."

"He's an officer and a pilot. He don't know nothing about struggling."

"Fool. Your ass is too dumb to realize how hard he must have *struggled* to get up in that club! You think they just welcomed him with arms wide open?"

"Man, I don't care about any of that noise. He's up there. I'm down here."

"It ain't just our batch of brothers, Rufus. It's the whole goddamn race."

He had Applewhite's attention.

"All the other brothers got it the same as us, and believe it when I say it's a hell of a lot better than it used to be."

Applewhite fired back, "Is it the same as them?"

Surico sipped his wine and looked off toward the bloated bag with a wooden stopper.

"Is it the same as them?" Applewhite asked again.

"No. Damn it. I know," Surico said. "But it ain't like flipping no damn switch. It's going to be gradual. Besides, would you rather be in the rice paddies stepping on land mines and getting shot at and shit?"

"It don't make our war any less shitty."

"We got jobs to do."

"Yeah, shit jobs."

"Whether I do this here or on the outside, I'm going to be

doing this. But this comes with a pension. And, to be blunt with your ass, I'm more suited to a ship's dark recesses than to wet jungles. So there. I'm getting what I want. The easiest way to get it is to play the traditional role with enthusiasm. I'll let them think I'm just here to serve them, because they get to believe the lowest form of their ranks is respectful of regulations and them."

"Never will understand why it matters," Applewhite said.

"Trust me, boy. The fewer reasons you give people to be pissed off, the higher quality of your life." He stopped talking and looked up at the rack of laces hanging on the far bulkhead. Without turning, he added, "Because the more they believe my lines, the easier my life becomes. Nobody bothers me down here. I do what I want to do, on my own time, which includes making this unauthorized alcoholic beverage and lots of cash from contraband."

Applewhite downshifted himself. Nobody argued with Surico. "I been meaning to ask, my man. Can you do something about the nasty taste of these potatoes?"

Surico laughed into his coffee mug. "Taste ain't the purpose of drinking it."

Applewhite nodded. "True, but no harm in being able to enjoy more flavor and less fumes."

"It's too late for the batch I've got going." Surico pointed toward the deep sink wedged into the corner, filled with a hot water bottle stretched a whitish-pink in the throes of the fermentation process.

"Has the XO been down here yet?"

"He brought down a pair of bowling shoes with the outside stitching split on the right shoe. Or was it the left? Anyway, he came down here like he was a politician looking for votes. Within the span of four minutes he shared a compliment about the orderliness of the shop, made a funny comment about me having to stay skinny to work in such tight quarters, and trusted me with something of value to him. He smiled a lot too. Seems like a really nice brother."

"He's no brother. He's one of them."

"I thought we settled this."

"Did he say anything about being the same race?"

"We didn't waste time with anything so obvious."

"So the highest-ranking black man on this ship comes down here to give you a dry hand job and that's all it takes to win you over. He's one of them and you can't see that."

"Look, man. No matter what you think of Porter, just make damn sure you remember that playing by the rules keeps your life less complicated so you can do the things you want without any trouble."

"But it ain't got to be like that."

"All the shit we take, we turn it into bricks, and we pave the road for our kids' generation, man. You're a father now. You want your kids to have it better than we both did, don't you?" Before Applewhite could answer, he added, "Along the way, we make some money and have some fun."

"Yeah. And do a lot of shitwork."

"It's all shitwork," Surico said. "Don't let nobody tell you different." He held up his mug. "That's why shit like this here is necessary."

"We could make a fortune—"

"Stop your gums about this or I'll kick you out of my shop."

CHAPTER 11

October tenth was a Tuesday, not unlike any other, except that it found Chaplain Phillips on the fantail in the humid air at 0200. He stood on the port side, near the trash dump spot, but it didn't stop him from choosing that exact location. Chaplain Phillips couldn't help but laugh.

The sound of water rushed past the hull two stories beneath him. High up as he was, he was closer to the water than he would've been on the flight deck above him. He looked into the dark and wondered if any of the battle group's smaller ships were nearby. He'd rarely seen them in the daytime.

As the humid wind whipped around, he raked brown hair across his forehead with his fingers. It was longer than it should've been. No one had said anything to him about it, though it wasn't near regulation. He avoided the ship's barbers as long as he thought he could get away with. Those boys were great with the clippers, but shaky with scissors. And they always got nervous when he came in.

The sky was all but starless and the ambient red glow from the ship's underway lighting provided just enough light to see ten feet in front of his nose. It was all the vision he'd need. He'd done the legwork, his homework, made the arrangements, had his shit in one sock, as the blue jackets liked to say.

Next to him, his sea bag sat erect on the deck—packed and

ready to go.

And still he waited. He stood there and breathed in the humidity.

"You're making this harder than it has to be," he said aloud. He winced, because the word *harder* was difficult for him to say without the old accent kicking in. He leaned an elbow onto the life rail behind him. He'd gotten this far without many people ever hearing that accent. His mother and Mary Alice had helped him neutralize the Rhode Island in him. As a way to sterilize his voice as much as possible, they had him repeat every word of the evening news, mimicking Walter Cronkite. For years. That kind of conditioning taught his mouth how to move around the letter R in many words. Most of the time, anyway.

Rhode Island seemed like a long, long way, not only in distance but in time. He could picture the faces of Mother and Mary Alice, but they were getting blurrier with each passing day. It seemed like the colors of those mental pictures were evaporating. Slowly lightening. Leaving behind plain, white spaces. He never knew if it was sadness or self-defense and there was no part of his faith that helped him deal with it when he was honest with himself in those pitch-black moments before he fell asleep. Too much darkness.

This made him think about a letter he hadn't yet written to his mother and Mary Alice. Of all the mail he'd sent and received, none of them were prepared for that unwritten note. Unless they could come over here and spend a year sleep-deprived on a floating prison listening to hundreds of young men with problems that stem from bad upbringings to weak constitutions, they'd never understand. Most of the time, though, Phillips didn't understand it himself. His patience stretched too thin. His faith lost.

He rested a hand on the upright sea bag at his side. From the outside, the sea bag looked like any other and no one would suspect it was loaded with various tools he'd picked up from around the ship, as well as a couple lengths of aircraft tie-down chains and a burned-out motor the size of a shoebox he'd tripped over in the hangar deck one night when he couldn't sleep. He'd wrapped each item individually in a T-shirt or a towel or a blanket as a way to prevent clanking and to keep the packed bag looking like a normal sea bag. The prized piece was a monkey wrench as long as his arm. That wrench, the chains, and the small motor weighed the most and helped push the bag's weight over eighty pounds or so. Heavy enough to get the job done, but not so heavy that he couldn't manage it.

He looked over his shoulder and removed Martindale's foil packet from his pocket and carefully unfolded the edges. Loose white powder covered the pills and the two rolled marijuana cigarettes, as well as the leaking bag of the powder. He brought the foil to his nose. He could sniff the loose powder, though he wasn't sure what it was. He could swallow the pills dry, one at a time, expecting to feel no pain. He could light the joints and risk the smoke giving away his position. His plan all along was to anesthetize himself to make it easier, but he'd never done drugs before and didn't know exactly how they would affect him. The notion of doing anything like that was the opposite of what his father and his grandfather expected of him.

But surely he couldn't be held to promises made in his early teens to a dead man, not minutes before he was going to do what he needed to do. No one would know. But still. He couldn't risk dulling his senses and getting caught. And he found himself not wanting anything to get in the way of doing what he had to do. He pushed the foil edges together, marrying the joints to the pills, all surrounded by the white powder, and he squeezed until the foil packet was a cylinder as long and thick as a hot dog. He leaned his chest against the life rail and watched as the foil fell through the air, slowly, into the water.

Even without the benefit of the drugs, he felt numb. He couldn't focus on anything other than the sound and the color of whatever it was that pulsed in his head. He could see it. Could feel and hear the wind gusting past his face.

He unbuttoned his khaki shirt with one hand as he untucked

the tail with the other. He yanked it off and stretched it out on the deck. He knelt and buttoned the shirt, smoothed away wrinkles and folded it neatly to show *K. Phillips* stenciled inside the back collar. He removed his work boots and placed each heel directly atop the silver LTjg collar devices.

No sooner had he placed them there than it struck him that he could use the extra weight. But with the sea bag, a couple pounds of wet boots wouldn't make or break him. Instead of putting them back on and lacing them up, he stripped off his socks and felt the nonskid surface dimpling the soles of his bare feet.

He squatted low enough to slip the sea bag strap over his arm and duck his head through so the strap rode his chest at a diagonal. The tug as he stood lifted the sea bag only an inch or two above the deck required every muscle in his thin legs. Once he got up, he tugged the strap across his chest, testing its ability to withstand the load. He walked back to the railing and swung a leg over. He paused for a moment, straddling the rail and felt it cutting into his groin. This sensation was the last time he expected to feel pain and he wanted to let it sink in. Holding the rail tight, he swung over his other leg and rested the balls of his feet on the deck's raised edge. The weight of the sea bag pulled at his back, but he gripped the railing and changed the position of his feet until the deck's raised edge dug into his heels with the weight of the sea bag rested on the rail. This made him feel more prepared.

As he drew in his last breath, the situation struck him as funny and he laughed. He'd never thought about his final breath. He didn't know how he could've overlooked that in his planning. Everyone had a last breath. Some weren't conscious to witness the inhalation. Others died mid-scream, which is just a fancy kind of exhalation. His laugh continued until his lungs were empty and he pushed the rest of the air out by tightening his abdominals. He held the sea bag strap and jumped in time to inhale a couple gallons of salt water.

* * *

The ship was at its quietest between two and five in the morning. With most of the crew asleep, the constant roar of male voices didn't fill the passageways. There was no activity on the flight or hangar decks to be heard. The red glow of nighttime electricity ran through the overhead lighting below decks and topside too. Instead of being asleep at 0300, Byrd headed to the galley to talk to a couple mess cranks in the scullery, where every surface above the deck was stainless steel and every inch of it was wet. One guy stood scrubbing, rinsing, and machine loading, while another guy danced a sequence of steps as he sorted all the clean pots and pans and plates and silverware and organized them on racks and carts that could be rolled back into the galley to get dirtied up again. Hot water sprayed around as the sanitizing machines steamed up the hundred-degree air. Byrd began sweating the minute he walked in.

He cleared his throat. "You better shape up in here."

Both guys looked at him, surprise on their faces more obvious than water down their gloves.

Byrd laughed. "I'm just playing. You're good, but you boys mind talking some?"

Before either one answered, the bosun on the bridge called, "Man overboard. Man overboard. Man overboard, port side. All hands muster within five minutes."

"Damn it," Byrd said.

When the call came, the XO had been asleep, dreaming of Sharon's pale breasts smashing against his chest as she rocked on top of him. He sprang from his rack, grabbed his khaki pants from the hook by his sink and stepped into his boots. He tugged on his khaki shirt and tucked it in as he double-timed it down the passageway.

Crewmen scurried to their muster stations. Those who saw

him got others out of his way with calls of, "Make a whole!" and "Gangway!"

He got to the bridge fast. The captain beat him there and stood with the phone pressed to his ear.

The officer of the deck, a skinny lieutenant with coffee-stained teeth, said, "Aft lookout is confident he saw a man in a T-shirt go over the rail on the fantail. The captain is talking to the chief engineer."

Porter wiped sleep from his eyes as he asked, "Directly aft? Into the screws?"

"Port side."

"Where they dump the trash?"

The lieutenant cocked his head sideways as he thought for a moment. "I have no knowledge of that, sir."

"Very well," Porter said.

The captain ended his phone call and turned to Porter. His eyes were fully open to show the red lines of exhaustion beneath enthusiasm and alertness.

"Why aren't we turning?" Porter asked.

"This is the kind of operational procedure you've got to know if you want to command a ship like this someday," the captain said.

Mustering for man overboard took top priority or there'd be hell to pay. Byrd didn't bother to say anything before turning around and jogging aft to take his place with the others as they mustered with Senior.

The scullery wasn't far from Byrd's muster station in the MAA shack, but that wasn't his main concern. Those pot scrubbers were on duty for only a couple more hours. This man overboard drill could drag on past their end of shift, leaving Byrd to search the ship to find them or wait until the next night. Neither option pleased him.

A deck painting of an old west sheriff's star proudly announced *"Salvation's* Finest" beneath Byrd's boots as he entered the MAA shack. The shack was actually a series of offices on the starboard side of the second deck, most of the way forward.

Senior came in a few seconds behind Byrd. If the man had gotten any sleep it didn't show. He looked like a loaf of bread pulled out of the oven halfway through. His hair still carried the shape of his pillow and his eyes were red. He wore khaki trousers, no shirt, and steel-toe boots, unlaced.

Senior said, "What the fuck, boy?"

Byrd didn't know how to react to that.

"You're not on duty," Senior said. "Why the motherfuck are you so bright-eyed this time of night, Byrd?"

Put on the spot like that, Byrd typically responded with something Senior might want to hear or some other type of lie. But on this night he said, "Can never fault a man for being too shaped up and squared away, Senior."

Applewhite slept. He'd heard something announced over the 1MC, but he rolled his face deeper into his pillow and ignored it. The thin yellow curtains on his rack remained closed as he heard talking in the aisles and boots stomping up the ladder outside the berthing compartment door. It wasn't long before everything got quiet again and he drifted off deep enough to drool.

He was awoken by a hand shaking his leg at the ankle where his foot stuck out of the wool blanket.

"Rufus," a voice called. "Rufus, we've got to muster. Man overboard. Come on, man."

Applewhite slid open his curtain to see his buddy, Tilly, buttoning his shirt. "Goddamn it," Applewhite said.

"I know, man. I know."

"Why can't they run these fucking drills during the motherfucking day?" Applewhite slid out of his middle rack, stepped into his dungarees he refused to button and boots he refused to tie. Tilly followed him up the ladder to their muster station on the aft mess deck by an ordnance elevator.

The foc'sle served as muster station for most of the clerical ratings aboard the *Salvation* and Brackert was one of the first to arrive. He stood by himself, leaning a foot atop a link of anchor chain the height and length of a shepherd at the shoulder. Hundreds of links connected the chain that ran the length of the space from the capstan to the hawser to the anchor.

A few guys from the disbursing office were the next to come into the foc'sle. They were cocky for office boys and they ran in a pack, which always made Brackert worry that if he pissed off one of them, he pissed them all off and they could delay his pay out of spite. Besides the corpsmen, the mail clerks, and a couple of the senior cooks, nobody got better treatment than the disbursing clerks. Nobody crossed them. The leader of this small group, a second class named Silver, called out, "I guess it's not our lucky day, boys. This piece of shit, Brackert, isn't the one who went over the side."

Silver's group of four buddies laughed. One pointed as he slapped Silver's back and said something Brackert didn't hear.

Brackert clenched his fist as he cleared his throat. No good would come from being provoked into a fight, he thought. Besides, he'd gotten used to this kind of vitriol from other sailors who didn't get what he was all about. It wasn't fear or hate for his country, but love, man. He wanted to tell them all. Instead, Brackert removed his foot from the anchor chain. "Ain't nobody wants off this ship worse than me, but not that way," he said.

Four minutes into the man overboard headcount, Porter stood beside the captain on the bridge. The captain crossed his arms. "Goddamn those slippery bastards."

Porter nodded. He hadn't gotten the results of the headcount yet. He didn't know what to say. He cleared his throat a couple times to stall for time.

"Don't be a Pollyanna, Smokey. In good conditions these things turn to shit more than thirty percent of the time and you know it. Darkness doubles those odds. Losses at sea don't help my chances of making admiral."

The captain's bluntness was a jab that hit Porter's chin with just enough impact to make a point. It was the first time Porter considered his boss's own ambitions. It made sense. Porter couldn't deny they had that in common.

Instead, he said, "Are you determined to call me Smokey forever, or just until you get a rise out of me?"

The captain laughed from the surprise, like Johnny Carson did when Don Rickles was on. The captain tried to hide his smile.

"I hope a frank conversation about it negates the need for losing my cool. With all due respect, Captain."

Captain Holt leaned a hand on the base of his conning chair. "You picked an odd fucking time to settle this."

Porter didn't want to be known as a leader who cared about himself more than his crew, but it was too late to stuff the words back into his voice box. He didn't detect any resentment, but he couldn't be sure. "The timing is not ideal, I'm aware."

The captain waved him off. "Do you prefer Robert or Bob?"

The feeling didn't tingle, but instead gave Porter the sense that he might just succeed in this job after all. "Either's fine, sir."

The captain nodded.

They didn't speak for a few minutes, until the captain said, "It's no secret I've lost a man overboard before. A gator freighter in the IO. Almost kept me from getting this command."

The confirmation of rumors caught Porter on his heels. He wondered if the captain had called that guy a slippery bastard, too. "I heard something about that, Captain."

Without turning to face Porter, the captain said, "Really? I thought you were the type of guy who did his homework, Bob."

Porter clasped his hands behind his back while holding his stare at the captain.

"Of the dozen or so deaths that took place on my watch," the captain continued, "the one lost at sea is the one that keeps me up at night."

Porter couldn't imagine living with that kind of weight pressing on his sternum every day and night. "I'm sure you did all you could, Captain."

"I don't know if that bastard slipped, jumped, or was pushed, but I'll guaran-damn-tee he had a pocket full of rocks or something. We looked and kept looking, but he sank down to the depths faster than he should've. I've got the same feeling about this one."

Porter studied the man in an effort to mentally record his actions, his words.

"We've got two helos and three boats out looking for him." The captain's chin wavered as he spoke. He looked nervous and needed a shave. "I'll bet this is some snot-nosed kid probably out of his mind on those filthy fucking drugs going around this ship behind my back, Bob." He didn't look at Porter, but the low end of his voice, the way he said his name, insinuated blame.

It was 0330 and Porter was tired. He would've hated the comment if fully rested, but under the circumstances, he felt a need to look away.

And he wanted this man overboard report to come back as a false alarm. As long as every man was accounted for, it would be worth the loss of sleep. *Please*, he thought. *Please*.

While the captain was on the horn again with the admiral, Porter walked to the starboard side, hopelessly staring at the water through the windscreens. This man overboard was the third loss of life in as many months that Porter had been aboard the *Salvation*. He worried about the ratio of deaths to his time aboard.

"Got to tell you, Don," he said to the officer of the deck, "I kind of feel like this is my fault."

Lieutenant Wicker shook his crew cut. "I don't see how that

could be remotely possible, sir."

The statement held no empathy. It assuaged no guilt. It simply pointed out the XO's illogic immediately following a shipboard emergency.

"Metaphorically," Porter said as he checked his gig line to make sure his shirt seam was lined up with his trousers' seam and both even with the edge of the belt buckle. "I was speaking metaphorically."

The headcount report took ninety minutes to confirm, because it had to be meticulous. The quartermaster of the watch, a young man going bald, held a piece of paper in this hand, which he delivered to the XO.

Porter read the paper and felt a surge of fear and regret speed through his bloodstream like Saturday night gin. He nodded and handed the paper over to be entered into the ship's log. "Captain," he said, "according to the headcount, one man from four thousand five hundred eighty-two officers and crew is missing."

"What's the name?" Captain Holt asked.

The captain's use of "the" instead of "his" felt like a raw nerve. He assumed the captain did so intentionally to distance himself and everyone on the bridge from the man overboard.

The officer of the deck looked down at his shoes, ready to say a prayer.

Porter looked at the captain. "Lieutenant j.g. Phillips, sir."

"Ken Phillips?"

"The chaplain, sir."

"Good Christ, that's the last person you'd expect to end up in the drink."

"That poor bastard," Porter said.

"He is literally the very last person I would ever guess could go over the side of my ship." Captain Holt looked up and gestured with an open palm. "Not because I thought he was a great Naval officer—far from it. I just never suspected he'd have the opportunity, the curiosity, or the balls to get anywhere near the edge."

Porter hadn't been close with the chaplain, but he'd met him a number of times and the thought of having lost him of all crewmen didn't sit well.

The captain would not secure from man overboard until he was sure.

Porter never knew what to expect of the captain. He didn't believe in drilling to excess and instead preferred to keep his men on routine as much as possible to streamline their every effort.

Captain Holt had the bosun of the watch call the chaplain over the 1MC. "Chaplain Phillips, please report to the bridge. Chaplain Phillips, please report to the bridge." The captain called the Marine commander to dispense a search party of ten men spread out to check spaces the chaplain might frequent.

Porter walked to his chair on the starboard side of the bridge. He looked out at swells three- to five-feet high. Calm waters to a ship that size. But he couldn't help thinking about the way Chaplain Phillips had welcomed him aboard. The honest smile of a politician with a handshake to match. He'd looked young. Had a face like a crooner from the previous decade. And now he was adrift in the South China Sea.

The captain said, "The degree of our loss can't and doesn't change our mission." He lowered his voice a little as he said, "I don't like this any more than you do, but wheels are in motion. You know that." He then picked up his voice. "We've got to meet the *Falls* and the *Sac* for gas, groceries, and guns so we can stay on point, at all costs."

The crewmen on the bridge nodded but did not speak.

Porter said, "Captain, I think under extenuating circumstances—"

The captain walked over and clasped his XO by the shoulder. "We got eyes in the sky and the destroyers in our battle group are making full sweeps. Under the circumstances, that's the best effort anyone could get."

* * *

Paul Martindale stood on the catwalk overlooking the flight deck. His buddy, Ant Pile, joined him on the twenty-foot stretch of steel grating and stood along the life rail with his hands cupped to facilitate Martindale lighting the joint. They were both aviation bosun mates who'd gotten permission to secure from man overboard a little early because they had watch in a couple hours. The only way to get the sleep they needed was to take the edge off and this was the last of his stash.

The joint lit. He took the paper hit, coughed, hit it again, and handed it to Ant Pile, whose acne was all across his face and neck, but thankfully wasn't on his mouth. They were buddies who had each endured bad jokes and insults from the crew for their most prominent features. That kind of shit left Martindale's mind when he smoked a joint. Almost all the shit went when he smoked a joint.

It was the kind of night civilians enjoyed on vacation in Miami or Hawaii—their women by their sides, piña coladas in hand, perhaps. Or a Mai Tai. A martini. A beer.

Martindale's hair blew around a fair amount and he frequently ran his fingers through it to put it back in place. It was hair like Elvis's, but he was running low on pomade so had cut down to half his usual amount to stretch out his last tin.

Ant Pile handed the joint back.

Before Martindale got a true buzz, the dogging handle slapped open behind them and the watertight hatch swung out. He wrapped his arms around his back, going into parade rest as he faced the door. "Whoever that is," he said, "we got to get rid of them."

The last person he expected to see walk through was the XO.

Martindale hadn't touched the hard stuff since that episode when the chaplain had found him like a zombie in a ladder well. This was just weed, but this was the XO. Martindale flicked the joint into the air behind his back, hoping the wind would carry it over the side. Even if it fell to the flight deck, there was no way it could be traced back to him. "Commander Porter," he said.

"Gentlemen," the XO said in that smooth register like a DJ on the soul station he'd heard one night in Memphis. In daylight Porter would cast a shadow. His shoulders were broad and he stood over six feet tall, while Ant Pile and Martindale were barely five-eight in boots.

Martindale feared the worst. Assumed they were busted. He looked to Ant Pile for help, but his buddy's eyes were half slits after that one massive hit of the joint. A slanted smile creased his face.

Part of Martindale was happy to be sober in this moment—to have his wits about him. The other part of him wished he could be high instead. As it was, he had no choice but to cover for both of them.

"I didn't realize the crew had been secured from man overboard," Porter said.

Ant Pile said, "We got permission to secure from muster early, sir, I swear."

Commander Porter nodded.

Martindale didn't know if the XO was indicating he believed Ant Pile or if it was one of those highway patrol kinds of nods that meant trouble was coming.

"We have watch soon," Martindale said. He figured he needed to sell a story to throw the XO off their scent. "We're just shook up about the chaplain. We came out here to be closer to heaven as we said a prayer for him." The lie came out like ashes from a can, but there was no taste to it. He couldn't believe he was saying the words, but once they began falling out, he couldn't stop mid-stream. He had to sound convincing. He feared he didn't.

"I just needed some fresh air," Commander Porter said.

Martindale exhaled as relief washed down his back. The chemical smell of the flight deck's coated steel wafted toward them along with the sweet stink of cigarette smoke.

Martindale hadn't even noticed that Ant Pile had lit a cigarette. Commander Porter held the hatch halfway open.

Martindale raked his hair into shape on his head and willed the XO to step back inside and shut it behind him. He clenched every muscle in his feet up through his shins, into his knees, to his hips, within his pelvis, his abdomen his upper torso, back, shoulders, arms, neck, even his brain squeezed in the hopes that the XO would get the fuck out of there and not bust them.

Porter stepped all the way out onto the catwalk and closed the hatch behind him.

All the clenched muscles in Martindale's body slacked, at least a little, from the exhaustion, the disappointment. He crossed his arms over his chest and scooted over to make way on the narrow catwalk platform.

Porter stepped to the life rail. "Either of you gentlemen spare a cigarette?"

Before Ant Pile could move, Martindale picked his pack of Chesterfields from his shirt pocket and a matchbook from his hip pocket.

The XO shook one from the pack and lit it with a match that fired on the first strike and stayed lit in the wind.

He smoked like a man who had only tried cigarettes a couple times. It didn't make him cough, but it didn't look like he enjoyed the taste. He exhaled straight into the dark above them. "Thank you," he said. "I appreciate it." Dark as it was and dark as he was, the XO's teeth shined like stars close up.

Martindale suspected something was up. He'd been in enough trouble to know when his principal or his father knew the score but gave him time to confess or to suffer. He always hated that, and if he was going to lose his chevron, they'd have to take it. He wasn't going to give anything away.

Awkward silence separated the three of them on that catwalk for a time until Porter asked, "Where you from?"

Ant Pile croaked, "Dallas."

Martindale admitted, "Long Beach, sir."

This led to talk of his being from Sacramento, as if they were adjoining neighborhoods, when the truth was Martindale had never been that far north. Never cared to.

Porter held the cigarette an inch from his mouth. "Since we're talking all nice and friendly and you're both clearly high, why don't you tell me everything you know about the drug ring aboard this ship."

Martindale coughed from the shock of it. He knew they'd been busted, but he wouldn't allow himself to believe it—until now. He looked over at Ant Pile. Neither of them looked the drug-using type. They both had good records. "We don't use drugs, XO."

Porter exhaled and looked at each of them without speaking or smoking his cigarette.

Martindale wanted nothing more than to believe this imposing black man believed him.

"I'll tell you what, boys. I'll give you both seventy-two-hour liberty chits if you can tell me something I don't know about it."

Martindale smoothed down the sides of his Elvis haircut. He looked at the deck for a long moment before facing Porter with second thoughts squeezing the skin over his brow bone. "I can't tell you how I know and you can't ever name me in this."

"What's this now?" Porter said

"That depends, sir."

Commander Porter's face had a sheen to it, even in the dark. His eyes squinted. "Depends? Depends?" A look of enthusiasm spread across the man's face. "If you have information, you are obligated by the oath you took, by the Uniform Code of Military Justice, by the Constitution itself, as well as the good Lord above to tell me."

Martindale broke eye contact by looking down and tapping a hand on the life rail. "I wasn't going to come to you with this," he said, "but since this opportunity dropped into my lap, I'd be crazy not to pursue it."

"Pursue what, exactly?"

"I want you to fast track advancement for me and my buddy, Ant Pile, here. And a thirty-day leave chit for me. For both of us."

"You boys shaking me down?" Porter's nose wrinkled and his head cocked to the side. He had a look that meant he might lash out. He easily could. It would be his word against the two lowlifes he caught smoking weed.

Martindale held his ground, despite the quivering in his knees. "No, sir. Could really just use the help and some time off."

Porter kept his face clenched, but said, "Seventy-two-hour liberty next time we pull into Subic. Ninety-six hours soon as we return to Thirty-Second Street. And I'll personally call your detailers before your next rate exams."

Before Martindale could counter that offer, Ant Pile blabbed, "Surico Hurasa."

Martindale stifled every instinct to throttle that stupid scar-faced bastard and nearly fell to his knees. That dumb shit.

Porter hit his cigarette and ashes blew away in the wind. "That sounds familiar."

"It's the name of the ship's cobbler," Ant Pile said.

Martindale couldn't believe his buddy rolled over like that. Days of liberty were more valuable than gold, but he left too much on the table.

Porter's head straightened, remained expressionless—blank as an erased chalkboard. The intimidation he wore disappeared. "The cobbler?"

Martindale still wanted to throttle Ant Pile. Instead, he looked toward his stoned buddy and then over at the XO. "You didn't hear that from us."

"Well," Porter stubbed out his cigarette on the heel of his boot and nodded. "I appreciate the smoke." He rolled the butt between his forefinger and thumb to knock off the extinguished ember. He tucked the butt into his shirt pocket. "That's certainly worth seventy-two hours of liberty, now isn't it?"

* * *

It was still dark, between four-thirty and five, when they secured from man overboard, and some of the crew were on the fence about going back to sleep. Byrd double-timed it to his rack to get a couple hours before having to be up for Quarters.

CHAPTER 12

Meanwhile, relief flowed through Applewhite that it wasn't a brother they'd lost, but he was hoping rumor control would've said that Surico had tossed another deadbeat over the side. Instead, the news made Applewhite uneasy. He wasn't the kind of guy who attended church services, but the chaplain had been the one to tell Applewhite that he was a father. After he relayed the height and weight, Applewhite was dying to know if it was a boy or girl. The chaplain grinned but didn't speak right away. This made Applewhite lurch forward, closer to his desk. His heart beat erratically and he felt he could hover three feet off the deck. He had to know and the chaplain was playing with him. "It's a boy," the chaplain said at last. "You have a son." Applewhite felt ten feet tall. He wished he'd had a telephone so he could call every friend, cousin, and every girl that ever broke his heart. Instead, he'd had a good talk in the chaplain's office. The chaplain told Applewhite about responsibility, and for the first time, it had made sense. Applewhite could never explain if it was the way the chaplain spoke or if it was being the father of a son that made Applewhite hear things differently, but that stork-like white dude laid it down in plain speak that had changed something in him. And now the chaplain was gone. A good man. A man of God, no less. If he could go, any of them could be wiped off the decks of that ship.

* * *

Ordinarily, Brackert would've been happy to get off the foc'sle where he'd been sitting alone, reading from his paperback copy of *Tropic of Cancer* he kept in his back pocket, but the news about the chaplain made him feel like a loaf of bread with a handful torn out of it.

Morning broke with the ship-wide announcement of, "Reveille, reveille. Heave out and trice up. The smoking lamp is lighted in all authorized spaces." Porter ignored the bullhorn directly above his head as he stepped onto and rode the escalator down five decks. He'd not been to sleep and he used the ride to close his eyes briefly enough to recall the times, not so many years ago, when he'd ride down the same escalator with all his gear after each successful sortie. Death-defying as those days were, it was a simpler time for him. His job was more defined back then. He'd had the whole sky to maneuver in, but much less gray area. He wished he could go back to the regular successes that came with being a fighter pilot. The escalator deposited him on the second deck, where he walked through the mess deck. He was in no mood to deal with any more crewmen, but this was the only path leading where he wanted to go.

He passed guys coming around the chow line with trays in their hands or filling their cups with bug juice, coffee, or milk, or already seated and eating something covered in red gravy. He took stock of all the faces. Some guys looked freaked out. Many others didn't seem to have a care in the world. Most of the ones affected were white.

Porter continued forward along the passageway. He hurdled knee knockers with precisely timed strides through the passageways and he almost never nicked his shins.

Just past amidships, he stopped outside the library door. The door wasn't a watertight hatch, instead like a household interior door but made of sheet metal and painted gray. He exhaled as he twisted the knob.

Somebody had left the lights on. Shelves filled with books lined the bulkheads and created aisles in the three-hundred-square-foot space. He walked down the center aisle to the door on the opposite side leading into the chaplain's offices.

There were two chaplain's offices, side-by-side, but as long as he'd been aboard there was only one chaplain. Ken Phillips. Now he was gone and the ship had no chaplain. This absence of a spiritual advisor made Porter worry for the crew. Having no one specifically trained to break the news of deaths in the family, or babies being born, or to provide guidance of that sort in these tense times could become problematic. Not to mention, there was nobody better suited to run the prevention group.

Porter flipped the light switch on in Ken's office. The trip down there had been a whim. He had no official reason for being there. Something drew him down there though. Something he didn't quite understand.

He picked up a picture frame on the corner of the desk. In the photo, Ken and his girlfriend held hands in front of a gate arbor, in the springtime it looked like. He wore dress whites and had his combination cap tucked smartly between his arm and ribs. The girl was not outwardly pretty—not homely, but plain. Likely a real smart gal. Well read. Fluent in French, perhaps. Her parents probably had money. Porter could always tell chicks like that.

Water ran through a pipe overhead. Porter exhaled. Thought about the letter he'd have to write her. A "Dear Jane" letter. He set the picture back on the desk, beside the blotter with a Bible centered, awaiting the chaplain's return.

Redness filled Porter's vision like being topside at night, except now, instead of a westerly breeze, Porter felt the bulkheads closing in on him. He pushed his arms across the desk, swept everything off its top. The picture frame crashed into the corner. The telephone clanged and the Bible thudded as they hit the deck. The blotter floated, while he turned and pounded the bulkhead with his fists. Porter's throat felt dry and sore, but he didn't recall speaking any words—maybe there were grunts or one sustained growl. He rested his hands on his hips.

Some of the crew might have heard him. He didn't know. He stared at the bare desktop, which saddened him. He walked to the corner, picked up the good book and centered it on the desk. He searched through the debris on the deck and found the picture of Ken and his girl. The glass was cracked. Ken looked out with that half grin of his. Porter wished he could talk to him now. He needed wise counsel on how he should proceed with the captain and crew. Worry caused his abdomen to burn hot twenty-four hours a day. Like his nerves, the glass in the picture frame held together despite all the cracks. He propped the picture atop the Bible and made his way through the library back into the passageway.

Etta Brown
1245 Barnabas St.
Sacramento, CA 95758

September 20, 1972

Commander Robert Porter
USS Salvation (CV-44)
FPO San Francisco, CA 95660

Hey there, Bobby.

I spoke to someone in the Navy office down there in San Diego. They wouldn't give me no specifics, but said your boat would be home sometime in November so I'll plan on you being here for Thanksgiving. I know you dyin' for my smashed potatoes and homemade apple pie.

You may not recognize Levon and Shonda. Levon is a natural born football player, like you. And fifteen year old, Shonda is a straight A student. She wants to study engineering in college, just like you. Wouldn't that be something if she studies that in college? And what if she wants to become a pilot too? Oh, Lord. A black man getting to be pilot is such a blessing, but a black girl flyin' a plane? That would be a miracle I never thought I'd live to see. It could happen, someday.

Until then, get your business done. See you for Thanksgiving. Jesus loves you, baby. So do I.

Auntie

CHAPTER 13

After morning chow Brackert dumped his tray at the scullery and walked forward, stepping over knee knockers all the way down to the library, through which the chaplain's office felt like a cavern ready to swallow him whole. If he were a smarter man, he'd be heading to the foc'sle to muster with the PNs like he was told to do, instead of standing in the chaplain's office. He couldn't help it. His life would always be different now and he wanted a taste of yesterday. Wanted to walk the same route, see the same sights, do the same things. Just wanted to start his day with one familiar act.

He needed the comfort that came with routine. His routine was mustering in the library with the chaplain and his group of lightweight criminals assigned there three weeks at a time. The added structure and rehabilitative properties of the chaplain's program had proven effective. Brackert's assigned duty with the chaplain's office came without word of duration, but it accompanied the proposition of being a model crewman, under the chaplain's supervision, or spend the rest of the deployment locked up in the brig until the ship returned to San Diego, where they'd kick his ass out with a dishonorable discharge.

The library sat forward on the port side, off the passageway on the second deck. He'd always appreciated the library more than any other space aboard ship. He'd spent much of his time sitting on the deck there, ankles crossed, back leaning against one of the shelves, reading about Hemingway's Spain or Jack London's frigid adventures. That was part of his routine since being ostracized by much of the crew.

On the far side of the library the chaplain had two offices, but only used one. Brackert had been using the other to do a few clerical duties, but mostly it had afforded him time to write letters to Chrissy.

As Brackert walked through the library to the vestibule outside the chaplain's office, he pictured the chaplain at his desk, signing a stack of liberty chits. He relived that moment with the chaplain explaining the picture on his desk of him and Mary Alice taken in the gardens behind his parents' club in Rhode Island.

Brackert didn't like to think about death. He'd managed to live twenty years without having to. But since that accident on the flight deck that he'd caused, he knew what it was like to hurt someone, perhaps a whole family. He'd think about it in those quiet moments in his rack between masturbating and falling asleep. So far, the image of the guy being dragged under the wing as it slid across the deck infiltrated his dreams almost every night. He'd ignored the images upon waking. Now, with the chaplain gone and his routine altered, Brackert would be forced to consciously think about death every day for the rest of this deployment.

The light was on in Chaplain Phillips's office. As soon as Brackert pushed open the door he sensed something in the room. It wasn't psychic, but rather visceral. He couldn't explain it, but he felt something deep, beneath his ribs, a weight, not a pressure, but an actual weight bearing down on his heart and lungs. It was suddenly difficult to breathe. He didn't know what it could be, but he checked his left arm to see if it was in pain as he'd been taught in first aid training. Nothing seemed wrong with the arm and his breathing slowly returned to normal. He was sweating now, salt dripping from brow to eye. The sting made him squint and he looked up at the overhead. Pain had been felt in this room. Perhaps nothing but. All the guys who got bad news here about a loved one passing. Perhaps Chaplain Phillips had nothing but pain inside himself. But there was also something more. Something besides the pain.

The two-year-old picture of the chaplain and his girl, in better times, now sat behind broken glass atop a Bible centered on the desk. The chaplain usually took his Bible to his stateroom in the evenings. Brackert had never seen the glass broken before, and he'd looked at the picture every time he'd entered because he couldn't believe any man could find a woman like that attractive once he sobered up. He never felt good about himself for thinking that way about the chaplain's future wife. His "betrothed," as the chaplain referred to her. Brackert felt doubly shitty for thinking about it now.

He noticed the phone on the deck. The blotter making a lean-to against the side of the desk.

"What the hell?" Brackert asked. He righted the desk chair, but just as quickly he returned it to its position on the deck. The MAAs should see this mess.

The chaplain was perpetually tidy. Always squared away. Kept his surroundings immaculate. He never would've left his office in such disarray. Someone had been here. Perhaps there was a scuffle and this someone threw Chaplain Phillips over the side. The possibility made Brackert's eyes well up for the first time in this whole ordeal. "No," he said. No to the potential tears bubbling up to his eyelids, and no to the son of a bitch who did this.

Brackert noticed a few links of silver ball chain sticking out of the top desk drawer. His heart sank into his stomach as he slid open the drawer to find the chaplain's dog tags. Not just his dog tags with the basics of name, serial number, blood type, and religious affiliation, but also a true symbol of his faith—his gold cross. Brackert pinched at the chain and lifted until the dull metal dog tags clanked together and into the shiny gold cross with a valley between the cross beam and the last quarter inch on the descending arm from the time the chaplain leaned too far over a life rail on the flight deck sponson—crushing it against his sternum.

Brackert cupped the whole affair in his palm and let the chain puddle there before shoving it into his pocket. He stood and exhaled, then righted the trash can and the desk chair and slid each under the desk. He dug into his pocket next. Pulled out the dog tags and dented cross. Placed the wad of it back into the drawer where he found it. He shut the light and closed the door behind him on his way down the passageway.

The chaplain's stateroom was spotless and devoid of anything out of the ordinary. Porter stood in the center of the ten-foot by twelve-foot space outfitted with two racks, two metal desks wedged between a locker and a bookshelf each, even though the chaplain had lived there alone. There were matching metal chairs and a sink with a mirror on the medicine cabinet door hanging above it. Today, a pair of broken-down boxes leaned against the opened door waiting to be shaped and taped.

After a few moments taking in the solemnity of the moment that came with standing where a dead man had slept, Senior Chief Rawlings walked in with a fresh cup of coffee. Porter watched the man's large hand holding the coffee cup as he brought it to his lips.

"Senior, good to see you," Porter said.

Senior nodded. "Why'd you want me to come alone, sir?" He sipped at his coffee again as if it were hot enough to burn the roof of his mouth.

Porter couldn't help being surprised by the man's bluntness. He waved Senior in. "Close the door."

The sound of steam compressing and expanding in the catapult equipment room twenty frames forward of the open stateroom door grew quieter with the door closed.

Senior had tucked his khaki shirt flawlessly into his khaki

pants and looked completely squared away. He was fit and had the vigor of a man half his age—but the face of a man twice as old. Porter hoped to get through this event with a better understanding of the man, and for Senior to better understand the XO. Aside from the sadness of the occasion, Porter feared an insurmountable gap between the two men, which could influence the captain.

As a result, he tried to be frank with Senior. "When a pilot checks out, his closest buddy packs him out," he said.

Senior sipped from his coffee mug before asking, "That's you?"

Porter smelled Senior's coffee as he suppressed his inclination to laugh. It would be disrespectful given the circumstances. He turned to open one of the lockers. He didn't know if his gasp was audible, but he couldn't hide the surprise. As neat as Porter kept his own lockers, he'd never seen anything like this. The chaplain's uniforms were hung on wire hangers equidistant from each other. His shoes lined up in the bottom of the locker, all shined with the toes facing out, laces tucked into the foot beds. His socks and underwear were rolled to regulations. He turned his attention back to Senior. "No one else seemed in much of a hurry to claim the title."

Senior nodded. "That doesn't surprise me."

Porter closed the locker door. "You're always so cynical, Senior."

"Technically, that's not true, sir."

"Then it's one hell of a coincidence every time I see you. Now why is that?"

"It's not like that."

"Do you not understand that I view us as equals? Our paths were different, but our destination is the same. Enlisted—officer. Black—white. We're both honorable men, well paid, each one step away from attaining our life's ambitions." As Porter spoke, Senior placed his hands on his hips and tilted his head to look up as he exhaled. It was a look of annoyance, but not total disrespect. Porter didn't like it, but he couldn't take the man to task for it either. "Do you have anything you'd like to say to that?"

Senior remained looking up as he said, "It's nothing personal." He then took a black pen out of his pocket and jabbed it into the air vent above his head. "I've just never worked for a black man before. But my best friend growing up was a black kid." Senior wiggled the pen as it clanked in the air register a few times. "Danny. We went to different schools, down in Atlanta, and I only got to see him in the summers when I stayed on my uncle's farm." Senior continued to focus on the air vent and his pen. "But one day…" he trailed off as he wiggled the pen. He pulled the pen out and looked at the XO, his face searching the memory.

"This would've been in 1940. I had a dime-store acoustic guitar that I'd gotten for my birthday. I practiced every day after school. Instead of playing outside between finishing home-work and eating supper, I was in my room trying to memorize chords from a wrinkled sheet of paper I kept under my pillow. Danny sometimes came over. He always listened to me play for a while, but he always asked to play it himself. He never wanted to look at the sheet of paper to learn the chords, he just wanted to strum and sing those old blues songs they used to play Satur-day nights on the radio."

Senior looked back up at the vent and dug his pen in again. "One day," he said, "Danny asked if he could borrow the guitar. 'Just overnight,' he'd said. I didn't know if Danny's mother let him play music late at night or early in the morning, but since my mother didn't, I figured there was no harm. What I did not know what that Danny's family would move out in the middle of the night and take Danny and my guitar with them. I cried that afternoon when my mother told me. That was the last guitar, as well as the last black friend, I ever had."

The notion raised a gasp in Porter's throat that his lungs didn't quite catch. He leaned forward and coughed. He didn't know how to play it off. He crossed his arms, but just as quickly abandoned the posture as it might appear hostile or closed off, when in reality he enjoyed this new insight into the man.

Senior grunted and then clenched the pen between his teeth. With his hands free, he reached for the air register. The screws were only finger tight and Senior removed them with little effort. As he tugged the register free, a stack of cards fell out. "What are they?" he asked, the pen still in his mouth, as the cards hit the deck.

Porter squatted to pick one up. It was a black-and-white photo of a Greek statue. He picked up another. It too was a Greek statue. They were all Greek statues. All male. All naked.

Porter's mind raced, as any man's might in the same situation. He didn't like to think the worst about people, but if he'd found these pictures in a photo album in a drawer, he could assume Ken Phillips had an interest in art history. Stashing them in the air register told him all he needed to know. It was the last thing he wanted to think about any man, let alone the religious authority for more than four thousand men at sea, in wartime.

"With all due respect, Mr. Porter, this ship is five years old." He pointed to the air vent above his head. "A dozen men could've slept here during that time. We can't say for sure these belonged to Chaplain Phillips."

The words struck Porter as sobering as the smell of Senior's overcooked coffee. "You're absolutely right, Senior." He swatted Senior's shoulder, only to watch the man back away with a disapproving head shake.

The air between them grew tense again. They remained quiet. After a moment, Senior said, "Well I suppose we should pull everything out of his lockers and stage it on his rack. I can have a couple MAAs come down and haul the boxes out of here later."

"I concur."

"By the way," Senior said. He drained the last of his coffee, set the mug on the empty desk, and pulled out his pouch of Beech-Nut. He scooped three fingers full into his mouth and compacted the sweet leaves with his tongue against the inside of his cheek. All the while holding eye contact with Porter.

Porter held steady.

Senior licked his thumb, tucked his Beech-Nut into his pocket. "That traitor, Brackert, burst through my door this morning jabbering on about foul play. Said the chaplain's office had been ransacked."

Porter realized for the first time that he'd left the place a mess after his emotional outburst the night before.

Senior continued, "Said he cleaned it all up for the chaplain. Said it would've been disrespectful to leave it like that mess. I was just down there. There's nothing left to see, but I believe that rat pussy bastard corncob."

Porter looked at Senior, tried to decipher his words, but he was in no mood for guessing games. "What do you mean, corncob?"

"Petty Officer, I mean, Seaman Brackert. The con-ob. The corncob. As in he's a faggot who takes it up the shit chute."

"You mean the conscientious objector?"

"Call him what you like, he's nothing but a pussy-ass traitor in my book."

Porter shook his head. The disapproval wasn't for Senior's name-calling of the kid, but of his own shortsightedness, his lack of self-control. "Well, Senior Chief, I believe I've got a bit of explaining to do."

Within the confines of that stateroom, Porter confessed. "I lost my cool, Senior. As we all do from time to time—in private ways. It was unfortunate, but we've all got traits we ought not have. I know you know what I mean."

Senior's face relaxed for a moment, the only tension was in the skin of his cheek as it stretched to a shine by the wad of chew in his mouth. It had been brief, but Porter saw in that instant that he didn't have to say the words. The man had been around a long while.

And just as quickly, Senior's face reverted to his dark-eyed scowl. "Are you insinuating something, Mr. Porter?"

"Come on. Really? You want me to talk about the underage girls in the PI and how that might affect your advancement to master chief?"

Senior's face clenched hard and got redder than Porter believed humanly possible. He spread his feet, distributed his weight evenly. "Are you threatening me and my whole retirement, sir?"

Porter's torso flooded with the perverse sense of power he'd never liked. "I'm simply stating my expectation is that we all keep our secrets."

Senior closed up his stance slowly, disbelieving there'd be no fight. "In that case, well played, Mr. Porter." Senior looked away for a moment. "And speaking of secrets." He looked up, holding a closed hand in front of him.

Porter played along and reached out and felt links of chain followed by dog tags left warm from the body heat of a stranger. "Are these?" he asked.

"Found them in his desk drawer." With Senior's hand empty, he held it up. "You know what that means. Right?"

"I'm afraid I do."

"So that's that, regardless."

"I suppose that's for the best, though it means I'll have to lie in the letter to his next of kin."

"So are we done here?"

"You'll send your men up?"

"Yes, sir."

As Senior reached for the door, Porter called out, "Hey, Dick? Have you ever heard of a guy they call Surico?"

Senior stopped and turned. His face clenched, not with displeasure or annoyance like usual, but in concentration. "Sounds familiar," he said. "Is he a barber?"

"Cobbler."

"That's right, yes. I've met him. Fixed my boots a time or two. Does good work."

"Did he impress you as being capable of organizing and running the drug operation aboard this ship?"

Senior's face so fully registered anger that when he actually smiled it looked like he was in a great deal of pain. He held this expression for a moment. "If you're talking about that guy who received a letter of appreciation last year for his inventiveness in remedying an incident when a woman touring the ship in Honolulu snapped one of her high heels in a ladder tread, then no."

"Is that so?"

"I'm not even sure if I could pick him out of a lineup, but he's hardly the type suited for that sort of thing."

The ship's constant vibrations reverberated through Porter's boots and up to his teeth. The taste of heat meant he'd been grinding too hard again. He shook it off and waved at Senior. "You're probably right."

"So, we through here?"

"Unless you'd like to move in." Porter kept his voice even and matter-of-fact, like all the best salesmen he'd seen operating in Sacramento when he was a kid. They always had a salesman's sample, no matter if it was a washing machine or a china cabinet. And if it was vacuum cleaners, you were getting the whole dog and pony show with the latest model. Porter didn't want to seem that eager, but he needed Senior on board the effort to stamp out the drug trade. This kind of upgrade in the man's accommodations might pique his interest.

"Yeah, right," Senior said, turning toward the door.

"I could arrange it."

"I'm fine where I am," Senior said. The second he opened the door, the fuller sound of the catapult equipment filled the space between them again. Over that noise, Senior added, "Good of you to offer, though."

Porter hated to see him go without confirming his commitment. "Suit yourself," he said.

* * *

Doris Rawlings
1934 Frost Line Rd.
Atlanta, GA 30304

September 19, 1972

Senior Chief Richard Rawlings
USS Salvation (CV-44)
FPO San Francisco, CA 95660

Dearest Dick,

We missed our wedding anniversary again. So we will have two things to celebrate when you get home. Three counting Thanksgiving in a couple months. But none of that matters. What matters is that I'm married to the most wonderful God damn man on this planet and I long for the day when these deployments are behind us and we can start our real lives together. I miss my sugar bear.

Betty Ann's braces are so God damn awful she won't open her mouth hardly but to eat. I told her as much as those God damn things cost she should be showing them off to everybody who'll look.

Ritchie issued strict orders that I'm not to tell you hello for him in this letter cause he's planning to write his own letter to you. Don't hold your breath. That kid has less follow through than a God damn bowler with a bad back.

Better sign off so I can get this in the box before Earl comes to collect the outgoing. I hope you're eating right and getting your rest. I know it's a war but you have to take care of yourself until I can take over that job.

Kick some ass and get yourself back home.

All my love,
D—

CHAPTER 14

As Brackert arrived on the O-3 level, he expected the smell of jet fuel could be avoided. This level was sandwiched between the flight deck and the hangar deck and was where the captain's in-port stateroom was located. Brackert knew from ship indoctrination the first week he'd gotten aboard that the auxiliary conn was all the way forward on that deck, at the very front, portholes like eyes and the flight deck like a solid unibrow. This room carried all the equipment and controls to navigate the ship in the event the island was attacked to the point of rendering the bridge inoperable.

Atop the escalator he walked forward toward the bow, cautiously stepping over the knee knockers. Over his past year aboard he'd seen a number of shipmates sprint through the passageways and clear each knee knocker without incident. Brackert hadn't developed that coordination and had to take things slower, which was just as well since he didn't know where he was going and didn't want to draw any attention to his trespassing.

The passageway was lit by white bulbs inside metal cages. He passed various pump rooms and pilot's staterooms and heads. After two more shin splitters, he found the arresting gear equipment room. His chest filled with air for a second and came down feeling like something kicked the wind out of him. This wasn't what he was looking for. His plan didn't involve causing problems for planes as they landed. His interest now was in the prevention of planes launching.

He walked past CIC and directly onto the blue tile of Officers Country. He knew he wasn't in the right place, but when he saw the guarded passageway it became clear that was the way to the captain's stateroom. A Marine stood sentry, while others shined brass and waxed the deck.

Brackert stopped and bent to retie his boot, hoping to buy enough time to come up with an idea to avoid raising the curiosity of armed Marines. He stood and checked his watch. He nodded once and backtracked amidships, where he crossed to the other side and turned aft. Slow as he was, he could tell right away that no one bothered to follow.

If he had a brain in his head, he would've scratched the whole idea. His inner voice hollered, *Get the hell out of here.* But his loyalty to Chrissy and the chaplain required more of him.

After more stalking of the decks just below the flight deck, he found a placard on a hatch that read *Catapult 2 Equipment Room.*

His heart quickened with the pride of getting there. He opened the hatch and poked his head in.

A guy wearing earmuffs and sweating through his T-shirt held a clipboard. The guy didn't look over at Brackert, like he didn't even see him. Brackert never figured the space would be occupied. The guy wrote down numbers from a whole host of gauges along the most elaborate piece of machinery Brackert had ever seen. From the outside it looked like two green tanks twenty feet in diameter and a hundred feet long. Steam collected in those tanks powered the hydraulic fluid fast enough to push even the heaviest planes into the air.

The noise coming out the hatch made him wish for ear protection. It was too loud to think. Brackert shut the hatch, dogged it, and tried to come up with a plan to incapacitate that beast.

As he retreated down the passageway and passed the wardroom, Senior Chief Rawlings swung open a stateroom door not ten feet from where he stood. Senior stormed down the passageway holding his coffee mug to his lips. If Senior saw him, he didn't acknowledge it.

Brackert felt himself holding his breath. He let out an exhale that was more of a sigh and walked in the opposite direction fast enough to crack his shins on a series of knee knockers. He didn't stop to rub the pain each time, and he didn't slow down enough to successfully hurdle each one. As his shins bled beneath his dungarees, he made his way to the escalator, where the five-story descent gave him time to catch his breath. At the bottom of the ride, Brackert walked through the mess deck without looking at anyone and continued on through the library and into the chaplain's office.

Byrd dumped his tray after lunch when a Marine in fatigues with the sleeves rolled up and *Gomez* printed above the left pocket approached him. "Well, if it isn't 'spic 'n span,'" Byrd said upon seeing his cribbage buddy.

They typically only saw each other in the brig to play cards, or when Byrd had business down there, but today Corporal Al Gomez said, "Fuck you, Byrd-shit. This ain't no social call. The XO wants to see you on the fantail."

Byrd laughed off the joke.

Gomez wasn't kidding.

Byrd felt his jaw drop wide enough to catch flies. He forced his trap shut just as quickly but couldn't prevent his curiosity. "For what? Why'd he send you?"

Gomez shrugged. "Don't know, Gringo."

Byrd didn't know if the XO was as good as everybody said he was, or if he was just average but got bonus points for being black. Byrd didn't give a shit one way or the other. He was curious, but it didn't matter.

If Byrd was in trouble, though, he'd know it by now. And more than the tactic of sending a buddy, he worried it was the lack of progress on the drug trade that had XO calling him out. Byrd cleared his throat and rolled his head around his neck a couple times in each direction. In that brief moment he allowed himself to think it could be good news. Perhaps he was scheduled to receive some award he didn't know existed. Plus, there was the story he'd heard of a boiler tech who got to have a beer with the XO of a carrier a year or so ago. That could happen today. It was early for a beer, but Byrd wouldn't complain about the refreshment it would bring.

He cleared his throat again. "He didn't say anything?"

"Nuh-uh. Sorry, man." Gomez clapped him on the shoulder. "I was just told to come get you."

Byrd nodded that he understood. He explored the notion that this surprise meeting with the XO might have something to do with the chaplain turning up missing. Maybe that's why they were to meet on the fantail. Byrd turned to go but stopped. "You coming with me?"

"Can't, my man," Gomez said. "We got an Un-Rep coming up." He held two thumbs up. "I got to get my weapon and get in position."

"All right. I better shape up then."

The two men shook hands and Gomez parted with, "All right, see ya. Let me know how it goes."

Porter leaned his elbows on the life rail at the extreme rear of the ship. Wind whipped around his head with enough of a gust to make his close-cropped hair move. He loved that feeling. Had loved it from his first experience in the Stearman crop duster in which he'd learned to fly. His enjoyment of that memory was cut short as Petty Officer Byrd walked up.

"You wanted to see me, sir?" The New York accent in the man's voice was unmistakable.

Porter stood. He liked Byrd. Saw the man not as short, but rather compact. Competent and thorough, as well as imaginative and resourceful. Byrd stood before him now, more squared away than most any other sailor aboard ship, his beard scrupulously groomed within regulations.

Porter pointed to the section of fantail facing the port side, which had always served as the garbage dumping station because it was as far aft as you could get without risk of damaging the propellers. "That's where we think the chaplain jumped."

Byrd nodded. "I was the one found his boots and shirt." He pointed. "Right over there."

"I didn't realize that," Porter said, his mind foggy from the memory of that night. On another night, Porter might console the petty officer or acknowledge how it might've affected him. On that night, he said, "Anyway, I wanted to hear about the progress we're making on the drug ring."

Byrd didn't physically move, but Porter witnessed a massive retreat in the guy's eyes. "Well, we've apprehended a dozen users in the past two months and gotten a good amount of narcotics and contraband out of circulation."

Porter couldn't sit on his latest intel any longer. "What can you tell me about the man they call Surico Hurasa?"

Byrd looked away and studied the water frothing from spinning propellers. "That's a complicated topic, sir."

"Break it down for me." Porter looked at his watch. "I've only got a few more minutes."

Byrd didn't flinch as he said, "I've had my eye on him since the last cruise and can't get anything on him. I've asked for clearance to have somebody go undercover and infiltrate Surico's operation, but Senior never signed off on the authorization."

"What reason did he give?"

"He's hard to press for answers, from my place on the pay scale, anyway."

Senior waited until everyone knocked off for the day so there'd be less traffic in the passageways. The crew would be headed from their workstations, to chow, or to their racks, leaving Senior free to walk with fewer eyes on him.

His footfalls clanged down the ladder, at the bottom of which he pushed open the lower half of the cobbler shop door and turned to close both halves behind him.

Surico looked up from his workbench. "Don't you close shit. If someone's coming we'll hear them on the ladder. If they see the door closed, they'll get suspicious."

Senior stepped close enough to Surico sitting on his stool that he was sure the cobbler could feel nostril wind blowing down on him. "We've got to hold your buyers to a higher standard, Surico." He pronounced it Sue-Rick-O, but it never got a rise out of the old guy.

Surico didn't move, despite Senior's proximity. "What are you saying?"

Senior detected Surico's accent in that simple question. "The XO is going to birddog this whole investigation, with or without me. Naturally, we've got to hold them to a higher standard so no one else talks."

"And how do you expect me to do that?"

"I don't know, Surico. They're your people. You'll figure it out."

Surico's face curled in, like the ankles of worn-out boots lining the far bulkhead.

"I don't care how you do it," Senior said.

After knocking off for the day, Applewhite climbed out of the heat of the ship's laundry and into the dry air on the second deck. His lungs quivered from the coolness. Eighty-five degrees was cold compared to the wet sting of one hundred twenty degrees down there. He wiped the corners of his mouth and put on his shirt but didn't take the time to button it. Headed aft. Down the passageway on the starboard side, past a couple flight squadron ready rooms with their doors shut. Their doors were always shut unless a pilot came or went. Inside, rows of high-backed chairs faced a podium at the front of the room with a chalkboard on the bulkhead behind it. He always pictured them sitting in there finding out who was dropping which bombs where.

Applewhite walked past the harmonica music of the ship's store, past various firefighting stations with hoses and nozzles at the ready, past fuel transfer stations with gauges and brass handles, past the access trunk to one of the shaft alleys, past the library and the dead chaplain's office, and through the mess deck, where the ordnance elevators shuttled bombs to the flight deck. Applewhite continued toward the cobbler shop. He didn't know if Surico was any closer to lining up any side projects he could get in on.

He'd been thirsty for a drink. More so than normal. More so than on bad days when all this bullshit got to him. A few years ago, Applewhite's grandmother would have sat him down and said, "Boy, you got something troubling you, so you better come out with it." She'd been gone three years now and he didn't have anyone who knew him like that anymore. If she were with him, she'd tell him, "It's the buildup of Tonya's letters." On some level, Applewhite knew that and felt better about himself. He needed to be reminded every once in a while, that no matter how he's caged every day that he was still a human being. He'd never tell anyone that the pressure to support the three of them weighed on him—a little heavier with each letter that came. He'd shoved the last three into his locker without opening them. Self-doubt, mostly. He'd already been gone for the kid's entire life. A real no-show father. He was determined to be able to look that kid in the eye someday, and he wouldn't be able to if he didn't take care of things and not become a no-dough father. He'd never earned a whole lot in the Navy, but now his left sleeve was empty, without the crow and chevron they took from him. But more than the rank, he hated them taking sixty-seven dollars from his pay every month.

In the passageway, the scent of detergents from the laundry gave way to the bite of jet fuel. Applewhite tried to cover his nose with the collar of his T-shirt, but the noxious fumes had already permeated it too. He slowed upon coming to the aft passageway intersection. In that instant, Senior Chief Rawlings climbed the ladder leading from the cobbler's shop. He held his coffee cup to his mouth as he spit and walked with purpose up the port side passageway.

Applewhite walked past a four-hundred-hertz circuit breaker. "Honky-cracker motherfucker," he said under his breath.

There was no way to know if the visit had brought shoes for repair or trouble for the best businessman aboard that ship. Applewhite's immediate worry became Surico's well-being. Theoretically, Senior could've threatened or even stabbed Surico when no one stood within view. It wouldn't be the first time.

At the bottom, he leaned over the lower half of the cobbler's opened door.

Surico smiled at him. "Hola, Rufus."

The cheerfulness surprised Applewhite. Made him rethink his approach to this situation. He bent down to Surico and asked how his day had been going.

"Fine."

"Nothing exciting happen today?" Applewhite gave Surico extra rope to hang himself.

Surico ignored the opportunity to tell Applewhite about the chief MAA's visit.

Applewhite felt disrespected. Like his head might implode. "All right, then. That's cool." Applewhite tried to hold in the smell of leather and polishes, because it was likely the last time he'd be there. "You take it light, man."

As Applewhite turned to leave, Surico called out, "What the fuck?"

Air caught in Applewhite's windpipe. "What?"

"Hold up, young blood. The hell you going already? Don't you want a drink? I've got to dump this all tonight. Might as well enjoy it before it's gone."

"Dump it? Why that is?"

"You should probably know that the XO's been asking about me, by name. I've got to shut down all but actual shoe business."

"This some straight-up-the-ass bullshit right here. I need that money."

"Hold up. You got this all turned around. This side business is just that, a side business. It's extra that we ain't supposed to be getting. But never forget they pay us to be here."

Applewhite felt his eyes close, as they were prone to do when he didn't want to hear something. He sensed that his head was leaning back, but he didn't remember putting it there. He straightened himself up. Applewhite nodded. "How did the XO come to learn your name in connection with any kind of contraband?"

"I got a couple guys looking into that."

Applewhite had his foot on the bottom tread of the ladder as he said, "I'll take care of it. If you like what I do, you pay me. If you don't, you don't."

Senior walked forward on the second deck passageway toward the post office. He could've delegated the task of buying stamps, but doing it himself somehow put him that much closer to his family. He never mentioned that to anybody, but it meant something to him. He loved his family. And at his age, each cruise was only fun for the first six months. That was tough shit though, and had been for the past couple months and counting. He didn't know when they'd make it back home. The briefing in the XO's office the past couple nights had focused on a delay in the arrival of the carrier sent to relieve the *Salvation*. No one knew for sure what that meant for the timeline, but in the meantime, writing letters was the only way of having any kind of closeness to Doris and the kids.

Up by the ship's store, the sound of harmonica music hit his ears. The instruments were sold in the store and one of the clerks routinely played one when he didn't have customers. There was no harm in it, so Senior allowed it. Besides, the kid was good and Senior always liked that part in "Moon River" that the kid was playing now.

His enjoyment was cut short by two black guys in the passageway outside the store who slapped each other's hands horizontally and then vertically and bumped fists and interlaced fingertips and wiggled their thumbs and that kind of handdancing bullshit they called dap. "On the black-hand side," one of them said.

"Let's break up that shit, boys," Senior called, walking toward them. "You're holding up traffic."

In the passageway on the other side of them, three kids formed a line, waiting to pass, probably coming from the foc'sle. They each held buckets at their sides. Senior didn't know what was in them, but they were obviously working and had the right of way.

Nobody moved. Senior hollered, "Make a hole."

Senior's real worry was not these two guys, but rather the trend aboard the ship of black guys prolonging this kind of dapping in an attempt to provoke a white guy into saying something that would start a fight. This was why Senior had recommended the captain enact a law of no more than two black men together at any time. Senior didn't see a problem with the white guys, so they could walk around however they saw fit. They weren't a threat to anyone as far as he was concerned.

The two black sailors looked at Senior and separated their hands and backed into the bulkheads on either side of the passageway, allowing the guys with the buckets through. These men nodded at Senior as they passed. The third guy said, "Write their black asses up, Senior."

Senior did his best to keep his face blank and not reveal any acknowledgment. Instead, he cleared his throat and said, "Let's all get where we need to be. Now."

CHAPTER 15

Friday, October 27, 1972

Byrd stood at a modified parade rest in the XO's office as Commander Porter said, "I'll give you until 2200 and then I'm raiding the cobbler's shop."

Porter didn't look like he was kidding. He never looked like he was kidding.

At the end of the XO's speech, Byrd nodded. "Ordinarily, I'd say that's excellent, sir, but no matter what we do it'll get back to Senior. We need clandestine operations here. Give me a couple days to do some recon and I'll let you know what I see."

The XO had said, "You've got until 2200 and then I'm busting down his door."

The air from Surico's Depression-era fan cooled the back of his neck as he tightened the last replacement eyelet on a gunner's mate's boot. As he finished, the clang of footfalls on the ladder outside filled the space. Instead of a crewman bringing a pair of shoes to be repaired, it was Petty Officer Byrd, that tight-ass MAA Surico never liked. It figured. "And here comes the scavenger bird after the bycatch," Surico said, putting his needle-nose pliers back into the galvanized drawer where they belonged.

Byrd leaned an elbow on the half-door counter. His forehead was beaded with sweat, which he swiped from the corners of his eyes with his right thumb. "Is that a voodoo curse or some shit?" Byrd asked. "You better shape up."

For some reason, Surico thought of the stick of Wrigley's gum in his pocket. The paper and foil came unwrapped easily and the fan blew them off the workbench. Surico folded the gum into a one-inch cube and popped it into his mouth. The double-mint flavor reminded him of his wife, but he didn't have time for sweet thoughts now. "I've been expecting one of you bastards since the XO got a bug up his ass."

Byrd held up lily-white hands that appeared unburdened by physical work. He held them out to his sides like a salesman. "That don't mean we can't be friends."

Surico laughed and then covered his mouth with the back of his hand to hide the laughter. "What the fuck does that even mean?"

Byrd leaned his elbows back on the customer's side of the counter. "Until this XO got here, I never bothered to look for you."

Surico shook his head and thumped himself in the chest with his thumb. "But I do nothing wrong." He got up and opened the lower half of the door wide enough to motion Byrd to get inside the workshop.

Byrd walked to the workbench, picked up one of the boots sitting there. He looked it over. "You might be able to talk all sorts of bullshit with your lackeys and your junkie customers but shut the fuck up with that."

The safe connected solidly beneath Surico's slamming fist and reverberated through the deck into his stiff shoulder. He felt his teeth grind as he said, "You come into my shop and talk to me this way?"

Byrd shook his head, crossed his arms. "Do you want to have a pissing contest or do you want me to save your ass?"

This guy had always impressed Surico as the type of man

who would never try drugs, not because he lacked curiosity or out-of-his-mind boredom for large portions of the day, but rather because he was following orders with blind devotion. Byrd enforced the rules merely because he was obedient to those in positions of authority, not because he actually liked them or agreed with them. Surico assumed the guy had grown up with everybody playing along—a lifetime of doing what his teachers, bosses, county sheriff in his hometown, and now Senior, the XO, the captain, the CNO, the secretary of the Navy, and even the president expected.

Reflexively, Surico began shaking his head. "And how exactly are you to save my ass?"

"Well, shit, forget it. If you've got it under control, who am I to interfere?"

"What are you proposing?"

Byrd seemed powerless to hold back that shit-eating smile he had. "Come on, Surico." He leaned on the workbench and into the path of the fan's wind. "If it was up to the XO I'd be bringing heat down on you right now. But if you cut me in, I can be cool as this breeze right here."

Surico never imagined this squared-away master-at-arms would ever flip for money. The notion of it spiked Surico's capacity for running scenarios in his mind. "Is that right?"

"I'll have to bust users once in a while to keep everybody happy, like we've been doing."

Surico didn't answer, but rather stared at Byrd.

The low overhead inside the cobbler's shop crowded them both. Surico sat beside his reel-to-reel tape player in the breeze of the wire fan mounted head height. His body curved to the shape of the space. As comfortable there as any place he'd ever been. Drug dealing was never his idea. Senior had roped him into it while deployed a couple of years back. Surico couldn't remember the weeks immediately after becoming the face of the drug trade aboard the *Salvation*, but he did recall how Senior had spent the previous year weeding out any competition.

Byrd shrugged. "Deal?"

"What about the XO?"

That smile returned to Byrd's face. "I'll take care of it all for thirty percent."

Surico had Senior on his side. A man in that position was better suited to managing the XO, but he couldn't share that information with this guy. "Fifteen."

Byrd backed up a step and shook his head like he'd heard a bad joke. "If I don't do my job, I can get in a lot of trouble. If I do my job, *you* will get in a lot of trouble. Twenty-five."

The speed in which that was delivered impressed Surico. Maybe this guy had something on the ball after all.

Byrd leaned on the bench and crossed his ankles, getting comfortable.

A laugh formed in Surico's chest, but he kept it buried. "Eighteen," Surico countered.

Byrd's jaw slid forward, either angry or deep in thought. Surico couldn't tell which. After a moment, Byrd said, "I skull-fucked a Czechoslovakian stripper behind a bowling alley in Scarsdale a couple summers ago. I've got mosquito bite scars on my ass, but I'll bet she's still burping up the asparagus I had that day."

"What the fuck is this?"

"So, what I'm trying to say is, don't let money stand between something great and going without." Byrd held out his right hand. "Let's round up to an even twenty and we'll get busy fixing this shitstorm."

Again, his words impressed Surico. He was clueless, but earnest. And until this minute, Surico hadn't considered the benefit of having two ship cops on the payroll. He imagined this guy running interference between Senior and the XO, which could benefit him in the long run. Even if it did, Surico wouldn't pay this fucking guy one red cent. "Deal," he said.

Byrd shook Surico's hand. "Deal!"

Surico said, "It would've been a bargain at thirty percent."

Byrd's smile reappeared. "I would've done it for ten."

"One more thing, Tin Badge." Surico leaned his elbows on his workbench, his nose inches from the openings of the boots still sitting there.

"What now, Surico?"

The smell of well-worn shoes never bothered Surico, or if it ever did, he no longer remembered. He took a moment to stare into Byrd's close-set eyes to make sure there was no misunderstanding. "I need to know who mentioned my name to the XO."

Byrd stroked the beard on his chin. "Is that right?"

"There's a hundred-dollar bonus in it for you if you get me the name before I knock off here for the day. If not, it drops ten dollars every hour."

He kept his hands on his beard as he said, "I'll see what I can do."

"Don't see, Byrd, do."

Izabella Hurasa
245 Lenox St.
Mangrove, FL 33704

October 10, 1972

Petty Officer Surico Hurasa
USS Salvation (CV-44)
FPO San Francisco, CA 95660

Hi Papi,

Me and Mommy wanted to write a letter saying hurry home. I show her your picture every day and she remembers, still. She always calls you "handsome." I see it, but it's probably just the uniform. Haha. I'm just kidding.

Mommy has had a good couple days. She's put on a

few pounds because she forgets that she's already eaten, but other than that she's still doing pretty good. How are you, Papi? Are you still drinking your milk with every meal like I do? I only get half a gallon on Mondays and no matter how much I try to make it last until Saturday it never does, so I drink it fast. Three days tops. Then gone. I won't get fat like Mommy. She's not fat, really. You may not even notice. I don't know if I would if I didn't see her every day. Did I tell you I gave my Wicked Witch costume to my friend, Beverly? She didn't have a costume, and I figured it might not be good to leave Mommy alone with kids knocking on the door and scaring her all night long. I don't need candy anyway. It might make me fat like, no never mind. She's not fat. I'm not saying that. Anyway, can you bring me back a red kimono? I'll save it for summer when I'm older, I promise.

Do you know how many more days you'll be away? I want to make a countdown calendar and cross off every day so you get here faster.

We love and miss you,

Me and Mommy

After securing from Quarters on Monday morning, Brackert walked aft on the second deck, past the mess deck on the port side, and made his way starboard and over to the master-at-arms area. The entire space consisted of a maze compartmentalized by painted aluminum walls with regular doors at each opening to various offices. The door to the brig, however, was solid steel with a sliding peephole behind chicken wire. Inside, eight cells awaited the next delivery of drug users or fighters, or even some dumbass intent on keeping airplanes from taking off. If Brackert was a smarter man he wouldn't show his face anywhere in the vicinity. It had nothing to do with intelligence, but rather an emotional curiosity. He had to know how the investigation was going—for the chaplain's sake, as well as his own.

Brackert opened the door and saw a Marine and a first class MAA standing in the passageway, staring at Brackert. Both wore immaculate working uniforms, while Brackert's looked like he slept in his. He felt that way too. He didn't like it much, but there was no point in trying to be 4.0 now. "I'm looking for Senior," he said.

Both guys pointed toward a closed door down a narrow hallway.

"Knock first," the Marine said.

"Yeah, you dumbass," the MAA added.

With his back to them, Brackert allowed his face to twist into an expressive "fuck you" to both of them as he made his way down the hall.

As his knuckles reached to knock, the door whipped open and Senior emerged in the doorway. The reflex of halting his forward progress caused his shoe to skid on the red painted deck. His sudden halt caused spillage from his mug.

Brackert braced for the sting of hot coffee, but the liquid was barely warm and it took less than a split-second to recognize that it definitely was not coffee.

Senior gasped. "Holy hell, where'd you come from?"

The Marine and the first class MAA turned. They each pointed to the tobacco spit running down Brackert's left shirt-sleeve as they laughed out loud.

Senior looked at the spit-streaked sleeve of Brackert's cleanest shirt and laughed.

Brackert took a step back and noticed his fists were clenched. He opened his hands, hoping the others hadn't seen. He was supposed to be a pacifist. His status as a conscientious objector depended on it. He said, "That'll wash right out. Besides, it's more of a problem for your deck."

Senior snapped his fingers as he pointed to the spill and

nodded at the other two guys. "What the hell are you doing down here, anyway, corncob? Are you turning yourself in or something?"

The three of them laughed again.

"I'm just here," Brackert lifted his voice above their laughter, "to ask about the investigation."

Senior spit into his mug. "What investigation? And what makes you think you're entitled to information?"

"Please, Senior. I'm itching to find out about the chaplain." That wasn't overstatement. His shins and arms had itched since he saw the chaplain's office in disarray.

"What are you talking about?"

"I have to know."

"You have to pay taxes and die. That's the only two things you have to do. And what you want don't mean shit to me."

"Please, Senior."

"Why don't you get your pansy ass out of here and crawl back under whatever rock you're living under until we kick your ass out of my Navy."

"Senior, please."

A vein on the side of Senior's neck swelled and his face got red. Brackert felt the hair stick up on his arms, but before he could back away Senior reached out and jacked Brackert by the neck with his free hand and lifted. "The day some pansy-ass fairy traitor tells me how to do my job is the day I exterminate that motherfucker. Do I make myself clear?"

Pain shot from Brackert's throat into his brain faster than he could catch a breath. Aside from that screwdriver incident a while back, he hadn't been in a fight since seventh grade, and this kind of attack was foreign to him. In the moment, he forgot about the disservice this was to the chaplain. This triggered a burst of rage and determination in him that he kept buried by clenching every muscle in his suspended body. He wanted to kick Senior in the balls, punch the Marine in the throat, and stab the first class MAA in the kidneys with an ink pen.

"You're about as useful as a deck of cards at an orgy."

The other two guys laughed.

"You're worth less than the laziest nigger aboard my ship," Senior continued. "You know that, Brackert?"

This was exactly the kind of bullshit Brackert would not miss when he got his freedom. People didn't get away with talking to anybody like that back home. But he wasn't home. He was on a ship. This man's ship, for all practical purposes. Making things worse here would get him locked up, and while it would be worth the hardship of being locked up, he couldn't risk any more delays in doing what needed to be done to impress Chrissy.

In an effort to smooth things over so he could get on with his day, he grunted through the chokehold. "I meant no disrespect."

As Senior dropped his arm, Brackert landed awkwardly on the deck. His left ankle twisted in the descent, but he remained upright.

"You're just a monkey fucking a football, you know that Brackert?" Senior said.

The Marines laughed as one swabbed up Senior's spilled spit while the first class MAA grabbed Brackert's arm and tugged him out the door and into the main passageway.

Porter didn't have any intention of waiting until 2200. At 1600 he met up with four Marines on the aft mess deck. He could've rounded the corner on the starboard side and met them in the MAA shack, but he wanted to stay as far away from Senior as he could. He needed the Marines to escort him down to the cobbler's shop—two to restrain Surico, and two to search the place.

If the cobbler had heard them coming, he never bothered to move. The sound of music Porter didn't know the name of filled the space, but it couldn't have been loud enough to drown out the sound of ten different feet bounding down the ladder.

Surico sat on his stool, his body bent to the limitations of this workspace. Porter could've come down here with one Marine to do the searching, because Surico didn't move from his stool until he had to raise his feet to allow the search on the lower portion of the workbench. Other than that, he just sat and watched the Marines rummage through tool chests and galvanized aluminum bins, bulkhead-mounted racks and shelves. The whole place was filled with leather in strips and in sheets. One bulkhead was filled with all manner of shoelaces. A manual sewing machine took up the near corner. Bins of galvanized grommets and rubber soles in various sizes.

When the Marines exhausted all possible hiding spots, Porter looked at Surico, then nodded toward the safe. "This should be interesting," he said.

Surico hesitated.

Porter's face tightened as he tried to prevent a smile.

One of the Marines shoved Surico forward. "You heard the man."

Surico took a knee in front of the combination wheel and looked over his shoulder at Porter. The cobbler's face was dark, the whites of his eyes a shade or two duller than his teeth. He held a certain paternal appearance, but Porter would cut this man no slack. He'd run him up before the captain and take full credit and get the shipboard television cameras out of Captain's Masts once and for all.

Surico spun the wheel to the right.

Porter's heart fluttered along with the numbers.

Surico spun the wheel to the left.

Porter's stomach clenched as he leaned forward.

On the final turn to the right, Surico hesitated, looked back at Porter, then clicked open the door.

Adrenaline surged from Porter's toes to his brain. He pointed and one of the Marines pulled Surico to his feet and away from the safe. Another Marine bent down and pulled out a green logbook and a metal lockbox with a busted hasp. Inside the lockbox was thirty-six dollars and forty-seven cents. Logbook entries for various repairs added up to that exact amount.

The four Marines sighed as Surico took his seat on his stool.

"Is there anything else I can help you fellas with?"

Porter never signed up to be a cop. Senior Chief Rawlings should've been down there experiencing this humiliation. The gut-twisting embarrassment. The captain would find out about this in only a matter of time. Porter had no power to stop that. Saying something to the five men crammed in that room would prove pointless without a way to enforce a gag order. He looked at Surico sitting on his stool like he didn't have a care in the world.

To be outsmarted by black drug users would be bad for anyone, but Porter was expected to have an inside track. He feared his fitness report would show negatives in his ability to carry out his duties. This could be the very thing that kept him from getting his own ship someday.

Porter looked at Surico. Wondered if he was this clean or if he might be this efficient at covering his tracks.

Surico picked up a pair of rubber boots from one of the repair lockers or maybe the sparky shop. He broke the silence by asking, "I go back to work now?"

"His locker," Porter said as soon as the idea flipped in his mind. "Come on." He tugged Surico's arm. "Let's go."

"Sure thing, Mr. Porter," Surico said, dropping the rubber boots. "I'm happy any way I can to help."

Two Marines climbed the ladder first, followed by Surico, the other two Marines, and Porter pulling shut the cobbler shop door behind him.

They walked single-file forward on the second deck about a hundred frames, and then down a ladder into Surico's berthing compartment.

The knockoff whistle had yet to blow, so all the racks were empty, as was the head and the lounge area.

"So, it's just us," Porter said.

Surico smiled and nodded, as pleasantly as any innocent immigrant.

Porter said, "Is this your rack?"

"My rack. Yes."

Porter gestured with his hand for him to unlock and open it.

Surico dug out his key. Porter felt the same sensation he'd felt while Surico opened the safe moments earlier. The rack locker opened like a coffin. The locker's lid was the piece of sheet metal he slept on with a mattress three-inches thick.

Porter wasn't totally surprised to find Surico's locker far from regulation, with uniforms and underwear and socks wadded up and smashed inside, but absent of any cash or contraband.

"I hope this some help to you, Mr. Porter." Surico stuffed wadded dungarees and T-shirts back into his locker as he spoke.

Porter banged a hand on the row of stand-up lockers on the opposite side of the aisle. "Which one of these is yours?" he asked.

Surico pointed to the one Porter had just hit and reached his key into the lock.

Porter jumped into Surico's face but made sure not to touch him. The temptation was strong to grab the bastard's collar, but such an altercation in such a venue would further alienate him and threaten his stature as XO. Instead he said, "I'm not trying to step on anybody's toes here, Surico." He spoke softly, but earnest enough to get his attention. "This is by no means personal. I'm looking to rid this ship of drugs and I'll take down you, him," he said pointing to one of the Marines, "anybody associated."

Surico removed the lock and one of the Marines stepped forward, yanked the handle and tossed through the hanging dress uniforms and sundry personal items.

Porter's stomach dropped ass height. *Fuck*, he thought to himself. He got in Surico's face again. "Taking down the drug supplier aboard this ship is my responsibility and it will happen. Now, we can do it the easy way or the hard way."

Surico didn't break character. His face crinkled a bit more into a mask of concern. "I don't know what you mean, Mr.

Porter." Surico retracted his body somehow and appeared to age ten years, like he'd put on a costume. It was still him, but he looked even less threatening. "I hear of these drugs and I never touch," he said. "Bad. Very bad. And expensive too, yes? I wish I could help more."

Porter stormed out, followed up the ladder by the four Marines.

CHAPTER 16

Sunday, October 29, 1972

After consecutive days of constant flight ops, the captain had called for holiday routine that Sunday, which meant only those scheduled for duty had to work. The rest of the crew could sleep, watch movies, play cards, write letters, or lay in the sun, if they wanted to. Many of the crew found themselves disappointed that CINCPAC had yet to replace the missing chaplain. Instead, an E-6 from the air wing filled in as some sort of proxy because his father was a preacher and he never missed a service. That met, but did not exceed, the crew's expectations. Byrd didn't care about that. He'd practically grown up in a church. His days of attending Sunday services were behind him.

With most of the aircraft stowed in the hanger deck below, Byrd took advantage of the flight deck being quiet and wide open as he sat on a towel in his PT shorts catching some rays. A few other sailors did the same, while a few of the fitness-minded ran laps around the steel acreage. Byrd raised his face to the near-noon sun and hummed "Good Vibrations" as he leaned back on his elbows. The air felt wet, humid, way more so than he'd ever felt before. One of his buddies hollered across the blank flight deck between them, "It's like Tampa in July out here."

Byrd nodded, taking the guy's word for it. He'd never been.

The smell of jet fuel clung to the air, likely permeated into the surface beneath him now, or on his own clothes, and permanently into the tender skin of his nostrils—the only scent in the breeze. Fat gusts of moist air wafted over the flight deck like playful shoves from a twin brother.

Just then he heard a voice somewhere close to him say, "Hey, man."

Byrd didn't want to open his eyes, didn't wish to engage in a conversation with anyone. He was knee-deep in a fantasy of May's darkened nipples and her tiny waist.

"Hey, man," the voice said again. Closer this time.

Even with his eyes closed, Byrd knew his face, maybe his whole torso, sat in the shade of this man. "Unless the ship is on fire, do us both a favor by shaping up and stop talking to me," Byrd said. "And you're blocking my sun."

The voice said, "It's me, fool."

Byrd squinted up over his sunglasses and left the fantasy world of May in her nude splendor. He nodded at Applewhite, and then over to his left.

Applewhite took the hint and sat five feet away from Byrd, but facing him and blocking out the other guy, who turned so as not to witness a casual conversation between the races. He said, "I don't understand you honky-cracker motherfuckers anyway. All you do is hate on the brown man and then you ignorant fucks come out to cook in the sun trying to make your white asses brown like us."

"I'd rather be in San Dog or in the PI, but this ain't all bad either. I'd blow the Pope for a beer right about now, though."

Applewhite laughed. "That's messed up, man."

"Do you know how impossible it is to get sun in New York this time of year?"

Applewhite flashed his pearly whites in a smile Byrd had never seen before. "It's not exactly Miami Beach, from what I've heard."

"You got that right," Byrd said. "Now why are you here, to

get a little more color yourself?"

Applewhite shook his head. "Don't try to be funny, Byrd. It ain't your strong suit."

Byrd laughed because he thought it was hilarious on a biological level. "Lighten up, it's holiday routine," he said, sitting up. "Nobody can be an asshole during holiday routine. Everybody knows that."

"I could give you a list of white devil assholes."

"They may be devils, but they don't hate you." Byrd leaned onto his right side. "They don't know you. They just prefer to continue things the way they've been done rather than think for themselves."

"That don't help us none." Applewhite's mouth closed around that fact. It contained no whine or complaint, but simply a statement as true as his name.

Byrd looked down at the hair atop his bare feet. "I suppose it wouldn't."

Applewhite shrugged, and his face twisted into a clench of puzzlement. "Whatever, man. Just tell me you got what I need."

"I did. I do. But I'm not sure I want to give it to you."

"What?" Applewhite's mouth stayed open for a second after his short question. But just as quickly, he added, "Come on, man. We agreed on a hundred bucks and me washing your laundry personally and separately from the rest of the crew's."

"I remember, but…"

Applewhite's face clenched again, even harder than the last time. "You trying to get more out of me?"

Byrd waved off Applewhite with an adamant hand. "It's not that."

Through the twisted clench, Applewhite smiled. "I could beat it out of you."

Byrd laughed. "Not by yourself, you couldn't. And quit fucking around."

"Then tell me what I need to hear so we can get on with our damn lives." Applewhite remained seated, but he seemed to vibrate from anticipation, like a relay runner waiting for the hand off.

Byrd's reservation stemmed from a brick in the center of his stomach. The brick only appeared when he found himself involved in something he probably shouldn't. "What makes you think this is a good idea?"

Applewhite's smile widened. "Never had a better idea in my life."

Byrd laughed. "That doesn't give me a lot of confidence."

Applewhite wiped sweat from under his eyes with the sleeves of his T-shirt. When he finished, he needed to do it again. Instead, he said, "You got a name for me or not?"

Byrd raised his hand to signal slow down and reached behind him to pick up his shirt. He angled his badge to reflect the sun into Applewhite's eyes, causing him to squint and to shield his face with his forearm, all while Byrd unbuttoned the shirt pocket and pulled out a green Navy-issue note pad the size of a pack of Pall Malls. He flipped to a page near the middle and tore out a single sheet. Byrd had gotten the name for Surico, but the notion of sharing that name never came up, so Byrd didn't see any real harm in sharing it with Applewhite. "This isn't going to come back and bite me in the ass, is it?"

"Don't worry about it, my man. It's cool."

Byrd's voice came out as serrated as hack saw as he said, "If something goes south because of this, I'll be the first one to personally deliver you to Captain's Mast, in a chokehold."

With that, Applewhite leaned forward and took the piece of paper. He read the name and tucked the paper into his back pocket. He then stood without using his hands to push off from the seated position on the flight deck and walked away, toward the island.

Byrd leaned back on his elbows, his stomach more than a little upset from doubt about trusting that damned guy.

* * *

Holiday routine was wasted on Brackert. Since he'd declared as a conscientious objector, he'd been stripped of his rank, rating, and all responsibilities, relieved of his duties for everything from UnRep, Sea and Anchor, General Quarters. Everything. He would help in emergency cases if he could, but no one trusted him to do what was in the ship's or the crew's best interests. So a day off was a day off from doing very little.

He spent a portion of his day in the chaplain's office. Former office. Brackert still had a hard time getting used to the past tense when thinking about Chaplain Phillips. He no longer got choked up just thinking about him, but he hadn't fully accepted his death, either.

Brackert sat in the chaplain's desk chair and looked again at the cracked glass in the picture frame that obscured the homely woman and the chaplain's goofy grins. Ordinarily the picture gave Brackert hope, as it reminded him there was someone for everyone and, just like Brackert, the chaplain had found his someone. Even with the stupid grin, the guy could've done better than her. He wouldn't have been able to get a girl like Chrissy. That was obvious. It was also a whole other kettle of fish, because Brackert didn't how well he had her sewn up. All this time away made it difficult to hold on to her.

At various points in the day he'd heard a couple guys come and go from the ship's library outside the chaplain's closed office door. The chaplain used to like big, fat Russian novels. He carried one under his arm throughout the day as if it was his combination cap. He read and underlined passages as he read. He once bribed Brackert with twenty bucks to read a Dostoyevsky book. Brackert tried, but he hadn't been able to stay interested for more than a minute at a time.

Brackert held the picture frame and shook out the shards of glass, right onto the desktop. The largest remaining portion of glass had remained stuck in the upper left corner. He felt better with it back together, looking squared away. The shine was gone from the photo, but despite the broken glass, its image was crystal clear to him. He threw a quick salute to the chaplain and his girl.

Sometime around 1000 Brackert heard someone in the passageway yell, "Bring me back a pack of smokes, will you?"

The voice was muffled, unlike Senior's voice the day before. Somebody was always hollering, which was bad enough, but Brackert hated the way Senior had gone off on him. If the chaplain hadn't disappeared, they might be having a conversation about that bullshit with Senior the day before.

He sank down into the chair.

The chaplain, he was gone. Just disappeared. Guys fall overboard sometimes. It's not that common. It happens on the best of ships, to the best of men. Brackert might be able to let it go and say goodbye if not for the way this office had been ransacked. Somebody was looking for something or a scuffle had broken out. Brackert didn't know for sure, but he was convinced. Maybe because of being sleep-deprived, or going crazy from the isolation, or from brain damage brought on by breathing JP-5 fumes all day and night, every day and night.

As he dozed in the chaplain's chair, Brackert had a dream that wasn't really a dream, but rather a vision. But that's not really it either. His only word for it was a visit, from Alan Houseman, Hydrant, the airman killed on the flight deck. Two-thirds of Hydrant's face looked like hamburger, as did one arm and both legs. His shredded dungarees flapped in the breeze.

"Why'd you kill me?" he asked.

Brackert recruited every muscle in his body to turn himself away from Hydrant, but doing so put him face-to-face with the chaplain. Brackert had never seen a ghost in his life. Never believed anyone who said they did, and there were a bunch of them back in Knoxville. Now, here he was seeing two, almost at the same time.

While Hydrant appeared the way he'd died, the chaplain looked normal, like he never left, like he wasn't fish-bitten and decomposing in the salty depths of the Pacific. They didn't take the time to exchange pleasantries. Instead, the chaplain gave Brackert an incredible idea, and it all made perfect sense.

"But," Brackert said, "someone could get hurt."

The chaplain laughed. "It's not hugs we're dropping from these planes."

Brackert's head lurched up from the desk. His eyes blinked too rapidly to focus on anything for a moment. His head felt like it floated a foot above his neck. As disoriented as he was, he felt moisture. He wiped drool from the corner of his mouth with one hand, then swiped at the puddle on the desktop with the other.

Applewhite sat at a table in the portside corner of the aft mess deck following evening chow. The key position in the back corner faced out to see everyone who walked by. It also removed the potential of anyone walking up behind him.

Five decks below the hangar deck, seven decks below the flight deck, but damn if that JP-5 didn't reek to high heaven down there too. The ship was twenty-five stories tall, overall. Prior to arriving aboard, he'd never been in a building as tall as that ship. Wasn't even sure if Kansas had any buildings as tall.

He sat in his corner with his arms behind his chair. His fingers found the loose piece of pipe lagging and tugged at it absently. Meanwhile, he stared at all the black faces, the white T-shirts, and dungarees in various shades of blue. A lot of guys around him. Unless he was working down in the laundry or taking a shit, at least four guys hung around Applewhite. He didn't think of them as his crew, but they were his boys, his brothers. They went to chow together. They played cards. Watched movies. Hung out on the mess deck. The minute a brother took off to grab Applewhite a pack of menthols from the ship store, another brother jumped up into that spot.

Along with the murmur of voices came the sound of mess cranks closing up—trays being stacked, silverware being replenished in the holders above the trays, stainless steel being wiped down. He had bits of meatloaf in his teeth and still smelled the stewed tomatoes he'd had over rice. His mother used to mix stewed tomatoes into her black-eyed peas and the smell always reminded him of her.

Downtime had made him reflective like that. And no one felt more deserving of this holiday routine than Applewhite. The crew had earned the day off, too, but like the cooks and cranks, Applewhite's job was never done. That whole month had been spent pressing and folding sheets for the officers and chiefs in triple-digit heat filled with steam and wet, hot metal, and there was more coming in.

He jutted his chin and leaned his head signaling his boys, Couch and Giles, to come over to his table.

Giles wore the heavy black frames the Navy issued with every sailor's eyeglasses. His head looked like a peanut. "What's up, Rufus?"

"I want you boys to spread the word that we're meeting at midnight tomorrow up at the foc'sle. Just tell the brothers you trust. We don't need no trouble."

"Something going down, Rufus?" Couch said the letter S funny, but no one laughed at a guy with arms as big around as most guys' legs.

Applewhite signaled Couch and Giles to come in closer. They both reeked of the weed they'd smoked down in the berthing compartment before chow. Their eyes were dilated, but their faces eager. "Between you and me, I got the name of that honky-cracker asshole who be trying to get me in trouble."

"No shit?" Couch asked, slurring the S.

"I'm going into a berthing space to blanket party the mother-fucker. I'm going to get caught and get in trouble if I do this alone. But if a bunch of fellas go down there with me, they'll never know who was the one that done it. You dig?"

"You want us to beat the shit out a white boy tonight?" Giles asked.

"Not tonight. Damn, fool. Everyone's off tonight. Too many eyes all around. No, man. Tomorrow night when they got flight ops planned all day and night. And it's just the one honky. And it's just me. You'll just be decoys. You hear me?"

"Decoys?" Giles asked.

"Because you'll be seen and the white bastards will give you up to the MAA and the Marines," Couch said.

Applewhite nodded. He absolutely could not afford to get caught. Byrd had been cool enough to make the deal he did, but Applewhite believed Byrd would gun for him if he crossed him. And if so, Applewhite knew he'd end up in front of the captain all bloodied and bruised and on camera for the crew to see. He couldn't risk that. That meant making sure there were no witnesses. "Getting that guy alone," he said, "would be almost impossible. The next best option is to make sure that I'm surrounded. Camouflaged. Like a black jellybean in a bowl of black jellybeans. You dig?"

"If there's a mess of us, no one will be able to know who did it," Giles said.

"We all look alike to them anyway," Couch said.

Applewhite smiled. "This time it'll be to our advantage."

"I can round up a group," Giles said.

Applewhite held out his hand and tapped the air, signaling slow down. "Just the fellas that can keep secrets."

"Damn right."

"And remind everyone to stay paired up," Applewhite said. "We don't need no trouble."

It had been more than a month since the captain had announced the two-man rule, making it illegal for black crewmen to walk in groups of three or more. No one found that order more insulting than Applewhite, but he wasn't willing to go against the policy with so much at stake.

He turned his attention back to his brothers. Many of them were high, but they all were just taking it easy. Hanging out. Around the group of twenty or so, the talk centered on what movie would be playing there later that evening.

"I don't care what it is as long as I see girls in tight sweaters and short skirts."

"Ain't never no sisters in them damn movies."

"Don't matter what color the outside. It's all pink on the inside."

Any movie would work to help distract Applewhite from the uneasy rattle in his gut from worrying that word would get out and his target would get tipped off and disappear into protective custody. That had happened in the first few weeks of this cruise, when a black guy needed protection, which came as no surprise to anyone back then. Before Applewhite had time to contemplate the topic much longer, and well before the movie began, the bosun of the watch on the bridge keyed the 1MC microphone. Applewhite heard the subtle click and felt the anticipation of words in the air. Movie time quickly approached, but instead of announcing what the movie would be, the bosun blew his pipe to signal attention and then all hands, followed by the announcement, "Standby to receive ship to starboard, at all stations."

Applewhite's blood felt like ice water. His lungs dried up and he struggled to suppress a cough. He failed, slapped the table, and hollered, "You've got to be kidding me."

"This is fucking bullshit," some of the guys said.

Another guy hollered, "They're fucking us out of a movie!"

"They're fucking us out of holiday routine," another guy said.

Applewhite said, "They're fucking us out of both." No one, least of all Applewhite, suspected an UnRep during holiday routine.

The announcement repeated over the 1MC and the crew vocalized their displeasure, which echoed throughout the passageways. One of the white guys on the escalator ride down from the hangar deck punched the bulkhead upon hearing the word.

As the group departed toward their UnRep stations, Applewhite looked over at the coffee maker, where Surico poured himself a cup that he took with three sugars.

"Hey Surico," Applewhite said, "don't you want to get one over on whitey?"

Surico waved his spoon. "Nah, Rufus, man. Not the way you're thinking."

"You for real?" Giles asked.

Surico nodded and tapped an index finger to his temple. "I think with logic instead of anger. You young bucks should look into it."

Applewhite couldn't help smiling. He shook his head. "You are one controlled brother, Surico."

"Don't play me, Rufus. I ain't having it." Surico sipped from his coffee before adding, "I won't stop you, but I don't think what you're planning is smart."

"Oh, it'll smart," Couch said, slurring the S.

CHAPTER 17

In the moments before the UnRep call piped over the 1MC, Brackert walked the ship. It was still holiday routine and the hangar deck showed no signs of life. If anything, there might've been a couple of guys in the jet engine shop all the way aft, and one guy on roving patrol, but that guy was probably standing in a doorway somewhere reading a magazine with his buddies who were off the clock.

Airplanes filled the hangar deck. Each stood at the ready with their wings folded in, parked at angles that maximized the space to accommodate aircraft and attendant vehicles driven on the flight deck: the two tractors that hauled the planes into position; the crash cart, a mobile repair locker that streamed hoses behind, ready to charge and battle flames; the dozen forklifts lined up against the forward bulkhead in a mirror image of the line along the aft bulkhead.

Brackert kept walking. Made his way to the island and stood in a room the size of a large closet back home. The room held Air Crew 4's coffee locker, where guys hung out between launch assaults. A coffee mess on a steel cabinet held a percolator, a gallon can of ground coffee, a half-filled sugar dispenser, and an empty box of powdered coffee creamer. Shelves lined with gear ran along the three bulkheads opposite the hatch. Between the angle iron and the folding chairs Brackert assumed six or seven guys could hang out there at any one time. But, as planned, he stood there alone, looking at the rack of off-white, weather-beaten helmets the airdales called cranials. He picked one up.

This skullcap, like most of the others, was made of cloth, with standard hearing protectors built in to block the noise of jet engines taking off mere feet from air crewmen. Protective pads covered the areas left vulnerable by the front and back shells. Attached goggles were secure enough to keep out sun, wind, and dust, with enough tint to make him unrecognizable. The name *Miller* in bold black marker filled a piece of silver duct tape across the top. Brackert had no way of knowing if the size was right, but the goggles looked unscratched and that afforded a better shot at accuracy when the time came. This item felt like a trophy in his hands and he wished he could bring it to the chaplain and brag about his plan. But it was too conspicuous to walk around with. He'd have to stash it somewhere for retrieval when he was ready.

The heat in the small space made Brackert sweat. Even after evening chow, temperatures remained high all over the ship. The tons of steel above the waterline made a giant heat sink in the South China Sea, absorbing sun all day that radiated all night. The coffee locker didn't have any forced air, but fresh air was one deck up and right out the hatch onto the flight deck. He didn't dare risk that. Getting caught would result in a lot of questions. Being watched too closely could thwart him and cost him Chrissy.

He had a red shirt from his old assignment to repair locker two. They'd never taken his shirt back and he kept it in his locker underneath folded dungarees, but he needed a cranial and safety glasses to make his disguise as complete as possible, and to make himself indistinguishable from any other airman to the plat camera mounted on the island and recording everything happening on the flight deck. He didn't know what he'd do, but if he had the cranial in his possession, he'd be ready to roll the next time they called flight quarters.

He wished the cranial collapsed. His life would be easier if it did, but the luck wasn't there. Putting it back meant losing it. Trying to sneak it out of there wouldn't get him five feet before somebody saw him, especially a chief or an officer. As he tried to decide his next step, the UnRep call came in over the 1MC. The call didn't register in Brackert's brain at first. A few seconds later, the sound of voices approached. Brackert's hands shook. Footsteps beneath those voices echoed in his chest. His thoughts smacked into the four bulkheads, surrounding him in a desperate attempt to solve this problem. There was no way to retreat unseen. He had no rational explanation for being in one of the spaces that served as break room and gear storage. His knees barely kept him upright, as spongy as the weakened springs on a 1952 Bel-Air. He could wobble back or forth, but he couldn't get away.

The captain wouldn't have called UnRep in the middle of holiday routine unless he got an order from CINCPAC or the CNO. Would he? They'd just taken on fuel the day before, so this was likely a weapons load. Gun shopping, as the chaplain used to call it.

As the group approached, Brackert feared the worst. He was busted. His mind raced with excuses, though technically he'd done nothing wrong. The UCMJ didn't expressly forbid holding a flight deck cranial, at least he hoped not. He wondered if the Navy had their own version of trespassing that he might get rung up on. That would be enough to get the badges involved. That was the last thing he was in the mood for. Any one of those dicks could lock him up in the brig or follow him around like a puppy and keep him from doing what he had to do.

The footsteps got louder in the passageway right outside the door. Brackert held up the headgear and rubbed the front of the goggles on his shoulder. He was out of options and pulled the cranial over his head.

It took everything in him to keep from reacting to the sour smell of sweat that came from the padding on his forehead. He tugged the goggles into place over his eyes. Instantly he felt it was a hood and this could turn into an execution. This piece of equipment normally protected airdales from injury, but now was getting a test to see if it protected his identity. His lower intestine spasmed. Sudden fright did that to him sometimes. He couldn't hold in the gas that pressurized like the catapult pistons. The door remained closed to the sound he emitted inside his dungarees, and for this he felt thankful.

He reached for gloves. By the time he donned the first one, a group of three guys entered the coffee locker hatch. They were all Brackert's height, thin with dark hair, and appeared unphased by the timing. The first guy twisted his nose back and forth as his mouth made anguished expressions. "Jesus, Miller. If you're going to rip farts, I wish you'd save it for up on deck so I can get up wind of you." The guy then picked up a mug from a shelf, looked inside, and filled it with coffee that had been in the percolator since the night before.

A second guy said, "You got here quick, Miller."

They pulled on their cranials and gloves and shoved Brackert toward the hatch as the third guy added, "The sooner we get this done, the sooner we can get back a few hours of holiday routine."

No one seemed to notice that he wasn't in his red shirt.

Doris Rawlings
1934 Frost Line Rd.
Atlanta, GA 30304

September 16, 1972

Senior Chief Richard Rawlings
USS Salvation (CV-44)
FPO San Francisco, CA 95660

Dearest Dick,

The Grand Jury indicted the president's men yesterday for conspiracy and a laundry list of underhanded shit. I don't know what the hell is going on and none of us know who to trust. No one seems willing to do things the right God damn way anymore. It just pisses me off and without you here I'm starting to lose perspective, like I do when your gone to long. Hurry up and come back already.

Everything else is much the same around here. Routine shit you don't need to concern yourself with today. The neighborhood might be going to shit though. The Anderson kids have grown to be a couple of hippie dipshits and they've got their dirty hippie buddies coming and going at all hours of the day and night. I never thought I'd have to close my windows so I don't hear bongo music at three in the God damn morning. I'm convinced they're taking drugs and smoking the marywanna. It's shameful. Bill moved downtown to shack up with his secretary and without a father those kids have gone to shit. Maybe you can straighten them out when you get home.

I hope it's soon. We need to make up for lost time.

Take good care of yourself, darlin'.

Doris

After securing from UnRep, Senior stayed up on the bridge with the officer of the deck, the quartermaster of the watch, the boatswain's mate of the watch, the helmsman, and the lookouts. He couldn't be sure anyone would still be up in the chief's mess and he didn't want to be alone. Things worried him in a quiet way that spoke to him only in absence of the roar of planes launching, the noises of shipboard machinery, or the rolling thunder of the crew's voices. Silence always got to him the most in those first few minutes his head hit his pillow. If in port, he'd hit the beach and drink every night and fall asleep faster as a result. As it was, he stewed each negative thought in the sour gasses of his herniated abdomen.

His biggest fear wasn't about the ship or its mission, or even that questionable ordnance just delivered. It was the future of his Navy and his country that kept him on edge these days. The lowering of standards, Navy wide, chipped away at him each day like a bosun's hammer on old paint. He wished Admiral Zumwalt's initiatives were more successful more quickly, but he didn't have faith the new chief of naval operations could turn things around. Too many guys still had too much hair on their heads and faces—thick beards or three-day stubble and pork-chop sideburns that didn't fall within guidelines. All the undesirables who'd gotten in when the DoD lowered the bar: deadbeats, dirt bags, and troublemakers. Busting them all would exhaust his staff and label him a tyrant. The last thing he needed to do was further twist the crew's tension. The blacks and the whites had a hard time ignoring one another as it was. As bad as all that looked to him at times, nothing equaled the depravity and decay he'd seen in the States over the years. Free love, pot, and peace occupied young people's time to where they hardly wore clothes or washed. One day in the not-too-distant future, the ragmen amongst the crew would work with or for people like that. He had kids who would someday walk amongst them. Lowering standards was bad for the Navy and worse for the country. He wanted everything to be held up the way his generation had inherited it.

In his day, everybody served in the military. He'd turned legal age to enlist only a couple years after his uncles got out, after the war. It was his turn and he had no interest in staying back in Atlanta and working at his family's filling station. The war in Korea made him stay, and once he reenlisted he knew he'd be on a ship the rest of his life. Being a cunt hair away from making E-9 made every night like Christmas Eve as a boy growing up in

Marietta at a time when his parents didn't always have a lot of money for presents. They were trying to grow the business and expand into other locations. He didn't know it then, but his parents were stretched thin with the assumption the time and money invested would pay off and take care of the whole family. He never knew if he'd get a bicycle or a baseball.

And any day now, he'd be officially promoted to the highest enlisted rank. Nine pay grades successfully achieved. As high on the pay chart as he could get. He loved the Navy and prized his position as command master chief. The title and the badge made him feel ten feet tall and twice as strong. He only wished it were possible to have elevated the crew to a level more in line with his own standards.

The old XO, in the months before his sudden heart attack, had said, "Any crew that performs this flawlessly is allowed a few special concessions, Senior Chief."

"But if they fuck up, we start cracking down, right?" he'd asked back then.

The old XO had smiled and replied, "I can't make any promises, Senior, but we'll see."

None of that mattered now. And all of it mattered.

And, on top of it all, following the early termination of holiday routine that night, he wasn't sure how the crew would react to anger pent up tighter than all the steam in the boilers. Before he had time to contemplate it further, Byrd walked onto the bridge. He had clearance to be on the bridge, but he was the last guy Senior expected to see there. Byrd nodded to the officer of the deck, who turned to stare at the supply ship steaming away off the starboard bow. Byrd walked over to Senior. "What the hell was up with the UnRep?"

Senior grabbed Byrd's arm and guided him to the starboard side. The captain had left the bridge to catch some sleep in his sea cabin, but this wasn't a conversation Senior wanted to have in front of all the men there. "Why?" he asked in almost a whisper as they stepped onto the steel box of the refueling bridge overlooking the starboard side of the ship. "Has the crew revolted?"

Byrd stared out the window facing aft but kept his voice low. "There's a lot of pissing and moaning, as you might imagine."

"Nobody ever promised the crew a whole day off. They should be happy they got to sleep late and lounge about all damn day. A couple hours work between dinner and taps ain't a bad way to earn your keep in my Navy."

Byrd shrugged and looked toward the disappearing supply ship.

Senior faced the younger man as he searched for a reason not to trust him. That wasn't possible. A man in Senior's position was paid to trust the men in his charge. He had to. Plus, Byrd had never given him reason not to.

They stood obliquely, shoulder-to-shoulder. Senior told him, "It was ordered by the joint chiefs. Outfitted us with a payload of fat bombs specifically for the non-stop assault we begin tomorrow afternoon at 1600. It's a big fucking deal."

Byrd's forehead slackened. "What'd they give us?"

"Shoeblack Hippos," Senior said.

"Like the ones we dropped on Okinawa?"

Senior nodded. "From the same damn vintage."

"Why give us old shit to load and go?"

Byrd was a good investigator because he was a nosy son of a bitch who never stopped asking questions. Senior couldn't help but like that trait. "Beats the fuck out of me," he said. "Ours is not to question why."

"Yeah, well, that's weak cheese when it comes to ordnance three decades old."

Senior spit into his mug. "They're perfectly safe," he said. "Besides, they'll be gone by the time you wake up Halloween morning. You big baby."

Byrd leaned a hand on the captain's chair. "Yeah, well. It just ain't right."

"How the hell you know so much about World War II ordnance?" Senior asked. "Your old man a Navy pilot?"

"No." Byrd laughed. "My father was a Marine. At Guadalcanal. He knew everything about the war. On both sides of the world. He lived and breathed it, especially after six highballs following a full day at the mill. He called me a pussy for enlisting in the Navy. It bothered me when he was alive. Every time I saw him, I heard those words coming out of his mouth." Byrd looked out the windshield. "That was buried with him though. I don't hold it against him. He didn't get it. I mean, I want to do my part, but all that hiking and camping is for the fucking bears, you know?"

Senior spit into his coffee mug. "They call it the past for a reason."

Byrd shrugged. "Has your informant given you any news about what's going on in the main black berthing compartment?"

"Since the drug investigation's heated up, he's been scared shitless to be seen talking to me."

"Can't blame they guy," Byrd said. "He gets caught, they'll stab him a hundred times and strain JP-5 through the holes."

Senior laughed as he brought his coffee mug to his lips. He held the cup there to conceal a smile as he spit. "Them coons can get violent when they want to."

Byrd nodded. "Are you heading down to the second deck?"

Senior spit into his mug and shook his head. "The quartermaster of the watch just put on a fresh pot of coffee."

CHAPTER 18

Monday, October 30, 1972

On Monday morning, following the abbreviated holiday routine, Porter made it his priority to get in front of as many crewmen as possible, as informally as possible. He walked the ship in fast strides, slowing only to step over the knee knockers of every frame.

He suspected most of the crew resented yesterday's UnRep timing, but he couldn't let on about that either. He had to tow the company line. Be the good cop to the captain's bad cop about the timing. The call had come down from Zumwalt himself. Porter figured if he could absorb as much of the crew's discontent as possible, the less there'd be for the captain to see. A happy crew would reflect favorably on Porter, which is what he needed with increasing urgency. With the events surrounding the chaplain's disappearance, the embarrassment with Surico Hurasa, and the lack of progress in busting the drug ring in general, Porter was pissed at himself and everyone in his way, but still, he smiled.

He'd spent last night fuming over a slideshow playing in his head. In the darkness of his stateroom, the carousel clicked to a shot of him arguing with the captain about calling UnRep in the middle of holiday routine. The picture didn't show Captain Holt insisting that the UnRep wasn't planned or that it was ordered when the floating armory was already parallel to their starboard side. According to him, he'd gotten the call from the admiral only minutes before the signal was given to the crew. Porter didn't believe him for one minute.

The carousel clicked to the next slide to show one-thousand-pound bombs sitting on pallets in various locations on the flight deck.

The next slide showed him embarrassed and perplexed by Surico Hurasa.

The next slide showed all that bullshit with the Marines in the cobbler shop.

The next slide showed the same clusterfuck down in the all-black berthing compartment.

The next slide showed their backs as they walked away with nothing but their dicks in their hands.

Click. Slide of the airman killed on the flight deck the day the XO arrived aboard.

Click. Slide of Ken Phillips being crucified to the mast of a pirate's galleon.

Click. Slide of Porter questioning his ability to ever captain his own ship.

Porter pushed that negativity toward the back of his brain. With flight ops scheduled all day, the captain would sequester himself on the bridge. This was a good opportunity for Porter to talk to the ship's company.

Porter rode the escalator down the five decks to the second deck, prepared to engage the crew in increments.

Much of his career to this point had involved accolades and medals and commendations, but on days like this he felt worthy of a best actor Oscar from Hollywood. He'd been sleep-deprived most of his time in uniform, but he could never let it show. This, however, was the first time he could remember being so angry.

He smiled despite sleeping so poorly for the past few nights that pressure behind his eyes and heaviness under his brow line felt like he had a work detail in his skull pulling at his eyelids like tarps.

On the mess deck, Porter found three black crewmen huddled around the bug juice dispenser draining the last of the purple liquid. In all technicality, they were not supposed to walk or congregate in groups of three or more, but he dismissed any notion of hassling them because he didn't believe in that particular policy either. It was blatant in its racism and nonsensical in its application. They weren't hurting anyone. Instead, he made sure they saw him. "Gentleman," he called as he passed by, slowly so as to afford them time to respond with any pertinent apologies or complaints.

They all turned their backs to Porter and continued drinking their grape bug juice.

Porter never broke stride. Those guys clearly held him in contempt for all he'd done to hamper their fun. They might be friends with Surico, for all he knew. He didn't let that get to him. There were other sailors, good sailors, who needed a little positive reinforcement and it was his job to provide that.

He heard the phrase "Uncle Tom" come from behind his back. The words locked his stride in place and he stood there, positive that group could still see him. He'd heard "nigger" and "coon" thrown around a few times in the past few weeks he'd been aboard, but he was used to ignoring that. This was the opposite and it ignited the boiler in his gut.

He turned, pointed at the group of three. "I don't want to know your names and I don't care how bad you think you are, but just remember this. I'm a black man that does a whole bunch of shit few brothers ever get to do, and let me tell you why. First, it comes down to ability. But second, I had to have the balls to put myself in that position. Yeah. You've got no motherfucking idea what I put into my life and my career. I'll spare you the gory details. Now, you fellas better break up your fence-line gossip session before you get written up for breaking the two-man rule."

He resumed walking through the passageway. Instead of holding on to anger or resentment over it, he checked the yellow emergency lights for signs of dust, deck drains for gunk, fire stations for leaking nozzles. Not everything was as polished as in Officer's Country, but it met his standards. Like those three knuckleheads, nothing shined bright enough to warrant praise, but there was a lot to be said for consistency of effort. Porter was pragmatic that way. While most of his fellow officers expected perfection from the entire ship, Porter held a different urgency in his regard for the crew below decks. As far as he knew, no one ever died from dust on the second deck. Other officers could easily set expectations of perfection, not just from the flight deck crew but from the entire crew. Porter's high standard included cleanliness, order, harmony, and compliance, along with the beefed-up drug policy.

As he walked into the MAA shack, Senior was the first man he saw. Porter smiled the kind of smile people always said could've made him famous on TV. He hated Senior for his intolerance. The guy walked across the room with a sure gait as he held a clipboard in one oversized hand and his coffee cup in the other.

The next face Porter saw belonged to Elliot Byrd, who stood half a head taller than Senior, but still shorter than Porter. His dungarees were pressed, with sharp creases in his sleeves. He nodded his chin upward. "Morning, XO."

Senior turned to look at them, frowned, then took a sip of coffee as he turned back to stare at his clipboard.

Porter nodded, chin down, and mustered all the enthusiasm he could. "How're you today, Petty Officer Byrd?"

Byrd put his hands on his hips. "Well, I wasn't going to say anything, but since you ask, I'm about as bitter as every other swinging dick on this ship, sir."

Senior turned to face them and three other guys came out doorways of small offices.

Porter felt blood rise in his face and through the tops of his ears. In other commands he'd tell them to suck it up, but today he needed diplomacy. "That's not a surprise," Porter said. "It's why I'm here."

Senior tucked his lower lip and whistled, then called out, "Fall in for Quarters."

A dozen men with badges filled the room, not in formal ranks, but orderly and respectful.

A fond sadness floated through Porter. It was partly because this was as squared-away a group of sailors as he'd seen on this ship and he wanted to commend each of them for meeting or exceeding standards, but he needed them to raise their game, not rest on their laurels. "The crew is going to be highly agitated today," Porter continued, "because of that ill-timed UnRep."

Heads nodded in recognition and agreement.

"We've got a long couple of days of flight ops so tensions will be wound even tighter as a result. I want all of you on your toes, covering as much ground as you can and preventing as many incidents as possible."

"We're all over that like white on rice," Senior said. He leaned his ass on a desk along the far bulkhead. "Ain't that right, gentlemen?"

Disappointment stung Porter in the back of the throat. He wanted to impale Senior with a nightstick. That cocky bastard let his mouth run instead of being open to the realization that shit was bound to happen. There were only a dozen of them, counting Senior. That was a jurisdiction of five hundred men each. Impossible to be everywhere at once. Senior should've said he couldn't make any promises, but they'd all do their best.

Porter smiled at Senior again. "I admire your confidence, Senior. I'm putting my faith in you and your men to rise to this occasion. Lead by example. Prevent problems before they happen. Calmly resolve those that've started."

A number of the assembled men nodded and bounced in their knees, eager to crack down. Too eager, perhaps.

"I'm not advising you to be hard-asses. No more than usual.

Just extra alert. Shit could get sensitive quick. Be prepared. But be fair and evenhanded. Is that clear?"

In a wave of agreement, each man said, "Yes," or "Yes, sir."

Senior stood from his spot leaning on the desk. "Thanks for coming down, Mr. Porter. We'll take care of it."

"Keep me posted."

"Roger that."

Porter left the MAA shack pleased with the showing of his masters-at-arms. Even with Senior's attitude, he felt confident in those men...as long as the races stayed calm.

Porter swabbed his forehead and under his eyes with the increasingly soggy handkerchief he kept folded in his back pocket. As he walked past the ship's store, he heard harmonica playing. He leaned in and applauded.

The clerk stopped playing. Three other crewmen there stood straight upon seeing their XO.

Porter said, "Sounds great! You are talented. Please play on."

"Okay, sir. This one here's an old train song that hobos have played for decades."

Porter tapped his foot as the shopkeeper led into the song and the others pulled mouth harps from their pockets and joined in. Blacks and whites harmonizing and taking turns with the lead. If only the world had its shit as together as musicians did. He applauded as they finished. "Keep up the good work, gentlemen," he said.

Porter walked across the mess deck and through the galley, where everyone was busy securing from breakfast and beginning lunch preparations. Porter smiled and waved at each man he saw, if even for a moment.

As he stood in the passageway mopping his brow with his soggy handkerchief, a crewman's Elvis Presley-style haircut caught

Porter's peripheral vision. Porter had always been glad that no one was required to salute inside the ship, but the downside of not having to wear covers inside was that he had to see a kid with hair flouting Navy regulations. Instantly, Porter's pulse rate quickened. He wanted to tell the crewman to march his ass down to the barbershop, but that wouldn't make him any friends.

The kid had *Martindale* stenciled above his shirt pocket. The name didn't ring a bell, but the kid looked familiar. Porter's heart rate elevated as he tried to piece it together for a minute. He clenched his teeth. Felt the heat of them grinding. This had to be about more than just the kid's haircut.

They'd each taken two steps in opposite directions when the context flashed in Porter's mind. "Hold on there, Martindale," he called out.

The kid with the Elvis hair stopped in the passageway and turned with a look of curiosity on his face. "Yes, sir?" he asked.

This is the son of a bitch that made him look like a fool. The same damn kid who told him about Surico Hurasa nearly three weeks ago. The embarrassment of coming up empty in the cobbler shop and in the black berthing compartment.

But deep down, he knew he should've verified the tip before acting on it. The Navy had taught him to live by CYA—cover your ass. As squadron commander, he'd given the exact advice he'd ignored because he was overanxious. Busting the drug ring and impressing the captain meant that much to him that he'd sidestepped one basic procedure. Civilians called it due diligence. He should've asked for proof that night on the sponson instead of running blind, driven by his need to succeed. He knew this on some level, but the bulk of his energy focused on his anger at this son of a bitch for being wrong.

He lunged for Martindale. Grabbed him by the collar of his dungaree shirt. Drove him into the bulkhead an inch from the cable run overhead.

Throttling the kid would satisfy the vengeance scratching

inside his chest. Sinking his fist into the kid's stupid face would be a relief and reward in the short term, maybe, but that would ultimately derail or at least delay his career goals. Porter took stock in that moment. Nothing could change the events that occurred in the cobbler's shop or in that berthing compartment. As he pinned the kid against the bulkhead, he heard the audible gasps of at least three men in the vicinity. This knocked off Porter's blinders and he saw what he was doing from the perspective of witnesses.

He eased Martindale down the bulkhead. He wanted to know who put him up to that bogus information, but he couldn't allow himself to do so publicly. "Be in my office tomorrow at 0900. Am I clear?"

The kid nodded, visibly shook. "Yes, sir!" he said.

Porter whispered, "God help you if you show up without any proof. You hear me, Elvis Presley?"

The kid nodded again, fear deep across his face.

Wendy Martindale
1866 Lebrundy
Long Beach, CA 90806

September 20, 1972

ABM2 Paul Martindale
USS Salvation (CV-44)
FPO San Francisco, CA 95660

Hay baby,

I called that number you gave me, but those morons don't know when you're coming home. This is crazy. I feel like you been gone half my life. I'll keep calling that number so I can get a motel down there so I can greet you on the pier and we don't have to wait any longer than we have to.

I'm doing ok. Missing you. Working a lot. I had a fight with your sister. She dropped that "Let me be me" line on me again yesterday and I lost it on that damn girl. I said "That's great ninety-nine percent of the time when you're wonderfully human with ups and downs like everyone else. But it's that other one percent when the whole maggilla is kicked into some extra gear." No shit. I swear I said those exact words. Then I says "This level you hit is difficult to be around. You're obviously wasted, but you insist that you're not. Just fucking own up to it and stop being such a bitch." She hasn't talked to me in two days.

Don't be mad. She had that coming. I know what you're saying. At least she has the sense not to drive, most of the time. But how much am I expected to take? It's on her to grow the fuck up. She's family but that don't give her no right to act the fool. Maybe remind her of that. She always listens to you.

Has your mother written you back yet? The other day she said she's been meaning to. I hope so. She has plenty of time in her day.

But any way. You stay safe baby. See you soon.

Love Wendy

CHAPTER 19

Senior sat at his desk, alone in the MAA shack. He'd allowed all but the two guys on duty to sleep in. Of the two MAAs on duty, one was on rounds, the other had to hit the head. If Senior needed any of the others, he could send someone to wake them.

Instead of a case file, he used the quiet time to open his inventory ledger listing all the shipments of product he'd received so far this cruise and his return from Surico. On those pages, columns were straight numbers in black ink. No names. No details. Not a code, but still totally untraceable to anything. It was just Senior's way of keeping score and keeping Surico honest. Their fifty-fifty split was more than fair. Surico had to pay labor out of his end. Senior had to buy the inventory out of his. The markup made it profitable. The demand made it a goddamn cash cow.

Senior drained the last of his coffee and looked at the bottom of the cup. The sight of the empty mug signaled his brain that it was time to stuff his cheek with a fistful of chewing tobacco, but before he pulled his pouch of Beech-Nut from his hip pocket, Brackert stormed in.

The only thing they had in common was their hairstyle, but even that was separated by a couple of decades and countless fistfuls of hair loss. Where Brackert's was long and bushy, swooping over the top left to right, Senior's was thin with more scalp visible than hair.

Brackert's shirt was wrinkled and his dungarees faded from repeated washes in the ship's laundry. He looked like a scared doe determined to get a drink from the pond.

Senior stared into his empty coffee cup. It was a rare moment when nothing was either going in or coming out of that cup. He patted his pocket with the Beech-Nut. "You're not going to ask me about the chaplain, are you?"

Brackert scratched the back of his neck with his index finger. "It's just answers to a couple or three questions I'm after, Senior."

This kid had always reminded Senior of a young Kirk Douglas. The jaw, for sure. The stone-faced stare, maybe. Certainly not the accent. "If you ask a single one of them, I'll tear off your head and shit down your neck hole. And then I'll lock your ass up."

Brackert's face widened to show the words soured his stomach. He shook his head. "I need to find out. We need to find out. He deserves that much."

Senior looked at his coffee cup and thought about the collision last time Brackert visited. The spill down the left side of this dumb bastard's shirt. "Last time we met," Senior said, "things didn't go so well for you."

Brackert didn't nod or look away, but rather stared at Senior, stone-faced. "Why was his office trashed?"

Senior looked down at the desk to his left. Ran his fingers over the opened ledger there. Who the hell was this lousy kid to ask questions? Especially that question? Senior wouldn't betray the XO's confidence to his best man. He sure as hell wouldn't share any information with this goddamn bum. Senior said, "I'll lock your ass up."

Brackert's jaw tensed and rode up over his top teeth before he said, "Why? Because I'm concerned about the chaplain?"

Senior picked up the ledger only to slap it down on the desk. "Because you're a goddamn good-for-nothing quitter."

Brackert winced at the slap on the wooden desk, but he stood his ground. "I ain't never quit nothing in my life. I simply refuse to be another cog in the wheel of the baby-killing machine."

"You really buy that load of bullshit?" Senior looked at the kid and pulled leaves out of his Beech-Nut pouch.

Brackert waved his hands like he'd touched wet paint. "Thousands of them kids is being blown up every day." He tucked his hands into his armpits and shook his head. "My girl writes me about all the bad stuff."

"Look, kid," Senior said, chewing a handful of tobacco leaves and stuffing in a few more. It tasted as sweet and soft as his first chew when he was thirteen and turkey hunting with his father and uncles out in Acworth that first season they all got back from the war. Ever since that day, each chew reminded him of the best times back home, despite the way people acted these days. "They're protesting in the streets back in the States," he said. "Some of those nutty broads are burning their braziers out in public for children to see. All hell is breaking loose everywhere. Over here, we're just trying to keep the bad guys out. A few lives lost now will enable generations to live peacefully when we're done. Don't you want that?"

Brackert shook his head. "I don't believe one life is worth sacrificing. Peace should be our human right."

This kind of logic made Senior wonder. "What inbred morons birthed a boy stupid as you, son? Or did some splittail put the notion in your brain that peace should be your human right?"

"Not just me, but everyone." Brackert unfolded his arms and held his hands out. "We all deserve peace."

Senior laughed into his cup. After he spit, he said, "The only way to get peace is to win a war. You know that."

"I've been taught that," he said, and then smiled. "But I don't believe it none."

"Your parents still alive?"

Brackert's smile disappeared. His chin tucked and his face clenched apparently by surprise. "They're not even forty yet," he said.

Maybe that was the problem. Maybe his folks had him when they were too young to implant some smarts into their kid. Senior shook his head. "What do they think of your shenanigans here?"

Brackert looked down at his boots as he scratched his arm. "They don't know my status, if that's what you mean."

"Why's that?" Senior asked as he sat on his desktop, pushing aside the ledger behind him. He had some free time to delve deeper into this kid's fucked-up existence. "Would they be mad? Embarrassed?"

"I'll tell them everything once I'm a civilian."

"That right?" Part of Senior found it difficult to believe the kid had any capacity for goodness in him.

"What does this have to do with the chaplain?" the kid asked.

"No, fuck that," Senior said, staring at the kid. Needling him. "I want to understand how a red-blooded American kid becomes a pinko-commie fag."

Brackert's chin tucked itself into his neck before it jutted out. He leaned forward like he would storm off, but his feet never moved. His lower eyelids tensed, became straight lines. His jaw moved forward and the right side of his top lip quivered into more of a snarl than Senior would've guessed could come from this goddamn guy.

Senior wanted Brackert to try something physical. That was all the excuse he'd need to beat the shit out of that rotten bastard.

"I'm only here to find out about the chaplain's investigation."

"That's it!" Senior hopped down from his seat on the desktop and lunged at Brackert. He hollered, "What did I tell you?" as he grabbed him by the collar. "What the fuck did I tell you about that?"

Brackert's unshaved chin trembled, but he didn't speak and he didn't fight back.

Senior's hands squeezed the kid's uniform tighter into his throat, ready to dismantle him if given any further provocation.

Instead of looking at Senior, Brackert made his line of sight focus on the deck. He shrugged his shoulders beneath Senior's grip. "I need to know what happened."

Senior squeezed the kid's collar with fists twisting into the kid's throat. "You're the last one who should be disobeying direct orders."

"I need to know it wasn't my fault."

Senior eased up on Brackert's collar but didn't let go. It was more confusion than adrenaline. "*Your* fault?" He jerked the collar tighter again. "Explain yourself."

Brackert's face washed out—went white as his T-shirt. He shrugged again. "Sometimes I think everything's my fault."

Before Senior could seek clarification, the bosun's whistle called attention over the 1MC, followed by the announcement, "Senior Chief Rawlings, please report to the bridge. Senior Chief Rawlings to the bridge."

This son of a bitch had been saved by the bell in this round, but Senior was determined to get to the bottom of what that kid meant by "his fault."

Senior released Brackert's collar. He could bounce this bastard off every bulkhead and wipe the deck with him and not fear a single repercussion. No one would take this pansy's word over Senior's. But Senior couldn't help feeling sorry for his dumb ass. Besides, his duty was to the captain of this ship, not to be delayed by his dislike for individual crewmen. "We'll continue this later."

Brackert stepped back a couple paces, his hand at his throat. "I'm not waiting."

"I'll find you later."

"I bet you will."

Senior opened the sheet-metal door leading into the passageway and left it open on his way to the bridge.

Shortly after calling Senior Chief Rawlings to the bridge over the 1MC, the bosun announced, "Sweepers, sweepers, man your brooms. Give the ship a clean sweep down both fore and aft. Sweep down all lower decks, ladders backs, and passageways.

Dump all garbage clear of the fantail. Sweepers."

Surico knew that would be a good time to catch Applewhite out of the laundry so they could have a conversation without having to climb down into the one-hundred-ten-degree heat.

He hung a makeshift sign of corrugated cardboard on the cobbler shop door. In black grease pencil, the sign read, *Back in 10*.

Surico climbed the ladders to the second deck. The fourteen steps made his thighs burn. He'd spent the whole morning sitting on his stool in his shop, hunched over his workbench, swapping out leather soles on officers' shoes and repairing eyelets on enlisted men's boots. The crew was worse on boots than jackals. His hand hurt down in the knuckles from squeezing the eyelet pliers. He no longer had the muscle or stamina of his younger days, but that's why he had guys like Applewhite and Wooly.

Surico stopped by the lower-aft berthing compartment they called "Downtown" to see if Wooly was down there. Within two seconds of entering the space, Surico heard a cheer.

"Hot damn!"

He followed the voice and found Wooly shooting craps with two brothers from back east.

Surico signaled with his head that Wooly should follow him. Together they doubled back to the second deck to find Applewhite. Surico wanted to talk to them both and wasn't willing to repeat his instructions later.

They found Applewhite sweeping the passageway between the laundry trunk and the imaginary line marking the end of the chow line. He stopped sweeping and watched them walk up. "I'm sick of sweeping this goddamn stretch of deck. I'll tell you that right now," Applewhite said. "I got to climb out of my laundry to push a broom three times a damn day? This is some straight-up bullshit, right here."

Surico never understood why some guys complain about the same things day after day. But more importantly, he didn't need Applewhite's bellyaching to draw attention to them. Surico looked down the passageway in both directions. Ship's policy didn't mean a whole lot to him, but this could be considered an obvious disregard for standing orders.

"Finish the deck later. Let's go down." Surico nodded toward the laundry's access trunk.

The crossroads between the chemical smells from the open laundry hatch and the food smells wafting from the galley snagged his attention. Someone was making a big batch of Salisbury steak gravy.

"I just got out of there and you want me to go back in?"

On another day Surico might point out that contradiction, but he understood the man's need for elbow room. And the ship's laundry wasn't just a tight space filled with equipment to wash, dry, press, or dry clean any garment aboard the ship. It was also home to two five-thousand-gallon desalination plants that turned seawater into water suitable for doing laundry.

Surico knew Applewhite was planning to blanket party some kid in one of the white berthings up forward. That's part of what he wanted to talk about. He didn't mind the notion of going down to the ship's laundry. That was a great place to talk privately. "I know it's hot down there, but this is important."

As they walked to the ladder leading into the laundry, Senior Chief Rawlings hightailed it down the passageway toward them. He'd been called to the bridge a while ago and should've been there long before now. He cleared each knee knocker in a precise and efficient manner and at a rate of speed that impressed Surico as skills honed over countless days at sea over many, many years. He held his coffee cup chest high without spilling a drop.

Senior was younger than Surico, but his face was more worried, more aged. Surico may have felt his years, but at least he didn't look ten years older than he was, like Senior.

Surico said, "Good morning, Senior." Surico had heard that dirty blowfish drank his own tobacco spit. He didn't know if it was true, but it's what everyone believed. As far as Surico was concerned, this *tonto* could drink whatever he wanted as long as he didn't blow their cover.

Senior didn't acknowledge Surico, which Surico assumed was in an effort to keep their business relationship secret. It wasn't every day their path's crossed in an official or public way. Senior stopped in front of the three of them, rolled back his shoulders. "I'm going to have to ask you boys to disperse," he said. "No more than two men can congregate or walk together."

Surico felt the shock of surprise right in his sternum.

Wooly seemed genuinely confused enough to count the three of them with his fingers.

Applewhite looked away as he dispelled air like the brakes on a city bus.

Senior looked over at Applewhite. Surico was worried about Applewhite getting into it with Senior. Applewhite was increasingly aggravated lately and unkind words could set him off.

Senior said, "I don't know who your friends are, cobbler, but one of you needs to disappear instantly or I'll write up all three of you."

Surico didn't know if Senior was joking, and he couldn't believe the man didn't recognize Wooly. He was glad for it. Less interference and resistance.

"Can I have a word with you, cobbler?" Senior leaned his head down the passageway and walked a few frames forward.

Surico signaled Applewhite and Wooly to sit tight for a minute and followed Senior.

"You can't flaunt the regulations like that. And what did I tell you about being seen with troublemakers?"

Surico wasn't surprised. "Don't worry 'bout my boys. They say nothing."

"I'm sure you're safe. It's me I'm worried about. They got no loyalty to me. I got no guarantee they won't drop a dime on me."

Surico could set Senior's mind at ease and confess that no one knew the alliance the two of them had. Instead, he said, "I don't hang with no rats."

"Is that right?"

"You can build houses on the foundation of my integrity."

Senior spit into his cup. "That's pretty fancy, cobbler."

"It is true."

Senior turned to continue down the passageway as he said, "No more than two at a time."

As Surico rejoined his boys, Applewhite said, "This is bullshit!"

Surico held up a hand and looked back toward Senior as he faded down the passageway. "You got to *go* along to *get* along, boy. Don't be forgetting that."

"White boys do whatever the fuck they want and three niggers can't talk in the motherfucking place I got to sweep three times a day? That's fucked up, my brother."

Surico laughed. "Play their game, Rufus. Play the game so the three of us can win the prizes."

"Racist bullshit," Applewhite muttered.

At the bottom of the ladder, Applewhite asked, "What did you want to talk to us about anyway?"

Surico's skin added to the wet heat in the room by perspiring immediately. The ship's laundry was a steel box within a network of steel boxes on the surface of the South China Sea, being cooked from the outside by the sun and from the inside by the hot water in washing machines, the high-voltage driers, and the constantly chugging desalination plants. He wiped at his forehead with a green bandana folded in his back pocket. "Never mind that," he said. "You got something you want to tell *me*?"

Applewhite propped his foot on the second ladder step and leaned his elbow on his knee. "I just spoke my mind. What else you looking for?"

Surico nodded as his nostrils filled with the scent of soap powder. As he tucked the bandana into his pocket, he asked, "Anything else I should know about?"

Applewhite rubbed the razor stubble on his throat and shook his head.

Surico knew he was lying, but he had to get back to the cobbler shop. "All right. We have to get out in front of something. I want you both on this one. Working as a team. This is a big boy we're talking about here. Not that I want it to get physical, but just in case. This is a brother. We hope he's got the money. If not, we remind him that he'd better get it by next payday or the interest and the level of pain increase exponentially." It was Big Detroit's first failure to pay, so Surico didn't want them going that hard after him. "If it comes to it, just maybe a couple cigarette burns along his collar bone should do it."

The crew was still at Quarters. All the passageways were empty. It reminded Brackert of having free reign of the hallways of his high school when classes were in session and he skipped class for just that feeling. He wished he had the luxury of enjoying it, but instead he only had a few minutes before every space he wanted to be got crowded.

While he was pissed about Senior, Brackert was excited about the idea that crusty bastard had given him.

He ran to his locker, stripped off his dungaree shirt, and took out his red shirt, but didn't put it on. Instead, he jogged to the escalator and rode up five decks. He'd abandoned the notion of damaging the catapult equipment when he found out where it was in O-country, eerily near the chaplain's stateroom, where the passageways were patrolled by Marines.

He had to hurry to get to the flight deck. On the way, he had to stop at his hiding spot to retrieve the cranial. He ripped the tape off the front that read Miller and put on his red shirt. He had the cranial halfway on when he heard voices in the passageway. He hightailed it up to the flight deck.

With the tinted goggles in place, he was unrecognizable as Brackert. As far as the plat camera and anyone else who saw him was concerned, he was supposed to be there.

His buddy, Hydrant, had told him that the aircrews all left the ordnance on planes, hot and ready to fire, as a way to save time in advance of launches.

If he pulled this off, no way would Chrissy be able to resist him.

He was amazed by the activity—planes, forklifts, fuel carts, pallets of bombs zooming by or standing at the ready. The ship had taken on tons of ordnance. Pallets of it would be stacked up on the flight deck, ready to be loaded and launched on the full day of massive bombings they had planned.

He worried about getting caught or, worse, failing.

May May
Barrio Barretto
Olongapo City 2200
Baloy
Olongapo City, Philippines

October 3, 1972

PO Harry Bird
USS Salvation (CV-44)
FPO San Francisco, CA 95660

Harry, yes my *pinsan*. Yo tell friend all go. Danilo meet at pier. This good. Very hoppy.

How long now? To long. Hurry here. Do biz-ness. Then come to me. I give ice blow job. Cold but fun.

Me need Harry. You need May

Mahal kita,

May May.

CHAPTER 20

Byrd joined his buddy, Gomez, near the jet shop on the fantail. Wind brushed past his nose and mouth and snuck in between his shirt buttons, puffing him up. The sun warmed his face as he leaned his abdomen into the life rail. This was the only place aboard ship where the smell of saltwater came close to masking the overwhelming smell of JP-5 and hydraulic fluid. If he had to guess, the wind carried a hint of what might be a late-season rain. It wasn't long after morning Quarters and the hangar deck issued sounds of early morning maintenance and repair, but not yet churning at full capacity. The pilots were in their ready rooms being briefed on the day's flight ops, flight crews were below decks in storage rooms gathering parts, and Byrd never got tired of being in the open air of the fantail.

Gomez carried a flashlight and a clipboard instead of a nightstick or gun—his job was simply to observe and report. Byrd was happy to have Marines on the job because the MAA shack didn't have the personnel to keep watch across the major spaces of such a large ship.

Two guys wheeled an engine on a dolly from the jet shop into the hangar bay. One guy pushed while the other pulled with the synchronized effort of having done so a thousand times together. Byrd envied their specialized knowledge. He didn't know much about planes. Could point out the F-8s and the F-4s, but not many of the others. None of the helicopters. He wouldn't be able to fix any one of them to save his life. He wasn't even sure he could hazard a guess which engine belonged to which plane.

"Walk and talk," Gomez said. "I've got to keep moving."

Byrd reluctantly turned from the blue sky beyond the fantail and followed Gomez on the perimeter of the hangar bay. This was too important to wait, but he didn't look forward to the actual discussion. He tasted metal, felt like he had pennies in his mouth.

"What's the matter with you?" Gomez asked. "Did you not get a letter from May at mail call?"

Byrd laughed for the first time that day. Each chuckle flooded his lungs with fumes of JP-5. He shook his head and remembered all the mistakes she'd made with the language, a smile on his face. "No, I got a letter." Thinking of the letter's content wiped away the smile.

"So what gives?"

Byrd looked back across the hangar deck. The sun was just about to crest the hangar bay door. Shadows would form in there in the matter of minutes, and he just might have to hide in them. "Have you ever done something against regulations?"

Gomez ran a hand over his high-and-tight haircut. "You mean paying a private to make my rack every morning? Sure. We all have. I went without a T-shirt one day because I had to hurry to make muster."

"No," Byrd said. "Important shit. Ever do anything really bad?"

"You mean like sleep on watch? Or gun deck maintenance on a rifle?

"Not exactly."

"My last name ends in Z, *hermano*, and I don't exactly look like the guy in the recruiting poster. That's two strikes against me. I do everything I can to avoid that third strike. But what are we talking about here?"

The starboard side a few yards ahead of him broke out in a

chorus of metal-on-metal clanging and pneumatic tools. Byrd had no idea what could be physically taking place over there. He wasn't raised mechanical.

"I don't know what's up your ass," Gomez said, "but you best keep your shit squared away or it could fuck up everything you've worked for."

"That's what I'm worried about!"

"What did you do?"

Before Byrd answered, he saw some guy standing awkwardly in front of an open watertight door, a flight deck cranial at his feet. As he and Gomez got closer, Byrd recognized the guy as Brackert. He thought it odd that guy would be up there, but it wasn't until they got a little closer and he read *Mk-5 Flare Locker* stenciled in bold, black paint beside the open door that his neck hairs stood. Brackert held the aluminum tube of one of the phosphorous flares between his hip and his elbow, aimed at the open doorway to the flare locker, his forefinger and thumb on the lanyard. There were fifty-five-gallon drums of paint in the elevator pits. Five hundred gallons of liquid oxygen in tanks one deck below. In various spots in the hangar bay and above on the flight deck stood pallets of five-hundred-pound and one-thousand-pound bombs, plus the fuel stations and the Zuni and Sidewinder missiles. All those flares igniting would set off a chain of events that would've been like a grenade in a soda can. This fucking idiot could send them all to hell by pulling that small string.

Gomez pointed his clipboard and yelled, "Hey! Put that flare DOWN!"

The two feet of aluminum tubing Brackert held was more combustible than anything on that ship. He could blind any eye within fifty feet as dim as the lighting was in the shadows of the far recesses along the hangar deck.

Byrd ignored protocol and sprinted toward Brackert.

Brackert got twitchy and swung his hips side to side, sweeping the flare back and forth between the locker and Byrd.

Before Byrd got to him, another crewman dashed across the deck so fast it was a blur and tackled Brackert. The flare dropped, unlit, onto the deck with more of a thud than a clang.

"No!" Brackert yelled. "No, goddamn it!"

With Brackert knocked to the deck, Byrd and Gomez watched Brackert try to protect his head as the guy rained hammer-fisted punches with speed and accuracy—saving Byrd the trouble of doing it himself. Byrd kicked the flare out of reach and stood over the two men, surprised how loudly each punch landed.

The fact he'd sprung into action without thinking made Byrd realize he had the basics covered and all his extracurricular activities didn't take away from his positive contributions to the ship, to the Navy. Every punch the guy landed was an exclamation point to the pleasure Byrd took in knowing he was good at his job and lived most of his life on the regulation side. More than that was the realization they could've all been killed had they not gotten there in time.

Gomez ran up next to Byrd, seemingly prepared to pull the Good Samaritan off of Brackert. Byrd reached out and grabbed Gomez by his rolled-up sleeve, silently saying, let this guy have his fun.

Byrd jutted his chin toward the flare locker. "This bastard could've ignited every flare in there. Do you know how fucked we all would've been it that happened?"

Gomez nodded. "Fuck, man." He crossed his arms. "I've dealt with these two before. They have history."

They both watched that guy pummel Brackert, who was now moaning, "Chrissy," over and over.

Byrd laughed and read the name *Corrigan* stenciled above the guy's shirt pocket. "Okay, Corrigan," Byrd said. "You've had your fun. We'll take it from here."

Corrigan stood to face Byrd. If he saw the badge, he didn't act like it. "You want some, too? You his accomplice?"

Byrd held up the badge affixed to his shirt pocket with a thumb and then pointed it at Gomez. "We saw what he was intending. You did good. Now it's time to let us do our jobs."

"How's the leg?" Gomez asked.

Corrigan nodded and looked back at Brackert, who remained in the fetal position with his arms covering his head. He mumbled the name Chrissy over and over through his bloodied mouth, but it was foolish to assume he was no longer dangerous. Byrd walked over and tugged Brackert's arm. As the arm came away from his face, blood raced down Brackert's forehead. His nose was flat. His lips busted like half-chewed tomatoes.

Gomez grabbed Brackert's other arm. "You just guaranteed yourself a spot in the Iron Inn, dirtbag."

Brackert didn't put up a fight. Maybe Corrigan had beaten out of him any fight the guy had. Instead, his head hung low, which made the bleeding worse and he dripped on the deck as they walked toward the brig. A few paces later, Brackert stopped and broke free of their grasp.

"What's your major malfunction, Brackert?"

Bracket punched himself in his already dented face. "Chrissy did it," he said, and punched himself again. "Chrissy killed him. The blood is on her hands. It's her should be locked up. Arrest her."

Before Byrd knew how to respond, Brackert commenced walking again without resistance.

Surico didn't lose sleep regularly, but for the past couple days, he hadn't let more than two minutes go by without worrying about Applewhite. He loved that motherfucker, but Surico knew Applewhite was behind the most recent scuttlebutt. Word was he'd planned something that might draw too much attention to the brothers. If Surico had his way, the young buck would work the system instead of rebelling against it.

As a way to bring him in close, Surico had Applewhite meet him just after Quarters.

Applewhite was supposed to be stuffing the washers with

sheets and towels from the chiefs' mess. Instead, Surico had him meet him on the mess deck with one of the canvas laundry bags.

Surico got there late. He'd gotten hung up with a shoe customer—a real particular pilot, Lieutenant Boggs or something he didn't bother committing to memory. Applewhite waited by the bug juice dispensers, the empty laundry bag draped over his neck hanging down both sides of his white T-shirt.

One of the mess cranks stopped behind them as he wiped down the stainless-steel serving line. They couldn't talk with ears around them. Surico nodded toward the passageway and Applewhite followed him forward, stepping over knee knockers along the way.

Even with a crew this size, there were still hundreds of places to find privacy, but they were all connected to a main passageway populated by hurried shipmates. They kept walking forward.

"It's a good thing Wooly ain't here," Applewhite said, "or some cracker would smack our asses down for being black-times-three."

Surico understood, but he couldn't condone it. Certain policies got to him, too, but he never let it show. It was easier to hide in plain sight, have a clean record, and profit from his crimes. "Man, don't sweat that shit."

"I've had it with that bullshit," Applewhite said. "I'm tired of these honkies acting like they better than me. Making me do they laundry and nothing else."

Surico laughed. Rolled out a couple middle-weight chuckles and slapped the bulkhead once.

Applewhite's nose twitched and he sniffed.

Surico looked down the passageway. "Wait a minute." He didn't care if the kid took offense or not, but he'd never embarrass him in front of shipmates—of any color. "I get your anger and shit, but what have you done to change things?'

"What do you mean?"

"I mean, what have you done to better yourself?"

"The fuck you say, 'better myself'?"

"Have you spent any time pursuing a rate that more suits your high-mindedness?"

"Rate" was the Navy's term for job, and Surico knew damn well that unless Applewhite was down in the laundry he didn't hang out with any of the white boys. No way a brother could get ahead if he didn't learn to get along. But just as Surico could've guessed, Applewhite had excuses out the ass.

"What time? I'm in that steam shithole all day long, man."

"So you expect an officer to come down there and hand you a better job?"

Applewhite looked at Surico like the man was speaking Greek.

"Seriously," Surico said. "You got to show an interest in the things you want. You can't go sulking around this big-ass boat thinking somebody owes you something. If you want something, you've got to work for it."

"Yeah, but—"

Surico lunged at Applewhite and clamped his hand on the younger man's throat and shoved him into a bank of pressure gauges for their firefighting water. "But my ass," he said.

Applewhite's eyes didn't pop wide in surprise, but rather squinted low, seethed with anger—unsurprised and unimpressed. He never dropped the bag.

The lack of respect pissed off Surico even more. "When you going to learn it's better to work the system than to cry about it?" Surico's thumb picked up the pulse in Applewhite's carotid artery. There were twenty years between them and Applewhite could easily tire him out and kick his ass, but he had to make a point. He knew Applewhite was dangerous, but he didn't fear him. He couldn't help liking him, either. The boy could be his son. They were opposites in many ways, but he always reminded Surico of a guy he served with on the *Iowa*. A pale brother from Louisiana who couldn't keep his tongue in his head. Surico had gotten along well with him and tried to tell him he was asking for trouble. He didn't listen and had a miserable time of the

Korean War.

Surico loosened his grip and shook his head. "It's business. They do their thing. I do mine. There's no room for emotion."

Applewhite shrugged his shoulder away from the gauges and stood in the center of the passageway, like that kind of physical altercation served as a hug. "Don't get your blood pressure up, Surico. We good. What the fuck, man? Where are we going, anyway?"

Surico kept shaking his head as they walked forward to a ladder, where they climbed down. The vestibule they entered rounded into a room thirty feet across with three stainless-steel freezer doors occupying most of the perimeter. A separate steel door held a padlock and had *Paper Products* stenciled across the top.

Applewhite rested his palm on one of the freezer doors as he leaned and crossed his ankles. "I'm surprised you wanted me to come down here with you."

"I trust you. Don't worry about that. I just thought it would be a good opportunity for us to talk."

"What you got on your mind?"

"Word is you're planning a blanket party. A white blanket party."

"Maybe I am, Surico. So what? It ain't like the honkies in charge are going to do anything to make shit right. We've got to do something."

"I'm not telling you not to do it."

"Ain't your place to say, Surico. All due respect. You run the drug biz, not my whole life."

"I dig," Surico said. "Just keep it to a minimum. This whole ship is a powder keg."

"It's one fucking guy. A fucking guy who deserves to have his dumb-ass head kicked in."

"That's what I'm worried about."

"You want in?"

"The fewer brothers you need down there, the better."

"Solid."

Surico opened one of the freezer doors by tugging on the heavy chrome handle. A fog of cold air wafted up into their faces. "Set your bag down and help me with these." Surico flicked on the light and pointed to stacked boxes of pickled okra and lima beans.

Without a jacket or glove, Surico's arms stung and his hands stiffened—the fingertips went numb.

"What are we doing?" Applewhite asked, hopping, attempting to generate heat.

"Take these stacks here and put them over there."

Applewhite didn't seem to understand, but he didn't argue. Instead, he dropped his laundry bag and began humping the boxes from one stack to another. "Might just freeze my dick off in this motherfucker."

"Quit your bellyaching. It won't take long." Surico had twenty-three guys on staff to perform fourteen different tasks. Some overlap occurred. Once in a while, he hired white freelancers to handle the white side. Surico didn't know if it was integrity or fear, but every one of those white motherfuckers had been straight up honest and delivered every penny, without exception. But still, he didn't trust anyone else to do this work.

He blew into a fist to warm his fingers. Once the stacks of boxes were removed, Surico popped open the false bottom of the shelving unit and pulled out three half-filled trash bags. One bag contained the remainder of his weed and pills, the others held stacks of cash, mostly singles and fives.

"How much is that?" Applewhite asked.

"Twenty-seven thousand, four hundred dollars in cash. Another three grand in product."

"Damn!" Applewhite said, cupping his hand over his mouth and hopping again.

"I've also got a shoebox of uncut horse in a storage compartment down by the shaft alley." The box wasn't full, but he hoped the exaggeration would further impress Applewhite.

As Applewhite put everything in the laundry bag, Surico said, "So what's your beef with this guy, anyway?"

Applewhite didn't look up. "I didn't plan on telling you."

"You keeping secrets from me now?"

"This is something you might be better off not knowing about."

"That so?"

"Believe it is."

Surico's jaw quivered from the cold, but he kept his teeth from chattering and pulled the door closed. If this was anybody else, Surico might've had a guy or two waiting down here to beat the shit out of them. "How's your baby doing?" he asked.

"From what I hear, he's doing fine," Applewhite said.

"Must've been hard taking that last pay cut."

"You know it is." Applewhite hopped, his head inches from the light fixture overhead. "Shit, that's why I work for you."

"Can I interest you in making more?"

"More?"

"Say the word."

"So why you bringing me in on this now?" Applewhite asked.

"You been a good friend. You earned my trust."

Applewhite seemed to flush from the compliment, inside and out. His skin, a shade darker than Surico's, never changed, but it read on his face. He was touched by the sentiment.

"You wouldn't have gotten into my inner circle if you ain't. People listen to you, Rufus. You can do some good things in the Navy or out. You're here now. Might as well get all you can out of it."

Applewhite wrapped his arms around his chest and hugged his shoulders. "Shit, man. This is all good of you to say, Surico, but I still don't know what direction you're going with this."

Surico exhaled a cloud of breath into the air between them. "I've got Byrd ready to wash this cash the next time we pull into Subic. Cost me ten percent, but I skimmed more than that."

"What's my end?"

Surico smiled. All told, he'd have earned more than three times his annual salary in one cruise. He had to be there anyway, but because he took on the side work, and ran drugs, he would have worked one year and been paid for three. Earning as much as a captain. He could afford to be generous. "You keep the peace until we get back to San Diego and you get the same cut."

"I told you. It's just one honky."

Surico's nose had gone numb and his lips frozen. This was the most private place to have a conversation and he needed to work this out with Applewhite here and now. He would use reason, their friendship, the threat of physical harm, anything, to make this agreement, which was just as important as the deals with Senior and Byrd.

"The XO could be getting closer to busting the up the whole enterprise." Surico rubbed his hands over his ears, trying to warm the tips. "We've got to move it. Hide it. But stage it to be ready to go the minute we hit port."

"How you expect to carry a laundry bag on a liberty launch and not get questions?"

"That's not for you to worry about. You just get it down to the laundry and hide it real good and it'll get taken care of."

"Hiding it in plain sight? Surico, my man!" Applewhite stepped up and dapped Surico longer than was necessary.

Surico ended it by pulling his hand away. "Do you know what a stool pigeon is, Rufus?"

"A snitch," Applewhite said with conviction in spite of the cold.

"Not necessarily." Surico walked to the lima bean boxes and sat on a short stack. Every muscle in his body clenched—some involuntarily—but he maintained control. "Back in the eighteen hundreds, settlers used to hunt pigeon, but the sound of gunfire scared the birds away. Some quick-thinking fella realized the best way to get pigeons to come back was to have a pigeon already in position so they knew it was safe."

Applewhite hugged his bare arms. "Yeah, so? We going to

hang out down here all day? I want to get back to some heat."

The impatience didn't surprise Surico. He tensed his abdomen to stimulate blood flow to help keep his organs warm as he continued. "Back in the old days, that fellow knew that pigeons flew away when they got the chance to live so he lashed a live bird to a stool and put it in the center of the field behind his house. It never failed to bring in dozens, sometimes hundreds of other pigeons, and then every motherfucker with a gun started blasting. All because of that pigeon tied to a stool."

"That's a real nice history lesson, Surico. So what?"

"You know why I told you that story, Rufus?"

"Come on, man. I didn't finish school, but I'm not an idiot."

"Then you'll be careful?"

"It's just one stupid honky."

"What is he to you? Surico asked.

"Damn, man." Applewhite held his hands in his armpits and bounced just enough to keep his knees moving. "I didn't plan on telling you, but I'm too cold to give a shit anymore. He's the motherfucker ratted you out to that Uncle Tom XO."

If not for his bodily fluid being frozen, a tear might've leaked from Surico's eye at that moment. He wiped at his face with the back of his hand anyway. Applewhite's gesture meant that much to him. "So you're doing this for me?"

"You my boy," Applewhite said, half a smile on his face, perhaps too shy to say it straight up. "Wanted to surprise you with this shit."

Surico forgot about the cold in that moment, stunned and flattered. In another setting he might've felt a warm flush rise up his limbs, but it was good enough to forget the pain for a minute. He walked to the door and pushed the metal knob. Before the door swung open, he turned and pointed a bent finger at Applewhite. "Load that bag and get it down to the laundry. And keep a low profile. This deal's on you either way."

CHAPTER 21

October 9, 1972

Seaman Elliot Brackert
USS Salvation (CV-44)
FPO San Francisco, CA 95660

Dear Elliot,

I want to tell you all about the carnage caused—the casualties on both sides, plus what they're calling collateral damage. That fucking Nixon and the plumbers and all that shit. Don't trust the government, man. They're rotten all the way to the top. You can't trust the squares, man.

With that said, I think it's time we end things with one another. You've been gone so long it's stupid to pretend anymore. Besides, you haven't done enough to prevent the killing. So let's part friends and maybe someday we'll be able to share a joint and laugh about all this. Ok man?

I do care about you so be safe.

Peace,

Chrissy

* * *

The chatter and laughter on the mess deck ceased as soon as the projector switched on. Byrd loved the sound of the projector ticking as it fed film past the bulb. He had a seat near enough to the screen that not many heads in front of him would be a distraction, but not so far back that he had to squint to see the characters on the screen. He pivoted in his seat to face the screen, anticipating the opening scene of *The French Connection*. On the tabletop in front of him he had a fresh cup of coffee and a Hershey bar from the ship's store that he refused to open until after the opening credits. It was perfect.

Through the smell of buttered popcorn and the various crunching sounds around him, he craved entertainment. Wanted distraction. Just a couple of hours to park his worries and lose himself in the world on the screen. A break from the deal he'd made with Surico and all the other bullshit hanging over his head with May's family. He needed every frame of this movie.

But before the opening credits ended and he unwrapped his Hershey bar, he felt a tap on his shoulder. He turned to see Gomez hooking his thumb toward the passageway.

Byrd whispered through his teeth. "What the fuck, man?"

Gomez hunched over so as not to block anyone's view of the screen. "XO wants to see you."

"Now?"

Gomez shrugged and nodded.

Byrd would rather scrape barnacles with his teeth than get pressure about busting the drug ring right now. "What is with that guy?"

"You tell me," Gomez said.

As much as Byrd wanted to, he couldn't tell his buddy what was going on. The time would come soon enough. He imagined he'd need backup in the near future, but for the time being, he had to keep his mouth shut. He exhaled hot and dry as he abandoned his seat, his coffee, and his Hershey bar, and then duck-walked beneath the projector's beam.

"Let me guess," he said to Gomez in the passageway. "You're not coming with me this time either."

Gomez nodded, and for a second Byrd thought he might have someone to share the burden of conversing with the XO. That eliminated some of the dread.

Then Gomez laughed. "Just messing with you," he said. "I ain't going up there. The less time I spend around officers the better."

"Asshole!" Byrd understood though. He wished he didn't have this kind of access. He liked it better when the old XO was there and they shared a mutual respect for each other's autonomy. Their only interaction was daily briefings. He missed that respectable distance.

Gomez and Byrd slapped each other five and went their separate directions.

The passageway angled the farther forward he walked. The bow of the ship narrowed and steel ribs rose from the deck and joined the hull to his left. All the way at the front of the ship, the passageway narrowed, jogged ninety degrees, and ended at an open watertight hatch with *Auxiliary Control* stenciled above.

Byrd had never been there before and didn't fully understand why the XO chose this spot for their meeting until he walked in and saw how isolated it was, and private.

Aux con replicated the bridge in the most basic ways so as to assume control of all the ship's movements in the event of damage or imminent threat to the bridge in the island structure above deck. This was the one space on the ship everyone hoped they'd never need to use. Use of this room other than for drills meant serious trouble was taking, or had taken, place. The room spanned the width of the bow, with five portholes that were black as coal at the moment except for the taillights of planes as they launched.

Commander Porter sat in one of two conning chairs raised so the seat was five feet off the deck with clear sight out of the portholes. A railing circled the chair beneath his feet, enabling full rotation and comfort even if reclined.

"The noise is muted between layers of steel, but the rush of energy that accompanies each launch is fully intact," Porter said.

For a split-second, Byrd considered hopping up into the matching captain's chair on the port side. Instead, he walked through an aisle formed by the conning console with its navigation equipment and radar. He stood at the auxiliary helm but didn't touch the wheel. He had no way of knowing if it was connected by cables to the primary helm on the bridge. He didn't dare alter the ship's course, especially during flight ops. His forward gaze lined up with the center porthole, which hung on the forward-most bulkhead on the ship, darkened by night. He leaned an elbow on the chart table.

Porter nodded. "That was good work. You and the Marine."

Byrd wouldn't know a sincere moment if it came with a singing telegram and skywriting. He had no experience with openness or integrity.

Porter snapped his fingers and asked, "What was his name?"

"Gomez, sir." As soon as Byrd said it, he regretted it. Gomez wanted to remain in the shadows, not have his name mentioned to the XO. "But to be honest," he continued, "that airdale, Corrigan, did all the heavy lifting. He dove on that whack job son of a bitch and saved us all from hell, sir."

"Does he have any connection to our other issue?"

"Corrigan or the corncob?"

"The corn—the conscientious objector, obviously."

"Not to my knowledge, sir."

The XO raised his voice for the first time Byrd ever heard. "Well, I don't mind telling you that I'm not very pleased with our progress on our main concern, Petty Officer Byrd."

This reminded Byrd of altercations with his father seventeen years ago, back home in Yonkers. He hadn't been yelled at since boot camp, where everybody got yelled at as a rule. Seventeen years as a sailor and here he was getting the business from his

XO. Byrd checked his gig line in order to stall—to verify he wanted to say what he had on his mind. His future rested in this man's hands. Byrd felt pressure to exceed the XO's expectations. Disappointing him could result in delays to one last promotion before he retired. He needed to make chief to help increase the numbers on his retirement checks so he could support his instant family. "To be honest, sir, we'd be farther along if I didn't have to do this myself, behind Senior's back."

Porter swiveled back toward the porthole, looked out over dark water.

"That takes planning," Byrd said. "Plans don't always go our way."

Without taking his eyes off the porthole, Porter said, "You think you got it all figured out, do you? You think you're real smart." He swiveled back to face Byrd. "Smarter than me, surely, a colored man."

Byrd shook his head. "No way, sir." Was this a setup? He couldn't believe how fast things went bad. "No, sir. Nothing could be farther from the truth."

Porter swiveled again. "You don't have that brand of hate in you. I know that. But I think that's just for your own personal gain."

Byrd cleared his throat, but his vocal chords felt knotted.

"Don't act surprised. I know your type," Porter said. "You might not hate me because I'm black, but you still look down on me. You think the only reason I'm here today is the color of my skin. Well let me tell you something, Petty Officer Byrd. I've had some doors opened, sure, but I'm the one who took the step and got the grades, earned my pilot's license, flew every mission—including two hundred off the deck of this very ship. I was the one taking hostile fire every time."

Byrd didn't know if that meant the jig was up or if he was playing a hunch. Sweat beaded on his upper lip and he wiped it away by placing his index finger there. The lack of success had Byrd feeling like he was backed into a corner. It seemed to him that if he kept quiet for Surico's three thousand dollars, he could wreck his service jacket. If he fessed up here, it could help his service jacket in a major way. But without that cash he'd be letting down May's family. Not only would there be no money, but surely Surico would find out and exact revenge. Byrd wasn't sure in that moment which outcome would be worse.

"Let's look at it objectively, Mr. Porter. You're still new here. You're black. The captain ain't exactly your best friend, no offense, but you need that man's approval if you got any chance in hell of getting any higher on the food chain. Am I right?"

Porter tilted his head and stared at Byrd. "I'm not your average stuffed shirt, Byrd, but I'm not pleased with the way you're speaking to me."

The fear of losing a live one on the hook made his breathing quicken. "Hold on, sir," Byrd said, a little breathless. "I meant no disrespect. It's simply the path of least resistance. I mean, I could kiss your ass and beat around the bush, but there's not a lot of time for that. We've been out here for-fucking-ever and we're bound to rotate back home sooner or later."

"Your point."

"What is busting this drug ring worth to you?"

Porter reclined the seatback to forty-five degrees and laced his fingers behind his head. "It, obviously, would mean the world to me."

Byrd squeezed down the urge to laugh. "Let me put it another way, sir. How much is busting this drug ring worth to *me?*"

"Surely you're not suggesting..."

It seemed like he'd jumped off a high dive and plummeted toward the water with no way to stop. The water's impact would be violent and wet and he braced for it. "I want to do the right thing, sir, but spilling the beans puts me at risk for some ugly shit. And to be honest, I've got people could use the money. Five grand, to be exact."

Porter crossed his arms over his chest and held a stare on Byrd for what seemed like an hour. "You're extorting money from me in exchange for information leading to those responsible for the drug ring?"

"Desperate times, sir. This will not make me popular with certain crewmembers. The hardships I'll face is what I want compensation for. Not for doing my job." The words came out harsh, but they had to be said. "Do I have your word?" he asked.

Porter nodded.

Byrd couldn't prevent or hide his surprise. He wanted verification. "Is that a yes, sir?"

"Yes," Porter said. "You have my word."

Byrd looked back down the passageway, then at Porter. "I can't reveal how I know this, and I can't even prove it, but somebody much higher up the chain is pulling the strings behind the scenes."

Porter climbed down from his conning chair and stepped within inches of Byrd. "Are you saying one of the officers in my ward room is responsible?"

"No, sir. It's worse than that."

"What's worse than that?"

Byrd spent the next twenty minutes laying out the structure and operations, the logistics and the bookkeeping that lead back to Senior.

"What proof do you have?"

"Proof? There's no proof. He's the chief of police, for Christ's sake. You expect me to go pick his lock when he's at GQ or something? Proof."

"So this is a hunch?"

"I know for a fact. And I'm willing to bet my balls."

"Okay, Petty Officer Byrd. We'll see about that. On two conditions. One: you will not be paid a penny until after the arrests. Two: you will perform whatever investigation is necessary, with my full support, of course."

"That's asking quite a lot of me, sir."

"Did you or did you not just bet your balls, Byrd? This is how the wager plays out. I've been burned once already by bad information and I can't let it happen again. If you're so sure, I'll give you whatever clearances you may require. But if this hunch of yours doesn't pan out, it's your face attached to it, not mine."

It was past taps, so the overhead lights in the berthing compartment had been switched to the red glow of auxiliary lighting reserved for sleeping hours. Applewhite stood at his open rack locker straining through the shadows of the red light as he rummaged through his socks. Taped to the underside of the rack above his was a poster of a fine sister in a loincloth. He'd stare at her every night before falling asleep. He didn't know her name, never really cared. Tonight he was focused on socks. He needed not a pair, but to find one sock without holes in it.

The dim light in the space allowed him to see that not many of the fellas were in their racks. Instead of snores and random farts, Applewhite heard waves of laughter as they crowded into the thirty-seat lounge on the starboard side, playing cards and talking shit. In a perfect world, Wooly would be up on the mess deck waiting for him with the other nine guys he'd selected. The odds were longer on that than any poker hand Wooly probably held at that moment.

All the brothers knew something was about to happen, but only ten of them knew any of the details. No one was more excited than Applewhite. He had that sensation like he used to get at Christmastime, even when he knew the gifts would be light, because back then he clung to the hope that his mother and his aunt would deliver a great surprise. This would be a different kind of gift tonight, but it felt exactly the same. His blood frothed at the thought of getting in his shots, making his point, and getting away with it. The physical display of his initiative and resourcefulness might make Surico more inclined to bring him in on an even higher payday. More money meant bringing home bigger surprises at Christmas. He rolled his head from shoulder to shoulder to stretch his neck, relieve the tension, calm himself a little.

Despite the anger and excitement pulsing through him, he had to keep the situation in perspective and not get carried away and kill the guy and get himself locked up in Leavenworth for good, though that would be a hell of a lot physically closer to home than being all the way over here. There was only forty-five minutes between the military prison and his hometown, but on the inside of the correctional barracks he'd have zero interaction with the outside world. That's why he needed Wooly and the rest of the boys.

He found a black wool sock that was intact and long enough to suit his purposes. He flipped the sock over his shoulder as he reached for a new bar of soap from his locker and unwrapped it so it would slide through the sock easier. His sinuses were too burned out from the industrial detergent powders down in the ship's laundry to notice any fragrance from the bar of soap, but that wasn't the point. A padlock or two would do more damage, but this was a message first and payback second. He pulled the sock off his shoulder and slid the soap into the opening. The sock stretched from the weight of the bar like a snake eating a rabbit until it bottomed out at the end, hanging at the side of his leg. Applewhite hefted it in his palm. He wrapped the wool around his hand once and felt the kinetic energy in the other end. With a smooth backhand motion, he smacked the improvised truncheon into the stand-up locker to his right. The locker must've been full, because the noise didn't ring out but rather thudded as it left a dent. The sound and the dent would've been greater if he'd shoved padlocks in there, but the soap was plenty of power and strength.

Just past midnight, in the lounge between the racks and the ladder well, Applewhite found Wooly covered in a white sheet with eyeholes cut out, hamming it for laughs with the other fellas.

That all-day scent of sweat hung in the air. He no longer registered the smell of jet fuel, but the animal musk of this many brothers packed this closely for this long never escaped him. Their asses covered every horizontal surface of Formica and Naugahyde, while many others stood around watching Wooly play the fool.

"What the fuck is this?" Applewhite asked.

All the brothers got quiet.

Wooly looked back at Applewhite through the crudely cut eyeholes and cocked his head. "Lighten up, man," he called through the sheet. "It's a disguise. And second of all, it's Halloween, my man. Trick or motherfucking treat. You know what I'm talking about?"

Applewhite felt like backhanding Wooly with the bar of soap. Instead, he tried to smell the soap through the sock. This did nothing to calm him. He reached out and snatched the sheet off Wooly. "The fuck's the matter with you?"

"What?" Wooly asked, grabbing for the sheet as it flew over his head and out of reach.

"Ain't none of us using sheets for nothing. When word gets out it was a bunch of niggers in sheets, the first place they'll come asking questions is the laundry. I ain't having it. So stop with this bullshit." Applewhite wadded up the sheet and dropped it in the trash barrel on his way toward the ladder, leaving Wooly and the others to follow.

Applewhite wasn't concerned with the rest of the guys, but Wooly couldn't have been happy about getting blasted like that. For a few steps, Applewhite wanted to turn and check on his buddy, but instead kept walking. This was his mission and only ten of them, counting Wooly, were meant to follow. It had to be a small group so they could stay tight and under the radar. They had to be guys he could trust. He had too much riding on the agreement with Surico to let some out-of-control brother wreck things out of revenge or opportunism.

Applewhite stopped in the passageway. He wanted to jump into the party mode they were all in, but he locked his facial features instead and crossed his arms over his chest. There must've been fifty brothers crowded there. Way more than he planned. He couldn't call it off without looking weak, and he really wanted to get that Elvis-looking motherfucker.

"Listen up," he hollered. "You ten," he pointed to Wooly and the original group, "continue forward two at a time, just like the racist fucking law says." His lungs caught awkwardly at the end of the sentence. He'd never given orders like this. He'd pushed around dozens of guys one at a time, and had felt comfortable doing so, but he never pictured himself in the leadership role, especially since there were older guys who were obeying him. He could live with that.

"The rest of you brothers hang back and stand sentry so we don't get ambushed down there. When we come out, you block for us all the way to the end zone of the aft mess deck."

The order was met with a smattering of, "Right on!" and "Black power!"

Simultaneously, a chill ran up his back and a flash of heat rose from his gut to his neck. It dissipated by the time he caught up to Wooly at the entrance to a white berthing space almost to the foc'sle. He walked to the front of them. "Okay, listen. Our brothers got our back, but if a honky wakes up from the noise and becomes a witness, Wooly will turn on the lights so he can see all of us. He'll never know for sure which one of us did what. You dig?"

The group of ten became a chorus of, "Hell yeah," "Yeah, man," "Damn straight," and "Black power!"

Wooly's voice was twice as loud as the rest.

Applewhite didn't tell them about the potential payday shortfalls or the dangers they may face down there. Explaining anything would only weaken his position. Instead he smacked the bar of soap into his palm a few times. He told himself this wouldn't be like the trouble back home in Lawrence. This was just one fucking guy. He'd get in and get out. Make an example out of him for all other crewmen to keep in mind.

"Remember boys," he said, "this is payback and not random

shit." His stomach felt like a volcano. He wasn't hungry or nervous, but rather dealing with the stress of keeping both extremes in check in order to collect that three grand from Surico. He could bring the best Christmas in the world back home to Kansas if everything went according to plan. He needed Wooly to pipe the hell down so nobody fucked this up for him.

He walked over to Wooly, pulled him aside. "I'm counting on you to make sure all our brothers stay cool. We don't want attention or trouble."

"I dig, Rufus, my man. We cool."

The eleven of them climbed down into the berthing compartment—a space with a hundred rows of racks stacked three high.

He followed the directions one of his guys gave him and made his way through the red glow of after-hour lighting and sounds of snoring, the smell of dirty socks and farts.

He found his target. It was a middle rack. Applewhite reached under the guy's closed curtain and clamped hard on the guy's throat until he gurgled. Applewhite slid open the curtain. The red light was bright enough in the aisle to see the Elvis hair without a flashlight. He tightened his grip on the guy's throat until more gurgles came out. Applewhite reared back and punched the guy in the face. It was solid contact that recoiled up his wrist and forearm, but he wasn't sure where it landed. He leaned into the guy's face. "You ever speak against me or my friends to anyone it'll be a knife blade where my hand is now. You got that? Keep your fucking mouth shut or you're dead."

The guy didn't move or try to speak.

Applewhite punched him again. His fists slammed into white flesh, his knuckles sore from hitting skull instead of landing clean shots to his face and neck. There was no precision. This wasn't an event he trained for, rather a wave of aggression growing and gaining momentum.

The guy's nose took the bulk of the punches that made solid contact. It wasn't a clean break, but Applewhite felt a good amount of give upon each successive impact. "That's the message, now here's the lesson." He pulled the guy out of his rack by his greasy Elvis hair and his T-shirt and stuck a boot in his ribs over and over. Each grunt fueled Applewhite's anger. Each kick was payback for every honky racist bastard who called him "nigger" or "boy" or spit on his mother or refused him service, or who had called him coon, darkie, spear-chucker, to every white woman who wrapped her arms around her pocketbook when he walked by; every teacher who called him stupid; every cop who presumed him guilty; every khaki-wearing mother-fucker in the entire Navy and the Pentagon for forcing guys like him into the menial chores of washing and cooking instead of being on the bridge or in CIC.

The guy cried out, "No. Please, God, stop," over and over again.

Wooly yelled, "Kill that honky motherfucker!"

The yelling woke sailors in the surrounding bunks. One of them reached out of his top bunk in the red glow of the after-taps lighting and grabbed Wooly by the back of his collar. "What the fuck are you doing in my berthing compartment?"

Wooly twisted himself free and climbed up to the top rack, reared back, and pounded the guy with a single punch to the jaw that simultaneously shut him up and knocked him out. "Happy Halloween, motherfucker."

The other brothers roared to action, hollering, "Black power!" as they threw punches into random racks and dragged half-asleep honkies to the deck, some requiring a struggle, but others with ease, and pulverized them with their fists and their boots.

The Elvis guy was unconscious. Applewhite hoped it was from the pain and not from being dead. There was too much riding on this. He wanted to calm his crew, but he had to make sure this bastard wasn't dead. He sat on the edge of a bottom bunk, dropped his weapon, and reached for the guy's arm. He placed his fingers near the wrist and was relieved to feel its rhythm. It made him think it wasn't too late. Then, Apple-white's energy plummeted. In the red light and smell of dirty socks and ass-gas, he watched the black-on-white retaliation—listened to the smacks on chins and bare abdomens—the hollers, yells, blood squishing. This was going to kill any chance he had at a big Christmas because Surico's deal had just been broken.

Part of him wanted to grab Wooly's shoulder and say, "Let's get the hell out of here." Neither of them needed any trouble with Senior, the XO, or any of the MAAs. But instead of running around and smacking every brother in an attempt to corral them back up the ladder and out of the berthing compartment, he stood back and watched them do their damage.

Because of his intensity of focus in the dim red light, Applewhite never saw the fist coming at his left temple and cheekbone. The force of the punch knocked his head to the right with a violent whip of his neck. He straightened and shook off the surprise of it and unleashed his aggression on the honky who sucker-punched him. He grabbed the guy's dog tags with his left hand and threw haymakers with his right. Landing one after the other into the damn guy's face until both surfaces were bloody and raw.

He heard footfalls coming down the ladder. More brothers stormed in. They must've followed the original ten.

The berthing compartment erupted into a flurry of fists and elbows flying. There was a chorus of "Fuck you, motherfucker!" and "Black power!" They swung brass nozzles, dogging wrenches, pipes, and lengths of chain into the sheet metal racks and lockers. The noise gave new meaning to steel drum. None of it drowned out the hollering that turned into a chant.

The white guys were unarmed and caught off guard.

One of them threw a full bottle of aftershave that bounced off the back of Wooly's head and cracked open when it hit the deck.

The noise brought more white guys forward.

Applewhite and his boys were outnumbered, but they all just started swinging.

CHAPTER 22

Porter sat at his desk in his stateroom, shirtless and barefoot, stifling yawns. He kept the overhead lights on as he wrote with black ink in a brand-new Navy logbook just small enough to fit in the safe in his stateroom. Despite the heat and being tired, he felt himself smiling as he stroked each word. Having an accurate list of facts related to the drug ring and all suspects could be instrumental in piecing together the whole thing. That certainly was worth losing a little sleep. These kinds of sacrifices were nothing new to Porter. He'd always had to study longer and train harder than his white classmates and fellow pilots, because no matter how he fared intellectually, any shortcomings would not be attributed to lack of effort. But it was exhausting.

He seemed more tired every day. He needed to sleep six hours to feel as refreshed as three used to leave him. He needed more coffee every morning. He'd pour a cup and not even sit, just stand there and down it as quickly as the temperature would allow. Then he'd pour a refill before thinking about food.

He angled the chair at his desk to be closer to the path of the air vent and wrote in the logbook, hoping to get all the fragments out of his head and onto paper, where he could make sense of it all. As a physical record of every name and detail he had bouncing around his brain, he even included the details about the bribe he agreed to pay Petty Officer Byrd. Before the ink even dried, he thought about ripping out the pages. He grabbed their edges and tugged lightly. The pages didn't give. The captain was the only one who knew the combination to his XO's safe. Porter envisioned showing the captain that page someday soon. In his mind, the old man would be impressed by the initiative his XO took for the benefit of the ship. Even if he wasn't, the simple act of generating such documentation might help him get to the truth. This log was a way of getting his shit in one sock, as his father used to say.

He was disrupted by the ringing phone. It was rare to get a call that time of night.

"Porter," he said as he pressed the phone to his ear.

"Sir, Lieutenant Wolinski calling from the bridge. Sorry to disturb you, but there's trouble on the second deck."

Porter's first assumption was a couple of crewmen fighting. That wasn't uncommon. Penalties were often days in the brig, which Porter didn't like, but he left it in place so as not to disrupt equilibrium between the captain and crew. "It's a little late to contact me about another fistfight isn't it, Wally?"

"It's much bigger than that, Mr. Porter."

"Are you talking a brawl? Is Senior Chief Rawlings on the scene yet?"

"I don't know what to call it, sir, but it's big and clearly racial."

Porter's anger rose and he squeezed the phone. "Are you talking about a lynch mob?"

"I don't know how to say this."

"Just say it!" Porter shouted.

The other end of the line went silent for a moment before Wally cleared his throat and then croaked, "The blacks are attacking the whites, sir."

A rush of adrenaline followed those words. It surged through him with equal parts anger and sadness. Porter hoped with everything in him that Wally was exaggerating the altercation, but deep down he felt the powder keg had finally ignited. His head shook until he realized it was. The thought pressed him in the chest with the heaviest sadness he'd ever known.

"Tell the captain I'm going to handle it personally," he said.

"He wants to talk to you. Standby."

The next voice Porter heard was that of Captain Holt. "Smokey, you know damn well that your station under these conditions is on this bridge. I recommend you hustle."

Porter imagined the captain half reclined in his chair, the heel of one shoe hanging on the foot rail, the other resting atop a mounted emergency light fixture.

"I've been briefed on the incident on the second deck," Porter said. "I was just telling the OOD that I'm going down to handle it personally."

The captain laughed. Porter heard the man's beard stubble brush the transmitter like sandpaper. "Is that right?"

"Captain Holt, this is the sole reason I'm here. Let me do this."

"Your station is on this bridge...but these are extenuating circumstances, I will have to give you that, Smokey. Yes. Very well. Okay, hotshot. Let's try it your way first. Go down there and see what you can do. Don't put yourself in jeopardy, but squash this thing. If you need backup, they'll be ready."

Porter's chest filled with the kind of air he usually felt before climbing into his plane. This mission was completely different, but the urgency and the fear were the same. "Aye, sir."

"You've got twenty minutes or I'm calling in the Marines," the captain said and hung up.

Porter slowly reached the phone to its stanchion-mounted cradle as he pictured the Marines being dispatched—fistfights and tools being thrown since there were no rocks or bottles. Porter longed for the days when sports and war were the only acceptable outlets for violence.

He reached for the shirt draped over the back of his desk chair and slipped it over his shoulders. Each button was an opportunity to imagine the worst.

Porter's ribcage clenched as it had while absorbing G-forces.

Unlike flying though, he couldn't readily pull out of this nosedive.

He didn't know how the crew might react to his presence. If he went down there, they could conceivably turn on him and kill him, or take him hostage. The thought of that made the skin on the back of his neck tense and he began to sweat. But, if he could bring this outburst under control and restore order, his service jacket would look even more impressive when his next review came around.

More than for his own safety or the way this might look for his fitness report at the end of the year, he needed to keep his crew safe and healthy so they could do their jobs and get back to their families when they finally returned to San Diego.

CHAPTER 23

Byrd climbed out of his middle rack and checked his watch in the glow of red light from the main aisle, happy to see he had almost four more hours to sleep. He stepped into his shower shoes for the fifty-yard walk to the head. He didn't have to piss, but he was up and figured he might indulge in a little quiet time on the shitter. Something wasn't sitting right in his stomach. He didn't know what the problem could be. He scratched at the stretched elastic of his boxer shorts as he walked.

Someone had left a year-old copy of *Reader's Digest* on the deck near the shitter, so he read about research being done on moon rocks. Science never appealed to Byrd, but he found the notion of bringing rocks back from a different planet a pretty big deal and worth reading about. The entertainment proved more productive than his bowels. He wiped, flushed, and dropped the magazine where he'd found it before washing his hands at the first in a row of sinks. He could've hopped in the shower and made some drain babies, but sleep was more important than pleasure, at that moment. As he rinsed the powdered soap from his fingers, four black crewmen walked in. Sweat beaded on their foreheads and their nostrils flared with each shallow breath.

Byrd felt naked in his underwear and shower shoes. He sort of recognized the fourth guy, remembered talking to him in the chow line a couple times. He was a ship's bosun with a dream of becoming a signalman. Hoarry, if he recalled correctly. A respectable kid. Clean-cut. Squared-away. Byrd wouldn't speak the kid's name now and acknowledge that he recognized him. Nothing good could come from that, for either of them. Instead, he said, "I don't want no trouble, fellas."

"Is that right, honky?"

As Byrd wasn't wearing his shirt or badge, he had no way of knowing if they recognized him as an MAA. "Straight up," he said. "Let's part strangers and we're good."

The main guy stepped up and waved a dogging wrench in Byrd's face. "How are we supposed to know you won't report us if we let you go?"

"First of all, I haven't seen you do anything wrong. And second, because I don't know your names. If anyone asks, I'll just use that bullshit white-boy line that you all look alike to me."

They laughed. The guy with the dogging wrench stepped close enough that Byrd felt the ions radiating off the rusted steel. "Is that right?"

"Won't tell this to nobody." Byrd's voice rippled in his throat, which undermined his attempt to look cool. "Trust me on that," he said with more authority.

"Can't trust none of you white devils, man," one of the other three guys called out.

"Yeah. Let's fuck him up," said another.

Byrd didn't know if it was Hoarry or not. It no longer mattered. In another situation, Byrd might've informed them that they were messing with a master-at-arms and their trouble would be exponential, as a result, but he kept his mouth shut. No need volunteering to be a trophy when he could get away with being just another obstacle.

The guy with the wrench held up his free hand. "I got this shit," without ever turning to them. He kept his focus on Byrd as he leaned in, their faces inches apart, the wrench held between them. "I think you need a taste of what would happen if you said anything."

"I won't say shit."

"I know you won't," he said, and then cracked the dogging wrench across Byrd's nose.

Byrd made no sound in response. He felt the blood flowing a split-second before the pain registered. As he covered his nose with his hands, blood filled his cupped palms and flooded his airway. Through the building pain and the spray of blood in the air, Byrd stomped the guy's instep and kicked his other ankle out from under him. Before the guy hit the deck, the other three charged. Byrd pushed one guy off with a forearm to the chin and threw blood at the others with each blind jab in the air. They all backed up then. Byrd hoped they'd move on in search of easier prey.

All four guys regrouped and faced Byrd, standing with fists at their sides, squeezed so hard the skin over their knuckles stretched yellow. They charged all at once.

Byrd didn't wait for them to get to him; he charged at them. Even in the red glow of after-hours lighting, he saw the whites all around their eyes and horror on their faces.

Their heads collided.

Blood and sweat smeared into Byrd's eyes and obscured his vision. He connected a couple of times with his own fists, but couldn't tell if he'd hit bone, skull, or parts of the bulkhead.

His jaw had held up well, until he took one on the right side. The only fight he'd ever lost was to a southpaw who clocked him on the right side. The percussive shock cranked Byrd's head sideways with enough velocity to crimp his brainstem. Motor function was lost. Gravity took him down, and once on the deck, kicks and boot heels pummeled without pause. Each kick to the ribs felt like a car crash.

He wasn't able to protect his head for long. Both forearms felt broken. His back was hamburger and every partial breath carried wads of fuel-stained air. He felt the cracks in his ribs, like skewers into his lungs. His first thought wasn't of his pain or how to survive this beating, but rather of May May and the sudden panic that he wouldn't be around to help her and her family. The blows continued. There was no way to know how long he huddled there, absorbing kicks and punches and elbows, as well as insults and spit.

At some point the abuse stopped and a new voice leaned over Byrd. "No. No, motherfuckers. Not this one. He's okay. Don't fuck with him no more."

Byrd grunted. He had no idea if it was anything intelligible, but through the blood smeared across his eyes and into his ears, he recognized Applewhite's voice and saw the outline of his face. He wanted to thank him. Before he could sit up, the sound of foot traffic passed by his ear and they left.

His next thought was of needing to warn the rest of the crew. He rolled onto his back, sore everywhere, but grateful the beating had stopped. The only parts of his body not bleeding were quickly swelling and he was fading. He forced himself to roll over onto his stomach. The piss-stained deck felt like a vice on his damaged ribs. With all his strength, he pushed. His left arm felt broken, but there was enough strength to lift his chest and hips high enough to crawl out into the passageway in search of help.

Senior stood inside the brig staring down at Brackert curled up on the foam pad on the deck in his cell. "In all the dumb stunts I've seen during my Navy career, and all the high-functioning retards I've encountered, nothing is more baffling to me than what your dumb ass tried to do. For the life of me I can't understand a man wanting to blow up the boat he is on. It makes about as much sense as shitting on your dinner plate."

Brackert remained in his fetal position. "It's all Chrissy's fault," he said. "She's the one responsible for all the bad shit."

It took everything in Senior to resist the urge to kick the fucker's head through the bars. Senior wasn't usually down there at that hour, but he'd gotten wind of Applewhite's plan.

He had many informants on both sides of the color line, and it was one of the blacks who'd told him about the rumor of a blanket party. Senior wanted to be in position in case things got out of hand.

He grew tired of listening to the caged animal ramble about some girl named Chrissy, so he nodded toward the Marine on watch and went to his office.

At his desk, he unlocked a drawer and strapped on his holster and .45, intent on keeping the peace.

The brothers were outnumbered, but through vengeance and the element of surprise, they swung fists and weapons and dominated the berthing compartment.

The unprepared white guys proved no match for the rampaging black crew, who pulled guys out of their racks with a series of tugs, slugs, yanks, kicks, and punches.

Applewhite left the Elvis-looking motherfucker bleeding in his aisle. Applewhite's chest swelled with the satisfaction. Surico would be pissed that the guy responsible for ratting on him had been dealt with even though he would never make that mistake again. Applewhite's rage burned in his veins until he sprang into the main aisle, looking for other white skulls to crack.

It no longer mattered if what they were doing was right or wrong. None of those white guys did anything to Applewhite, but they were all part of the system that made life more difficult than it needed to be for him and his brothers. He spit on mattresses and pillows as he passed. Wiped his feet on blankets. He'd make every one of the white bastards pay if he could, even if that meant death. This was one small step in that direction. "Make whitey pay," he yelled. None of them were totally innocent.

After five minutes or so, Applewhite grabbed Wooly by the arm. "Spread the word to the brothers that we're moving on."

They moved as a mob through the berthing space to the far end and out that door, up the ladder, down the passageway, hooting and hollering and ripping memos and schedules off of squadron room doors. Some grabbed dogging wrenches and firefighting nozzles and bashed any white boy in their path.

They walked into workshops and storage rooms and trashed them. Airplane parts would take days to reorganize, especially the small parts, loose in bins. Those spilled like boxes of nails. The mob cheered and pounded on bulkheads, pipes, electrical panels, and transformers. He recognized the collective breathing—all those brothers around him taking in oxygen and using it to cool their engines reminded him of the riot in his hometown when he was a kid.

They stopped at a ladder well in the passageway. "That's another berthing compartment down there, right?"

"A bunch of office boys down there," Wooly said. "White ones."

Applewhite dapped Wooly. "They's about to be shitting themselves."

"Walk on with your bad self," Wooly said as he pulled a firefighting foam applicator off the bulkhead. The Navy called it a wand, but it was a pipe bent like a hockey stick and with a chunk of brass the size of a grapefruit at the business end.

Applewhite took the steps confidently into the berthing compartment. A group of thirty brothers crowded behind him. The shouts and smacks echoed down the narrow aisles of racks.

On the opposite end, a white boy lunged and flipped on all the light switches, flooding the room in fluorescent light as bright as daylight. "The blacks are on a rampage," he hollered. "Wake your asses up and defend yourselves."

Applewhite saw a pale postal clerk cowering in his rack so pathetically that he looked like a little kid during a storm. At first the image made Applewhite recall his childhood summers down at his aunt's house in Alabama. But after that initial flash, Applewhite saw his own son being afraid, all alone. "It's your lucky day," he told the postal clerk and then walked off, only to turn back to see Wooly holding onto the top rack for the leverage of getting enormous kicks into the postal clerk's bottom rack.

Applewhite kept walking to the sound of the postal clerk calling out, "Oh, God, please, no!"

Applewhite figured there were more than two hundred brothers fighting all over the ship by this point. He knew it wouldn't take long before the bridge got wind of it and dispatched the Marines. Applewhite went from group to group of rioting brothers and told half to meet him on the aft mess deck and the other half on the foc'sle, figuring the split would confuse the Marines and maybe buy them time.

With the red devils he'd swallowed fully circulating through his system, he felt invincible and hungry for blood. He didn't question why they looked to him as their leader. He took a couple more red devils and told Wooly, "Find that punk-ass mess crank that denied me a second sandwich that day and bring him to the aft mess deck."

Surico went forward to check out the scene on the foc'sle. They were all going to be in trouble over this, but there wasn't anything he could do to stop it. He figured he'd allow himself to enjoy witnessing as much of it as he could. He was sick and tired of the bullshit his damn self, but he didn't have the anger about it that the younger bucks did. It was like the ship's softball games. He didn't play anymore, but he always went to watch because he loved the game.

On his way to the foc'sle he figured he'd better take a piss before going up there, so he turned down and athwart ship's passageway to find a head. Before he got there, he saw a white dude crawling toward him.

Through the blood smeared all over his face there was no way to recognize a face. He wore no uniform, only boxer shorts. Surico enjoyed seeing one of the white crew so badly beaten, without having personally thrown a single punch.

Surico looked past the blood, the sweat, and the swelling and recognized the cool MAA laying facedown on the deck. A wound in his scalp bled in a river toward a deck drain. "Byrd?" Surico asked. This wasn't just a white boy to Surico. This was a business partner. They had a lot of money on the line. The more he looked at Byrd, the more he wondered how much time he'd be laid up in sick bay and if he might still be able to orchestrate everything from behind the scenes—under the radar, but still as they'd planned.

Byrd reached up and grabbed the bell-bottom near Surico's shin. He saw not fear or even pain in the man's eyes, rather only resignation. The guy's eyes were swollen to look like boiled onions with knife slits. Surico expected to hear pleas of, "Help me!" or, "Get a corpsman!" Instead, the guy said, "Tell May I'm sorry."

Surico didn't know what that meant. Despite the business at stake, he couldn't risk being seen helping a white boy. Surico tucked his hands into his hip pockets and stared at the guy. If the situation had been reversed, Surico was sure, this dude wasn't likely to help a black man.

Byrd remained semi-conscious as Surico picked him up in a fireman-carry and hauled him to the door just outside sick bay. He knocked and ran off without looking back, hopeful the Byrd man would receive the medical care he needed.

The captain sat upright in his chair on the bridge, his fingers pressed together and fanned under his chin.

Lieutenant Commander O'Neil, the officer of the watch, walked over. "The corporal of the watch is on the line and standing by, sir."

"Send them to the flight deck and have all the lights turned on. Light up the hangar bays and the flight deck like noontime."

O'Neil straightened for a second and then leaned in again. "Don't you want the Marines on the mess deck, captain?"

The captain didn't look at O'Neil. "I want them protecting

the planes."

"What about the crewmen, sir?"

The captain swiveled to face O'Neil. "Launching planes pays the bills, buddy boy. Besides, if the coloreds are in a tizzy, armed Marines will only burn their asses more. I'd like to avoid publicly acknowledging whatever this skirmish may be, and I damn sure don't want the admiral being bothered with any of this. I've personally sent Mr. Porter to diffuse the situation."

This was the ultimate test for his XO. The man had yet to dismantle the drug ring, so Holt was curious to see if ol' Smokey might redeem himself by calming the irate horde of his people.

CHAPTER 24

They stood on the aft mess deck, more than a hundred strong, and caught their collective breath, more exhilarated than exhausted. Like most of them, Applewhite was sweaty with splotches of blood—mostly not his own—on his white T-shirt. These men had gathered there because Applewhite had told them to. It was his meeting. This was his gang. He'd dispatched the rest of his brothers to the foc'sle. He loved the feeling of being in charge of all the angry brothers. This group stood among the empty tables and chairs beneath fluorescent bulbs that made their sweaty skin shine. A clock mounted high on a bulkhead read 0210. The air smelled of pot smoke. Their fists were still clenched. Applewhite wanted another couple of red devils.

His confidence in Wooly bringing back a white boy was strong, but there was no certainty that it would be the right one. There were already dozens of white boys laid out along the decks. Applewhite had no idea the amount of damage they'd caused already, but they were just getting started.

Someone set a firefighting nozzle on a table. The nozzle was ten pounds of brass, shined by one of the crewmen within the last seventy-two hours, if Applewhite had to guess. If it had been used as a weapon during the rampage, it wasn't bloodied. Applewhite walked past and picked it up by the water-flow handle and kept walking. Its weight tugged Applewhite's arm, which sent a signal to his brain in the form of a memory. Pain. The physical kind that accompanied a dislocated shoulder as a fourteen-year-old. The white cop never got in trouble over the incident that left Applewhite's reach shorter on that side, which ended his basketball career, but there was no use complaining about any of it. It was better to pretend the whole thing never happened.

Within ten minutes, Wooly and Ray dragged in the blond-headed honky mess crank. At the sight of a white boy, the crowd of brothers erupted with hoots and hollers Applewhite felt all his organs and tissue lift in more happiness than he'd felt in almost a year. He wanted to smile but had to stay strong.

His boys threw off heat and the anticipation of exacting more vengeance. The deck had a pulse from all the energy in the room. The icemaker did its thing.

Applewhite couldn't ignore the good work of getting the right guy, instead he channeled his happiness into an elaborate dap with Wooly that lasted thirty seconds straight. "On the black-hand side," he said, slapping knuckle-to-knuckle.

Fear and acne scars covered the blond kid's face. He'd been dragged out of his top rack to flop to the deck, banging a shoulder violently on the way down. At one point, two black guys shoved him along with his arms bent back so tightly the pain shifted to numbness. He wore only Navy-issue briefs, with *ROLLINS* stenciled on the white fabric across his wide ass. His torso was thick and the skin flabby enough to hide the waistband. He'd always had a sweet tooth and working in the galley gave him opportunities to swipe squares of sheet cake and donuts from the rolling racks outside the bakery.

He wished that was why he was up here. He didn't know what was about to happen, but by the looks of all the busted-up white guys limping or laid out in the passageway, it wasn't anything good. The two black guys dragged him into a section of the aft mess deck, where a whole gang of black guys huddled together. He was shoved into the center of the crowd. He covered his crotch with both hands in preparation for the onslaught. He'd heard of lynchings of black people and understood the black crew's anger, but he'd never even met a black person before he joined the Navy and didn't really care one way or another about them. In place of genuine opinions, he just echoed whatever his buddies said, and he had no idea why he was singled out for added attention, when other white crewmen were simply dismissed.

They shoved Rollins down to his knees by an ammo elevator. He knew an ass beating was coming and he just wanted to get it over with. Get his cuts stitched up in sick bay, maybe an icepack for a lump he'd likely get on his noggin from a kick or two, and then get back to his rack for some much-needed sleep. He would heal while all these misbehaving darkies were getting their clocks cleaned at Captain's Mast.

As Rufus Applewhite emerged from the crowd surrounding him, Rollins recognized him from that incident with the sandwich a few months earlier. Rollins didn't want to think about that altercation. He wanted to climb into his rack and dream of sitting across from Linda Leaf, the girl he'd taken to two movies and three different restaurants. They were never steady or intimate, but he'd gotten some over-the-sweater boob in the movies a couple of times and a kiss good night every time. She promised to be on the pier when he returned, but he never even got a letter from her. He'd convinced himself that she'd be waiting for him on the pier as the *Salvation* pulled in, maybe wearing a yellow dress and those little round sunglasses, but he couldn't see any of that now. Instead, his field of vision was completely dark.

Applewhite swung the brass firefighting nozzle with all the rage and revenge in him. Just before impact, a lone voice shouted, "No!"

It was too late to stop the momentum even if he'd wanted to, and it wasn't until after brass met bone that Applewhite saw the XO charging through the crowd. All the brothers cheered, some hooted or whistled, as the kid's body slumped, and his shoulder hit the deck.

Applewhite took no pleasure in the act. The satisfaction of crossing a task off a list, perhaps, but no true enjoyment, and not just because of the numbing effects of the pills. The pills did, however, prevent him from worrying about repercussions. He knew there'd be some price to pay, but it wasn't time to worry about that yet. For now, his mind allowed him to believe he'd hallucinated seeing the XO standing there. But there was no mistaking the nausea that washed over the XO's face. He was real.

Porter covered his mouth with the back of his fist. His eye twitched. The icemaker hissed. The brothers stood in random packs among the tables and chairs and shifted side-to-side. They opened and closed their fists. Some held weapons improvised from firefighting equipment and aircraft tie-down chains.

Applewhite couldn't think with all the adrenaline and noise. He dropped the nozzle and the brass thunked hard onto the deck. He was in no mood to speak, let alone shout, so he kept pushing a hand downward until the air got quiet. He expected Porter to rant and rave about the blond-headed mess crank slumped by the ammo elevator.

Porter still looked nauseous, but also with determination set in his jaw. "You boys are having one hell of a Halloween," he said calmly, despite the stiff jaw.

The brothers stared at Porter.

The XO could react any number of ways, and Applewhite had no idea which way it would be. With Porter being such an Uncle Tom, Applewhite expected him to run and call in the Marines. He didn't turn to run though. He was a big dude. Applewhite wondered if he should storm over and take him into custody himself. But of all the words spoken about the man since he'd arrived aboard ship, none of them ever called him stupid. Applewhite didn't figure there was such a thing as a dumb pilot, let alone one as highly decorated as this Uncle Tom.

Applewhite walked up to the man. Stood toe-to-toe with him and stared him in the eye. Before either man flinched, Applewhite nodded and then relaxed onto the top of a table and rested his elbow on his knee, intent on observing the man's next move. Meanwhile, a tornado churned through his brain, his mouth felt like it was full of sand. Red devils always did that to him, but he reached into his pocket and popped a couple more into his mouth and dry swallowed. By his estimation, he had fourteen left. That would be enough to get him through the night under different circumstances, but the XO complicated things.

The crowd's energy pulsated.

"Go home, Uncle Tom!" a voice called out from the crowd.

"Let's kill that black honky, too!" another voice said.

An explosion of hoots and applause followed that suggestion. Brothers slapped palms and some banged tables with their weapons.

Applewhite felt throbbing in his chest. The way he responded would dictate the rest of his life. He might get away with killing that mess crank, but he didn't know if he could live with himself for taking out a brother that never did nothing to him. The red devils mixed with his anger and clouded his judgment, made it seem like a good idea to get the XO out of the way. The Navy couldn't give all the black crew the death penalty. And he'd already made peace with the fact he'd never be a suitable father to his kid. The enthusiasm of the crowd and the buzz of the pills was about the only thing he had going for him. He saw no reason why he shouldn't go all out.

The crowd chanted, "Put him down!"

All Applewhite had to do was lift his voice or snap his fingers and a dark tsunami would obliterate the XO.

Just then, Surico came into Applewhite's line of sight. Applewhite didn't know how long he'd been standing there, staring at him. But it was clear he saw Rollins on the deck and the XO looking worried. Applewhite held his place without movement.

Applewhite felt the pressure building up so strongly inside him that he spared Porter not because of Surico, or to spite what Wooly wanted, but because there weren't enough pills left on that ship to make him sink that far.

Porter had run to the aft mess deck as fast as he could, but he hadn't been fast enough to save a life. The brass nozzle had torn through the blond kid's skull, which had exploded blood and bone in all directions. He died right before their eyes. The impact of brass and bone knocked the wind out of Porter in that same instant it knocked the life out of the kid. Porter blinked often to keep his eyes dry. If he'd been smart, he would've ducked out unseen. Porter hadn't meant to call out, but he was unable to stop himself. It was too late now with his torso and limbs locked rigid as the group turned to face him. His mouth ran dry, and no matter how many times he licked his lips, he couldn't end the discomfort.

The group of black sailors converged like fingers closing to make a fist.

Porter felt breath all around him. His eye twitched and sweat ran down his back. He'd never wanted a drink more in his life.

Applewhite's chin was raised high enough to reveal flaring nostrils. Porter assumed Applewhite was high on something because his eyes were glossed over and dark. The smell of marijuana floated in the space between them and the low overhead, but it had to be something more.

Despite the blood splattered on the stomach, side, and shoulder of his T-shirt, Applewhite appeared simultaneously calm and out of his mind.

Porter forced himself to breathe deeply. *Stay calm*, he told himself. Meanwhile, his focus jerked from Applewhite and Wooly to the rest of the room—at the crowd and for the nearest egress. The noise he heard was his own grinding teeth.

Applewhite and Wooly exchanged words, but Porter wasn't listening. While he was surprised to see them fighting amongst themselves, he just couldn't stop looking over toward the dead kid near the ammo elevator.

Each black man in this group was a stick of dynamite to Porter. Individually they could make some noise and do some damage, but collectively they could change minds Navy-wide. Nation-wide.

He had to act quickly, but he couldn't just pull rank and yell at them. This didn't seem a crowd in the mood to honor the chain of command any longer. He could plead or reason, but that would make him appear weak, and this kind of mob feasted on weakness.

The crowd yelled, voices overlapping.

"Uncle Tom!"

"Black Elmer!"

"Whose side you on?"

"You with us or against us?"

The crowd swayed in an unconscious rhythm. Everything was closing in on him. Breathing became more difficult. The mood grew darker as they banged their weapons on the tabletops. He kept his back to the least threatening of the bunch. Felt his eye twitch. His upper lip and forehead puddled with sweat. The dryness in his mouth turned into a persistent knife in his throat. He wondered if they could see his knees shaking no matter how hard he tried to keep them still. His legs felt weak despite the adrenaline coursing through him. He'd never feared death before. Being confronted by the prospect of it now made him realize he had to win over every black man aboard that ship. At first he didn't speak, but he didn't try to hide either. He didn't shrink down or hug himself or wish this wasn't happening. Instead, he looked around, purposefully, taking time to look into faces long enough to establish eye contact. He forced the corner of his mouth into a smile.

Shouts of, "Kill the motherfucker, already!" and "Take him

out!" fired from the outer rows of brothers like shotgun blasts. Horror echoed in his brain at the thought of what they'd be capable of in their collective animosity. If they killed him tonight all their lives would be made worse. If he lived, he could help each of them improve their situations. The image of his father came sharply into focus. Porter shook his head to clear his mind of the hallucination, but the image stayed with him. He was doing something good here. Or could be. They'd never believe him if he said it, but who else would fight for them?

Porter had only one chance to win them over.

He composed himself as he cleared his throat. "I don't care," he said, pointing to a few of the guys in the front row, "what has happened up to this point. I just want to help you—"

"What you talking about helping us?" someone in the crowd hollered.

"I've been helping you since I landed on that flight deck above each of your damn heads," Porter said.

"You ain't helped nobody but yourself," the same voice said.

Porter shrugged off the insult.

"If you're slinging accusations like that around, I'll take it," he said. "What of it? There wasn't anyone else studying for my tests in college. And as far as I recall, I was the only one doing the work to get me into OCS and flight school. And I flew my own plane off this very damn flight deck, in the face of much danger, often. So unless you count the man upstairs as my copilot, I did help myself, but I did the work." Porter cleared his throat, changed tactics. "You see me as the XO, but would you believe I started loading cargo holds on airplanes when I was nine years old? My father was the janitor at the airport." Porter stood in the center of an opening in the crowd shaped like a banjo.

The table where Applewhite rested his ass occupied the top of the narrow part. His view of Porter unobstructed.

"Save your bullshit, Black Elmer!" Wooly's voice blasted from the front row of the crowd. He then stepped up to Applewhite. "Shit, Rufus. He sure as shit turn your ass in. You know what you gots to do now to this black honky."

Porter laughed again and scanned all the brothers standing around him. He rolled his eyes and exhaled, "My blood is just as African as each of yours. That's what makes this so laughable. You know, in most of the world I've got to face issues of black and white. With guys like all of you, I've got to face black and not-black-enough. The real world isn't as black and white as you boys make it out to be. Most of it is, like this fucking ship, gray. You've got to live in the gray, man."

"Tough shit."

"That's not our problem."

"We all took an oath to defend our country and each other," Porter said. "We are connected. You, me, us, and all our white shipmates. But I'm as black as you."

"Prove it!" somebody shouted from the back of the crowd, which was followed by half a dozen calls of, "Yeah!"

"What the fuck you doin', Rufus?" Wooly slapped his thigh with a hand he then pointed at the XO. "You best be getting all up in Uncle Tom's ass or this is some bullshit right here."

Applewhite nodded toward Surico and then turned to face Wooly. "When I want your opinion, I'll ask for it," he said.

Wooly spun to his left and stared down Applewhite, either daring him to fight or evaluating his own options.

Porter was the only one in that room who posed a risk of letting the word get out. Murder, under the UCMJ, carried a mandatory life sentence unless it was proven at court martial that it was premeditated, in which case Applewhite would receive the death penalty.

Porter felt the vacuum sucking hope from his skin, leaving him to confront the distinct possibility that they would kill him, too. He lifted his chin and looked out over the crowd.

"You ain't no brother!"

"Traitor!"

"Uncle Tom!"

The taunts were loud and plentiful. Porter's eye twitched, but he shrugged it away.

"My black brothers," Porter said at the top of his voice. "My job is being a commander in the Navy. My *life* is being a black man." He tore off his khaki shirt, buttons flying. He ripped open his T-shirt and shrugged out of it. He slapped his bare chest. "All black!"

Porter raised his fist overhead. "Black power!"

The crowd erupted with cheers. Applewhite's eyes were barely slits, but he smiled at Porter.

Part of Porter wasn't happy about giving them what they wanted. But a portion of doing it felt good. Their reaction lifted him three inches off the deck.

Porter turned his focus up toward his fist. "What does it mean?" he asked aloud. "I'll tell you what it means. It means different things to different people." He jutted his chin toward Wooly. "Which kind are you?"

"The fuck you talking about?"

"You boys have an opportunity to change the way white people think and the way they treat you. You can make life better for all black sailors—that is if you're not so bent on violence that you ignore good advice."

Porter no longer knew if he was doing this to save his own ass or prevent further violence in general and keep the ship's readiness intact. He didn't have a plan and he didn't care about taking credit or blame. He was too far in and it was working on almost everyone.

He still couldn't shake the image of that blond kid's death, murder...execution. That's what it was. If Porter survived this night, he'd see to it that Applewhite paid for his actions. The rest of them though, he'd help chip away at the foundational racism of which they were sick and tired.

"Just because you don't kill him," Wooly said, "don't mean I got to listen to him anymore." He scratched at his chin then removed a pick from his back pocket and stuck it in his hair.

Applewhite turned toward Wooly and threw two jabs into

his right eye socket. The jabs came rapid-fire, before Wooly had time to lift his arms to defend himself. Each jarring enough to knock the pick loose and to the deck. His eye puffed up almost immediately as millions of inflammatory cells converged to protect it from more abuse. "What did I tell you about your opinion?"

Wooly covered his eye and started to speak.

Porter pointed at Wooly. "Don't be ignorant, young blood." In that instant, Porter felt like his father had inhabited his body. Those were his old man's words, not his. "This isn't about me and you or you and him. It's about every black kid that steps on a ship. It's about making the Navy better for them, for all of us."

The crowd rumbled. To a man, they all talked at once.

Porter thought of the pictures he saw of his father in his Army uniform, being as pissed off as these brothers before him now. He could easily have been like Applewhite. And if Porter hadn't been good at football, he never would've gone to college and could've been just like these guys. Young, angry, and indignant.

"Where are the others?" Porter asked.

"What the fuck he talking about, Rufus?" Wooly held a hand over his eye as he spoke.

"Foc'sle," Applewhite said.

Porter put his hands on his hips and inhaled as deeply as he could. "We need to have all of us together," he said on the exhale. "This is too big a deal."

CHAPTER 25

Senior walked down the passageway with his .45 drawn, locked, and loaded. His steps were slow and deliberate. A number of crewmen, mostly white, lay wounded or sprawled unconscious on the deck. Avoiding their spread limbs took effort with each footfall. The corpsmen hadn't made it down that far yet and the smell of pain flooded the passageway as strongly as the stink of fuel.

This was one of the rare times aboard ship he didn't have his coffee cup. Nothing going in or being spit out. He could go for a chew about now. His lips were chapped. His collar and armpits soaked enough to smell himself. He'd showered after evening chow but being clean didn't last long in shipboard heat. As he swabbed his face with a handkerchief from his back pocket, he heard a ruckus in the back corner of the aft mess deck.

A voice emphasized certain words Senior couldn't make out. Feet stomped, and tables were smacked. Those sounds were unmistakable.

Senior shook his head and cleared his throat as quietly as he could. He raked his fingers through his sweat-damp hair and his scalp felt electrified. He looked over his shoulder, unable to shake the feeling he was being watched. He tiptoed through the galley toward the scullery to peek in at the action.

A group of black crewmen surrounded somebody or something. After a few moments, a black fist raised above the crowd's head height. Just outside earshot. The colored crew responded with jumps and hoots and foot stomping and laughing. Senior couldn't tell who it was in the center of all the commotion, but a hunch knotted his intestines. He hoped he was wrong, but that knot almost never lied. As the mob continued their display or celebration and loosened their tight ranks, between two darkies, each the size of linebackers, Senior saw Commander Porter. Shirtless. Black fist raised overhead. The knot in Senior's gut tightened so hard it cut off his breathing. He expected that kind of bullshit from the lower ranks, but not from his XO.

Senior felt unclean—and not from sweating. He rubbed a forearm with the butt of the .45 and wished he was somewhere else, because this was too much to bear. This ship was as much a part of him as his own home. The men aboard were as important as his family.

Without his chewing tobacco, his teeth clenched and grinded. His mind jumped to the worst possible conclusion. Flight ops were only a few hours away and any disruption would be unacceptable.

Senior backed out of the galley and double-timed it down the passageway and pushed into one of the flight squadron's ready rooms. He hadn't moved that fast in a while and he had to catch his breath in one of the leather chairs lined up in rows. His heart rate slowed enough for him to hold a conversation by the time he dialed and the quartermaster answered.

"Put the captain on," he said. "Now!"

"Who's this?"

"This is Senior. The Senior. Just get the old man on the motherfucking phone. Now!"

Senior's grip on the phone tightened as he waited. His knees ached, but his breathing slowed. In a way he was anxious to see the uppity XO knocked down a peg or two. Senior fidgeted as he breathed in. He couldn't imagine a breath without JP-5 fumes. The longer Senior had to wait, the hotter his body temperature rose. His heartbeat quickened and the muscles in his forearms and jaw clenched tightly. He had regained his composure by the time the captain got on the line, "Captain," he said. "Go."

"Sir," Senior said. "I must inform you that I witnessed your executive officer displaying alliance with the rioters, sir."

"Slow down," the captain said. "Was he under duress, Senior?"

"He was holding court," Senior said without taking a breath. "All the black crew huddled around him—three and four deep."

"Do you believe they're conspiring, Senior?"

Something in the captain's tone made Senior feel guilty for breaking this news to him. He also felt kind of happy about the XO, a man he never liked, being the goat for this whole fucking thing. With him disgraced, the drug trade could carry on unhindered.

"I couldn't hear Porter's words, sir," Senior said, "but his facial expression and that dirty fist in the air told me all I needed to know. I fear mutiny, Captain. My recommendation is to call out the Marines. Let them handle it. This is treason and this is a violent mob."

The captain's only response was half a dozen exhales from his nose whistling around snot. If Senior had learned anything since this man took command of the ship it was never to ask him if he heard you. He always responded in his own time, and interrupting that time angered his face fireman red.

"What do you mean by 'that dirty fist in the air'?" the captain asked.

This caught Senior off guard. He reached over to the leather seat a row in front of him, leaned a hand on it for support. "The black power salute," he said. "You know."

"We have reports of casualties. Are you saying Porter's behind this?"

"He's definitely in on it," Senior said. "That's for sure. Yes, sir. I saw that fist with my own two eyes." Spittle flew from his mouth as he spoke.

"Don't let them out of the area."

"Aye, sir."

Applewhite felt himself blinking too much. The pills had him hyper aware of all the brothers standing around him and Porter, but of little else. Applewhite scratched the side of his throat where razor bumps hadn't settled from yesterday's shave. Adrenaline kept surging through his limbs. "What you mean, all together?"

"The whole black crew," Porter said. "We'll all get together and talk this through."

Applewhite, Wooly, and Surico crowded closest to Porter, who stood with tight shoulders, a dead stare, and sweat beading on his forehead. He kept scratching at his forehead to cover up his twitching eye. This made Applewhite trust him less. He stood, arms crossed, noncommittal. "You telling me what then?"

Porter stared across the mess deck toward the serving line for a moment.

Wooly stepped up. A sheen of sweat coated his face. He breathed heavy for standing still and rubbed the back of his neck, looked like he just wanted to fight. His legs spread wide. A vein on the side of his head throbbed. He nodded continually— shoulders back, bouncing on his toes, hyper alert like he had six cups of coffee. "How we know you ain't just aiming to get us all in one place to make things easier for the jarheads?"

"Yeah!" a number of guys in the crowd hollered.

Porter didn't back away. He kept his gaze alert and searching the eyes of every brother in the room, even as Wooly walked his nose an inch from Porter's shoulder and fidgeted with his pick.

Porter rubbed his lips with a knuckle on his index finger and leaned over to Applewhite. "Can we speak privately for a minute?" His breath smelled of sour milk, which made Applewhite think about the cereal he may never be able to eat again.

"All right, Mr. Porter." Applewhite nodded toward Surico

and Wooly. "I'll be right back." Porter followed him toward the serving line, where Applewhite propped an elbow on a stack of trays. "Okay. This is as private as it's getting. What you got?"

With a quick look over his shoulder, Porter seemed surprised by the way the crowd closed ranks around Surico and Wooly. He turned back to Applewhite. "I'm going to level with you," he said with a half-smile, flashing a couple of teeth on his right side. His voice was neither quieted nor raised. His smile thinned as he continued. "You're in charge down here, Applewhite. I'm not questioning or challenging that. Rank hasn't mattered aboard this ship for hours. But no matter how bloodthirsty you and all these men may be," he held out his hands in acknowledgment to the angry mob, "there's no future in it. Certainly, you know the Marines are coming and will shut this down with deadly force if necessary."

"We deadly, too," Applewhite said, while looking straight ahead. "As you've seen for yourself." His free hand bounced the monkey fist on his thigh.

Porter followed Applewhite's line of sight toward the blond kid's corpse leaning against the bulkhead. "That's precisely my point," Porter said. "I have. And no matter if I don't live to testify, the mathematical odds are at least three people will link you directly to the killing of that kid. That's all it will take. But above and beyond that, you don't want your name forever tied to some bullshit that will set our cause back fifty years."

Applewhite kept his elbow on the trays and propped his head in his hand there. "And what cause is that?"

"All of us. Our lives in the Navy, especially shipboard. We have a responsibility to the entirety of our race—especially our seagoing brothers. If we put our heads together, we can accomplish much more by hurting no one else. Without your cooperation, word will spread that 'some of us blacks' couldn't take the deployment and went native or something equally ugly."

"That right, Mr. Porter?" Applewhite rested his free hand on his hollow abdomen, still thinking of that cereal. "You think it's just about being gone so long?"

"What I think doesn't matter. I'm on your side. I also know you're part of the drug ring." Porter spoke in a deliberately lower tone and watched Applewhite's face for reactions.

At first Applewhite remained stone-faced. The nerve of Porter to make him responsible for the whole race when all he wanted was better treatment on this one ship. That worried Applewhite. He had no way of knowing if Porter had definitive proof of the drugs in addition to the dead blond kid, and now was not the time to worry about that shit.

Porter leaned in and again, in an even lower tone of voice, said, "I'll get you immunity for all of this if you agree to stop the violence now and convince the others to air grievances through proper channels."

Applewhite knew enough about the law to know that immunity meant freedom. Freedom to eat cereal and raise his kid. The idea made his hollow stomach rumble into his chest. He wiped sweat from the back of his neck on his way to pointing at Porter. "And you got to guarantee none of my boys will get mast for this shit here tonight."

Porter brought a hand to his chin and scratched at the stubble. "I can't make a promise like that, but I give you my word I'll do everything I can."

Applewhite looked at Porter without blinking. Maybe it was relief or maybe it was the red devils, but a comforting sort of warmth spread through his limbs.

"I can keep you out of it," Porter said, "but there's a dead kid over there. A couple of your boys will have to do time. As many as a dozen, depending how badly injured some of those other white boys are stacked up in the passageway."

Applewhite laughed.

"This shit isn't funny!"

Applewhite crossed his arms. He wanted to keep cracking skulls, but Surico stood with his hands behind his back, parade rest-style, seeming to suggest that everything was going to be okay as long as they listened to the XO. Surico had a calmness on his weathered face that Applewhite only saw while the man listened to his reel-to-reel tapes in his shop. Despite the pills and the anger coursing through Applewhite, he couldn't come up with a decent reason why more violence would do them any better in the long run. They'd made their point.

"These brothers are pretty geared up."

"While cracking more honky heads might be fun for a while, there's no way to win against Marines with M16s."

Applewhite didn't care if a honky died, but getting a brother, somebody's black son, killed was the last thing he could handle right now. His mind was clouded. He feared that he was leaning toward something that might be best for him but bad for the brothers.

"We don't need no dead brothers," Applewhite said. "All right. Shit. I got your back, Mr. P. Don't worry none."

"You can present the notion to the men." Porter clapped Applewhite's shoulder. "Lead them down a rebellious but peaceful path."

"Nah, Mr. Porter." Applewhite removed his elbow from the stack of trays and stood as tall as he was able. "You go on and explain it to all of us. I back you up."

Applewhite returned to his spot in front of the mob. "All right. Listen up." He rarely raised his voice above a conversational volume, but everyone stopped and gave their undivided attention.

Porter followed, drawing his shoulders toward his ears. Sweat beaded on his forehead and his right eye twitched. He tugged at his collar and cleared his throat.

Applewhite addressed the crowd. "Yo. My brothers. We are all cool with Mr. Porter. Anyone hurts him answers to me. You dig?"

Most of the crowd held looks of surprise on their faces. A few shouts of "No shit?" followed, before everyone nodded and looked at one another as if they'd go along just to see where it took them.

"Now our man, Mr. Porter here, wants to say a few words." Applewhite pointed to Porter, but remained facing the crowd, checking their faces. Every eye was on Porter. "We're going to listen to him until he's done and we're going to vote on what we do next. You dig?" Without waiting for the crowd to respond, he added, "Go ahead, Mr. Porter. Tell these men your plan."

Applewhite felt dizzy, not from the red devils, but from the risk he was taking. He bit his lip and stared off for a moment, second-guessing his decision.

Porter cleared his throat again. Licked his lips. Exhaled deeply. The sound of electricity coursing through transformers along the far bulkhead was the only noise between them. Porter looked at the assortment of black men on the mess deck through a squint. He cleared his throat again. "Each of you is human dynamite." He laughed a little without cracking a smile. "Each one of you is dangerous on your own. But assembled like this, you are powerful enough to sink this ship."

The crowd hooted and slapped skin.

Porter continued. "But nothing has to explode to make significant change and notable progress aboard this ship tonight."

That quieted the crowd. Applewhite stood with his arms crossed, unsure how the crowd might respond.

"It's not about us and it's not about them." Porter nodded as he spoke. "You can't fault men for doing their jobs, especially since that's all they know. They're following orders and don't know any better. We've all had to do things we didn't want to. We can't go bashing skulls any more than they should be bashing ours. It's not about black and white or us and them. It's about the Navy, at the institutional level. Faceless bureaucrats in Washington, DC who've been slow to change. If we crack a white skull, thousands of other whites will use that as fuel to power more hatred against all of us, your little brothers, cousins, sons, too. Instead we need them to see we're just like them. No different. And we should be treated as such. The best way to achieve this is to change the Navy, from the inside. The best way to make the Navy change is by presenting our case and winning over a portion of white sailors, the captain, the admiral—all admirals, on up to the Department of Defense. It's incumbent upon all of us here to show the Navy that it's not just about us here tonight, but about every black sailor fleet-wide."

The warmth in Applewhite's limbs progressed into a floating sensation that made it impossible to suppress a moment of hopefulness. He didn't know where the XO learned to talk like that, but to hear the man voice such support meant something to him.

"How many of you heard of the National Black Political Convention? It was held in Gary, Indiana, back in March, while you all steamed circles out here." Porter stopped talking for a minute.

Applewhite looked at the brothers, who shrugged at each other.

"Even better than that," Porter said, "Doctor King got more respect than any of the rioters in Washington just a few years ago. Each of you can be a Sailor King. Make your case like men instead of words they can call you—criminals, animals, and so on. Be reasonable, but firm. Get heard. Build a strong foundation for future generations of brothers."

The crowd looked to Applewhite, who redirected his focus on Mr. Porter. For a split-second, it looked like he was going to cry, but the urge seemed to pass before any water fell. Applewhite didn't know why he noticed that in Porter. He also didn't understand why he related to the sensation so strongly.

Porter continued. "Together we can sail mighty ships across great oceans and return home successful and proud. Together we can run corporations and towns and our voices join like the braids of a mooring line making it strong enough to keep things together."

The crowd murmured. As Applewhite began to applaud, they all joined in.

Porter held up a hand to quiet them, or to thank them. Applewhite stepped forward and hollered to his boys. "Take this here party to the foc'sle and tell the other brothers. If we hurry, we can get there before the Marines gear up."

They organized themselves with Applewhite and Porter in front, Surico and Wooly next, in preparation for mobilizing forward to the foc'sle.

CHAPTER 26

Surico kept looking at his watch. Seconds ticked too fast. Mobilizing a couple hundred brothers up to the foc'sle would take a single-file line snaking through passageways and over knee knockers, all before the Marines caught up to them. The knot in Surico's throat told him the odds were not in their favor. He just wanted all the bullshit calmed down so he could get back to business, but the knot was never wrong. Yet, after the XO's speech, anything seemed possible. All the other brothers agreed to go along and that gave him hope.

Before they took their first steps, Senior appeared in the passageway, advancing toward them. His khaki uniform wasn't as squared away as usual. His shirt had come untucked at some point. With his chin in the air it was easy to see his shave wasn't fresh. On another day, he might kick over a trash can or two to get the attention of large groups of crewmen. Instead, he'd drawn his .45 and held it straight out in front of him. On the other end of that pistol, sweat glistened on Senior's red face and his free hand jerked to wipe his brow and beneath his eyes.

The hair on Surico's arms and neck stood. His leg muscles tightened, coiled up and ready to run. He wanted to take off and hide, but he had no egress. His vision distorted like being under strobe lights and he couldn't stop himself from blinking. He felt cold. His heartbeat was a chipping hammer as Senior approached, locked and loaded.

"Afraid I can't let you boys walk out of here," Senior said. "I heard your little speech, Commander Porter, but even if I was the type to change sides, I'm under orders by the captain to keep you all quarantined right here. The Marines are en route."

Many of the brothers reached slowly to pick up the weapons they'd wielded in the berthing compartments and passageways. They acted like their slow and soundless efforts also made them invisible. Applewhite held up a hand and shook his head.

Porter faced Senior. "This is all under control, Senior Chief. Why don't you supervise the corpsmen's triage efforts down the passageway?"

Senior clicked back the hammer with his thumb. "No way you bastards are going to mutiny aboard my ship."

Surico stepped back, checked his proximity to others. His mouth ran dry and an old pounding in his ears returned. His stomach hardened. This bastard was off the rails. Surico stood still and tried to fake calmness.

"This is no mutiny," Porter said as he stepped toward Senior.

"You fucking traitor!" Senior said as he fired a shot from his Navy-issue .45 pistol.

Before Surico's ears absorbed the percussive force, he saw blood darken the whole in the XO's shoulder and roll in rivers down his arm to spot the deck. The XO looked surprised and patted at the blood flowing.

Surico leaned away, tried to make himself as small as possible and, certain that the next shot had his name on it, squeezed his eyes shut. He bit the inside of his cheek. Tasted blood. Thought about the time Izabella sliced her foot on a broken bottle near the front stoop.

Senior's second shot came a split-second after Surico opened his eyes.

Applewhite had anticipated the shot and jumped to push Porter out of the way.

The bullet hit Applewhite in the center of his back. The

impact knocked him from the air just as blood and a small portion of his innards followed the bullet's exit. His momentum propelled him across the deck.

"Nooooo!" Wooly yelled.

Applewhite's lifeless body thumped like a wet sea bag on the far edge of a table. His head was on the wrong end of the landing and Surico looked away. He'd miss that boy, but it was his own fault for not listening. Surico watched Porter struggling to keep his balance after being shoved out of the line of fire. He stilled himself on a bulkhead behind a row of brothers, who helped lean him against a table. Other than a squint to his eyes, you wouldn't have known he was in pain.

Wooly's hands clenched into fists. Before Senior could fire a third shot, Wooly rushed Senior, knocking the pistol out of his hand, and proceeded to beat him.

Surico kept all the other brothers back by raising his hand like a traffic cop. He shook his head as he looked at Applewhite's boots sticking up above the tabletop.

After a few minutes, Wooly tired. He stood, wiped his nose with his bloodied knuckles.

Surico looked once more to Applewhite laid out on the deck and felt his face twist in rage. He walked over and mashed the heel of his work boot through the side of Senior's knee. Wooly gasped as he threw an air punch from ten feet away. Surico got in a few more kicks before signaling the rest of the brothers to join in.

Senior cried out, "You motherfuckers!" as darkness descended.

The brothers chanted, "Tread stomp! Tread stomp!"

Surico looked back toward Mr. Porter, prostrated on the deck. There was no way to know if he'd live or die.

Wooly shook a thumb over his shoulder. "The escalator," he said. The ship's escalator had been secured for the night but was still usable as sharp metal stairs. They dragged Senior to it as he struggled beneath the grips of so many black hands. Wooly held Senior's arms behind his back. Surico moved in and unbuckled

Senior's khaki belt and pulled it free. He handed it to a thick-necked brother, who tied Senior's wrists behind his back. Wooly kicked him in the same knee and got him on the deck again. He pulled Senior by a thick handful of hair toward the escalator. The injured knee slowed down Senior. Pain gave him a limp. Wooly held Senior's hair as he positioned his head and pushed until the tread was firmly in his mouth.

Senior squirmed and grunted as Wooly took the first stomp. His boot slammed into the base of Senior's skull with the sound of ice cracking off a roofline. The crowd hooted and hollered again. Surico's turn was next. He looked toward Applewhite and then to the blood spreading out on the tread in Senior's mouth. With an exhale that came out half scream, Surico stomped the heel of his boot onto the back of Senior's head and felt the skull break like an egg. He held up his fists as the crowd cheered.

As the succession of brothers waiting in line took their turns, Surico walked toward the serving line. He supposed it had to happen. Fine. So be it. But he wanted it over with. Now.

The line stomped one by one, leaving Surico to wonder if the head would completely sever from the body.

CHAPTER 27

As the group had swarmed Senior, somebody handed Porter a towel retrieved from the galley. He kept it folded and applied direct pressure on his shirtless wound. He'd always believed in his line about all their bones being the same color, but when forced to be on the receiving end of such complete and vile hatred, Porter was repulsed that Senior's bones were the same color as his own. And nothing he could've done would've stopped the mob from killing Senior.

And there was no way to bring back Applewhite.

Sadness crept across his shoulders and into his neck and he bowed his head. In that position, he noticed a drop of blood resting on one side of the monkey fist hanging out of Applewhite's pocket. Porter wiped at the blood with his thumb, but instead of removing it he'd smeared it into the line. He pulled out the monkey fist keychain from Applewhite's pocket. The edges had gone dark from wear and tear. It held just two keys— one to his locker and the other to the main door of the forward laundry. That was the sum total of his responsibility in this world. He demanded more, but never showed interest in going after it the right way. All horsepower and no rudder. It was something that could've been addressed and overcome through mentoring, which Porter would've gladly given had Applewhite's life been spared. Porter didn't shed a tear, but he clenched the monkey fist in his palm until the keys cut into his fingers. He held that grip for a moment, then tucked it into his own pocket.

As the black crew beat and kicked Senior, Porter's first two priorities were making sure everybody else in the crew survived the night and securing Senior's weapon.

The blunt surface pain in his shoulder was like the worst toothache ever, but a hundred times worse, and with what felt like a heated wire coat hanger poking all the way through it while someone cranked it around. He'd never imagined getting shot at such close range. Face-to-face. He could still move his shoulder and get a decent breath. Best he could guess, the shot went between the clavicle and lung. There was a little less blood flowing, and he hoped he'd be okay until Doc could take a look at it.

Blood loss made his head feel like a stale loaf of bread. He breathed rapidly to oxygenate himself. He wanted fresh air, but there was no time to get up on deck, or even out to one of the sponsons. The stuffiness made him think worst case, which made his sour stomach rise up in his throat.

Most of the men laughed and hollered, "Tread stomp!" as they danced around Senior's mangled body. The celebration involved many boots stomping the deck. The display struck Porter as primal. Proud of themselves, no doubt. As if they could nourish themselves on the carcass of another man.

A moment later, a chubby second class with his T-shirt on backward ran up breathless. "The Marines are coming," he panted. "Loaded for bear."

Defensiveness swept over the mob. The energy on the mess deck transformed from laughs and stomps to retrieving their weapons and facing the widest opening leading toward them. There were calls of, "Fuck them motherfuckers," and "Bring it on," among the nervous chatter.

Porter nodded toward Surico and then back at the black crew.

Surico took the hint and whistled through his fingers loud enough to get the black crew's attention. "Listen up," he said, then gestured an open palm toward Porter.

Porter pushed himself to one knee, then stood. His head felt full of bees, but he stepped into the clearing in front of the angry mob. He felt heat radiating off the bulkheads and pipes and cable runs just above their heads. Their faces held expressions not of anger or of joy, but rather of excitement. He tried to make direct eye contact with everyone in the front row, but all eyes scanned the passageway, waiting.

Surico stood with his feet spread, ready to move quickly in either direction.

"Who has Senior's weapon?"

No one answered.

"Hand over Senior's pistol so none of us gets shot if the Marines see it."

The crowd murmured for a moment as they passed the gun to the front of the mob and into Porter's hand.

"Thank you," he said as he released the magazine and cleared the chamber, surprised how much the motion hurt his shoulder. He stayed on the deck, leaning to one side, emptied the magazine with his thumb. "This is evidence. We want a clear case of murder to hang over Senior's memory forever."

The crowd cheered.

Porter cleared his throat. This opportunity wasn't going to come again. Decide, commit, execute. Just like landing a plane on the flight deck. "What's done is done," Porter said as he made his way to his feet. "If you want to be animals, you'll have to face the Marines. But worse than that, those of you who survive will forever be the villains. Matters might get worse for brothers on every ship in the fleet. Don't fuck them over. They deserve better. We all deserve better."

He applied pressure and said, "If it's not enough that you men can make life better for every brother that serves in the Navy from now until the end of time, consider that you and even those who died today can be remembered for sparking change. You will be written about. Despite your crimes tonight, don't you want to be shown as someone who did just enough to change the system? Do you want to fight and set our cause back by decades? Or do you want to stay alive and be remembered as noble freedom fighters?"

"You still going to take their side?" someone hollered.

"I'm on all sides. The health and welfare of everyone aboard this ship is my responsibility. I know you're unhappy and you've got the right to be, but one night of blowing off steam is only going to get you thrown in Leavenworth. Not only locked up, but without changing anything. The next brother coming up is still going to have to endure all the policies that pissed you off. It would be a smarter play to drop the weapons and peacefully protest."

"And then what?" a shirtless kid with glasses asked.

"You hit them, not with fire hose nozzles, but rather a list of your legitimate grievances. It is the only way to make anything good come from all of this."

To a man, their jaws were loose and they turned to look at one another, perhaps for verification they'd heard that right.

"Now it's too late to join the rest of our crew on the foc's'le," Porter continued, "but we can send two men on two different routes to better our odds of delivering the message." He checked his blood-soaked compress after he spoke.

"What if neither of them makes it?" a sturdy non-rate asked.

Porter pressed the compress back to the wound. Winced at the pain. "We can't control every black man on this ship," he said. "At least we're on record as being peaceful, now. Don't fuck that up."

The crowd mumbled, considering it.

"You." He pointed to a squared-away black kid with his uniform surprisingly intact. "Run up the port side to the foc's'le and tell them the plan. You." He pointed to another skinny kid who looked like he wanted to run. "You go up the starboard side. Same thing. I've got a seventy-two-hour liberty chit for the first one to deliver this message. Now go!"

He didn't know if he'd be salvaging the dignity of the black crew, or if he'd just signed two death certificates.

"The rest of you, if you want to survive the Marines' arrival and also enact permanent change for all our brothers, we have to hustle. You two, take Applewhite over to the ammo elevator. You two, do the same with Senior. Everyone else, take a seat on the deck and do as I say. Exhibit no hostility. Don't make yourself a target. And keep your mouths shut."

The bodies of Applewhite, the mess crank, and Senior were lined up parallel to the ammo elevator, out of view. The passageways were bad enough, and surely word had gotten out about the berthing areas. Porter couldn't figure out why the GQ alarm hadn't sounded yet. His doubts about news reaching the bridge were swabbed away like drops of blood on the deck. He wondered what the chaplain might've advised.

The Marines charged in formation, helmets on and M16s drawn. The barrels aimed over the heads of the black crewmen, who sat on the deck, hands atop their heads.

Porter had no way of knowing if another twenty-man Marine Reaction Force had already stormed the foc'sle with no regard for compromise, or if they'd shot and killed any men.

His head pounded. His shoulder felt like it had been hit with a Zuni rocket instead of forty-five-caliber lead. Despite that and the corpses lying in the ammo elevator, he needed this to look like one of the sit-ins he'd seen on the six o'clock news.

The captain walked in behind another group of Marines who hollered, "Attention on deck!"

The seated black crew around Porter stayed seated. Their weapons within reach, but they did not react when the Marines charged in. Nor did they jump to attention upon seeing the captain. *Stay strong*, he told himself for their benefit as well as his.

Captain Holt's khaki uniform was starched and squared away, which made Porter self-conscious about being shirtless, bloodied, and sweat sodden. They locked eyes.

"The hell's going on here, Porter?" The captain spoke with inquisitiveness thinly veiled behind a truckload of contempt by his lack of "mister" or "commander."

"Captain," Porter cleared his throat and remained seated. "My orders were to secure the black crew."

"Where is your shirt? How were you injured? Have you seen the carnage in the passageways?"

A shiver made Porter's shoulders clench as the images of triage being set up in the passageways and the murders he'd witnessed since.

"The violence that has taken place is regrettable," Porter said, as nonconfrontationally as he could. "We sit here now in peaceful protest of the treatment and conditions of black sailors aboard this ship, and likely Navy-wide."

The captain crossed his arms and reclined an inch or two. His head cocked to his right as he swept his stare across the mess deck. Taking it all in, Porter supposed.

"On your feet," Captain Holt said.

Porter felt like his chest was being pulled into his stomach and he couldn't breathe. "I'd rather not stand while everyone else has to sit for his own safety."

"I want a word with you in private."

Porter pulled Applewhite's monkey fist out of his pocket and squeezed it in his hand. "I'd rather have all my brothers hear what you have to say."

The captain crossed his arms and clenched his jaw. "Have you thought this through, Bob?"

The mention of his first name made Porter laugh. He gripped Applewhite's monkey fist. Worked it between his fingers and thumb, rubbing the spot of smeared blood. "Well, Captain," he said, "the best I figure it, Dr. King had the Edmund Pettus Bridge, and we have this ship."

The captain laughed in a way that encouraged the Marines to laugh too. "So now you're Martin Luther King?" he asked, sarcasm thick on his voice.

Porter shook his head. "No, Captain. I'm Robert Louis Porter, and conditions for these men have to change immediately."

The captain stopped laughing and the Marines tightened their grips on their rifles.

Blood drained from the captain's face for a moment making him paler than usual. The blood returned all at once and his face looked hot as a boiler ready to explode. He raised a hand, not to stop traffic, but to halt others from speaking. He cleared his throat with a bark. "What the hell is all this?"

Though he didn't move, Porter said, "This is a complicated mess, Captain. I have a plan in mind. It'll just take a moment of your time." His words came out steady and pitched low enough to make the captain lean in, but also to appear as not yelling. The whole time he spoke, Porter's muscles tensed, and he held pressure on his wound with the little energy he had to spare. He inhaled as deeply as he was able to avoid what had been intensifying and now felt stabbing pains if he went too far. His heart pumped blood against the steady pressure he held to his chest.

The black crew remained seated, but constricted in their proximity, like a snake coiling to strike. Sweat was visible on every neck.

"First off, Captain, eighty-four days without a port visit is cruel and unusual punishment for any crew."

"You know as well as anyone, I like land just as much as the rest of you. If it was up to me, we'd visit more ports than you ever imagined. But war means doing what's necessary. When CINCPAC says 'stay' we stay."

"That's just the start of it, Captain."

"All right," the captain said. "That's enough, Porter. On your feet, you're coming with me to sick bay."

Porter remained seated. The only times Porter felt fully present, "in the moment" as the philosophers say, was while flying. That was one of the reasons for his addiction to it. Without that in his life, he'd spent most of his time looking forward and looking back as if the present was merely a series of activities. Until now. Now he was focused on the moment and not Sharon back in Rhode Island. Not about flying. Not about becoming captain someday. Not even about the gunshot wound whistling in his chest. Just this. Nothing but the lives and welfare of the men he was compelled to help.

"The divide is too great to do anything else," Porter said. "These men have assured me there will be no more violence if our demands—"

"You're making demands, Mr. Porter?"

"Not me, sir. All of us. We've been quiet too long. *I* have been quiet too long. I've finally figured it out. The way to fix this ongoing problem is to get at the root of it. To begin, we want you to send messages to the CNO and every newspaper and station in San Diego and Washington, DC."

The captain leaned back as if flinching a punch. "We'll need to go through proper channels."

"We do it just as I said."

Captain Holt shook his head three condescending times. "This really the way you want to play it, Bob?"

Porter resisted the urge to raise his voice. Nodded.

"I took a bullet for this, Captain. From Senior himself."

"Dear God. Where is Senior?"

"He's dead, Captain."

The news stunned the captain slack jawed. "He shot you and now he's dead?"

"That's right," Porter said. It was all that needed saying, but those two words held horsepower that rumbled within his ribs. The pain lessened if he stayed still. He sat, cradled his other arm to alleviate pressure on the wounded side. The pain didn't let up and it was hard to get a decent breath. "And instead of doing what you might want me to," he said through gritted teeth, "I'm doing what's best for the crew, the entire crew."

"Is that so?"

"Not just this crew, but every crew Navy-wide. This is the

first step toward a Navy made fair and equal. We've been treated poorly for too long."

"You would hold this ship hostage?" the captain asked.

"Nothing of the sort, sir." Porter took a moment and inhaled a jagged breath deep enough to recharge himself. "We're simply asking for your cooperation."

The captain's face turned as red as the faded Confederate flag tattooed on his chest. "We'll do it your way, Commander Porter. That's how confident I am in my XO. But to be clear, as to the duties aboard this ship, each man was informed of the role they'd be playing before arriving here. And if I'm not mistaken, the XO is a great argument against your assumptions. As for the berthing spaces, you people segregated yourselves. And I've recently heard that you don't allow anyone else down there." He paused. Looked up and sucked his teeth. "What was next, oh yes, the decisions at mast are mine for reasons that aren't always made public. Suffice it to say that if you've been to jail as a civilian, that factors into my decisions. As for the days at sea, we go where our country needs us. As I said earlier." He stopped talking long enough to scan the faces of those in front.

The hard, impassive faces he saw must've made him feel something. Porter wished he knew what that might be.

"And," the captain continued, "the two-man rule was an attempt to prevent the events of this evening from happening. Since it didn't work, many of you will be detained by these Marines." He made a neutral look take over his face. Diplomatic. He nodded to a Marine corporal, who jogged up the passageway to deliver the news.

Porter held the monkey fist in his hand down by his lap, rolling it as he looked at the light fixtures and cable runs attached to the overhead. He didn't want eye contact with anyone. His only goal in that moment was to conceal the pure and simple joy he couldn't help feeling. That satisfaction made him forget about his wound enough to smile. "We send the statements and then we all hit the rack and get up in couple hours to perform another day's duties. Right, Captain Holt?"

The weight of that rhetorical question chilled his bare torso. He shivered. Doing so fired every nerve ending around his bullet wound. He doubled over and choked back a groan. For the first time in his life, he was positive his father was smiling down from his cloud.

CHAPTER 28

December 15, 1972

CMDR Robert Porter
Naval Training Center
San Diego, CA 92106

Dearest Robert,

Your last letter made me cry. I'm more than ready for another visit out there, too. I wish California was closer. I really wish they weren't keeping you until after the hearings, but we'll make up for lost time when you become a civilian.

I saw Eddie the other day. His aunt didn't know he moved out and sent a letter I had to give him. He couldn't believe that beneath your recruiting poster image beats the heart of a freedom fighter. You fully earned his respect. Somehow that makes me want you even more.

Have you decided what you want to do?

Anxiously,
Sharon
XOXOXO

* * *

May May
Barrio Barretto
Olongapo City 2200
Baloy
Olongapo City, Philippines

January 12, 1973

PO Surico Hurasa
USS Salvation (CV-44)
FPO San Francisco, CA 95660

Hary Bird do nice better now Sir rico. Thank you very mush for monee you send. Hary no walk good but he eat more and talk like Hary now. Better all days.
You visit. We meet. I hug you.

May May

ACKNOWLEDGMENTS

Tremendous debts of gratitude are owed to many people who helped or at least humored me during the writing of this book. Instrumental in this process were (and continue to be) Tracy Crow and James R. Duncan, who have been deeply patient, helpful, and inspirational. To Mark Fleeting, Pinckney Benedict, Fred Leebron, who praise and chide and are never wrong. To Matt Flaherty, Mike Kobre, Tim Wright, Carol Dee Turner, and everyone in the DD-214 Writers' Workshop, the Queens University MFA program, as well as many of the journal and magazine editors who've published my stories, essays, and articles, particularly: Jonathan Sturak and Eddie Vega at *Noir Nation*; Anthony Neil Smith at *Plots with Guns*; Steve Weddle at *Needle: A Magazine of Noir*; Nicholle M. Cormier at *The MacGuffin*; Jerri Bell and Ron Capps at *O-Dark-Thirty*; Jon Chopan, Tracy Crow, and Cliff Garstang at *Prime Number Magazine*; Mary Akers at *r.kv.r.y.*; Ralph Pennel at *Midway Journal*; and to Ron Earl Phillips at *Shotgun Honey*. (It's my sincere hope that everyone reads all these fine publications.) I'm immensely thankful to Eric Campbell, Lance Wright, Chris Rhatigan, and David Ivester. I'm also thankful to Zach McCain for such a great cover, and to Elizabeth White for some mighty-fine guidance, as well as to Emily Bell, Dan Wickett, Donald Maas, Lorin Oberweger, Kim Wright, Elaine Ash, and Gene Garrett for their insights along the way. I'd also like to thank those whose presence influenced me in the early years of this adventure: Susan Wolf Johnson, James O'Neil; Willie Reader; my third-grade teacher, Mrs. Dickerson; Ronald "Bo" Walston; the Wilsons of Mobile, Alabama; Mark Amen; Mark August; Lyn Biliteri; H. Kermit Jackson; Ty Jones; Denny Sawyer; my

Navy buddies, Joe Paul, Curt Jarrett, John Louthan, Perry Chastain, James "Bubba" Smith, Scott Dickerson, and all the San Jacinto Plank Owners; and my lifelong friends who are like brothers to me, Jeff Prince, Chris Hartnett, Anthony Acitelli, William Barnes, David (Hezy) Hemed, Paul Drew, and Kurt Hopson. And I'm forever thankful for my entire family, but especially my parents, Carol and Jack, who showed me the way and kept me on the path. The biggest thanks of all goes to my beautiful and infinitely understanding wife, Lauren, who got on this rollercoaster with me when I thought it would be easy and loved me even after finding out that it never is. I wouldn't trade you for anything in the world!

JEFFERY HESS is the author of the novels *Beachhead* and *Tushhog* and the short-story collection *Cold War Canoe Club* as well as the editor of the award-winning Home of the Brave anthologies. He served aboard the Navy's oldest and newest ships and since 2007, he's led the DD-214 Writers' Workshop for military veterans and their dependents.

BOOKS

On the following pages are a few
more great titles from the
Down & Out Books publishing family.

For a complete list of books and to
sign up for our newsletter,
go to DownAndOutBooks.com.

Walkin' After Midnight
Joe Ricker

Down & Out Books
May 2019
978-1-948235-83-9

This collection of stories is set in the darkest corners of New England, where the damaged American underbelly emerges.

The characters in these stories will challenge every notion you have of right and wrong, and you'll quickly realize that you've probably passed some of the characters in these stories on the streets.

Be glad you kept walking.

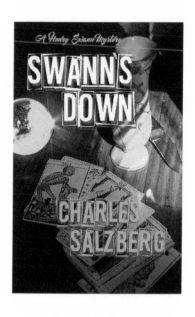

Swann's Down
A Henry Swann Mystery
Charles Salzberg

Down & Out Books
May 2019
978-1-64396-011-1

At skip-tracer Henry Swann's weekly business meeting with Goldblatt at a local diner, his inscrutable partner drops a bomb. He wants to hire Swann to help out his ex-wife, Rachael, who's been swindled out of a small fortune by a mysterious fortune-teller, who has convinced the gullible young woman that she's made contact with her recently deceased boyfriend.

At the same time, Swann receives a call from an old friend and occasional employer, lawyer Paul Rudder, who has taken on a particularly sticky case…

The Hurt Business
Stories by Mike Miner

All Due Respect, an imprint of
Down & Out Books
March 2019
978-1-948235-75-4

"We are such fragile creatures."

The men, women and children in these stories will all be pushed to the breaking point, some beyond. Heroes, villains and victims. The lives Miner examines are haunted by pain and violence. They are all trying to find redemption. A few will succeed, but at a terrible price. All of them will face the consequences of their bad decisions as pipers are paid and chickens come home to roost. The lessons in these pages are learned the very hard way. Throughout, Miner captures the savage beauty of these dark tales with spare poetic prose.

Main Bad Guy
A Love & Bullets Hookup
Nick Kolakowski

Shotgun Honey, an imprint of
Down & Out Books
February 2019
978-1-948235-70-9

Bill and Fiona, the lovable anti-heroes of the "Love & Bullets" trilogy, find themselves in the toughest of tough spots: badly wounded, hunted by cops and goons, and desperately in need of a drink (or five).

After a round-the-world tour of spectacular criminality, they're back in New York. Locked in a panic room on the top floor of a skyscraper, surrounded by pretty much everyone in three zip codes who wants to kill them, they'll need to figure out how to stay upright and breathing...and maybe deal out a little payback in the process.